John Russell Bartlett, Roger Williams

Letters of Roger Williams

1632-1682

John Russell Bartlett, Roger Williams

Letters of Roger Williams
1632-1682

ISBN/EAN: 9783337137731

Printed in Europe, USA, Canada, Australia, Japan

Cover: Foto ©Andreas Hilbeck / pixelio.de

More available books at **www.hansebooks.com**

PUBLICATIONS

OF THE

NARRAGANSETT CLUB.

(*First Series.*)

VOLUME VI.

PROVIDENCE, R. I.

MDCCCLXXIV.

Providence Press Co., Printers.

THE

LETTERS OF ROGER WILLIAMS.

EDITED BY

JOHN RUSSELL BARTLETT.

LETTERS

OF

ROGER WILLIAMS.

1632-1682.

NOW FIRST COLLECTED.

EDITED BY

JOHN RUSSELL BARTLETT.

PROVIDENCE:

PRINTED FOR THE NARRAGANSETT CLUB.

1874.

EDITOR'S PREFACE.

———o———

In publiſhing for the firſt time, all the letters of Roger Williams, as far as they have come to the knowledge of the editor, it is proper to mention the ſources from which they have been obtained.

With the exception of a very few letters, printed in various controverſial books of the period when Williams lived and wrote, the firſt which appeared in print were in Backus's Hiſtory of New England with reference to the Baptiſts, printed in 1777. A few iſolated letters next appeared in the early volumes of the Collections of the Maſſachuſetts Hiſtorical Society, and a large number in Profeſſor Knowles' Life of Williams, publiſhed at Boſton in 1834, few of which had before appeared in print. But the moſt conſiderable acceſſion was in the "Winthrop Papers." Theſe letters were written by Williams to Governor Winthrop of Maſſachuſetts, and to his ſon John Winthrop, Jr., Governor of Connecticut, and had remained in the poſſeſſion of the Winthrop family until preſented to the Maſſachuſetts Hiſtorical Society. They were publiſhed by the Society at different times, as they came into its poſſeſſion ; hence, are not found in one volume, but in many ; the larger number being in volume VI., of the fourth ſeries of its "Collections."

Williams doubtleſs had other correſpondents, but his letters to ſuch were unknown to thoſe who have written upon his life, or who have edited the recent republications of his ſeveral works. The editor of the preſent compilation of theſe letters has made further ſearch in various Hiſtorical Collections and in other books, and he has alſo conſulted gentlemen familiar with the writings of Williams ; but only in a ſingle inſtance has he been able to find a letter, not already in print. For this letter, which is an important one, the editor is indebted to Charles Deane, Eſq., of Cambridge.

In preſenting the letters of Williams, it was the deſire of the editor to give them preciſely as they were written, by preſerving the language and the original orthography ; a plan which was found to be impracticable. Had all been printed as thoſe are in the later volumes of the Maſſachuſetts Hiſtorical Society, where the language

B

and orthography remain as originally written, this plan might have been carried out; but, unfortunately, in nearly one-half the letters, the language, as well as the spelling, had been modernized, so that it was impracticable to attempt a presentation of all the letters as originally written. Under these circumstances, the editor was compelled to modernize the whole, in order to preserve a uniformity. In doing this, he has printed all the letters found in Backus's History of the Baptists; in Knowles' Memoir of Williams; in Elton's Life of Williams, and in some of the Historical Collections which had been modernized, precisely as they appear; no alteration being neceffary. Those among the " Winthrop Papers" printed in the later volumes of the Collections of the Maffachusetts Historical Society, have been modernized in their spelling, but preserve the original language.

In spelling the Indian names, no syftem seems to have been followed either by Mr. Williams or other early New England writers. Thus we find Narraganfett spelled *Naniganfick, Nanihiggonfick, Narrogonfett, Nariganfet, and Nanbiggonfet.*

For Connecticut, we have *Quinnihticut, Qunnticut.*

For Nyantic, we have *Nayantakick, Nayantaquit, Nayantuqiut.*

For Mohawks, *Mauquahogs, Mawquawogs, Mohowawogs, Mowhauogs,* and *Mawhauogs.*

For Uncas, we have *Okace, Owokace, Wocafe, Onkace, Onkas,* and *Oncas.*

For Mohegan, *Monahiganenchs, Monahig, Monhiggin, Monahiggen.*

The spelling of these and other Indian names have been changed into the orthography of the present day.

Many of the letters of Williams are without dates; some only bear the day of the week, while a majority of them are dated in the manner following: (Nar. 16. 12. 49. fo call'd) meaning Narraganfett, the 16th of the 12th month, i. e. the 16th February, 1649–50; according to the Old Style, then in vogue, when March was the firft month. Where the date is entirely wanting the editor has endeavored to fix upon the month and year, by the subject of the letter, or by the endorfement of Gov. Winthrop when the letter was received by him. The editors of the " Winthrop Papers " have labored to ascertain the dates of many, which dates in almoft every inftance have been adopted; but ftill some remain, the contents of which are of fuch a general character, that it has not been poffible even to fix the probable year when they were written. The date of every letter, however obfcure, if it hore any, is given as it appears in the original, while the probable or affumed date is given in brackets. But with every effort to arrive at the truth, it is poffible that errors have been made.

The notes which have been added are neceffarily numerous, and might have been extended, but it was deemed advifable not to enter into any of the controverfies in which Mr. Williams was involved.

In the notes the fource has been given whence all the letters in the volume were obtained. The larger number is from the " Winthrop Papers," which papers include letters from men prominent in New England during the feventeenth century, all being a portion of the correfpondence of three generations of the Winthrops.

The public eftimate of fome men famous in hiftory has been leffened by the reading of their letters ; but no one can read thefe from the founder of Rhode Ifland in this volume without having his refpect and admiration for him increafed. Mr. Knowles was the firft of Williams's biographers to introduce his letters. Even thefe tended to elevate his character ; but their were periods, relating to which no letters from his pen were known to be in exiftence The publication of the Winthrop papers brought letters to light, which tend to elucidate many events in Williams's life.

In fpeaking of the correfpondence of the Winthrop's, Mr. Lowell in his charming effays (*"Among my Books,"* p. 246) thus writes :—

" Let me premife that there are two men above all others, for whom our refpect is heightened by their letters,—the elder John Winthrop and Roger Williams. Winthrop appears throughout as a truly magnanimous and noble man in an unobtrufive way,—a kind of greatnefs that makes lefs noife in the world, but is on the whole more folidly fatisfying to moft others." . . . " Charity and tolerance flow fo noticeably from the pen of Williams that it is plain they were in his heart. He does not fhow himfelf a ftrong or very wife man, but a thoroughly gentle and good one. His affection for the two Winthrops is evidently of the warmeft."

For the better underftanding of certain letters of Mr. Williams's in this volume, it has been deemed advifable to include a few from other perfons. Among thefe are the letters of Mrs. Sadlier, daughter of Sir Edward Coke, in reply to Williams's letters to that lady during his vifit to England in 1653—and two from Sir Henry Vane.

J. R. B.

PROVIDENCE, October, 1874.

LETTERS OF ROGER WILLIAMS

PUBLISHED IN THIS VOLUME.

WITH THE PLACES FROM WHERE WRITTEN AND THE DATES.

PAGE.

c

LETTERS OF ROGER WILLIAMS.

For the right Worſhipful John Winthrop, Eſq., Governor of the English in the Maſſachuſetts.[1]

PLYMOUTH.[2] [1632.]

MUCH HONORED AND BELOVED IN CHRIST JESU, — Your Chriſtian acceptation of our cup of cold water is a bleſſed cup of wine, ſtrong and pleaſant to our wearied ſpirits. Only let me crave a word of explanation : among other pleas for a young councellor (which I fear will be too light in the balance of the Holy One) you argue from twenty-five in a Church Elder : 'tis a riddle as yet to me whether

[1] John Winthrop, the friend and correspondent of Roger Williams, came from England to Salem in 1630; but ſoon after removed to Charleſton, and ſelcted the ſite where the city of Boſton ſtands. He was annually elected Governor of Maſſachuſetts Bay until 1634; again in 1637–40, 1642–44, and from 1646 to his death, March 26, 1649. In 1636, when Sir Henry Vane was elected governor, Winthrop was choſen Deputy-governor. Vane and Winthrop were on oppoſite ſides in the Hutchinſon controverſy. Winthrop was oppoſed to an unlimited democracy ; and when the people of Connecticut were forming a government, he wrote them a letter, in which he ſaid that "the beſt part of a community is always the leaſt, and of that leaſt part the wiſer are ſtill leſs." His firm and decided management of affairs ſometimes made him unpopular. His private character was moſt amiable. His eldeſt ſon John was the founder of the Saybrook colóny, and governor of Connecticut. His valuable "Journal" of the public occurrences in the Maſſachuſetts Colony from March 29, 1630 to January 11, 1649, was firſt printed in 1790, and again with notes by James Savage, in 1826 and 1853.

[2] 4 *Maſſ. Hiſt. Coll.* vol. vi. p. 184.

Moſt of the letters of Roger Williams printed in this volume are without full

you mean any elder in thefe New Englifh churches, or (which I believe not) old Englifh,—diforderly functions, from whence our Jehovah of armies more and more redeemed his Ifrael,—or the Levites who ferved from twenty-five to fifty, Numb. 8., 24; or myfelf but a child in every thing, (though in Chrift called, and perfecuted even in and out of my father's houfe thefe 20 years), I am no Elder in any church, no more nor fo much as your worthy felf, nor ever fhall be, if the Lord pleafe to grant my defires that I may intend what I long after, the natives fouls, and yet if I at prefent were, I fhould be in the days of my vanity nearer upwards of 30 than 25;[1] or whether Timothy or Titus be in thought, &c., at your leifure I crave interpretation. Sorry I am fince Rationals fo much circumround and trouble you, that *beftiale quid* (and mine efpecially) fhould come near you: but fince the Lord of heaven is Lord of earth alfo, and you follow him as a dear child, I thankfully acknowledge your care and love

dates. Some give only the day of the week, and others only the day of the month. In many, the year is omitted; while fome have neither the month or year. In moft of them the editor has been able to affign dates which have been adopted by hiftorians, or by the biographers of Williams.

This letter was probably written between June and October, 1632. The queftion arofe in the "Congregation at Bofton" whether one perfon might be a civil magiftrate and a ruling elder at the fame time. Nowell affigns his pofition as ruling elder, doubtlefs from that caufe. Gov. Winthrop vifited Plymouth in October, 1632. This letter was probably written between thofe dates.—DRAKE

Hift. of Bofton, p. 140. WINTHROP, *Hift. of N. Eng.* vol. 1, p. 108–109,

[1] This, with other authorities, has given the year 1599 as the date of Williams' birth. See Roger Williams' teftimony in favor of Richard Smith's title to his land at Narraganfett, 1679. This date 1599 is now generally conceded as the year of Williams' birth.—ARNOLD, *Hift. R. I.* vol. 1, p. 50. GUILD, *Mem. of Williams,* Narr. Club, vol. 1, pp. 5 and 6.

The order for Williams's banifhment was paffed Sept. 3, 1635. He is fuppofed to have left Salem about January, 1635–6; and to eftablifhed himfelf at Providence in the following June.

about the cattle, and further entreat if you may (as you give me encouragement) procure the whole of that fecond, and let me know how, and how much payment will be here accepted, or in money in England. The Lord Jefus be with your Spirit, and your deareft one, and mine, in their extremities. To you both and all the Saints our due remembrances.

Yours in all unfeigned and brotherly affections,

ROGER WILLIAMS.

The brethren falute you.

You lately fent mufic to our ears, when we heard you perfuaded (and that effectually and fuccefsfully) our beloved Mr. Nowell to furrender up one fword: and that you were preparing to feek the Lord further; a duty not fo frequent with Plymouth as formerly : but *Spero meliora.*

For his much honored, Mr. John Winthrop, Deputy Governor thefe.

[1636 or 1637.][1]

MUCH HONORED SIR,—The frequent experience of your loving ear, ready and open toward me (in what your confcience hath permitted) as alfo of that excellent fpirit of wifdom and prudence wherewith the Father of Lights

[1] *4 Maff. Hift. Coll.* vol. vi. p. 186.
This letter, which is without date, is addreffed to Winthrop, as Deputy Governor, which office he held for the po- litical year ending May 17, 1637. It was evidently written fhortly after hefettlement at Providence, which it is bet lieved was in June, 1636. The letter

hath endued you, embolden me to requeſt a word of private adviſe with the ſooneſt convenience, if it may be, by this meſſenger.

The condition of myſelf and thoſe few families here planting with me, you know full well: we have no Patent: nor doth the face of Magiſtracy ſuit with our preſent condition. Hitherto, the maſters of families have ordinarily met once a fortnight and conſulted about our common peace, watch, and planting ; and mutual conſent have finiſhed all matters with ſpeed and peace.

Now of late ſome young men, ſingle perſons (of whom we had much need) being admitted to freedom of inhabitation, and promiſing to be ſubjeɛt to the orders made by the conſent of the houſeholders, are diſcontented with their eſtate, and ſeek the freedom of vote alſo, and equality, &c.

Beſide, our dangers (in the midſt of theſe dens of lions) now eſpecially, call upon us to be compaɛt in a civil way and power.

I have therefore had thoughts of propounding to my neighbors a double ſubſcription, concerning which I ſhall humbly crave your help.

The firſt concerning ourſelves, the maſters of families : thus,

refers to preparations againſt the Pequots, probably to Endicott's expedition which failed from Boſton the laſt of Auguſt of that year. After deſtroying the Indian ſettlement on Block Iſland, it failed for Thames River. Endicott reached Boſton on his return on the 14th of September.—Winthrop, *Hiſt. N. Eng.* p. 231–233. Drake, *Hiſt. Boſton,* p. 201. The letter, therefore, was probably written in Auguſt or September. Winthrop

refers to letters received by him from Williams, July 26th and 30th, and Aug. 26th, but neither allude to the matters ſpoken of in the letter in queſtion. (vol. i. p. 227–230.) The letter is intereſting, inaſmuch as it is the earlieſt account extant relating to the ſettlement at Providence and of the manner in which the civil affairs of the little community there were conduɛted.

We whofe names are hereunder written, late inhabitants of the Maffachufetts, (upon occafion of fome difference of confcience,) being permitted to depart from the
limits of that Patent, under the which we came over into
thefe parts, and being caft by the Providence of the God of
Heaven, remote from others of our countrymen amongft
the barbarians in this town of New Providence, do with
free and joint confent promife each unto other, that, for
our common peace and welfare (until we hear further of
the King's royal pleafure concerning ourfelves) we will
from time to time fubject ourfelves in active or paffive
obedience to fuch orders and agreements, as fhall be made
by the greater number of the prefent houfeholders, and
fuch as fhall be hereafter admitted by their confent into
the fame privilege and covenant in our ordinary meeting.
In witnefs whereof we hereunto fubfcribe, &c.

Concerning thofe few young men, and any who fhall
hereafter (by your favorable connivance) defire to plant
with us, this, —

We whofe names are hereunder written, being defirous
to inhabit in this Town of New Providence, do promife
to fubject ourfelves·in active or paffive obedience to fuch
orders and agreements as fhall be made from time to time,
by the greater number of the prefent houfeholders of this
Town, and fuch whom they fhall admit into the fame fellowfhip and privilege. In witnefs whereof, &c.[1]

Hitherto we choofe one, (named the officer,) to call the

---

[1] This agreement was afterwards
adopted by the people of Providence,
in much the fame language, bearing
thirteen fignatures, among which, however, the name of Williams does not appear.—*R. I. Col. Records,* vol. i. p. 14.
See alfo " Confirmatory Deed " of Roger Williams and his wife of lands tranf-
ferred by him to his affociates in the
year 1638. *Ibid.* vol. i. p. 22.

meeting at the appointed time: now it is defired by fome of us that the houfeholders by courfe perform that work, as alfo gather votes and fee the watch go on, &c.

I have not yet mentioned thefe things to my neighbors, but fhall as I fee caufe upon your loving counfel.

As alfo fince the place I have purchafed, fecondly, at mine own charge and engagements, the inhabitants paying (by confent thirty fhillings a piece as they come, until my charge be out for their particular lots: and thirdly, that I never made any other covenant with any perfon, but that if I got a place he fhould plant there with me: my query is this,—

Whither I may not lawfully defire this of my neighbors, that as I freely fubject myfelf to common confent, and fhall not bring in any perfon into the town without their confent: fo alfo that againft my confent no perfon be violently brought in and received.

I defire not to fleep in fecurity and dream of a neft which no hand can reach. I cannot but expect changes, and the change of the laft enemy death, yet dare I not defpife a liberty, which the Lord feemeth to offer me, if for mine own or others peace: and therefore have I been thus bold to prefent my thoughts unto you.

The Pequots hear of your preparations, &c., and comfort themfelves in this, that a witch amongft them will fink the pinnaces, by diving under water and making holes, &c., as alfo that they fhall now enrich themfelves with ftore of guns, but I hope their dreams (through the mercy of the Lord) fhall vanifh, and the devil and his lying forcerers fhall be confounded.

You may pleafe, Sir, to take notice that it is of main confequence to take fome courfe with the Wunnafhowa-

tuckoogs[1] and Wufquowhananawkits,[2] who are the further-
moft Neepnet men, for the Pequots driven from the fea
coaft with eafe, yet there fecure and ftrengthen themfelves,
and are then brought down fo much the nearer to you.
Thus with my beft refpects to your loving felf and Mrs.
Winthrop, I reft,

Your Worfhips unfeigned, praying to meet you in this
vale of tears or hills of mercy above.

R. WILLIAMS.

PROVIDENCE the 24th of the 8th.

SIR, WORTHY AND WELL BELOVED,—I was abroad about
the Pequot bufinefs when your letter arrived, and fince
meffengers have not fitted, &c.

I therefore now thankfully acknowledge your wifdom
and gentlenefs in receiving fo lovingly my late rude and
foolifh lines : you bear with fools gladly becaufe you are
wife.

I ftill wait upon your love and faithfulnefs for thofe poor
papers, and cannot but believe that your heart, tongue, and
pen fhould be one, if I were Turk or Jew, &c.

Your fix queries I welcome, my love forbidding me to
furmife that a Pharifee, a Sadducee, an Herodian, &c.,

---

[1] Or *Showatucks.* Perfons going by
land from Maffachusetts Bay Colony to
Connecticut, paffed through the country
of this tribe.

[2] *Wufkowhanan–auk–it* "the pigeon
country." The place "where thefe

fowl breed abundantly."—WILLIAMS'
Key, p. 176. This was in the northern
part of the Nipmuck country, in what
is now Worcefter County, Mafs.—
TRUMBULL's notes to WILLIAMS's *Key,*
Narr. Club, vol. i. p. 116.

wrote them; but rather that your love and pity framed
them as a phyfician to the fick, &c.

He that made us thefe fouls and fearcheth them, that
made the ear and eye, and therefore fees and hears I lie
not, but in his prefence have fadly fequeftered myfelf to
his holy tribunal, and your interrogatories, begging from
his throne thofe feven fiery lamps and eyes, his holy Spirit,
to help the fcrutiny, defirous to fufpect myfelf above the
old ferpent himfelf, and remembering that he that trufteth
in his own heart is a fool.   Prov. 28.

While I anfwer let me importune from your loving
breaft that good opinion that you deal with one (however
fo and fo, in your judgment yet) ferious, and defirous in
the matters of God's Sanctuary to ufe (as the double
weights of the Sanctuary teach us) double diligence.

Your firft Querie then is this.

What have you gained by your new-found practices? &c.

I confefs my gains caft up in man's exchange are lofs of
friends, efteem, maintenance, &c., but what was gain in
that refpect I defire to count lofs for the excellency of the
knowledge of Chrift Jefus my Lord: &c.   To His all
glorious Name I know I have gained the honor of one of
his poor witnefles, though in fackcloth.

To your beloved felves and others of God's people yet
afleep, this witnefs in the Lord's feafon at your waking
fhall be profperous, and the feed fown fhall arife to the
greater purity of the kingdom and ordinances of the
Prince of the kings of the earth.

To myfelf (through his rich grace) my tribulation hath
brought fome confolation and more evidence of his love,
finging Mofes his fong and the Lambs, in that weak victory
which (through His help) I have gotten over the beaft, his

picture, his mark, and number of his name, Revel. 15. 2. 3.

If you afk for numbers, the witneffes are but two: Revel. 11., and how many millions of Chriftians in name, and thoufands of Chriftians in heart, do call the truths (wherein yourfelf and I agree in witnefling) new found practices?

Gideon's army was thirty-two thoufand; but cowardice returned twenty-two thoufand back, and nine thoufand feven hundred worldlings fent but three hundred to the battle.

I will not by prophecy exafperate, but wifh (in the black and ftormy day) your company be not lefs than Gideon's, to fight (I mean with the Blood of the Lamb and Word of Witnefs) for what you profefs to fee.

To your fecond, viz.:   Is your fpirit as even as it was feven years fince?

I will not follow the fafhion either in commending or condemning of myfelf.   You and I ftand at one dreadful, dreadful tribunal : yet what is paft I defire to forget, and to prefs forward towards the mark for the price of the high calling of God in Chrift.

And for the evennefs of my fpirit.

Toward the Lord, I hope I more long to know and do His holy pleafure only, and to be ready not only to be banifhed, but to die in New England for the name of the Lord Jefus.

Towards yourfelves, I have hitherto begged of the Lord an even fpirit, and I hope ever fhall, as

Firft, reverently to efteem of, and tenderly to refpect the perfons of many hundreds of you, &c.

Secondly, To rejoice to fpend and be fpent in any fervice, (according to my confcience) for your welfares.

2

Thirdly, To rejoice to find out the leaft fwerving in judgment or practice from the help of any, even the leaft of you.

Laftly, to mourn daily, heavily, unceffantly, till the Lord look down from Heaven, and bring all his precious living ftones into one New Jerufalem.

To your third, viz.: Are you not grieved that you have grieved fo many ?

I fay with Paul, I vehemently forrow for the forrow of any of Zion's daughters, who fhould ever rejoice in her King, &c., yet I muft (and O that I had not caufe) grieve be- caufe fo many of Zion's daughters fee not and grieve not for their fouls defilements, and that fo few bear John company in weeping after the unfolding of the feals, which only weepers are acquainted with.

You thereupon propound a fourth, Do you think the Lord hath utterly forfaken us ?

I anfwer Jehovah will not forfake His people for His great name's fake 1. Sam. 12. That is, the fire of His love towards thofe whom once He loves is eternal, like Himfelf: and thus far be it from me to queftion His eternal love to- wards you, &c. Yet if you grant that ever you were as Abraham among the Chaldees, Lot among the Sodomites, the Kenites among the Amalekites, as Ifrael in Egypt or Babel, and that under pain of their plagues and judgments you were bound to leave them, depart, fly out, (not from the places as in the type,) but from the filthinefs, of their fins, &c., and if it prove, as I know affuredly it fhall, that though you have come far, yet you never came out of the wildernefs to this day : then, I befeech you, remember that yourfelves, and fo alfo many thoufands of God's peo- ple muft yet mournfully read the 74, 79, 80, and 89

Pſalms, the Lamentations, Daniel 11th, and Revel. 11th, 12th, 13th, and this, Sir, I beſeech you do more ſeriouſly then ever, and abſtract yourſelf with a holy violence from the dung heap of this earth, the credit and comfort of it, and cry to Heaven to remove the ſtumbling blocks, ſuch idols, after which ſometimes the Lord will give His own Iſrael an anſwer.

Sir, You requeſt me to be free with you, and therefore blame me not if I anſwer your requeſt, deſiring the like payment from your own dear hand, at any time, in any thing.

And let me add, that amongſt all the people of God, whereſoever ſcattered about Babel's banks, either in Rome or England, &c., your caſe is the worſt by far, becauſe while others of God's Iſrael tenderly reſpect ſuch as deſire to fear the Lord, your very judgment and conſcience leads you to ſmite and beat your fellow ſervants, expel them your coaſts, &c., and therefore, though I know the elect ſhall never finally be forſaken, yet Sodom's, Egypt's, Amalek's, Babel's judgments ought to drive us out, to make our calling out of this world to Chriſt, and our election ſure in him.

Sir, Your fifth is, From what ſpirit, and to what end do you drive ?

Concerning my ſpirit, as I ſaid before, I could declaim againſt it, but whether the ſpirit of Chriſt Jeſus, for whoſe viſible kingdom and ordinances I witneſs, &c, or the ſpirit of Antichriſt (1 John 4) againſt whom only I conteſt, do drive me, let the Father of Spirits be pleaſed to ſearch, and (worthy Sir) be you alſo pleaſed by the word to ſearch : and I hope you will find that as you ſay you do, I alſo ſeek Jeſus who was nailed to the gallows, I aſk the way to loft Zion, I witnefs what I believe I fee patiently (the Lord affifting) in fackcloth, I long for the bright appearance of the Lord Jefus to confume the man of fin: I long for the appearance of the Lamb's wife alfo, New Jerufalem: I wifh heartily profperity to you all, Governor and people, in your civil way, and mourn that you fee not your poverty, nakednefs, &c., in fpirituals, and yet I rejoice in the hopes that as the way of the Lord to Apollo, fo within a few years (through, I fear though, many tribulations) the way of the Lord Jefus, the firft and moft ancient path, fhall be more plainly difcovered to you and me.

Laftly, You afk whether my former condition would not have ftood with a gracious heart, &c.?

At this Query, Sir, I wonder much, becaufe you know what fins, yea all manner of fins, (the fin unto death excepted,) a child of God may lie in, inftance I need not.

Secondly, When it comes to matter of confcience that the ftroke lies upon the very judgment, that the thing practiced is lawful, &c., as the polygamy of the Saints, the building of the Temple, (if David had gone on,) the many falfe miniftries and miniftrations (like the ark upon the new cart) which from Luther's times to this day, God's children have confcientioufly practiced. Who then can wonder (and yet indeed who can not but wonder) how a gracious heart, before the Lord's awakening, and calling, and drawing out, may lie in many abominations?

Two inftances I fhall be bold to prefent you with. Firft, do you not hope Bifhop Ufher hath a gracious heart? and fecondly, Do you not judge that your own heart was gracious even when (with the poifoned fhirt on your back) you, &c.?

But while another judgeth the condition fair, the foul that fears, doubts, and feels a guilt hath broken bones, &c. Now, worthy Sir, I muſt call up your wiſdom, your love, your patience, your promiſe and faithfulneſs, candid inge-nuity, &c. My heart's deſire is abundant, and exceeds my pen. My head and actions willing to live (as the Apoſtle Paul) καλῶς ἐν πᾶσι. Where I err, Chriſt be pleaſed to re-ſtore me, where I ſtand, to eſtabliſh. If you pleaſe I have alſo a few Queries to yourſelf, without your leave I will not: but will ever mourn, (the Lord aſſiſting,) that I am no more (though I hope ever) yours,   R : Will :

Sir, Concerning natives: the Pequots and Nayantaquits reſolve to live and die together, and not to yield up one. Laſt night tidings came that the Mohawks, (the canni-bals,) have ſlain ſome of our countrymen at Connecticut. I hope it is not true.[1]

To John Winthrop, Governor, &c.

[1] The editor of the "*Winthrop Papers,*" (4 *Maſs. Hiſt. Coll.* vol. vi.) does not aſſign any date for this letter and the one that follows. This one is dated "the 24th of the 8th month," (or October 24th.) Williams begins by ſimply allu-ding to the "Pequot buſineſs." We in-fer from this that the Pequot war had not begun. With the exception of this paragraph, the letter relates wholly to religious affairs: with replies to queries put to him by Winthrop, about his "new found practices." May not this refer to his entire freedom in the exerciſe of his religious opinions in his new abode? In the letter which follows, Williams begins by ſpeaking of reports of a league between the Pequots and Mohawks, that the Pequots had "ſlain both Engliſh and natives at Connecticut Plantations." This muſt have been before the deſtruc-tion of the fort at Myſtic, which oc-cured on the 26th of May, 1637, for the Pequots were ſo completely annihi-lated in that fight, that there could have been no chance of making a league with the Mohawks; and it is known that, from fear of the Engliſh, the Mohawks des-troyed ſuch of the Pequots as ſought ſhelter among them. We think, therefore, that the firſt letter was written in Oc-tober, 1636, and the ſecond ſoon after; or, at any rate, before the attack on the Pequot fort.

To John Winthrop.[1]

NEW PROVIDENCE, 2ndo 7manæ, inflantis.[2]   [1637.]

SIR,—I have nothing certain to acquaint you with at
prefent: there have been reports thefe ten days, that the
Pequots are entered league by the hire of three or four
bufhels of beads, (black and white,) with the Mauquawogs
or Mohawks which fignifies men-eaters in their language; Thefe cannibals have been all the talk thefe ten
days, and the Narraganfetts are much troubled at them.

Two days fince came tidings that thefe Mohawks
and Pequots have flain many, both Englifh and natives, at
Connecticut Plantations. As yet I believe it not, and hope
in the Lord's mercy it is falfe, yet fince you pleafe to make
fuch good ufe of (poifon) bad and lying news, (which for
that end to awaken people I confefs) I fent the laft: I
would not conceal this: I hope to fend better in like manner after this; yet I fadly fear if the Lord pleafe to let
loofe thefe mad dogs, their practice will render the Pequots
cannibals too, and fecondly (at the leaft) cut off all hopes
of fafe refidence at Connecticut, and yet they are one hundred miles to the weftward of Connecticut Plantations. I
hope it will pleafe the Moft High to put his hook into
their nofe, &c., as alfo to give wifdom in the managing of
the war, that if it be poffible a league may rather be firm-
ly ftruck with them: they are moft favage, their weapons more dangerous and their cruelty dreadful, roafting
alive, &c.

Sir, I hear of the danger of the innovation of your
Government. The God of Heaven be pleafed to give you
faithfulnefs and courage in his fear: I fear not fo much

---

[1] 4 *Mafs. Hift. Coll.* vol. vi. p. 239.   [2] *Secundo feptima.* i. e. the 2d day of
the prefent week.

iron and fteel as the cutting of our throats with golden knives. I mean that under the pleafing baits of execution of juftice to the eaftward, and enlargement of authority, beyond all queftion, lies hid the hook to catch your invaluable liberties. Better an honorable death than a flave's life.

Sir, I may not forget due thanks for your intended requitals of my poor endeavors towards the barbarous : if it pleafe the Lord to ufe (with any good fuccefs) fo dull a tool, *fatis fuperque,* &c.

One kindnefs (yet according to true juftice) let me be bold to requeft. I have not yet got a penny of thofe two unfaithful ones, James and Thomas Haukins, of Bofton, concerning whom myfelf and wife have formeily troubled you. Mr. Coxall hath long had their bills : agreement of mitigation hath been made fince by arbitratois but to no purpofe. Their great earnings (if I had not lovingly releafed them) were mine own : my own debts lie unpaid, daily called for, and I hear for certain (though they can flatter and lie) they have fpent lavifhly and fared daintily of my purfe, while myfelf would have been glad of a cruft of their leavings, though yet I have not wanted, through his love that feeds the ravens, &c. John Throckmorton hath often demanded but in vain, he will now attend your loving helpfulnefs, and He who is moft holy and bleffed, all mercy and all pity, help you mercifully to fteer (by his holy compafs and alfo with his own moft holy hand) in the ocean of troubles and trials wherein we fail. It is no fmall favor that once again (though the occafions are fad) we may fail and fpeak togethcr, but the Harbor (fafe and large) will pay for all. Thus praying for our meeting, with beft falutes to Mrs. Winthrop and all yours, and my true refpects to Mr. Deputy, Mr. Bellingham, and other loving friends, I reft,

Your worfhip's unfeigned,

ROGER WILLIAMS.

For his much honored Mr. Governor, and Mr. WINTHROP, *Deputy Governor of the Maffachufetts, thefe.*

NEW PROVIDENCE, this 2d of the week.[1]   [May, 1637.]

Sir,—The latter end of the laft week I gave notice to our neighbor princes of your intentions and preparations againft the common enemy, the Pequots.   At my firft coming to them Canonicus (*morofus æque ac barbarex fenex*) was very

---

[1] 3 *Maff. Hiff. Coll.* vol. i. p. 159. *R. I. Hiff. Coll.* vol. iii, p. 137.

Written probably a few days before the attack on the Pequot fort, May 26, 1637. On the 10th of April, the authorities at Bofton concluded to fend Captain Underhill with twenty men to aid Connecticut Colony, in her attack againft the Pequots. To this Williams probably refers in his opening paragraph, and poffibly to the expedition under Captain Patrick.   The Narraganfetts concluded a treaty at Bofton, in October 1636, making the Pequots a common enemy.   In the third of Williams' "obfervations" in this letter, he recommends Niantic as a place of rendevouz.   This was apparently adopted, as Mafon, Underhill and Gardiner, the leaders of the expedition, arrived there May 25, (by way of Narraganfett Bay, May 23,) and

on the next day taking "Wequafh" for their guide, the Pequot fort at "Miftick" was reached.—DRAKE, *Hiff. of Bofton*, p. 205–209. *Book of the Indians*, p. 105–106. WINTHROP, *Hiff. N. Eng.* vol. 1. p. 268.

Capt. Daniel Patrick in a letter of May 23, 1637, writes Gov. Winthrop, that "Mr. Williams informs your worfhip at large" about the expedition againft the Pequot fort,—poffibly referring to this letter.   We are difpofed to believe that the date of this letter is May 22, which was Monday, from the apparent reference to it in Capt. Patrick's letter above quoted of fame date, and that the "rude view" was a copy of the above defcription, having been probably explained to R. W. at the date of the previous letter.

four, and accufed the Englifh and myfelf for fending the plague amongft them, and threatening to kill him efpecially.

Such tidings (it feems) were lately brought to his ears by fome of his flatterers and our ill-willers. I difcerned caufe of beftirring myfelf, and ftaid the longer, and at laft (through the mercy of the Moft High) I not only fweetened his fpirit, but poffeffed him, that the plague and other fickneffes were alone in the hand of the one God, who made him and us, who being difpleafed with the Englifh for lying, ftealing, idlenefs and uncleannefs, (the natives' epidemical fins,) fmote many thoufands of us our-felves with general and late mortalities.

Miantunnomu kept his barbarous court lately at my houfe, and with him I have far better dealing. He takes fome pleafure to vifit me, and fent me word of his coming over again fome eight days hence.

They pafs not a week without fome fkirmifhings, though hitherto little lofs on either fide. They were glad of your preparations, and in much conference with themfelves and others, (fifhing de induftria for inftructions from them,) I gathered thefe obfervations, which you may pleafe (as caufe may be) to confider and take notice of:

1. They conceive that to do execution to purpofe on the Pequots, will require not two or three days and away, but a riding by it and following of the work to and again the fpace of three weeks or a month, that there be a fall-ing off and a retreat, as if you were departed, and a falling on again within three or four days, when they are returned again to their houfes fecurely from their flight.

2. That if any pinnaces come in ken, they prefently prepare for flight, women and old men and children, to a fwamp fome three or four miles on the back of them, a

3

marvellous great and fecure fwamp, which they called Ohomowauke,[1] which fignifies owl's neft, and by another name, Cuppacommock,[2] which fignifies a refuge or hiding place, as I conceive.

3. That therefore Nayantaquit,[3] (which is Miantunno-mue's place of rendezvous,) to be thought on for the riding and retiring to of veffel or veffels, which place is faithful to the Narraganfetts and at prefent enmity with the Pequots.

4. They alfo conceive it eafy for the Englifh, that the provifions and munitions firft arrive at Aquedneck, called by us Rhode Ifland, at the Narraganfett's mouth, and then a meffenger may be defpatched hither, and fo to the bay, for the foldiers to march up by land to the veffels, who otherwife might fpend long time about the cape and fill more veffels than needs.

5. That the affault would be in the night, when they are commonly more fecure and at home, by which advantage the Englifh, being armed, may enter the houfes and do what execution they pleafe.

6. That before the affault be given, an ambufh be laid behind them, between them and the fwamp, to prevent their flight, &c.

7. That to that purpofe fuch guides as fhall be beft liked of to be taken along to direct, efpecially two Pequots, viz. : Wequafh[4] and Wuttackquiackommin, valiant men, efpeci-

[1] Koko'kehom, Oho'mous, An Owle. WILLIAMS' *Key*, vol. i. p. 174.

[2] Afterwards known as the Pine or Maft Swamp of Groton, Ct.—CAULKINS' *Hift. of New London*, note, p. 376.

[3] The Niantics were a tribe fubfidary to the Narraganfetts. They occupied the fouthermoft portion of Rhode Ifland, being feparated from the Pequots by the Pawcatuck River. Their principal refidence was at Wekapaug near Wefterly, R. I.—DRAKE, *Book of Indians*, p. 67.

[4] Wequafh died previous to 1643. He was a renegade Pequot fachem and as a

ally the latter, who have lived thefe three or four years with the Narraganfetts, and know every pafs and paſſage amongſt them, who defire armor to enter their houfes.

8. That it would be pleafing to all natives, that women and children be fpared, &c.

9. That if there be any more land travel to Connecticut, fome courfe would alfo be taken with the Wunhowatuckoogs, who are confederates with and a refuge to the Pequots.

Sir, if any thing be fent to the princes, I find that Canonicus would gladly accept of a box of eight or ten pounds of sugar, and indeed he told me he would thank Mr. Governor for a box full.

Sir, you may pleafe to take notice of a rude view, how the Pequots lie:

River Connecticut.
_____

O a fort of the Nayantic men, confederate with the Pequots.

Mohigadic
_____
River.

   Wein **O** *ſhauks, where*   *Ohom* | | | *owauke, the swamp,*
   Saſſaeus the chief Sachem is.   *three or four miles from——*
     Mis O *tick, where is* __Mamoho__, *another chief ſachim.*
_____
River.

     Nayantic, **O** *where is* **Wepiteammock** *and our friends.*
_____
River.

Thus, with my beft falutes to your worthy felves

guide did good fervice to the Englifh. They attempted to convert him to chiftianity, and according to fome authorities were evidently fuccefsful, but Roger Williams was not fo hopeful. Wequafh is the Indian name for Swan.—WILLIAMS' *Key*, p. 175. Mr. TRUMBULL'S notes to *Key*, pp. 26–27.

and loving friends with you, and daily cries to the Father
of mercies for a merciful iſſue to all theſe enterpriſes, I
reſt

    Your worſhip's ʼunfeignedly reſpective

                   Roger Williams.

To John Winthrop Governor of the Maſſachuſetts.[1]

     New Providence, this laſt of the week.[2]   [May, 1637.]

Sir, — I am much deſired by Yotaaſh (the bearer hereof, Miantunnomue's brother) to interpret his meſſage to
you, viz.: that Miantunnomu requeſts you to beſtow a
Pequot ſquaw upon him.

I object, he had his ſhare ſent him, he anſwers that Canonicus received but a few women and keeps them : and
yet he ſaith his brother hath more right: for, himſelf and
his brother's men firſt laid hold upon that company.

I object that all are diſpoſed of, he anſwers, if ſo, he
deſires to buy one or two of ſome Engliſhman.

I object that here are many run away, which I have deſired himſelf might convey home to you: he replies, they
have been this fortnight buſy (that is keeping of a kind
of Chriſtmas): and ſecondly, at preſent Miantunnomue's
father-in-law lies a dying: as alſo that ſome of the runaways periſhed in the woods ; three are at the Narraganſett,
and three within ten miles of this place; which I think

---

[1] 4 *Maſs. Hiſt. Coll.* vol. vi. p. 241.   were written juſt before the attack on
[2] This letter and the one that follows   the Pequot fort.

may beft be fetched by two or three Maffachufetts Indians who may here get fome one or two more to accompany and help.

Sir, you were pleafed fome while fince to intimate fome
breach of league in Miantunnomu. I would not dif-
hearten this man (from coming by my fpeech any way :
but I could wifh you would pleafe to intimate your mind
fully to him, as alfo that if there be any juft exception
which they cannot well anfwer, that ufe be made of it, (if
it may be with the fafety of the common peace,) to get
the bits into their mouths,[1] efpecially if their be good affurance from the Mohawks. So with my beft falutes and
earneft fighs to heaven, I reft

Your worfhip's unworthy

ROGER WILLIAMS.

---

*For his much honored, Mr. Governor of the Maffachufetts,
thefe.*[2]

[May ,1637.]

MUCH HONORED SIR,—I was bold to prefent you with
two letters by Thomas Holyway, fome weeks fince. I am
occafioned again at prefent to write a word by this bearer
Wequafh : whom (being a Pequot himfelf,) I commended
for a guide in the Pequot expedition.

I prefume he may fay fomething to yourfelf, or to fuch
other of my loving friends as may report unto your worfhip, what befel him at Cowefet.[3]

---

[1] "I mean the bit of awful refpeft, that they fall not into mutinies at home." *Note by Williams.*

[2] *Mafs. Hift. Coll.* vol. vi. p. 242.

[3] Eaft Greenwich. *Cowawefuck,* a pine tree.

He hath been five or six days now at my houfe, in which time I have had much opportunity to fearch into particulars, and am able to prefent you with naked truth.

He came from Monahiganick to Cowefet within night and lodged with his friend called Pananawokfhin. At Cowefit, an old man (Weeokamin,) hath made great lamentation for the death of two fons in the Pequot wars. This Weeokamun with divers of his conforts in the night time laid hold upon Wequafh, intending to bind him, charging him with the death of his two fons. Much bickering there was between them, but no hurt done, only Weeokamun ftruggling with one of Wequafh his company was fore bitten on the hand, and alfo bit the young man's fingers which are well again. So that their hoft kept peace in Canonicus his name, and brought them fafe to me the next day: yet in the fray they loft a coat and other fmall things, which (coming forth before day) they left behind them.

I fent up a meffenger to the Sachims to demand a reafon of fuch ufage and their goods. Canonicus fent his fon, and Miantunnomu his brother (Yotaafh) who went to Cowefet and demanded the reafon of fuch ufage, and the goods, and fo came to my houfe, caufing the goods to be reftored, profeffing the Sachim's ignorance and forrow for fuch paffages, and given charge to all natives for their fafe travel.

Having thofe meffengers and Wequafh at my houfe, I caufed them folemnly to parley of what I knew was grievance betwixt them, and what elfe I could any way pick out from either of them, concerning ourfelves the Englifh, or the Pequots, or themfelves. All which I carefully writ down the particulars, and fhall readily, at your worſhip's pleaſure, acquaint you with them : either concerning ſome ſquaws which Wequaſh acknowledgeth he parted with (and juſtly) to Canonicus and Miantunnomu, or other brablings which I thought not fit to trouble your worſhip with, without commiſſion.

Dear Sir, (notwithſtanding our differences concerning the worſhip of God and the ordinances miniſtred by Antichriſt's power) you have been always pleaſed lovingly to anſwer my boldneſs in civil things : let me once more find favor in your eyes to gratify myſelf, Mr. James, and many or moſt of the townsmen combined, in adviſing what to ſay or do to one unruly perſon who openly in town meeting more then once, profeſſeth to hope for and long for a better government then the country hath yet, and lets not to particularize, by a general Governor, &c. The white which such a ſpeech or perſon levels at can be no other then the raiſing of the fundamental liberties of the country, which ought to be dearer to us then our right eyes. But I am always too bold in prolixity, &c., therefore at preſent with humble reſpect remembered and cries to Heaven for mercy to you and yours, root and branches, and the whole country by your bleſſing, I reſt

Your worſhip's moſt unworthy

ROGER WILLIAMS.

For his much honored Mr. Governor [*Henry Vane,*] *or Mr. Deputy Governor,* [*John Winthrop,*] *theſe with ſpeed.*

This laſt of the preſent week in the morning.[1] [May 13, 1637.]

SIR, — Miantunnomu with a great train arrived the ſame

---

[1] 4 *Maſs. Hiſt. Coll.* vol. vi. p. 189. The editors of 3 *Maſs. Hiſt. Coll.* vol. vi., gives the date of this letter, as perhaps May, 1637, and probably be-

day that Anthony Dike[1] departed hence with his sad
tidings, and confirmeth. with the most the report of Anthony. The Narragansetts are at present doubtful of
reality in all our promises : I have alledged the best arguments I have heard or could invent, to persuade reality of
purpose and speedy performance, as also reasons of delay.
Miantunnomu and his best Council here with him, have
requested me earnestly to make this proffer to you. The
Pequots are scarce of provision, and therefore (as usually so
now especially) they are in some numbers come down to
the seaside (and two Islands, by name Munnawtawkit[2] and

fore the 17th of that month. We think
the date of the letter is previous to the
attacks on the Pequot fort, or rather
prior to the march of the Narragansetts to Niantic, May 22. The letter
gives information of the Indians (Pequots,) having gone down to the islands
to fish. Winthrop, under date of May
17, speaks (p. 265,) of having "received
intelligence from Miantunnomo, that the
Pequots had sent their women and children to an island for their safety," &c.
Roger Williams, under probable date of
May —, says, "Miantunnomo lately at
my house held his barbarous court.—
DRAKE, (*Hist. of Boston*, p. 212,) says,
May 22, a company of forty men under
Capt. Patrick was hastened away *because
of intelligence received from Miantunnomo
about the Indians having "sent their women to an island."* A mistake in its date,
as Patrick must have been at Providence
on that day.—See 4 *Mass. Hist. Coll.*
vol. vii. p. 328.

The letter was probably written Saturday, May 13, the bearer in accordance with Puritan customs not leaving until Monday 15, would possibly not reach
Winthrop until after the 17th, on which

day the election took place, promoting
Winthrop from Deputy Governor to
Governor. As this election was very important it probably had been thoroughly
canvassed, and Williams conversant with
the fact addresses Winthrop.

[1] Anthony Dike or Dick, came to Boston in 1623, and was lost on Cape Cod
in a very cold storm December 15, 1638.
WINTHROP, *Hist. N. Eng.* vol. i. p. 345.
"Anthony Dike master of a bark, having his bark at Rhode Island in the winter, was sent for by Mr. Vane, then
Governor. Anthony came to Rhode
Island by land, and from thence he came
with his bark to me with a letter, wherein was desired that I should consider
the best way I could to quell these Pequots, which I also did, and with my
letter sent the man's rib as a token."
GARDINER'S *Pequot Warres*, 3 *Mass.
Hist. Coll.* vol. iii. p. 144. The news
brought by Dike was probably the attacks by the Indians on the settlements
at Saybrook and Weathersfield, on the
Connecticut River.—4 *Mass. Hist. Coll.*
p. 7–398.

[2] *Munawtawkit*, Montauk Point, formerly Montauket, Montacut, and by

Manittuwond efpecially) to take fturgeon and other fifh, as alfo to make new fields of corn, in cafe the Englifh fhould deftroy their fields at home.

Miantunnomu defires to go himfelf with one Wequafh[1] here at prefent with him, in this pinnace here left by Anthony, or any other that fhall take him in at the Narraganfett.

He will put in forty or fifty or more as the veffel will ftow.

He will put in victuals himfelf for his men. He will direct the pinnace to the places, and in the night land his men, defpoil them of their canoes, cut off the men he finds, (the greateft number being women and children, which for the moft of them he would cut off,) as alfo fpoil their fields : and this he proffers to do without landing an Englifhman, with whom he will remain on board in Englifh clothes which he defires for himfelf.

John, a feaman aboard, calls the Ifland, Plum Ifland, and is very willing to go on the defign, and thinks, as alfo Miantunnomu doth, that if within two or three days they went forth, they would be here again within four or five or lefs.

Sir, for myfelf I dare not advife : but if my thoughts be afked I fhall (with all due fubmiffion) fay this : —

It will at prefent wedge them in from any ftarting afide until your forces fhall follow.

If they fpeed it will weaken the enemy and diftrefs them, being put by their hopes : as alfo much enrage the Pequots for ever againft them, a thing much defirable.

Roger Williams Munnawtawkit, is probably from *Manati, auke*, and *it* locative ; in the Ifland country, or country of the Iflanders.—*Conn. Hift. Coll.* vol. ii. p. 23.

[1] " The Pequot of whom I have formerly wrote."—*Williams' note.*

Befide, the charge or danger of the Englifh will be none, unlefs Miantunnomue's coarfe clothes and a large coat for Wequafh, the Pequot guide, a man of great ufe. The Moft Holy and only Wife be pleafed to fmile upon the face of the Englifh that be his: (we have all, if ever, caufe to examine ourfelves, our errands and work) in the face of Jefus Chrift.

While I write, a Meffenger is come to Miantunnomu from Neepemut, reporting a far greater flaughter then that Anthony brought word of, and fince the former a great number at the Plantations, and fome perfons are mentioned, but I will not name either, but hope and long to hear it countermanded.

In cafe that Anthony or other feamen cannot be gotten fuddenly, here is one with us willing to make up a third man, (to the other two left with the pinnace,) to carry the veffel, though I judge Anthony himfelf the fitteft.

Sir, Miantunnomu defired me to give you a hint that the fix fathom of beads which he gave for the flaying of Audfah[1] be repaid him, and fent now if it may be; his wars keep him bare.

> Your worfhip's unfeignedly refpective
>
> ROGER WILLIAMS.

For any gratuities or tokens Canonicus defires fugar; Miantunnomu powder. My humble refpects to all my loving friends.

Sar, Miantunnomu is clofe in this his project, and therefore I think the meffenger is fent only for the beads: it is very convenient that Miantunnomue's clothes and Wequafh his coat be fent by him.

---

[1] "Audfah the chiefe murtherer" of Oldham.—4 *Mafs. Hift. Coll.* vol. vi. p. 208, 214, 216.

To his much honored Governor John Winthrop.[1]

NEW PROVIDENCE,
this 6th of the prefent week, towards midnight.   [June 2, 1637.][2]

SIR, — By John Throckmorton[3] I was bold to advertife of the late merciful fuccefs it hath pleafed the Father of Mercies to vouchfafe to the firft attempts of our country-men againft thefe barbarians.

After his departure toward you, I went over to the Narraganfett, partly for intelligence and partly to encourage the Narraganfetts in cafe the fad news of all their men and yours defeated were true.

I found the firft news of the cutting off the whole Fort of the Pequots at Myftic to be certain and unqueftionably true, as I fent, with little or no variation, of which hereafter.

The news of the cutting off three hundred Narraganfetts and all the Englifh held ftill for current and confirmed that they were oppreffed with multitudes, their provifion being fpent and the Englifh wanting powder and fhot and the Narraganfetts arrows.[4]

---

[1] 4 *Mafs. Hift. Coll.* vol. vi. p. 191.
[2] Probably Friday, June 2, 1637, juft one week after the deftruction of the Pequot fort, May 26, 1637.—WINTHROP, *Hift. of N. Eng.* vol. i. p. 268.
[3] Probably Mr. Williams fent by John Throckmorton news of the capture of the fort at Myftic, and the fubfequent tidings of the "cutting off three hundred Narraganfetts and all the Englifh." *This* letter is to correct the laft "fad news." John Throckmorton came to America with Roger Williams in 1630, was excommunicated at Salem at the fame

time and for the fame offences as Williams, and was one of the original thirteen firft fettlers of Providence. Removed to Monmouth, N. J., and died before 1687. SAVAGE, *Genealog. Dic.* vol. iv. p. 294. *R. I. Col. Rec.* vol. i. pp. 17–22 and 299.
[4] "Prefently upon this came news from Narraganfett, that all the Englifh, and two hundred of the Indians were cut off in their retreat, for want of powder and victuals. Three days after, this was confirmed by a poft from Plymouth, with fuch probable circumftances, as it was gen-

I gave the beſt reaſons I could to perſuade that they were all either gone together to Connecticut for proviſion, or upon ſome ſecond aſſault upon the other of the Pequot Forts.

As alſo I was bold to promiſe (in Mr. Governor's name) that although all theſe or móre were cut off, yet there ſhould be freſh ſupplies of the Engliſh who would never ſheathe their swords, &c.

This fifth day paſt toward night I have received tidings (bleſſed for ever be the Lord of Hoſts,) that the Narraganſetts are all came ſafe home yeſternight, (at noon I came from thence,) and brought word that the Engliſh were all ſafe, but the three firſt ſlain at the Fort with two of their own.

As alſo that indeed they fought thrice that day of their firſt victory with no loſs of their ſide, and with the loſs of two Pequots more.

That themſelves and the Engliſh prepared next day after for their other Forts, found all ſled, made themſelves lords of one, in which both Engliſh and Narraganſetts now keep.

That Maumanadtuck[1] one of their biggeſt, with great troops, (as before he gave out he could) is gone to Wun-naſhowatuckqut (the further Neepmucks.)

---

erally believed. But three days after, Mr. Williams having gone to the Narraganſetts to diſcover the truth, found them mourning as being confident of it; but that night ſome came from the army, and aſſured them all was well, and that all the Pequots were fled and had forſaken their forts."—WINTHROP, *Hiſt. N. Eng.* vol. i. p. 269.

[1] In a letter from Capt. Stoughton to Gov. Winthrop, he writes: "We ſhall the next week join in ſeeing what we can do againſt Saſſacus, and another great Sagamore, Momorrattuck."—DRAKE, *Hiſt. of Boſton,* p. 215. This is probably the ſame, Indian names being variouſly written by different perſons. Capt. Daniel Patrick, writes July 6, 1637 to Increaſe Nowell, "Mamenatucke is at Quenepiage, or lately gone to the Mohawks."—4 *Maſs. Hiſt. Coll.* vol. vii. p. 326.

That Safacus[1] faid he would go to Long Ifland, and thither is gone or hid in the fwamps, but not a Pequot is to be found.

That Miantunnomu is come from Pequot to Nayantaquit, and was refolved homeward to fend out to Wunnafhowatuckqut where the enemy fhelters and have Forts.

Now Sir, confidering the work is effected (through the mercy of the Moft High) in thefe parts, and that the Connecticut Englifh, together with Capt. Patrick[2] and his, are fufficient to maintain what they have gotten, and purfue Safacus in all his motions thereabouts: I conceived (with fubmiffion) that it might fave the country no fmall charge, and hazard, and lofs, timely to advertife and give intelligence.

The Wunnafhowatuckoogs and Pequots with them are about the diftance from you that we are: on them I conceive and underftand the Narraganfetts next fall.

If you fee caufe and grounds to make a ftop for a day or two, if the Lord pleafe, the fecond day or third of the next week I hope to acquaint you with Miantunnomues and Caunonicus their advice and defire, which it may be well to meet his companions at the hither Nipmucks and none to come this way, or fome the one way and fome

---

[1] "Saffacufe chief fachem of the Pequots." "This Saffacufe, (the Pequots chief fachem) having fled to the Mohawks, they cutt off his head, with fome other of ye chiefs of them, whether to fatisfy the Englifh, or rather the Narraganfetts (who as I have fince heard, hired them to do it,) or for their own advantage I now know not; but it was thus this war took end."—BRADFORD, *Hift. of Plywouth Plantations*, p. 361.

[2] Capt. Daniel Patrick came to America in 1630, and fettled in Watertown, and was there admitted a freeman. His manner of life was very unpuritanic, and he therefore removed to "within twenty miles of the Dutch and put himfelf under their protection." His death in 1643 was occafioned by being fhot by a Dutchman; who had charged him with treacherous dealings between the Dutch and Indians.—WINTHROP, vol. ii, p. 182. 4 *Mafs. Hift. Coll.* vol. vii, p. 412.

the other. This morning, I go over (if the Lord pleafe) to confult with them, hoping to be at home (if poffible) to-morrow evening, and fo to difpatch fome meffenger the fecond in the morning.

Sir, your late meffage to the Nipmucks (through the Loi d's mercy) have wrought this effect, that whereas they ftaggered as neuters, they brought this prefent week divers bafkets of their nokehick and cheftnuts to Canonicus towards his wars.

Sir, I underftand that the caufe why the Englifh hurt fo many of the Narraganfetts, was want of figns or marks. You may pleafe therefore to provide fome yellow or red for their heads: The Connecticut Englifh had yellow but not enough.[1]

Thus befeeching the God of Peace to be at peace with us, that all the fruit may be the taking away of our fin, (which if not removed will unftop worfe vials) to guide your confultations and profper your expeditions to the praife of His own moft holy name, I reft

Your worfhip's faithful and affectionate in all civil bonds,

ROGER WILLIAMS.

Sir, for the young man that accompanies my man, the country may pleafe to recompenfe his time, or I fhall.

Our beft refpects to Mrs. Winthrop and all your and our loving friends.

---

[1] Divers of the Indian friends were hurt by the Englifh, becaufe they had not fome mark to diftinguifh them from the Pequods as fome of them had.—WIN-THROP, *Hift. N. England*, vol. i. p. 268.

NOTE ON THE PEQUOT WAR. Without entering into the particulars of the caufes which led to the war between the Englifh and the Pequots, it is fufficient to ftate, that, in confequence of the many murders of the colonifts, committed by this tribe. the Governor and Council of Maffachufetts declared war againft the Indians on Maniffes, (Block Ifland). and late in September, 1636, fent Capt. John Endecott there with a force to subdue them. The Pequots now commenced more ferious depredations, fo that the Connecticut government determined to fend a force againft them. In May, 1637, Capt. John Mafon, with a command of ninety men; and Uncas, the Mohigan chief, with a body of Indians failed down the Connecticut. The latter encountered the Pequots near Saybrook fort and defeated them. They were now joined by Capt. John Underhill with nineteen men, when the two Captains at once refolved to make an attack upon one of the forts of Saffachus, the Pequot chief, fituate in or neat the prefent town of Myftic. The Englifh, with their Indian allies, about five hundred in number, arrived in the vicinity of the fort on the 25th of May, where they were joined by a party of Narraganfetts. Before daylight the following morning they had completely invefted the fort. Both the Mohegans and Narraganfetts manifefted great alarm in attacking this ftronghold of the Pequots and their fuperior force; and the Englifh had reafon to fear that they would be abandoned by their Indian allies.

The Englifh having fent a portion of their force from Saybrook back to Hartford, were now reduced to feventy-leven men. Thefe were divided into two companies, one led by Capt. Mafon, the other by Capt. Underhill. The fort had two entrances on oppofite fides, into which each party were led, fword in hand. The enemy being afleep were aroufed by the barking of a dog, and were heard to cry out *Owanux* (Englifhmen.) Their wigwams were now fet on fire, while the poor creatures with their fimple weapons, could make little defenfe, and in vain, attempted to efcape. They were purfued from wigwam to wigwam, and flaughtered in every fecret place. Men, women and children were alike cut to pieces or confumed by the flames, which foon enveloped the entire enclofure. Such as fucceeded in getting outfide the pallifade were fhot down by the foldiers pofted there. "And thus" writes Mafon " in a little more than one hour's fpace was their impregnable Fort, with themfelves, utterly deftroyed, to the number of fix or feven hundred, as fome of themfelves confeffed. There were only feven taken captive and about feven efcaped."—*Hift. of the Pequot War*, p. 10.

Of the Englifh, two were killed and about twenty wounded. "All our Indians" fays Mafon, "except Uncas, deferted us." Saffachus was in another fort, and hearing of the fuccefs of the Englifh, deftroyed his fort, and, with about eighty of his followers, efcaped to the Mohawks, who beheaded him and fent his fcalp to the Englifh.

The Pequot war was a memorable event in the early hiftory of New England, refulting in the annihilation of this powerful tribe. Befides what is faid by Winthrop aud other hiftorians, there are four feparate works in relation to it as follows :

1. JOHN UNDERHILL's *News from America; or a New and Experimentall Difcoverie of New England, containing a True relation of their warlike proceedings thefe two yeares laft paft, with a figure of the Indian Fort or Palazado.* LONDON, 1638.

2. P. VINCENT. *A True Relation of the late Battell fought in New England, between the Englifh and the Pequot Salvages. In which were flaine and taken prifoners about 700 of the Salvages, ana*

For his much honored Mr. Governor thefe. Mr. Stoughton or Capt. Traſke, on their way, may pleaſe to read this.

NEW PROVIDENCE, this 4th of the week.   [June 21, 1637.][1]

SIR,—John Gallop (bleſſed be the Lord) is ſafely arrived at our doors, and hath brought from the Lord and you a merciful refreſhing to us. He be graciouſly pleaſed to recompenſe it a thouſand fold to the whole land and yourſelves eſpecially.

thoſe which eſcaped had their heads cut off by the Mohocks: with the preſent ſtate of things there. LONDON, 1638.
  3. MAJOR JOHN MASON. *A Brief Hiſtory of the Pequot War; eſpecially of the memorable Taking of their Fort at Miſtick, in Connecticut in* 1637. BOSTON, 1736.
  4. LEIFT LYON GARDINER. *His Relation of the Pequot Warres.* (1660.) A manuſcript. Printed in 3d ſeries *Maſs. Hiſt. Coll.* vol. iii.
  Underhill, Maſon and Gardiner were prominent actors in the war. Of Vincent nothing is known.

[1] 4 *Maſſ. Hiſt. Coll.* vol. vi. p. 194.
  This letter muſt be of later date than June 19, 1637, as Capt. Daniel Patrick writing to Winthrop from Providence on that day, ſays " William Quicke has been here this ten days, but none but he has yet come." Probably written in the latter part of June, 1637, either 21st or 28th; more likely 21st, as Drake, (p. 214) concludes that Stoughton muſt have arrived at the mouth of the river before June 26. Trumbull, (pp. 1–35) ſays " the party arrived at Pequot harbor the latter part of June. Maſon, ſays "About a fortnight after our return home which was about one month after the fight at Miſtick, there arrived in Pequot River

ſeveral veſſels from the Maſſachuſetts, Captain Iſrael Stoughton being Commander-in-Chief, and with him about one hundred and twenty men ; being ſent by that colony to purſue the war againſt the Pequots.— *Hiſt. of Pequot War,* p. 14.
  John Gallup was with his pinnace at the Pequot River at the time when Stoughton's force was there. Hubbard, (p. 127) ſays of the capture of ſome hundred Pequots, " The men among them to the number of thirty were turned preſently into Charon's Ferry, but under the command of Skipper Gallop, who diſpatched them a little without the harbor." Probably Gallop was on his way to join Stoughton, or poſſibly he was in command of one of the veſſels of Stoughton's ſquadron. Stoughton having "ſailed" from Boſton, this letter was probably ſent by water conveyance to Winthrop.
  John Gallop was of Dorcheſter, in 1630, and afterwards removed to Boſton. He was a fiſherman and pilot, and alſo an Indian trader. On one of his expeditions he diſcovered the murder of John Oldham by the Indians and bravely captured Oldham's boat and all the murderers. A ſtorm coming up, he was obliged to let them go, taking only one

He relates that there is now riding below three pinnaces, (the names of the maſters, Quick,[1] Jigles and Robinſon,) and the two Shallops, as alſo that the other, whereof —— Jackſon[2] of Salem, is maſter, was in company with them the night before, and weighed anchor together, but being not able to turn about was fain to chop to an anchor again, but they hope is in by this time.

Sir, I hear our loving friends, Mr. Stoughton,[3] Mr. Traſke,[4] &c., are on their way, and one hundred and ſixty (the intended number) with them. I hope the continuance of the number will be ſeaſonable, if not for purſuit of Saſacous and the Pequots, (of whom it is ſaid that they are gone far and finally,) yet for the quelling of their con-

Indian to Boſton. He and his ſon John rendered valuable ſervices during the Pequot wars, and after the death of the father in 1650, the ſon received "with reſpeŝt unto ſuch ſervices," grants of land amounting to four hundred and fifty acres. Gallop's Iſland and Gallop's Point in Maſſachuſetts Bay were probably named for thoſe men.—Caulkins' *Hiſt. of New London.* Savage, *Genealog. Dic.*

[1] William Quick, mariner, was of Charleſtown in 1636, and afterwards removed to Newport, where he was admitted a freeman, Dec. 27, 1638.—Savage, *Genealog. Dic.* vol. iii. p. 499.

[2] John Jackſon, of Salem, who came to New England in 1635, from London. His houſe was deſtroyed by fire Oŝober, 1636; he died June, 1656.—Savage, *Genealog. Dict.* vol. ii. p. 529. Winthrop, vol. i. p. 239. "a goodly man and experienced ſeaman."—vol. ii. p. 23.

[3] "We alſo provided to ſend one hundred and ſixty more men after them

to proſecute the war; and Mr. Stoughton, one of the magiſtrates, was ſent with them."—Winthrop, *New Eng.* vol. i. p. 263.

Col. Iſrael Stoughton, an early ſettler of Dorcheſter. Member of the firſt General Court convened 1634, and again in 1635, 1636 and 1637; diſabled from holding office for three years for publiſhing a pamphlet denying to the Governor and Affiſtants ſome of the powers they claimed, but was reſtored in 1636. He returned to England and there died 1645.—Drake's *Dic. Am. Biog.*

[4] William Traſk one of the early ſettlers of Salem, and a repreſentative from that town a number of years. He was an important man in the colony, and one on whom Gov. Endicott greatly relied. In this expedition he commanded the Eſſex men, having Richard Davenport as his Lieutenant. He died in 1666, aged 77

federates the Wunnafhowatuckoogs and Monafhackotoogs, &c., who live nearer to you on the weftward, &c. Some two hundred of thefe (fince the flaughter at the Fort) came in revenge upon the Narraganfetts : which the Narraganfetts themfelves knew not until three Pequots (now fallen to them) related it : for it pleafed the Lord to fend a great mift that morning that they durft not fight, and fo returned : fo that there is caufe to take fome courfe with them, and efpecially if it be poffible for the clearing of land paffage to Connedicut.

I underftand it would be very grateful to our neighbors, that fuch Pequots as fall to them be not enflaved, like thofe which are taken in war : but (as they fay is their general cuftom) be ufed kindly, have houfes, and goods, and fields given them : becaufe they voluntarily choofe to come into them, and if not received, will go to the enemy or turn wild Irifh themfelves : but of this more as I fhall underftand ; thus in hafte with beft falutations to Mrs. Winthrop and all yours, with my poor defires to the Lord for yours, I reft

Your worfhip's unfeigned,

ROGER WILLIAMS.

My beft refpects to Mr. Deputy, Mr. Bellingham, theirs, and other loving friends.

For his much honored Mr. Governor, [*John Winthrop.*]

NEW PROVIDENCE, this 6th inftantis. [July, 1637.] [1]

MUCH HONORED SIR,—It having again pleafed the Moft High to put into your hands another miferable drone of Adam's degenerate feed, and our brethren by nature, I am bold (if I may not offend in it) to requeft the keeping and bringing up of one of the children. I have fixed mine eye on this little one with the red about his neck, but I will not be peremptory in my choice, but will reft in your loving pleafure for him or any, &c.

Sir, Capt. Patrick gives me a hint of the likely return of moft of your forces (Safacous and about a fcore of men with him and other companies, four fcore in one, furviving,) I fhall humbly propound whether it be not confiderable, that better now then hereafter the purfuit be continued.

1st, Becaufe it may ftop a conglomeration between them and the Mohawks, which longer time is like to make.

2ndly, Longer time will put many opportunities of occafional revenge into their hand, as we fee in the three laft cut off upon the Connecticut river, after the fort cut off.[2]

Capt. Patrick alfo informs me of a great itch upon the soldiers to fall foul upon our neighbors. Little fparks

---

[1] *4 Maſs. Hiſt. Coll.* vol. vi. p. 195, DRAKE fays, it appears by a letter from Capt. Stoughton received in Bofton, July 6, that Mr. Haynes and Mr. Ludlow were at Pequot River with the colonial forces. The letter was probably carried by Jiglies, (previoufly mentioned) whofe pinnace arrived at Bofton, on the fixth of July, with forty-eight Indian prifoners. Poffibly Williams may have received his letter from Capt. Patrick by this pinnace and then felected the "little one with the red about his neck."—*Hiſt. of Boſton,* p. 214.

"There were fent to Bofton, forty-eight women and children. There were eighty taken as before is expreffed. They were difpofed of to particular perfons in the country."—WINTHROP, *Hiſt. N. Eng.* vol. i. p. 278.

[2] "Saffachus, flying towards Conetticot plantations, quartered by the river fide; there he met with a fhallop fent down to Seabrooke fort, which had in it three men; they let fly upon them, fhot many arrows into them. Courageous were the Englifh, and died in their hands, but with a great deal of valor."—UNDERHILL, *News from America.* London: 1638.

prove great fires. The God of Peace who is only wise be pleafed to guide us. Capt. Patrick confeffeth that they were the chief actors in the laft captives, and had taken all by a wile and flain two before the Englifh came. I hear no speech at prefent about inequality, but content and affection towards us.

I much rejoice that (as he fayeth) fome of the chiefs at Connecticut (Mr. Heynes[1] and Mr. Ludlow,[2]) are almoft adverfe from killing women and children. Mercy outfhines all the works and attributes of him who is the Father of Mercies, unto whom with earneft fupplications for you and yours, I reft

Your worfhip's unfeigned

ROGER WILLIAMS.

My beft refpects to good Mrs. Winthrop, Mr. Deputy, Mr. Bellingham, and theirs.

[1] John Haynes came to New England in 1633 with the Rev. Mr. Hooker. He was one of the beft educated of the early fettlers of the country, and during his life was always in prominent official pofitions. Affiftant in 1634 and 1636, he was in 1635 Governor of Mafs. In 1637 he removed to Connecticut, was elected Governor in 1639, and was re-elected every alternate year until his death in 1654.

[2] Roger Ludlow, Deputy Governor of Maffachufetts and Connecticut, emigrated from England in 1630 and was one of the firft fettlers of Dorcheffer. He was an affiftant judge for four years, having received his appointment in England. Failing to be elected Governor in 1634, he complained of the election as having been a fraud. He removed to Windfor, Connecticut, in 1635, where he was, for nineteen years one of the moft ufeful and diftinguifhed men. He was every year elected either a magiftrate or Deputy Governor, and was alfo one of the Commiffioners of the United Colonies. In 1653, the Commiffioners, in confequence of an alleged plot of the Dutch, voted to make war againft them; but Maffachufetts refufed to concur. At this period the inhabitants of Fairfield determined to make war upon Manhadoes, and chofe Mr. Ludlow commander-in-chief. The General Court of New Haven, difcountenanced the proceedings and punifhed his officers for attempting to create an infurrection. In confequence of this affair he removed to Virginia with his family in 1654. He compiled the firft code of laws adopted in Connecticut, which was printed in 1672. Ludlow was brother-in-law of John Endecott.—BLAKE, *Biog. Dic.*

For his much honored John Winthrop, Governor of the Maſſachuſetts.

NEW PROVIDENCE, this 2d 7 næ. [July 10, 1637.] [1]

SIR,—Concerning your priſoners taken at Block Iſland, I have informed the Sachems of your care not to injure them and deſire to have them cleared; accordingly Cut-ſhamaquene[2] (now come from purſuing Saſſacous who is fled Southerly, far out of reach,) I ſay he hath received teſtimony from the Sachems Princes that they are Nayan-taquit men, (Wepiteammocks[3] men) and ſo all are Narra-ganſett men, and ſo indeed Sir, I had thought to ſend you word at this preſent, had I not received your letter, for it was continually affirmed to me for truth by all the Narra-ganſett men occaſionally being here.

Sir, the laſt meſſenger that carried letters from you to Pequot, related to the Sachems at Narraganſett, that you were diſpleaſed that the captives brought to the Bay lately, were taken by the Engliſh from the Narraganſetts, as alſo the

---

[1] 4 *Maſſ. Hiſt. Coll.* vol. vi. p. 197. 2d Septimanae; or ſecond day of the week. Probably Monday, July 10.

[2] "A pinnace returning (from Capt. Stoughton's expedition) took a canoe with four Indians near Block Iſland. We ſent to Miantonomoh to know what they were, and after we diſcharged all ſave one, who was a Pequot, whom we gave Mr. Cutting to carry into England.— WINTHROP, vol. 1. p. 277.

[3] "Kuchamakin, Cutſhamoquin, who was the firſt ſachem, and his people to whom Mr. Elliot preached."—1 *Maſſ. Hiſt. Coll.* vol. i. p. 166. "In 1636, Kutſhamakin ſold to the

people of Dorcheſter, Uncatquiſſet, be-ing the part of that town, ſince called Milton. This it appears was at ſome period his reſidence."—DRAKE, *Book of Indians*, p. 52.

"The Bay Men killed not a man, ſave that one Kichomiquin, an Indian Sachem of the Bay, killed a Pequit ; and thus be-gan the war between the Indians and us in theſe parts." — GARDINER. *Pequot Warres*, 3 *Maſs. Hiſt. Coll.* vol. iii. p. 140. This man was often employed as an in-terpreter, he being "acquainted with the Engliſh language," and alſo as a guide in the various expeditions of the colo-niſts.

ſpoil upon them, which was given to the Engliſh ſoldiers.[1] I have anſwered that I think it was not ſo, but I ſhall underſtand the truth ſhortly ; and therefore, Sir, be pleaſed in your next to intimate a word, that I may ſatisfy them, for though I would not fear a jar with them yet I would ſend off from being foul, and deal with them wiſely as with wolves endowed with men's brains.

The laſt week is a battle fought between the hither Neepmucks and the further, the Wunnaſhowatuckoogs, &c., the ſucceſs is not yet known : it will be of conſequence, for it is ſaid they fortify, joining with ſcattered Pequots.

Sir, The laſt day of the week Wequaſh the Pequot guide, near hand, ſlew his countryman Saſſawwaw, a Pequot, alſo Miantunnomue's ſpecial darling,[2] and a kind of General

---

[1] Wepiteamock, was Miantunnomu's brother-in-law The "Eaſtern Niantics" were located about Weſterly, R. I., and were tributary to the Narraganſetts. The "Weſtern Niantics" were located between the Connecticut and Niantic Rivers, and were allies or tributaries of the Pequots. Early in the ſeventeenth century before the Engliſh came to New England, the Pequots migrated from the North to the country about New London, ſeparating the Niantics, who until that time had probably been one tribe. The confanguinity of the tribes was well known to the Engliſh at the time.

[2] Saſſawwaw, otherwiſe known as Soſoa or Socho. He did not die at this time but was living in 1662. In 1660, he ſold a tract of land called Miſquamicoke, what is now known as Weſterly,

R. I., to ſome Newport parties, which land having been claimed by Ninigret, a number of depoſitions were taken to prove Soſoa the rightful owner. All theſe teſtimonies proved that before the Engliſh "had any warr with the Pequots, the Pequots, croſſing the Pawcatuck, ſeated themſelves on the neck called Miſquamicook, which were the Narraganſett lands and territories : whereupon the Narraganſett Sachims, Canonicus and Miantonumy, employed a captain of thoſe parts, their ſubject, to deſtroy or beat off thoſe intruding Pequots, and in caſe he ſo did, they gave to him and his forever the ſaid land Miſquamicook."— "and that the aforeſaid Sachim was named Soſoa ; and is ſtill living."—TRUMBULL, note to *Williams' Key*, p. 79. POTTER'S *Narraganſett*, p. 243.

of his forces. There was yefterday fome tumult about it, becaufe Wequafh lives with Canonicus, and Miantunnomu purfues the revenge and juftice, &c.

By the way, although Wequafh it may be have treacheroufly almoft flain him, yet I fee the righteous hand of the moft High Judge, thus: Saffawwaw turned to the Narraganfetts and again pretends a return to the Pequots, gets them forth the laft year againft the Narraganfetts and fpying advantage, flew the chief Pequot Captain and whips off his head, and fo again to the Narraganfett: their treacheries exceeds Machiavelli's, &c.

Sir, Captain Stoughton, left fick at my houfe one foldier, a Bofton man, Thomas Roberts,[1] his mafter is abfent, and Mr. Harding hath charge of him. I have fent to him, &c. The man was near death. Through the Lord's mercy my wife hath got him upon his legs, though very weak, only his hearing is quite gone, and I fhould be glad to receive any help for him in that great lofs. So with my refpective falutations to Mr. Deputy, Mr. Bellingham, yours and theirs, and other loving friends and my poor fighs to heaven to meet you there if not here below, I reft

Your Worfhip's unworthy yet unfeigned

ROGER WILLIAMS.

[1] Thomas Roberts was afterwards a freeman of Providence, holding honorable pofitions. He married a fifter of William Harris, and died 1676. Poffibly he may have been the fame, although a Thomas Roberts died in Bofton, 1654.

To his much honored Governor John Winthrop, these.

NEW PROVIDENCE, 2ndo Septimanæ. [July 10, 1637.] [1]

SIR,—In the morning I wrote to John Throckmorton, what I heard and thought in general. It hath pleafed the Lord now this afternoon to fend this meffenger, (Affotemuit)[2] with variety and plenty, and ftrangenefs of news and tidings, I hope true, and for ought I can difcern, true, bleffed be the holy name of the moft High, who breaks the bow and cuts the fpear, &c. Pfal. 46.

This man was fent this morning from Miantunnomu and Canonicus (as I conceive alfo from all their chiefs in council) with charge to bring relation to myfelf of what hath lately happened amongft the Pequots: as alfo that with my letter he fhould make fpeed to yourfelf with tidings.

He relates that a Pequot man and fome five Pequot women came two days fince to the Narraganfett,[3] and with their ordinary fubmiffion begged their lives, and liberty to declare in the name of many others what had happened amongft them: before that Pequot came one fquaw, and a fecond came, but was queftioned much for their truth; but upon the coming and report of the old Pequot, he faith, they all take his report for true.

This man himfelf, Affotemuit, is a noted meffenger from

---

[1] 4 *Mafs. Hift. Coll.* vol. vi. p. 198.
Probably written on the fame day as the preceding letter.

[2] I find no other notice of this man, except that his name appears as witnefs to Deed of Canonicus and Miantunnomue of Acquedneck lands to William Coddington and others.—*R. I. Col. Rec.* vol. i. p. 46.

[3] In a depofition made in 1682, Mr. Williams faid, "that being inquifitive of what root the title or denomination *Nahiganfet* fhould come," he heard that it was "fo named from a little ifland, between Puttiquomfett and Mufquomacuk, on the fea and frefh water fide." For further remarks on this name fee Mr. TRUMBULL's note to WILLIAMS' *Key to the Language of America, Narr. Club Pub.* vol. i. p. 22.

the Sachems, and one whom Miantunnomu hath commended to me for an efpecial meffenger from him.

This Pequot and the women report that (as I alfo heard before) all the Pequots were affembled fome ten days fince with Safacous in council : fome perfuaded to fight and fall firft upon the Narraganfetts, (this alfo I heard before) the greater part diffented and were for removal : Safacous and about four fcore[1] refolved for Mauquowkit, alias Waukheggannick, where the men eaters are ; a hundred more for Long Ifland ; another company, the leaft, for Connecticut, fome part of it, with purpofe to take final leave of their country. Seventy men, women, and children, (of men between twenty and thirty,) refolved for the Narraganfetts to beg their lives, &c.

Safacous and his company were wroth with thefe refolved for the Narraganfett, and a fkirmifh paft between them where fome were wounded, but away they got, and each company packed up and departed their intended journeys.[2]

[1] " The Pequots having received fo terrible a blow and being much affrighted with the deftruction of fo many, the next day fell into confultation. Affembling their moft ableft men together, propounded thefe three things: Firft, whether they would fet upon a fudden revenge upon the Narraganfetts, or attempt an enterprife upon the Englifh, or fly. They were in great difpute, one amongft another. Safachus, their chief commander, was all for blood ; the reft for flight, alledging thefe arguments : We are a people bereaved of courage, our hearts are fadded with the death of fo many of our dear friends ; we fee upon what advantage the Englifh lie ; what fudden and deadly blows they ftrike ; what advantage they have of their pieces to us, which are not able to reach them with our arrows at diftance. They are fupplied with everything neceffary ; they are flote and heartened in their victory. To what end fhall we ftand it out with them ? We are not able ; therefore let us rather fave fome than lofe all. This prevailed. Suddenly after, they fpoiled all thofe goods they could not carry with them, broke up their tents and wigwams and betook themfelves to flight."—UNDERHILL, *News from America*, Lond. 1638.

[2] " The news of the flight of Saffachus, their fagamore is confirmed. He went with forty men to the Mohocks,

6

Miantunnomu sent word to this company remaining in the midway between Pequatit and Nayantakick, that he was in league with Mr. Governor, and therefore of himself would say nothing, but desired them there to rest (at Cuppunaugunnit) in the midway, until he sent to Mr. Governor, and what he said that he would affent unto.

They told Miantunnomu that they had brought three guns with them. He sent the women for the guns, who fetched them from that place, Cuppunnaugunnit, and there they are with him. Only he claims a promise of one to himself, which he desires may be out of these three, as also some powder and shot to it, as indeed was promised.[1] I have much labored with this man to find, if it were possible, any deceit or falsehood, but as he himself and the Sachems question not the Pequot man and women, so I cannot question him.

I ask him (in discourse) what he thinks were best to be done, he answereth that as Miantunnomu himself when he sent to Canonicus to speak his mind, and Canonicus refusing, sent him to speak first, Miantunnomu would say nothing, but would say as Mr. Governor said so himself would likewise say nothing. Yet in discourse I fished out divers hints of their own desire and good liking.

As first, that there is not amongst these any Sachem or

---

which are cruel, bloody canibals."— VINCENT, *Pequot War*, 3 *Mass. Hist. Coll.* vol. vi. p. 40. "This Saffachus, (the Pequots chiefe sachem) being fled to the Mowhakes, they cutt off his head, with some other of ye chiefe of them, whether to satisfie the English, or rather the Narragansetts, (who I have since heard hired tnem to do it,) or for their own advantage, I well know not; but this their warr tooke end."—BRADFORD, *Hist. Plymouth Plantations*, p. 361.

[1] "When Mr. Vane was Governor." WILLIAMS' note. Probably at the time of the treaty when Miantonomy, at the request of the authorities, Oct. 21, 1636, went to Boston.

any of thofe who were murderers of the Englifh; if there were they fhould die.

2. That if Mr. Governor were fo minded, they incline to mercy and to give them their lives: and I doubt not but your own breafts are far more tender, like the merciful Kings of Ifrael.

3. That divers more befide thefe remain in the woods, and refolve to come in and fubmit if thefe be accepted.

4. For the difpofing of them, I propounded what if Mr. Governor did defire to fend for fome of them into the Bay; leave fome at the Narraganfett and fo fcatter and difperfe them: this he liked well, that they fhould live with the Englifh and themfelves as flaves. I then propounded that if they lived amongft the Englifh or themfelves, they might hereafter be falfe to the Englifh, &c., and what if therefore they were appointed and limited to live upon Nayantacawnick or fome other Ifland: and this he thought alfo well of, if not beft, becaufe they were moft of them families.

5. That they defire you would pleafe to fend fome Englifh to take poffeffion of the Pequot country and there to inhabit.[1]

6. That for their own hunting fake, Miantunnomu defires that the Englifh would inhabit that part neareft Connecticut, and that Myftic[2] and thereabout might be free

---

[1] "Captain Stoughton and his Company having purfued the Pequots beyond Connecticut, and miffing of them, returned to Pequot River, where they were advertized, that one hundred of them were newly come back to a place fome twelve miles off. So they marched thither by night and furprifed them all. They put to death twenty-two men, and referved two Sachems, hoping by them to get Saffachus, (which they promifed.) All the reft were women and children, of whom they gave the Narraganfetts thirty, and our Maffachufetts Indians three, and the reft they fent hither."— WINTHROP, *Hift. N. Eng.* vol. i. p. 277.

[2] "Which is neareft, and where the flaughter was."—WILLIAMS' note.

for them. I told him that they might hunt in the woods as they do at Maffachufetts and here, notwithftanding the Englifh did generally inhabit : and this fatisfied [him].[1]

7. That they defire the Pequot's corn might be enjoyed by the Englifh and themfelves, as Mr. Governor pleafe.

8. That the Wunnafhowatuckoogs are alfo afraid and fled, fo that there is hope of a fafe paffage to Connecticut by land.

9. That there is no hope that the Mohawks or any other people will ever affift Safacous, or any of the Pequots, againft the Englifh, becaufe he is now, as it were, turned flave to beg his life.

If all this be true (as I hope it is) we may all fee the God of Heaven delights in mercy, and to draw by love and pity than by fury and wrath. I hope Sir, now that troubles may arife from other parts, his holy Majefty is pleafed to quench thefe nearer fires. He be pleafed to confirm this news, and tune all hearts to his prayers in the ordering of our converfation aright. So I reft praying

Your worfhip's unfeigned,

ROGER WILLIAMS.

This man relates that yefterday, the Lord's day in the morning, a Pinnace arrived, but he knows not yet what fhe is.

I pray Sir, forget not to reward this meffenger with a coat, as alfo fome powder for Miantunnomu.

My loving refpects to Mrs. Winthrop, Mr. Deputy, Mr. Bellingham, and theirs, &c.

[1] Thefe propofitions met with favor with the Englifh, and the lands of the Pequots were divided among the foldiers and fai- lors. Pequot town was fubfequently fet- led and called London, but afterwards changed to New London.

To his much honored John Winthrop, Governor of the
Maſſachuſetts.[1]

THIS 3rd. 7æ. [July 11, 1637.][2]

SIR,—Yeſterday by our neighbor Throckmorton I
wrote concerning thoſe Nayantaquit men your pinnace
took. This bearer, Juanemo,[3] (one of the chief Sachems
of that place and chief ſoldier) came laſt night with
near a ſcore of his men to enquire after them. He was

[1] 4 *Maſs. Hiſt. Coll.* vol. vi. p. 202.
[2] The third day of the week; probably July 11, 1637.
[3] Alias "Ninigret," Sachem of Niantick. A portrait of this chief is in poſſeſſion of the Winthrop Family, from a
copy of which (made for the late Lieut.
Gov. Winthrop) an engraving was made
for Drake's Hiſtory of Boſton. There
is an intereſting tradition that the life of
John Winthrop, Jr., was once ſaved by
him. Winthrop records the arrival of
"Ayanemo" at Boſton, on the 12th July, with ſeventeen men. This was Wed-
nesday. Williams's letter was written
on Tueſday, "3rd 7æ" (that is, 3d ſepti-
manæ): probably the day before, or
July 11. It appears by the letter which
follows, that the bearer had returned to
Williams by the next "Lord's day;"
which fell on the 16th.—Note, 4 *Maſs.*
Hiſt. Coll. vol. vi. p. 202.

Winthrop under date of July 12th,
1637, ſays "Ayanemo, the ſachem of
Niantick, came to Boſton with ſeventeen
men. He made divers propoſitions,
which we promiſed to give anſwer unto
the next day; and then, underſtanding
he had received many of the Pequots,
ſubmitting to him ſince the former defeat, we firſt demanded the delivery of

them, which he ſticking at, we refuſed
further conference with him; but the
next morning, he came and offered what
we deſired. So the Governor referred
him to treat with our captains at the Pequot, and wrote inſtruĉtions to them how
to deal with him, and received his preſent of ten fathom of wampum. He
was lovingly diſmiſſed with ſome ſmall
things given him."—*Hiſt. of New Eng-*
land, vol. i. p. 278. He returned to
Williams on the next Lord's day, July
17. See ſucceeding letter.

This Indian is better known as Ninigret. He was couſin to Miantunnomo,
and his reſidence was at Wekapaug, now
Weſterly, R. I. Having viſited the
Weſtern Indians and the Dutch Governor, Stuyveſant, he was ſuſpecĉted of plot-
ting with them for the deſtruĉtion of the
Engliſh; and Sept. 1653, the Commiſſioners for the United Colonies declared
war with him, but owing to oppoſition
from Maſſachuſetts it was not proſecuted.
War was afterwards (1654) again declared, Major Willard leading the expedition, who captured one hundred Pequots; but Ninigret had fled. He joined
in the war known as "King Philip's
War," and died prior to 1680.

very defirous of a letter to you : I told him I hoped he
would find his men at liberty. He hath brought a mus-
ket and a barrel of a leve [lever ?] piece which his men
took from the Pequots.

There was a fpeech that three of thefe men were Na-
yantakoogs, and one a Pequot : it feems he is a Pequot
born, but hath long fince been theirs, fallen to them, and
done good fervice in their wars againft the Pequots.

Sir, this Juanemo is a notable inftrument amongft them,
&c., your wifdom, I know therefore, will lay hold of this
his vifit, to engage him the more to you.

Thus humbly begging mercies from the God of heaven
for you and yours in all affairs, I reft, in hafte,

Your worfhip's unfeigned

ROGER WILLIAMS.

All due refpects and falutations, &c.

To John Winthrop, Governor of Maffachufetts.

NEW PROVIDENCE, this 15th of the 5th. [July 15, 1637.][1]

SIR, — For the captives and booty, I never heard any of
thefe Natives queftion the Acts of the Englifh, only that
Native who brought letters to you from Capt. Patrick,
and was twice at Bofton, related fo much as I wrote of in
my former, at his return to the Narraganfett, viz. : that
yourfelf fhould be angry with the Englifh, &c. I met

---

[1] 4 *Mafs. Hift. Coll.* vol. vi. p. 203.

fince with him, and he faith he had it not from yourfelf, but an Englifh man at Roxbury. I thought good to clear your name, and remove fufpicions from Mr. Stoughton, &c.

Wequafh is alive, fo is alfo the other like to recover of his wound: I never heard that Miantunnomu was dif- pleafed with Wequafh, for any fervice to the Englifh, but that Wequafh was fufpected to deal falfely when he went to hunt for the Pequots at the rivers mouth. 'Tis true there is no fear of God before their eyes, and all the cords that ever bound the Barbarians to Foreigners were made of felf and covetoufnefs: yet, if I miftake not, I obferve in Miantunnomu fome fparks of true friendfhip, could it be deeply imprinted into him that the Englifh never in- tended to defpoil him of the country, I probably conjec- ture his friendfhip would appear in attending of us with 500 men (in cafe [he is wanted]) againft any foreign enemy.

The Neepmucks are returned with three heads of the Wunnafhoatuckoogs, they flew fix, wounded many, and brought home twenty captives.

Thofe Inlanders are fled up toward the Mohawks: fo they fay is Safacous: our friends at Connecticut are to caft a jealous eye at that people; they fay (unlefs they are be- lied) that they are to war with the Englifh, &c.

Truely Sir, to fpeak my thoughts in your ear freely, I blefs the Lord for your merciful dealing, &c., but fear that fome innocent blood cries at Connecticut. Many things may be fpoken to prove the Lord's perpetual war with Amalek extraordinary and myftical; but the 2 Kings, xiv. 5. 6. is a bright light difcovering the ordinary path where- in to walk and pleafe him. If the Pequots were murder- ers (though pretending revenge for Safacous his father's death, which the Dutch affirmed was from Mr. Governor)

yet not comparable to thofe treacherous fervants that flew
their lord and king, Jofhua, King of Judah, and type of
Jefus, yet the fathers only perifh in their fin, in the place
quoted, &c. The bleffed Lamb of God wafh away iniquity and receive us gracioufly.

Thus with beft falutes to your loving felf and yours, Mr.
Deputy, Mr. Bellingham, and other loving friends with
them, and daily cries to the Father of Mercies for you,

I reft your worfhip's unfeigned

ROGER WILLIAMS.

Poftscript.—Sir, to yours brought by Juanemo on the
Lord's day I could have little fpeech with him; but concerning Miantunnomu I have not heard as yet of any un-
faithfulnefs towards us; I know they belie each other;
and I obferve our countrymen have almoft quite forgotten
our great pretences to King and State, and all the world,
concerning their fouls, &c. I fhall defire to attend with
my poor help to difcover any perfidious dealing, and fhall
defire the revenge of it for a common good and peace,
though myfelf and mine fhould perifh by it: yet I fear
the Lord's quarrel is not ended for which the war began,
viz.: the little fenfe, (I fpeak for the general that I can
hear of) of their foul's condition, and our large protefta-
tions that way, &c. The general fpeech is, all muft be
rooted out, &c. The body of the Pequot men yet live,
and are only removed from their dens. The good Lord
grant, that the Mohawks and they and the whole at the
laft unite not. For mine own part I cannot be without
fufpicions of it.

Sir, I thankfully expect a little of your help (in a way
of juftice and equity) concerning another unjuft debtor of

mine, Mr. Ludlow,[1] from whom alfo (in mine abfence) I have much fuffered. The good Lord fmile upon you and yours in the face of his anointed.

Your worfhip's unworthy

ROGER WILLIAMS.

To his much honored Governor John Winthrop.

NEW PROVIDENCE, 21 of 5th monthe.[2] [July 21, 1637.]

MUCH HONORED SIR, — My unfeigned love and refpect to your foul's eternal comfort, and firm perfuafion of your leveling at the higheft white,[3] have emboldened me once more to tell you of fome poor thoughts of mine own, penned and fent to fome friends amongft you ; which happily, (if the good Lord fo pleafe) may fome way conduce to your foul's fatisfaction in the midft of all your troubles.

[1] George Ludlow is fuppofed to have been a kinfman of Roger Ludlow, as before appears. He applied to be admitted a freeman of Maffachufetts Colony in 1630 ; but does not appear to have fettled in New England. Roger Williams complains frequently of him as will be feen by feveral fubfequent letters. In 5 *Mafs. Hift. Coll.* vol. i. p. 250, is printed a letter from Ludlow to Roger Williams, to which is appended a note by Williams, which is as follows: "Mr. Coxall hath a letter of particulars, but in this Mr. Ludlow acknowledgeth 1ft an heifor, which was mine 4 years fince, the increafe of her is mine. 2ndly. Upwards of 4 fcore weight of tobacco. 3rdly. confideration above 8li for 3 goats due to me when they were almoft 2 yeare fince, about 4li a goate ; as allfo their increafe. 4thly. an houfe watch. 5thly. Another new gown of my wives, new come forth of England, and coft between 40 and 50 fhillings." By *Coxall*, is doubtlefs meant the name of *Coggefhall*.

[2] 4 *Mafs. Hift. Coll.* vol. vi. p. 205.

[3] "Higheft white." Mark at which an arrow is fhot, which ufed to be painted white.

I have been long requefted to write my grounds againft the Englifh preaching, &c., and efpecially my anfwers to fome reafons of Mr. Robinfon's[1] for hearing.

In the midft of a multitude of barbarous diftractions, I have fitted fomething to that purpofe : and being not able at prefent to tranfcribe the whole ; yet having been long folicited by Mr. Buckley[2] (from whom I received fome objections,) and by many others, and of late by my worthy friend Mr. Peters,[3] who had fight of them, I have

---

[1] Rev. John Robinfon of Leyden, born in England, 1575, was educated at Cambridge. Removed to Holland fhortly after 1608, was paftor of the church at Leyden, remaining there until his death in 1625. He was very active in promoting the emigration in the Mayflower in 1620, intending fhortly to follow, but died before the confent of the affociation of Englifh merchants who controlled the enterprife could be obtained. His widow and children came out in 1630. He publifhed a number of his writings, but the one to which this probably refers is "A treatife of the lawfulnefs of hearing of the minifters in the Church of England," was not printed until 1634, nine years after his death and three years prior to the date of this letter. A complete edition of his writings was publifhed at Bofton, in 1851 in 3 vols.

[2] Rev. Peter Bulkley, of Concord, Mafs., one of its founders in 1636. He was a nonconformift in England and was therefore removed by Archbifhop Land. He was the author of fome Latin poems contained in Cotton Mather's Hiftory of New England, and alfo of "The Gofpel Covenant Opened." London: 1646.

[3] "Hugh Peters, born in 1599, arrived in America in Auguft, 1635, with Richard Mather ; and in the following year, took charge of the church in Salem, as fucceffor of Roger Williams. Such was his fuccefs as a preacher, that during the five years of his miniftry in this place, one hundred and fixty perfons joined his communion. He was, at the fame time, occupied in mercantile purfuits, alfo engaged in political matters, and was one of the moft diftinguifhed citizens of that period in America. In 1641 he failed for England, with a view of procuring fome alteration in the laws of excife and trade ; but he did not again return to America. During the civil wars in England he advocated the caufe of Parliament, and contributed much to its aid by his preaching. He was accufed of great violence in urging the King's condemnation, but he affirmed that he was oppofed to it. Be that as it may, Cromwell appointed him to feveral public trufts. After the reftoration he was tried for confpiring with Cromwell, and compaffing the King's death. His trial terminated in his condemnation ; and he was executed on December 16, 1660, at the age of 61 years. His eloquence was of a peculiar and ftriking character, was calculated to gain the attention of the lower clafs. He had thoufands of hearers in London."— DRAKE, *Biog. Dictionary.*

thought good to fend fo much as I have tranfcribed, to the hand of my loving friend, Mr. Buckley.

Sir, I am bold to give you this intimation, becaufe in thefe firft loofe leaves, handling the ftate of a National church, from the thirty-eight page I have enlarged the differences between Ifrael and all other ftates. I know and am perfuaded that your mifguidings are great and lamentable, and the further you pafs in your way, the further you wander, and have the further to come back, and the end of one vexation will be but the beginning of another, till confcience be permitted (though erroneous) to be free amongft you.

I am forry my ftraits are fuch that I cannot tranfcribe the remainder, and efpecially what concerns the matter moft concerning your dear felf, and therein efpecially the affoiling of fome objections, but if the Lord pleafe I live I fhall endeavor the reft, and thankfully receive any intimation from yourfelf, yea from the leaft, whereby I might myfelf return from any wanderings. The Lord Jefus be to you and me the Way, the Truth, and he will be the Life alfo. So prays

Your worfhip's moft unfeigned

ROGER WILLIAMS.

I have no news, but from Connecticut, the receiving of Safacous, his prefent and company by the Mohawks, and fome promifes of theirs to him to fettle him again at Pequot. This week Souwonckquawfir,[1] old Sequin's[2] fon,

---

[1] William Pynchon of Springfield, in 1648, fpells this name Sowoquaffe.— WINTHROP, vol. ii. Appendix P.

[2] "Sequin (in 1635) gave the Englifh land there, (Weathersfield,) upon contract that he might fit down by them,

cut off twenty Pequot women and children in their paſſage to the Mohawks, alſo one Sachem who three years
ago was with you in the Bay with a preſent.[1]

For his much honored Mr. Governor, John Winthrop.

MUCH HONORED SIR, — I am bold to interpoſe (in all
humble reſpect) a word or two concerning the bearer,
Mr. Greene.[3] Being at Salem this laſt week to take order

and be protected, etc. When he came
to Weathersfield and had ſet down his
wigwams, they drove him away by
force." — WINTHROP, vol. i. p. 312.
This chief was otherwiſe known as Sow-
heag.

[1] Under date of Nov. 6, 1634, WIN-
THROP, vol. i. p. 176, writes " There
came to the Deputy Governor about
fourteen days ſince, a meſſenger from
the Pequot ſachem, to deſire our friend-
ſhip . . . . . He brought a ſmall preſent with him, which the deputy received."

[2] 4 *Maſſ. Hiſt. Coll.* vol. vi. p. 212.

[3] Auguſt 1, 1637, "Mr. John Greene,
of New Providence, having ſpoken
againſt the magiſtrates contemptuouſly,
ſtands bound in 100 marks to appear at
next quarter court to be held the firſt
Tueſday of the 7th month enſuing," —
Maſſ. Col. Rec. vol. i. p. 200. " The
quarter court was adjourned from September 5 to September 19, becauſe of
the Synod meeting at Newtown," at that
time. — *ibid*, vol. i. p. 202. September
19, 1637, "Mr. John Greene, of New

Providence, was fined 20 pounds, and
committed until the fine of £20, be
payed, and enjoyned not to come into
this juriſdiction upon paine of fine or impriſonment at the pleaſure of the court,
for ſpeaking contemptuouſly of the magiſtrates. — *Maſſ. Col. Rec.* vol. i. p. 203.

We differ from the editors of the
Williams' letters (*4th Maſſ. Hiſt. Coll.*
vi. 212, note,) as to the date of this letter. It cannot be of Sept. 18th as there
ſtated, as the General Court, as appears
by the Maſſachuſetts Records, was held
Tueſday, Auguſt 1. As Greene, doubtleſs attended the court, the letter is probably of the Monday previous, or July
31ſt.

"One of the inhabitants of Warwick,
was John Green, ſurgeon, a native of Sal-
iſbury, England, who coming over in the
next company after Roger Williams, with
his wife and five children, had followed
Williams to Providence, and Gorton to
Shawomet, thus becoming an original
proprietor in both places. — GEO. W.
GREENE, *Life of Gen'l Nath'l Greene*,
vol. i. p. 4.

about the fale of his houfe, and coming away an ancient acquaintance meets him (Ed. Batter) and queftions whether he would come and live there again, unto which he anfwered, how could he unlefs he might enjoy the freedom of his foul and confcience. Ed. Batter[1] replied, he might fo, to which he again replied he knew that could not be, for the power of the Lord Jefus was in the hand of civil authority ; upon this came by Mr. Endecott,[2] calls Ed. Batter and queftions him (as himfelf related to Mr. Greene) what was their conference : the fum whereof being told, Mr. Endecott warned Mr. Greene to appear at this General Court.

Sir, for myfelf I have no partial refpect to Mr. Greene nor relation, but of neighbors together : only for the better following of peace, (even when it flies from us), I am bold to acquaint with paffages of truth (as I cannot but hope) before hand : I fhall grieve much that any moleftation or trouble fhould arife unto you from hence, or that there be the appearance of any further jar. Sir, I know to whom I fpeak. Mr. Endecott had need have a true

[1] Edmund Batter, maltfler, came from fame place and in fame veffel with John Greene.

[2] John Endecott, Governor of Maffachufetts, who was fent to America by a company in England, as their agent, to fuperintend the plantation of Naumkeag, or Salem, arrived in September, 1628, and there laid the foundation of the firft permanent town in within the limits of Maffachufetts patent. In April, 1629, the company chofe him the Governor of "London's Plantation" ; but in Auguft it was determined to transfer the charter and the government of the colony to New England ; and John Winthrop, who arrived in the following year was appointed Governor. In 1636 Mr. Endecott was fent on an expedition againft the Indians on Block Ifland and in the Pequot country. He continued at Salem until 1644, when he was elected Governor of Maffachufetts, and removed to Bofton. He was alfo Governor from 1649 to 1664, excepting in 1650, and from 1655 to 1665. He died in 1665, in his 77th year.—BLAKE, *Biog. Dictionary.*

compafs for he makes great way, &c. : the Father of
Lights and Spirits merciful be pleafed to guide all our
fteerings.

Mr. Greene here is peaceable, a peacemaker, and a lover
of all Englifh that vifits us. I conceive he would not
difturb peace in relating his judgment to his friend, (if I
may fo call him) demanding it firft alfo of him, or elfe I
prefume he fhould not have heard a word of fuch matters, if I know Mr. Greene.

Sir, I hear yet nothing of any of the runaway captives
amongft our neighbors. Yefterday I heard that two efcaped
from them to the Pequots. If any be or do come amongft
them I fuppofe they fhall be fpeedily returned, or I fhall
certify where the default is.

Sir, I defire to be truly thankful for the boy intended :
his father was of Safquankit, where the laft fight was : and
fought not with the Englifh, as his mother (who is with
you and two children more) certified me : I fhall endeavor
his good and the common, in him. I fhall appoint fome
to fetch him, only I requeft that you would pleafe to give
a name to him.

Sir, concerning captives (pardon my wonted boldnefs)
the Scripture is full of myftery and the old Teftament of
types.

If they have deferved death 'tis fin to fpare :

If they have not deferved death then what punifhments ?
Whether perpetual flavery.

I doubt not but the enemy may lawfully be weakened
and defpoiled of all comfort of wife and children, &c.,
but I befeech you well weigh it after a due time of training up to labor, and reftraint, they ought not to be fet

free: yet fo as without danger of adjoining to the ene-'
my. Thus earneftly looking up to heaven for you and all
yours, I reft

Your worfhip's unfeigned,

ROGER WILLIAMS.

My beft refpects to Mrs. Winthrop, Mr. Deputy, Mr.
Bellingham, &c.

To his much honored Governor, John Winthrop.

NEW PROVIDENCE, 20th of the 6th.[1] [Auguft 20, 1637.]

MUCH HONORED SIR, — Yours by Yotaafh[2] (Miantunnomue's brother) received, I accompanied him to the
Narraganfetts, and having got Canonicus and Miantunnomu with their council together, I acquainted them faithfully with the contents of your letter, both grievances and
threatnings; and to demonftrate, I produced the copy of
the league, (which Mr. Vane fent me,) and with breaking
of a ftraw in two or three places, I fhowed them what they
had done.[3]

---

[1] 3 *Mafs. Hift. Coll.* vol. i. p. 162.
KNOWLES. *Mem. R. Williams,* p. 134.

[2] Otherwife Otafh and Yotnefh. This
chief and Roger Williams were witneffes
to the deed of the ifland of Rhode Ifland to William Coddington and others,
March, 1636-7.

[3] October 21, 1636, Winthrop "notices the arrival of Miantunnomoh and
other indians at Bofton, and the conclufion of a treaty of peace,"—which the
Governor fubfcribed, and they alfo fubfcribed with their marks, and Outfhama-
kins alfo. But becaufe we could not
make them underftand the articles perfectly, we agreed to fend a copy to Mr.
Williams, who could beft interpret it to
them.—WINTHROP, *Hift. of N. Eng.* vol.
i. p. 237.

In fome their anfwer was, that they thought they fhould prove themfelves honeft and faithful, when Mr. Governor underftood their anfwers; and that (although they would not contend with their friends) yet they could relate many particulars, wherein the Englifh had broken (fince thefe wars) their promifes, &c.

Firft then, concerning the Pequot fquaws, Canonicus anfwered, that he never faw any, but heard of fome that came into thefe parts, and he bade carry them back to Mr. Governor, but fince he never heard of them 'till I came, and now he would have the country fearched for them. Miantunnomu anfwered, that he never heard of but fix, and four he faw which were brought to him, at which he was angry, and afked why they did not carry them to me, that I might convey them home again. Then he bid the natives that brought them to carry them to me, who departing brought him word, that the fquaws were lame, and they could not travel. Whereupon he fent me word, that I fhould fend for them. This I muft acknowledge, that this meffage I received from him, and fent him word, that we were but few here, and could not fetch them, nor convey them, and therefore defired him to fend men with them and to feek out the reft. Then, faith he, we were bufy ten or twelve days together, as indeed they were in a ftrange kind of folemnity, wherein the Sachems eat nothing but at night, and all the natives round about the country were feafted. In which time, faith he, I wifhed fome to look to them, which notwithftanding, in this time, they efcaped; and now he would employ men inftantly to fearch all places for them, and within two or three days to convey them home. Befides, he profeffed that he defired them not, and was forry the Governor fhould think he did. I objected, that he fent to beg one. He anfwered, that Saffamun, being fent by the Governor with letters to Pequot, fell lame, and, lying at his houfe, told him of a fquaw he faw, which was a Sachem's daughter, who while he lived was his, Miantunnomue's great friend. He therefore defired, in kindnefs to his dead friend, to beg her, or redeem her.

Concerning his departure from the Englifh, and leaving them without guides, he anfwered, firft, that they had been faithful, many hundreds of them, (though they were folicited to the contrary,) that they ftuck to the Englifh in life or death, without which they were perfuaded that Uncas and the Mohigans had proved falfe, (as he fears they will yet,) as alfo that they never had found a Pequot, and therefore, faith he, fure there was fome caufe. I defired to know it. He replied in thefe words, Chenock eiufe wetompatimucks? that is, Did ever friends deal fo with friends? I urging wherein, he told me this tale: that his brother, Yotaafh, had feized upon Puttaquppuunck, Quame and twenty Pequots and three-fcore fquaws, they killed three and bound the reft, watching them all night, and fending for the Englifh, delivered them to them in the morning. Miantunnomu (who, according to promife came by land with two hundred men, killing ten Pequots in their march) was defirous to fee the great Sachem, whom his brother had taken, being now in the Englifh houfes, but (faith he) I was thruft at with a pike many times, that I durft not come near the door. I objected, he was not known. He and others affirmed, he was, and afked, if they fhould have dealt fo with Mr. Governor. I ftill denied, that he was known, &c. Upon this, he faith, all my company were difheartened, and they all and Cutfhamo-

8

quene defired to be gone ; and yet, faith he, two of my men (Wagonckwhut and Maunamoh) were their guides to Sefquankit from the river's mouth.

Sir, I dare not ftir coals, but I faw them to be much difregarded by many, which their ignorance imputed to all, and thence came the mifprifon, and bleffed be the Lord, things were not worfe.

I objected, they received Pequots and wampum without Mr. Governor's confent. Canonicus replied, that although he and Miantunnomu had paid many hundred fathom of wampum to their foldiers, as Mr. Governor did, yet he had not received one yard of beads nor a Pequot. Nόr, faith Miantunnomu, did I but one fmall prefent from four women of Long Ifland, which were no Pequots, but of that ifle, being afraid, defired to put themfelves under my protection.[1]

By the next I fhall add fomething more of confequence, and which muft caufe our loving friends at Connecticut to be very watchful, as alfo, if you pleafe, their grievances, which I have labored already to anfwer, to preferve the Englifh name ; but now end abruptly with beft falutes and earneft prayers for your peace with the God of peace and all men. So praying, I reft

Your worfhip's unfeigned

ROGER WILLIAMS.

All loving refpects to Mrs. Winthrop and yours, as alfo to Mr. Deputy, Mr. Bellingham, theirs, and Mr. Wilfon, &c.

[1] Under date of July 26, 1637, Winthrop (voi. i, p. 283) writes "and Wiantunnomoh fent here fome Pequot fquaws which had run from us."

To his kind friend, Mr. Richard Collicutt, these.[1]

This 12th of the 7th mon. (commonly called) 1637. [September 12.] .

KIND FRIEND,—I lately wrote unto you : once when I sent home your boy, and again when I sent the girl : concerning either of them, if you be minded to put either of them away, I desire to give you your desire : otherwise I wish you much comfort in the keeping of them.

As I am many ways indebted, so I have many debts coming to me. I take it very lovingly that you please to help me concerning Mr. Ludlow.[2] I have accordingly sent you power to deal in it. In three respects I request you to be serious and punctual.

1st. It is now an old debt, especially my cow was mine, left behind four years ago, for me in Virginia, and some goats.[3]

2ndly. I have requested the last year divers to help me and gave them power, but all failed me, so that I shall have cause to be thankful to you above others.

3rdly, If his payment like you, I shall request you first to satisfy yourself, and shall remain

Yours most unfeigned
ROGER WILLIAMS.

I shall gladly satisfy not only your charge, but also your time and pains in dealing with M. Ludlow.

---

[1] 4 *Mass. Hist. Coll.* vol. vi. p. 211.

[2] Richard Collicott or Colcott, settled in Dorchester before 1633, and was a sergeant in the Pequot war. He was one of the twenty-three original or charter members of the "Ancient and Honorable Artillery Company" of Boston, whi-ther he removed before 1656. He died in 1686, aged 83. Winthrop, who apparently believed in the doctrine of special Providence, reports (vol. ii. p. 336,) his preservation from drowning by the influence of prayer in 1648.

[3] See note to Letter of July 15th.

[POWER OF ATTORNEY FROM ROGER WILLIAMS TO RICHARD
COLLICUT.]

MEMORAND: that I, Roger Williams of New Providence, doe conftitute & ordaine Richard Collicut of Dorchefter my true & lawfull Atturney, for me and in my
name to afke or demaund, fue or arreft, acquit or releafe
George Ludlow of all fuch fummes of money or goods as
are due unto me from him.

per me   ROGER WILLIAMS.

---

*To his much honored John Winthrop, Governor of the
Maffachufetts.*[1]

[No date; probably October or November, 1637.]

MUCH HONORED SIR,—I was fearful that thofe dead
hands were no pleafing fight (otherwife than a remarkable
vengeance had feized upon the firft murderer of the Englifh, Wauphanck,)[2] yet I was willing to permit what I
could not approve, leaft if I had buried the prefent myfelf,
I fhould have incurred fufpicion of pride and wronged my
betters, in the natives and others eyes : I have always fhown
diflike to fuch difmembering the dead, and now the more,
(according to your defire) in your name.

I was alfo fearful that mine own hand (having no commiffion from my heart (which is not in mine hand but in

---

[1] 4 *Mafs. Hift. Coll.* vol. vi. p. 207.
[2] "The Narraganfetts fent us the
hands of three Pequots; one the chief
of thofe who murdered Capt. Stone,"
Auguft 31, 1637.—WINTHROP, vol. i.
p. 283.

the hand of its Maker, the Moſt High) to write you ought of mine own return in ſpirituals,) I ſay fearful that mine own might not be ſo grateful and pleaſing to you : but being called upon by your meſſage and your love, (your paper), I am emboldened.

Concerning the Pequots, the ſoldiers here[1] related to me that Uncas[2] the Mohiganie Sachem had about three hundred men with him on the Pequot river,[3] ſome ſixteen miles from the houſe, which I believe are moſt of them Pequots and their confederates the Wunnaſhowatuckoogs and their Inlanders (whom he charged under pain of death not to come to Canonicus) and with whom he hath made himſelf great. This man is but a little Sachem, and hath not above forty or fifty Mohigans, which as the Engliſh told me were all he could make.

It is generally confirmed that Thomas Stanton,[4] (as him-ſelf alſo confeſſed to me at my houſe) was groſſly cou-

---

[1] Winthrop under date of Aug. 26, records "The captain and ſoldiers re-turned all from Pequot," (vol. i. p. 283:) Oct. 12, "A day of thankſgiving kept in all the churches for our victories againſt the Pequods."—*Ibid*, vol. 1, p. 290.

[2] *Uncas*, was originally a Pequot. He revolted from Saſſacous in 1634, became friendly to the Engliſh, and was made chief of the Mohegans. His authority being ſo recent, perhaps is the occaſion for the ſlighting remark of Williams at the cloſe of the paragraph. He has been characterized as treacherous, vicious and "an old and wicked wilful man." He died in 1683 at a great age.

DRAKE, in his *Book of the Indians*, (p 149,) gives the following epitaph from a tombſtone of one of *Uncas'* ſons:

Here lies the body of *Sunseeto* Own ſon to *Uncas* grandson to *Oneko* Who were the famous sachems of Mohegan But now they're all dead, I think it is *Wer-heegan.*

[3] "The reſt of the Pequots were wholly driven from this place, and ſome of them ſubmitted themſelves to the Nar-iganſetts and lived under them: others of them betooke themſelves to the Mon-higgs under Uncas their ſachem, with the approbation of the Engliſh at Con-ighteecutt, under whoſe protection Un-caſs lived."—BRADFORD, *Hiſt. Plymouth Plant.* Boſton : 1856. p. 361.

[4] Thomas Stanton at the age of 20, emigrated in 1635 from London to Vir-ginia. He afterwards removed to Con-necticut, and was one of the original pro-

fened and deluded by one Wequafhcuck[1] (a Nayantaquit
Sachem) who fheltered four Pequot Sachems and fixty Pequots at Long Ifland, where now they are, where peace
was made with promife from the natives not to permit one
Pequot; yet Wequafhcuck marrying Saffacous his mother
hath thus deceived you. This Wequafhcuck was the man
(to my knowledge) that fheltered Audfah, the murderer of
Mr. Oldham, and kept his head fo upon his fhoulders: yet
to this man Thomas Stanton (as it appears) did too much
liften, flighting I fear, too much the Narraganfetts.

I find our Neighbors very eager to purfue thefe four
Sachems and the fixty Pequots there, I preffed them to patience till Mr. Governor's mind be known, and Miantunnomu (to my knowledge) doth all he can to reftrain them,
or elfe long fince they had been there. They plead that
Mr. Governor may pleafe to accompany, or fend himfelf
againft them, but cannot by any article in the league bind
them to fuffer fo many of their enemies in a knot fo near
them.

I prefs them to humane confideration of fo much blood
fpilt, they anfwer if they have the Sachems heads they
will make the reft Narraganfetts, and for the Long Iflanders themfelves and Wequafhcuck, they will not meddle
with them, becaufe of the peace Mr. Stoughton made with
them.

Concerning the kettles : Miantunnomu anfwers, that he

---

prietors of Hartford, and in later years
was of Stonington, where he died in
1678. He is many times mentioned in
thefe letters, and was conftantly employed
during his life as an indian interpreter.

[1] This man has often been confounded

with Wequafh. Winthrop in fpeaking
of the death of the latter, calls him Wequafh Cook; Williams is more accurate.
He was living in 1648, while Wequafh
died prior to 1643.

hath been much wronged by the reports of enemies and falfe friends to whom fome of us (as he faith) hath hearkened before himfelf.

He faith he never knew of more than two, one of which the Englifh ufed at the houfe, and the other as he hears is at the Fort ftill: he faith, he hath many of his own, and indeed when I came firft hither I faw near ten or twelve which himfelf or Canonicus had.

He repaid me with a grievance about a Pequot canoe which he defired might be ordered by your own hearing, but it was denied him: his plea feems very fair: thus this brother Yoteafh having taken the great Sachem (Puttaquappuonckquame who was was kept in the pinnace alive fometime) took his canoe, which, faith he, the Englifh Captains fitting all together were very willing unto: this canoe Mr. Stoughton afterwards brought about homeward: Miantunnomu and his brother claim it: 'twas denied: he requefted that it might be left at my houfe till Mr. Governor's mind was known. Capt. Stoughton would not yield, but defired him to go along to me, but faith he, I would not truft myfelf with him, feeing he would not ftand to Mr. Governor's determination about the canoe: I would not have mentioned this leaft it might provoke Mr. Stoughton or any: but I know to whom I intimate it: and I have pretty well appeafed the matter already.

He anfwers, all I can object to him with this: let Mr. Governor have the hearing of it: I will reft in his word, and objecting to him in the particular before divers, that the Englifh complain he was proud, he defired that I would prefent to Mr. Governor thefe particulars, that he had caufe to maintain his right, becaufe the Connecticut Englifh equalled Uncas and the Mohigans with himfelf and his men

Whereas faith he, thefe Mohigans are but as a twig, we are as a great tree.

They fell to the Englifh but laft year, we have been ever friends, &c.

Uncas and his men had a hand in the death of all the Englifh and fought againft the Rivers mouth (at Connecticut) we never killed nor confented to the death of an Englifh man.

When the Dutchmen and we fought with the Pequots the Mohigans joined againft us.

When Capt. Endicott came againft the Pequots the Mohigans received the Pequot women and children and kept them, while the men fought with him, &c.

Uncas brought prefents to Canonicus, and Miantunnomu, yet at the fame time killed two of his women treacheroufly.

They fell to the Englifh this year in fear or other policy, and we, (faith he) have continued friendfhip and love ever fince they landed. Thus he pleaded, &c., and yet proud and covetous and filthy they are, &c., only I was willing to gratify him in this, becaufe as I know your own heart ftudies peace, and their foul's good, fo your wifdom may make ufe of it unto others who happily take fome more pleafure in wars: The bleffed God of Peace be pleafed to give you peace within, at home, and round about you abroad, So prays

Your worfhip's unfeignedly refpective

ROGER WILLIAMS.

To Mrs. Winthrop, Mr. Deputy, Mr. Bellingham, &c., all refpective falutations.

I have at prefent returned Richard Collicut's Pequot girl which Miantunnomu found out, and defired me to fend home, with promife of further enquiring.

To his much honored Governor John Winthrop.[1]

[No date.][2]

SIR, — Having ufed many means and many Attornies (in my abfence) to recover a debt of Mr. George Ludlow, and failed by all, and now laft of all by Richard Collicut who undertook ferioufly, but comes off weakly in it: let me humbly beg what help in a righteous way may be afforded (now in his departure) to caufe him to deal honeftly with me who have many years and in many wants been patient toward him. The debt was for mine own and wife's better apparel put off to him at Plymouth. My bills are loft, but his own hand which the bearer will deliver is teftimony fufficient. He hath ufed fo many flights and told fo many falfehoods, that Sir, if you believe more than you fee, I muft patiently give my debt for defperate : however with my beft refpects to your kind felf and Mrs. Winthrop, and fighs to heaven for you, I reft

Your worfhip's unfeignedly faithful till death,

ROGER WILLIAMS.

[1] 4 *Mafs. Hift. Coll.* vol. vi. p. 212.
[2] This letter is of later date than the one preceding, as it evidently refers to it. It probably enclofed a letter received from George Ludlow, and which is printed in full in 5 *Mafs. Hift. Coll.* vol. i. p. 250. To this R. W. has added a note. (See previous letter.)

9

To his much honored Governor John Winthrop.[1]

[No date ; probably October, 1637.]

SIR, — Some while since you were pleased to desire me to signify to the Sachems, the promise of the Block Island-ders to yourselves, and therefore their exemption from all other submission and tribute.　Their answer was, that as they had left them to Mr. Governor formerly upon Mr. Oldames death, so have they done since, and have had no other dealing with them then for the getting of the head of Audsah the chief murderer : as also that they under-stand the one hundred fathom of beads to be yearly paid to Mr. Governor, in which respect they have been far from desiring a bead from them, and do acknowledge them to be wholly Mr. Governor's subjects.

Sir, I hear that there is now at Pequot with the Mohe-gans,[2] one William (Baker[3] I think his name is) who was

[1] *4 Mass. Hist. Coll.* vol. vi. p. 214.
In this letter Roger Williams men-tions the probability of Miantonomo going to Boston in a day or two.　The letter of November 10th, reports the return of this "big indian."　WIN-THROP, (vol. i. p. 291) records under date of November 1st, "Miantonomo the Narragansett Sachem came to Bos-ton."　He also reports that Miantono-mo acknowledged that "all the Pequot country and Block Island were ours."　He was also given "leave to right him-self for the wrongs which Janemoh and Wequash Cook had done him."　The letter is probably of a date not later than October 28, and perhaps not much ear-lier.

[2] *Monahiganeucks* — Mohegans.　By the revolt of Uncas, the Pequot territo-ries became divided, and that part called

Moheag or Mohegan, fell generally un-der his dominion, and extended from near the Connecticut River on the south, to a place of disputed country on the north, next the Narraganfetts.

[3] "William Baker, Plymouth, 1643, may I think, have been first of Rhode If-land, as early as 1638, and probably went thither again, being counted among the freemen 1655 at Portsmouth " SAVAGE, vol. i. p. 100.　*R. I. Col. Rec.* vol. i. Williams in subsequent letters speaks of him as of Plymouth, and that he was whipped at Hartford in the same year. The next year November 12th, 1638, he was admitted an inhabitant of New-port.　There was in Plymouth in 1632 a William Baker an apprentice to Rich-ard Church, and possibly this was the man to whom Roger Williams refers.

purfued, as is faid by the Englifh of Connecticut for uncleannefs with an Indian fquaw, who is now with child by
him. He hath there gotten another fquaw and lies clofe,
unknown to the Englifh. They fay he came from a trading houfe which Plymouth men have at Connecticut, and
can fpeak much Indian. If it be he, when I lived at Plymouth, I heard the Plymouth men fpeak much of his evil
course that way with the natives.

The occafion that our neighbors know of him was this :
fome eight days fince, fix Narraganfett men were coming
from Connecticut, and by the way fell upon fome Pequots,
who were refcued out of their hands by the Mohegans,
who alfo bound thofe fix Narraganfetts many days together at Monahiganick (upon Pequot river, where this
William was) and fpoiled them of their coats and what
elfe they had.

The Sachems and the men are greatly incenfed, affirming that they can not but revenge this abufe offered to their
men ; yet I have got this promife that they will not do
ought without Mr. Governor's advice.

Sir, I have long heard, and thefe fix men affirm, that
there are many of the fcattered Pequots rendezvoufed with
Uncas the Mohegan Sachem and Wequafh the Pequot,
who being employed as one of the guides to the Englifh
in their late wars, is grown rich, and a Sachem with the
Pequots : and hath five or fix runaways. There are all
the Runaways harbored (which upon long and diligent
inquiry) I am certain and confident of, and can give good
affurance that there is not one amongft all the Narragansetts.

Mr. Stoughton hath been long affured that Meikfah,
Canonicus' eldeft fon hath his fquaw, but having enquired
it out, I find fhe was never at the Narraganfetts, but is mar-

ried to one Meikſomp a Sachem of Nayantick, which being nearer to Pequot is more friendly to the Pequots: and where as I hear that Wequaſhcuck ˎwho long ſheltered Audſah and ſo groſſly deluded Tho : Stanton in the late wars) hath filled many baſkets with beads from Pequots Sachems and one hundred and twenty Pequots which he ſheltereth now at Nayantick.

Uncas the Mohegan and Wequaſhcuck were lately at Long Iſland, from whence ſome few days ſince, Uncas carried away forty Pequots to Monahiganick, and Wequaſhcuck thirty to Nayantick.

While I write, Miantunnomu is come to my houſe and affirmeth the ſame; profeſſing if I would adviſe him, he would go over to Mr. Governor to acquaint the Governor that Canonicus[1] and himſelf hath no hand in theſe paſſages.   He aſks me often if he may ſafely go, and I aſſure him if he have an honeſt heart he need not fear any deceit or treachery amongſt the Engliſh ; ſo I think within a day or two he will be coming towards you.

He tells me what I had not heard that of thoſe Pequots to whom at the firſt by my hand you were pleaſed to give

[1] "Canonicus, a Narraganſett chief, uncle of Miantonomoh, was born about 1565 ; died June 4, 1647 ; was the firm friend of the Engliſh, eſpecially of Roger Williams.   From him Williams obtained, March 24, 1638, the grant of land for his ſettlement of the future State of Rhode Iſland.   In 1622, two years after the Pilgrims landed at Plymouth, Canonicus ſent as a challenge a bundle of arrows tied with a ſnake-ſkin. The ſkin was returned filled with powder and ball; but the peace was unbroken. In 1632–35, there was a war between the Pequots and Narraganſetts, about the ownerſhip of lands lying between Pawcatuck River and Wecapang Brook.   Canonicus, after loſing his ſon, burned his own reſidence and all his goods in it. Roger Williams calls him " A wiſe and peaceful prince."   During his life, the Narraganſetts, though engaged in war with other Indians, remained at peace with the whites.   Many years after his death, however, under the famous King Philip, they made war on the Engliſh and were exterminated."—DRAKE. *Dic. American Biography.*

life, but feven came to them, of which five alfo long fince are gone to Monahiganick.

Sir, I forget not your loving remembrance of me concerning Mr. Ludlow's debt. I yet know not where that tobacco is : but defire if Mr. Craddock's agent, Mr. Jolly would accept it, that it may be delivered to him in part of fome payments for which I have made over my houfe to Mr. Mayhew.

Sir, your fervant Reprieve lodged here two nights, and Miantunnomu[1] tells me that five days fince he lay a night with him and is gone to Block Ifland. He is very hopefully improved fince I firft faw him : and am bold to wifh that he might now take his laft farewell of his friends, to whom you would be rather pleafed to give leave to vifit him at Bofton, for you cannot believe how hard it is for him to efcape much evil, and efpecially uncleannefs while he is with them. The good Lord be pleafed to blefs him to you and to make you a bleffing to him and many others. . . . run headlong (without once hearing of it,) into everlafting burnings. So prays daily

Your worfhip's unfeigned,

ROGER WILLIAMS.

To Mrs. Winthrup, Mr. Deputy, Mr. Bellingham, and theirs, refpective falutations.

---

[1] Miantonomo, Sachem of the Narraganfetts, was the nephew and fucceffor of Canonicus, and affumed the government in 1636. He was the friend and benefactor of the fettlers in Rhode Island, to whom he gave their territory. In 1638 he entered into an agreement with Uncas, Sachem of the Mohegans, not to make war upon one another without firft appealing to the Englifh. Cited in 1642, upon a mere rumor of intended hoftilities to appear at Bofton before the Governor and Council, he declared his innocence, and called upon the Englifh

To his much honored Governor John Winthrop [1]

The laſt of the week, I think the 28th of the 8th.   [Oct. 28, 1637.]

SIR,—This bearer, Miantunnomu, reſolving to go on his viſit, I am bold to requeſt a word of advice from you concerning a propoſition made by Canonicus and himſelf to me ſome half year ſince. Canonicus gave an iſland in this bay to Mr. Oldham, by name Chibachuweſe, upon condition as it ſhould ſeem, that he would dwell there near unto them. The Lord (in whoſe hands all hearts are) turning their affections towards myſelf, they deſired me to remove thither and dwell nearer to them. I have anſwered once and again, that for preſent I mind not to remove; but if I have it from them, I would give them

to produce his accuſers. None appearing, he was diſmiſſed with honor. Gov. Winthrop, in his Journal, teſtifies to the reſpect in which the ability of the great chief was held. The rivalry between the Mohegans and Narraganſetts, which it was the policy of the Engliſh to foment, produced its inevitable reſults. Driven by the inſults and injuries of the unprincipled Uncas, he attacked him, but was defeated and made priſoner ; and by the advice and conſent of the Engliſh magiſtrates and elders, was executed. Brave and magnanimous, he was doubtleſs the moſt able of the Indians of New England. DRAKE. *Biog. Dictionary.*

[1] 3d Ser. *Maſs. Hiſt. Coll.* vol. i, p. 165, aſſigns October 28, 1637, as the probable date of this letter ; in which opinion ARNOLD, in his *Hiſtory of Rhode Iſland* agrees. Vol. i. p. 105. KNOWLES, and *R. I. Col. Records* copy from the *Maſs. Hiſt. Coll.*

[2] The *R. I. Col. Records*, (vol. 1. p.

45) quotes the Deed from Canonicus and Miantonomo of the iſland of Aquedneck to William Coddington and others, under date of March 24, 1637, "excepting Chibachuweſa, *formerly ſold* unto Mr. Winthrop the *now* Governor of the Maſſachuſetts and Mr. Williams of Providence."

We cannot reconcile the difference of dates, except that Winthrop's date refers poſſibly to the time Gov. Vane ſent for Miantonomoh. Miantonomoh alſo was at Boſton on Nov. 1, 1637, (WINTHROP, vol. i. p. 291.) If the date of the deed above mentioned is correct, and the formerly ſold is the "*whole truth*" this letter is probably of 1636, if otherwiſe, probably 1637. We incline to the latter date. Winthrop retained his half of the iſland leaving it by will to his ſon Stephen. Williams ſold his half with other lands to pay his expenſes in England when on ſervice for the colony.

satisfaction for it, and build a little house and put in some swine, as understanding the place to have store of fish and good feeding for swine. Of late I have heard, that Mr. Gibbons, upon occasion, motioned your desire and his own of putting some swine on some of these islands, which hath made me since more desire to obtain it, because I might thereby not only benefit myself, but also pleasure yourself whom I more desire to pleasure and honor. I spake of it now to this Sachem, and he tells me, that because of the store of fish, Canonicus desires that I would accept half, (it being spectacle-wise, and between a mile or two in circuit, as I guess,) and he would reserve the other; but I think, if I go over, I shall obtain the whole. Your loving counsel, how far it may be inoffensive, because it was once (upon a condition not kept) Mr. Oldham's. So, with respective salutes to your kind self and Mrs. Winthrop, I rest

Your worship's unfeigned, in all I may,

ROGER WILLIAMS.

[No date.   Probably written soon after July, 1635.]

The Church of Jesus Christ at Salem, to our dearly beloved and much esteemed in Jesus, the Elders of the Church of Christ at Boston.

Your letters (dear and well beloved in Christ) dated the 22 of this 5th month, have been read openly before us, wherein we understand you see not your way clear before you, for delivering of our humble complaint unto the

Church of Chrift with you ; as alfo your reafons why you
dare not publifh to the body our letters.　Our dear Brethren, according to your loving and Chriftian defire, we
dare not but gently and tenderly interpret this your delay
as fpringing from your holy care and fear leſt difhonor
fhould redound to our Lord and King, in thefe weighty
affairs of his holy government.　We give you many and
hearty thanks for your loving and faithful dealing in returning us a reafon of your holy fears and jealoufies.　And
we befeech you [in the bow]els of Chriftian tendernefs to
bear with us while we firſt add a word unto your felves,
and afterwards to your reafons.　We have not yet apprehended it to be the choice of the officers of a Church,
when public letters are fent from fifter Churches, to deliver
or not to deliver the letters unto the body ; we acknowledge
it their liberty and duty to order wifely for convenience
and due feafon of prefenting the Church with them, but
wholly to conceal or fupprefs the letters of the Church, we
yet fee not.　Our reafons are, amongſt others, thefe two:
1ſt, becaufe they are the Church's, not the officers'.　The
Church hath the right which the officers may not affume
unto themfelves, and therefore it hath been queſtioned
whether public letters fent to [a Church of] Chriſt, ought
not to be delivered publicly to the elders in the face of the
Church met together according to what is written, [Aɛts]
15. 30, when they had gathered the multitude (that is, the
Church) together, then they [deliv]ered the letters. If this
be the power and liberty of the officers, for ought we fee
[if there] be but one elder in the Church that he may privately put up the public letters of the whole.　Our 2d reafon is, becaufe the prefence of our Lord Jefus is moſt
efpecially promifed and . . . . to the whole body

met together in his name, than to one or all the elders; and
therefore in folemn feeking of God's face by the whole
Church (his fpoufe and wife) we conceive a more clear and
diftinct apprehenfion of the mind of Chrift concerning an
anfwer to be returned back doth ordinarily arife, than from
the officers apart from [the Church.] For however it hath
been the Prelate['s p]lea, the people are wea[k . . . .
giddy and rafh, and therefore fhould not enjoy fuch liberties, we con[ceive per]fons truly gathered in his name fhall
find a wifdom great[er than theirs] in the midft amongft
them even Jefus Chrift, who himfelf is made their wif[dom]
. . 1 Cor. i. 30. [Y]our reafons of not reading are three;
two againft reading a[t all, the third,] againft reading on the
Lord's day. The firft, more exprefly concerning . .
. . our admonition, you fay is a gift which fhould not be
offered up [until we have] reconciled ourfelves to our much
honored and beloved the majiftrates [who are] againft us.

Now we befeech you humbly, our dear brethren, confider . . . a gift; our prayers and thanks and offerings,
are alfo gifts, Mat. v. [23, 24.], and then if no gift may
be offered while a cafe of offence de[pendeth, then furely]
1. a brother, yea, a whole Church muft intermit their holy
meet[ings, and] for a while the ordinances, yea, for the
prefent, be un-churched. 2. And fo fecondly, if we fhould
meet together to confider about, and find out the offence,
we fh[ould not] offer up the incenfe of our prayers to the
Lord for the difcovery of the offence unto [our brethren.]
3. Further, for ought we fee we fhould not at all come together, for the prefence of our fouls and bodies together in
the prefence of the Lord is a gift. 4. Nay more, by that
rule no Church in her members might have fellowfhip
with us, nor ourfelves with them, in cafe we have not pow-

10

er to offer up a gift while a matter of offence dependeth,
though ourfelves are ready to receive light from our
brethren concerning the offence. 5thly. If this rule be
abfolute ye have failed fo far to communicate with us as to
fend us thefe your letters, if [we cannot] meet together
to read them and confider and feek the face of our God in
Chrift for anfwer. 6th. Since that fome times brethren
may be offended at a good and righteous act, pleafing to
Chrift, as fome were, Acts xi. [17, 18], by this ground
it will follow that the Churches fhall offer up no gift to
God nor man until they have repented of their duties and
confeffed them as fin, both to God and man, in cafe others
be offended.

Laftly, be you pleafed to remember that hitherto in a
church way (the way of Chrift for Church failings) we
have not heard of any one brother offended with us, which
fhould have been in . . . . . might any way have
held forth . . . . argument unto us ; our reafon is
. . [gre]at difference between a Church way, and the proceeding of a Commonweal.

Your fecond argument feems to be, the act of the
majiftrates gave . . [pub]lic offence, and befide that,
a public action offenfive may be but private offence: unto
this with all due fubmiffion we conceive the Court of Juftice is as public [as the gate of the city.] Amos. v. 12 :
"They turn afide the poor from their right in the gate."
2dly, we acknowledge in fome obfcure and dark paffages,
one or two may fpy a blemifh where thoufands do not ;
this is a fecret, and we defire to walk by the rule, Prov.
xxv. 9., "debate the caufe with thy neighbor himfelf, and
difcover not a fecret to another;" *but to [punifh befor]e fhe
hath been conve[n]ted, to deal with a church out of a church way,*

[*to*] *punish two or three hundred of our town for the conceived failing of the Church*, we fee [not] how any cloud of obfcurity can hide this evil from the eyes of all; and therefore not two or three of ourfelves, but many of the prefent court, and many others, and ourfelves [of the] Church of Chrift who cry to the Lord for mercy to ex . . . . fee a failing, yea fome hundreds of the whole town fmarting in their . . . . and the whole land may, and other lands hearing of it cannot choofe [but be bli]nded, weakened, ftumbled; and therefore we conceive as the fun [cannot] be fhut up in a chamber, public finnings muft be openly [complained] of: 1 Tim. v. 20. "Them that fin rebuke before all, that others may fear." [Yo]u fay you cannot judge of our right and title, for our matters are only [ft]ayed; we fignify thus much to your felves and humbly requeft if there be caufe you will fignify fo much to the brethren, that we are far from arguing our right with any in a church way. We hoped the proof that was defired by the court would have given fatisfaction might they have had leave to fpeak; and furthermore the delay of a petition in cafes of prefent neceffity (as ye well know) may be as grievous by the delay of a few months (fuch ftood the prefent ftate of the town) as if it was a whole year; and therefore the Lord provides againft delays of a poor man's wages, Deut. xxiv. 14 15, not only becaufe of his prefent need, but alfo becaufe of the grief of his fpirit, which will make him cry unto God for redrefs againft the injurious. We doubt not but a petition may be both delayed and rejected, but we muft needs profefs our exceeding grief that a Church of Chrift fhall undergo a punifhment before convented, be punifhed (if there were due caufe) before exhorted to repentance in a rule of Chrift, and hundreds of

innocents punifhed of the town . . . . as the conceived nocents of the Church.   This, to our apprehenfion,
is fuch an evil as which (whether we refpect the perfons,
or the public nature of the evil, as) God is not wont to
expiate without fome public ftroke of jealoufly and difpleafure.   We hope we fhall ever be with the foremoft in all
humble refpect and fervice to all higher powers, according to God.   We fpeak now of our much honored brethren as brethren, whofe fouls are dear and precious to us
in holy covenant, and therein conceive the only way to
honor them in the Lord, is to befeech them to wafh away
the difhonor of the moft high, by true, godly forrow and
repentance; and in this your fervice we conceive in the
e[nd] you will find that moft true which the fpirit of G[od]
writes, " open rebuke is better than fecret love."

Your 3d argument is, that you dare not upon the Lord's
day deal in a wordly bufinefs, no[r bring a] civil bufinefs in
the Church.   Firft, pleafe you to remember (our dear and
well beloved in Chrift) that for any civil matter we open
not our mouth.   We fpeak of a fpiritual offence againft
our Lord Jefus, and againft the holy covenant of brethren,
and fo we do]ubt not though unclean . . . . oppreffion be offences againft the c[ivil ft]ate which the Church
meddles [not] with, yet the Church deals with members
lawfully for their breach [of cove]nant, and difobedience
againft the Lord Jefus.

Again, we are not bold to limit you (our beloved) to the
Lord's day; we leave [it to your] wifdom and the wifdom
of the Church, when to confider of the matter: yet
hither[to] we have conceived that the kingly office of our
Lord Jefus ought to be as well adminiftered on the Lord's
day, as his Prieftly and Prophetic [office,] and [alfo] that he

is as much honored in the [act of] censuring or pardoning of sinners from his throne, Zach. vi. 13, in case of transgression against his crown, as against the administration of other his sweet and blessed ordinances.

Now our blessed C[hrist Jes]us, who holdeth his stars in his right hand, and out of whose mouth goes a sh[arp two-] edged sword, and whose countenance shines as the sun in his strength, Rev., shine mercifully and clearly upon your souls in all holy . . . consolations and . . . lvations.

Your most unworthy brethren, unfeignedly respective and affectionate in Christ Jesus.

ROGER WILLIAMS.   SAMUEL SHARPE.

This letter for which we are indebted to CHARLES DEANE, Esq., of Cambridge, was not received in time to insert it in its proper place, according to its date. It was accompanied by the following note from that gentlemen :

NOTE.—I copied this letter some years ago from the original, in Roger Williams's hand, belonging to the Prince collection in the keeping of the Massachusetts Historical Society. The letter was considerably imperfect, many of the words quite obliterated and gone, so that the meaning is in many places quite obscure. Enough however is preserved to shew the general thought of the writer, and to indicate the occasion on which it was written. It bears no date, but must have been written in 1635, and was a reply to a letter from the elders of the Church of Boston, dated "ye 22 of this 5th month"—ie. the 22d July. I apprehend the occasion on which the letter was written was this: We learn from Winthrop, under date July, 1635, that the "Salem men had preferred a petition, at the last General Court, for some land in Marblehead Neck, which they did challenge as belonging to their town ; but because they had chosen Mr. Williams their teacher, while he stood under question of authority, and so offered contempt to the magistrates, &c., their petition was refused, till &c. Upon this, the Church of Salem wrote to other Churches, to admonish the magistrates of this as a heinous sin, and likewise the deputies; for which at the next General Court, their deputies were not received until they should give satisfaction about the letter." (Vol. i p. 164.) It would appear that the letter sent to the Boston Church was retained by the elders and not laid before the

For his much honored Mr. Governor, John Winthrop.

10th of 9th.   [November 10, 1637.][1]

SIR,—I acquainted this Indian Miantunnomu,[2] with
the contents of your letter fent by him, who refts well
perfuaded that if it break not firft with them, the league
is firm and lafting, and the Englifh are unfeigned.

I have bought and paid for the Ifland,[3] and becaufe I
defired the beft confirmation of the purchafe to yourfelf
that I could, I was bold to infert your name in the original
here enclofed.

The ten fathom of beads and one coat you may pleafe
at leifure to deliver to Mr. Throckmorton : who will alfo
be ferviceable in the conveyance of fwine this way.

Your native, Reprive,[4] requefts me to write a word for
himfelf and another for the Sachem of Block Ifland, Jac-
quontu.

For himfelf he tells me when he departed hence, being
alone, he wandered toward Neepmuck : At Nayantick,
Juanemo faid he was a fpy from Mr. Governor, and threatened to kill him, denied that there were Pequots, faying

Church, they giving their reafons for fo
doing in their reply to the Salem Church.
The letter from the Bofton elders called
forth, as I fuppofe, this letter from Williams, figned by himfelf as teacher, and
Samuel Sharp, as ruling elder, of Salem
Church. Sharpe was foon afterward called
to account by the General Court for his
hand in this bufinefs. In copying this
letter of Williams, I have indicated the
omiffions by . . . I have modernized the orthography in this copy. c. d.

[1] *4 Mafs. Hifl. Coll.* vol. vi. p. 217.

[2] See previous letters. This letter was
probably written fhortly after Miantunnomoh's vifit, Nov. 1, to Bofton.—WIN-
THROP, vol. i. p. 291.

[3] The deed of Prudence Ifland, is
dated Nov. 10, 1637, the fame day of
this letter. (See *R. I. Hifl. Coll.* vol. iii.
p. 29.) The confideration paid Miantunnomoh and Canonicus was twenty
fathom of wampum and two coats, which
Williams paid, and now afks to be reim-
burfed one-half.

[4] *Reprive,* an Indian fervant of Gov.
Winthrop. See letter of October.

though Reprive faw many himfelf) that they were all gone to Monahiganick. So he came back in fear of his life to Wepiteammock (Miantunnomue's brother-in-law) who lent him a canoe to Block Ifland where he ftaid but fix days.

From Jacquauntu,[1] Block Ifland Sachem, that he is preparing thirteen fathom of white, and two of blue to prefent you with about the firft month.

That they are greatly in fear of the Nayantick men who threaten them, in cafe the Englifh fall upon Nayantick.

I am glad to fee this poor fellow Reprive careful to pleafe you, for he faid you gave him leave for twenty-eight days and though he could ftay but fix days where he defired to ftay longeft, yet he will not lie.

He fays his brother goes along with him to ftay fome while, till the fpring.

Sir, There are two Pequot fquaws, brought by the Narraganfetts, almoft ftarved; viz.: Mr. Coles his native, and one girl from Winifimmit: there was a third (I think Mr. Blackftone's,) who had efcaped before to Nayantick. I promifed thefe, if they would ftay at my houfe and not run away, I would write that they might be ufed kindly. The biggeft, Mr. Cole his native, complains that fhe of all

---

[1] Referring to the tribute as required by treaty made by Jaquauntu, the Block Ifland Sachem.

[2] His name in fome of the records of the period is fpelled *Blaxton*. William Blackftone or Blaxton, firft fettled on the peninfula, now the city of Bofton; removed to Rehoboth in 1633, and thence to Cumberland, R. I., near the river fince called Blackftone River, in reference to his name. He died juft before King Philip's war, when his refidence and his fine library were confumed. See note to letter of June 13, 1675.

natives in Bofton is the worfe ufed: is beaten with fire-
fticks, and efpecially by fome of the fervants.

The little one makes no complaint of ufage, but fays fhe
was enticed by that other fquaw, which I think was Mr.
Blackftone's. I afked the biggeft, who burnt her and why,
fhe told me Mr. Penn[1] becaufe a fellow lay with her, but
fhe faid, for her part fhe refufed.

My humble defire is that all that have thofe poor
wretches might be exhorted as to walk wifely and juftly
towards them, fo as to make mercy eminent, for in that
attribute the Father of mercy moft fhines to Adam's miferable offspring.

Sir, I fear I am tedious, yet muft I crave leave for a line
more: I received a letter from fome in Charleftown, (in
fpecial from one Benjamin Hubbard)[2] intimating his and
others defire (with my help and furtherance) to be my
neighbors in fome place near adjoining: Mr. James[3] hath
not declared himfelf to be one, but I guefs he is inclining
to accompany them. On the Narraganfett fide the natives
are populous, on the fide to Maffachufetward Plymouth
men challenge, fo that I prefume if they come to the
place where firft I was, Plymouth will call them theirs.[4] I

---

[1] James Penn who at this time was one
of the overfeers or magiftrates of the
town of Bofton.

[2] Benjamin Hubbard came to Charleftown in 1633, was a prominent man,
poffibly removed, fays SAVAGE, to Bofton, but he is known to have returned
to England, and probably never returned
to America.

[3] Thomas James, probably one of the
thirteen original proprietors of Providence, being firft mentioned in the "in-
itial deed," fo called in 1638, and then

more fully in the confirmatory deed of
1666 which bears his name. BRADFORD,
calls him "a phifitian."—*Hift. of Plymouth,* p. 364.

[4] No deed has ever been difcovered,
we think, of the lands of Seekonk and
Rehoboth; but a depofition of John Hafell, taken in 1642, confirms fuch a pur
chafe. "John Hafell affirmeth that Af-
famequime chofe out ten fathom of beads
at Mr. Williams's and put them in a bafket, and affirmed that he was fully fatiffied therewith for his land at Seacunck ;

know not the perfons, yet in general could wifh (if it be either with countenance or connivance) that thefe ways might be more trod into thefe inland parts, and that amongft the multitudes of the barbarous, the neighbor-hood of fome Englifh Plantation (efpecially of men defi-ring to fear God) might help and ftrengthen. I fhall be thankful for a word of advice, and befeeching the Moft Holy and only Wife in mercy and goodnefs to know and guide the fouls of his in this remote wildernefs, and in this material defert, to difcover gracioufly the myftical where twelve hundred and three fcore days his faints are hid. Revel. 12. I rest

Your Worfhip's, forry that I am not more yours and neither of us more the Lord's.

ROGER WILLIAMS.

To Mrs. Winthrop all refpective remembrance.

I fhall beg (this winter in fome leifure) your help with my bad debtors, James and Tho: Haukins, from whom as yet I get nought but words.

---

but he ftood upon it that he would have a coat more, and left the beads with Mr. Williams, and wifhed him to keep them until Mr. Hubbard came up."—*Plymouth Col. Rec.* vol. ii. p. 87. Our impreffion is that the Charleftown men firft pro-pofed to go to Seekonk, but afterwards gave it up, and the lands were then taken in 1641 by Rev. Samuel Newman and others of Weymouth and Hingham. We can trace no fettlement near Providence to Charleftown men.

11

To his much honored Governor John Winthrop.

20th of the 9th. [November 20, 1637.][1]

SIR,—I reft thankfully fatisfied in your propounding of
my motion to the Court, and the anfwer. (The earth is
Jehovah's, and the plenitude of it.)   I am not a little glad
that the lot is fallen upon a branch of that root, in whofe
good (prefent and eternal both of root and branches) I
rejoice.   For his fake I wifh it ground, and grafs, and
trees ; yet what ufe fo ever he pleafe to make of it, I defire he would not fpare to make ufe of me in any fervice
towards the natives on it or about it.

Miantunnomu in his relations of paffages in the Bay
with you, thankfully acknowledges to myfelf and others
your loving carriage to him, and promifeth to fend forth
word to all natives to ceafe from Prudence, trees, &c.
Since your letter I travelled up to Nayantick by land where
I heard Reprive was : there the Sachem (to whom he ad-
heres, Wepiteammock) and the people related that he was
gone to his wife at Mohegan : alfo that he, Wepiteammock, had fent to Uncas advifing and urging their return,
but he could not prevail, and that if Reprive come within
his reach he will fend him (though alone without his wife)
however.

I traveled to Mohegan and underftood that they were
all at Pequot, Nayantick, but Uncas not being at home
(but at New Haven) I could not do ought.

Sir, I have often called upon your debtor, Jofhua,[2] but
his ill advifenefs of refufing my fervice and fpending of
his time upon a houfe and ground hath difabled him.

---

[1] 4 *Mafs. Hift. Coll.* vol. vi. p. 220.   of land was adjoining Mr. Williams's
[2] Probably Jofhua Verin, whofe grant

Upon this occafion of your loving proffer of the half of the debt (8*li*) to myfelf, I fhall be urgent with him to feek fome courfe of payment of the whole to yourfelf, from whom in recompenfe of any pains, &c., I defire no other fatisfaction but your loving and wonted acceptation, yea, although the bufinefs had been effected. Sir, I had almoft been bold to fay my thoughts what I would do in this cafe, were the runaways[1] mine, but I will not more at prefent. If you fhall pleafe to require account of what my obfervation hath taught me, I fhall readily yield it in my next, ever begging mercy and truth to you and yours, and my loving friends with you. The Lord Jefus return us all (poor runaways) with weeping and fupplications to feek him that was nailed to the gallows; in him I defire to be (and mourn I am not) more

Your worfhip's unfeigned

Roger Williams.

Sir, I received fix fathom of beads from Mr. Throckmorton, which though I will not return, yet I account them yours in my keeping.

Sir, I pray my refpective remembrance to Mrs. Winthrop.

---

[1] Poffibly refers to Reprive and other Indian fervants, before mentioned.

To his much honored Governor John Winthrop.

PROVIDENCE, 10th of the 11th month. [January 10, 1637–8.][1]

MUCH HONORED SIR,—It having pleafed the Moft High to befiege us all with his white legions,[2] I rejoice at this occafion from Connecticut (thefe letters fent to me by Mr. Hooker)[3] that I may hear of your welfare and health, which I wifh and beg unfeignedly of the Lord.

Mr. Hooker intimates a report to me that they hear from the Monahiganeucks that Miantunnomu intends Tho: Stanton's death. I have taken fome pains in it, and other paffages fent me, finding them flanders: and fince (for many good ends and) for keeping a paffage open between yourfelves and Connecticut by natives, fummer and winter, a peace is much to be defired between the Mohegan and the Narraganfett. I have proffered my pains in procuring a meeting of the adverfe Sachems, if it pleafe the Magiftrates of Connecticut to order Owokace (the Mohegan Sachem) to touch in at the Narraganfett mouth, where I hope to get the Narraganfett Sachems aboard, and it may pleafe the God of Peace to fave much blood and evil, &c.

Only it behooves our friends of Connecticut, as I have writ to them, to look to the two or three hundred Pe-

---

[1] 4 *Mafs. Hift. Coll.* vol. vi. p. 221.

[2] Snow. WINTHROP fays, "This was a very hard winter. The fnow lay from November 4 to March 23 half a yard deep about the Maffachufetts," &c., vol. i, p. 317.

[3] The Rev. Thomas Hooker, of Hartford, to whom Williams here alludes, was an eminent divine, and one of the founders of the colony of Connecticut. He arrived at Bofton in company with John Cotton, September 3, 1633, and the following month became paftor of the church in Newton. In 1636, with his whole congregation, he removed to the banks of the Connecticut river, where they founded Hartford. In this new colony, Hooker was very influential in eftablifhing churches. He died in 1647, aged 61. He was the author of feveral volumes, the moft celebrated of which is *A Survey of the Sum of Church Difcipline*, printed at London, in 1648.

quots harbored by Wocafe[1] the Mohegan, as alfo William Baker[2] of Plymouth, (of whom formerly I wrote) who is there hid, is turned Indian in nakednefs and cutting of hair, and after many whoredoms, is there married: this fire-brand with thofe Pequots may fire whole towns: I have intimated how they may with eafe take him.

Sir, let me be humbly bold to requeft a favor of you: I am at prefent deftitute of a man fervant, and much defire, if you light on one that defires to fear the Lord, remember me. I have a lufty canoe, and fhall have occafion to run down often to your Ifland[3] (near twenty miles from us) both with mine own and (I defire alfo freely) your worfhip's fwine, fo that my want is great. I would fpare no charge, either out of thofe beads and coat in your own hand: the tobacco from Mr. Ludlow, and 8 or 10 *li* in James and Tho: Hawkins hand of which I hear not yet.

Sir, if any letters from yourfelf or other friends are for Connecticut, I intreat you make hafte and fpeed by this meffenger, for I caufed four natives who came from Connecticut to ftay his coming: I have already paid him, fo that his expectation is not great. Thus longing to hear of your healths, and with earneft and daily wifhes for that peace which this world cannot give nor take from you, and my poor wife's and mine own beft falutes to your deareft companion, I reft

Your worfhip's to my power faithful

ROGER WILLIAMS.

My due refpects to Mr. Deputy, Mr. Bellingham, theirs, and other loving friends, &c.

---

[1] Probably Uncas.
[2] See note to letter of October preceding, relative to William Baker.
[3] Prudence Ifland.

To his much honored Governor John Winthrop.

PROVIDENCE, 28th of the 12th.   [February 28, 1637-8.][1]

SIR, — Some few days fince I received letters from Mr. Hooker, who had fafely received your packet with thanks, &c.

He intimated that according to Miantunnomue's information by myfelf, William Baker was hid at Mohegan, but they had made Uncas and Wequafh to bring him in. Since which time (Seargeant Holmes bailing him) he is again efcaped.

He alfo fignified the defire of the Magiftrates at Connecticut that there the meeting fhould be: as alfo that in the mean feafon they had charged the Mohegans not to moleft any natives in their paffage and travel, &c., requiring the fame of the Narraganfetts towards the Mohegans.

Accordingly I have been fince at Narraganfett[2] and find Miantunnomu willing to go to Connecticut by the time limited, the end of the next month; only firft he defired to know Mr. Governor's mind: fecondly, in cafe his father-in-law Canonicus his brother, (whom I faw near death with above a thoufand men mourning and praying about him) in cafe he recover, otherwife it is unlawful for them (as they conceive,) to go far from home till toward midfummer.   Thirdly, he defires earneftly my company, as being not fo confident of the Englifh at Connecticut, who have been (I fear) to full of threatnings: fecondly, he cannot be confident of Tho: Stanton's faithfulnefs in point of

---

[1] 4 *Mafs. Hift. Coll.* vol. vi. p. 223.
[2] The Narraganfett country which occupied much the fame diftrict as Wafhington County now embraces, except a fmall portion lying eaft of Pawcatuck river; and extended a little north of the prefent line of Kent County.

interpretation. Thefe things make me much defire (as I have written back) that you would both pleafe by fome deputed to make my poor houfe the centre where feems to be the faireft offer of convenience, and I hope no queftion of welcome.

Vifiting Canonicus, lately recovered from the pit's brink this winter, he afked how Mr. Governor and the Englifh did, requefting me to fend him two words : firft, that he would be thankful to Mr. Governor for fome fugar (for I had fent him mine own in the depth of the winter and his ficknefs.) Secondly, he called for his fword, which faid he, Mr. Governor did fend me by you and others of the Englifh, faying Mr. Governor protefted he would not put up his fword, nor would he have us put up ours, till the Pequots were fubdued, and yet faith he, at Mohegan there are near three hundred, who have bound and robbed our men (even of the very covering of their fecret parts) as they have paft from Connecticut hither : after much more to this purpofe, I told him that Mr. Governor had promifed him to fet all in order this fpring.

Sir, I underftand that Uncas the Mohegan hath Safacous his fifter to wife, and one of the wives of Safacous his father Tattoapaine, and that is one reafon, befide his ambition and nearnefs, that he hath drawn all the fcattered Pequots to himfelf and drawn much wealth from them : more I could trouble you with, &c.

Canonicus and Miantunnomu both defired that there might be a divifion made of thefe furviving Pequots (except the Sachems and murderers) and let their fhare be at your own wifdom.

I fhall be humbly bold to prefent mine own thoughts concerning a divifion and difpofal of them : fince the Moft High delights in mercy, and great revenge hath been already taken, what if (the murderers being executed) the reft be divided and difperfed, (according to their numbers fhall arife, and divifion be thought fit) to become fubjects to yourfelves in the Bay and at Connecticut, which they will more eafily do in cafe they may be fuffered to incorporate with the natives in either places: as alfo that as once Edgar the Peaceable did with the Welfh in North Wales, a tribute of wolves heads be impofed on them, &c., which (with fubmiffion) I conceive an incomparable way to fave much cattle alive in the land.

Sir, I hope fhortly to fend you good news of great hopes the Lord hath fprung up in mine eye, of many a poor Indian foul enquiring after God. I have convinced hundreds at home and abroad that in point of religion they are all wandering, &c. I find what I could never hear before, that they have plenty of Gods or divine powers: the Sun, Moon, Fire, Water, Snow, Earth, the Deer, the Bear, &c., are divine powers. I brought home lately from the Narraganfetts the names of thirty-eight of their Gods, all they could remember, and had I not with fear and caution withdrew, they would have fallen to worfhip, O God, (as they fpeak) one day in feven, but I hope the time is not long that fome fhall truely blefs the God of Heaven that ever they faw the face of Englifh men. So waiting for your pleafure and advice to our neighbors concerning this intended meeting for the eftablifhing of peace through all the bowels of the country, and befeeching the Moft High to vouchfafe his peace and truth through all your quarters, with my due refpects to Mrs. Winthrop, Mr. Deputy, Mr. Bellingham, &c., I reft

Your worfhip's in all true refpect and affection

ROGER WILLIAMS.

Sir, I heard no more as yet from Charleſtown men coming this way. Mr. Coxall and Mr. Aſpinwall[1] have ſent to me about ſome of theſe parts, and in caſe for ſhelter for their wives and children.

Indorſed by Gov. Winthrop, "Proviſions to be ſent by the Salem Bark to Mr. Williams and Mr. Throckmorton, Mr. Harlackenden knows more."

To his much honored Governor John Winthrop.

PROVIDENCE, 16th of this 2d. [April 16, 1638.][2]

MUCH HONORED SIR,—I kindly thank you for your loving inclination to receive my late proteſtation concerning myſelf, ignorant of Mr. Greene's letter,[3] &c. I deſire unfeignedly, to reſt in my appeal to the Moſt High in what we differ, as I dare not but hope you do : it is no

[1] William Aſpinwall, was one of the ſigners of the compact at Portſmouth in 1638, and was choſen Secretary. The following year he had lands aſſigned him in that town. SAVAGE, ſays he moved to New Haven and afterwards returned to Boſton.—*Genealogical Dict.* vol. i. p. 71. It is to be inferred from this letter that ſome of the family were ſtill in the colony of Rhode Iſland.

[2] 4 *Maſs. Hiſt. Coll.* vol. vi. p. 226.

[3] March 12, 1638. "Whereas a letter was ſent to this Court, ſubſcribed by John Greene, dated from New Providence, wherein the Court is charged with uſurping the power of Chriſt over the Churches and men's conſciences, notwithſtanding he had formerly acknowledged his fault in ſuch ſpeeches;

it is now ordered, that ſaid John Greene ſhall not come into this juriſdiction upon paine of impriſonment and further cenſure : and becauſe it appears to this Courte that ſome other of the ſame place are confident in the ſame corrupt judgment and practice; it is ordered, that if any other of the inhabitants of the ſaid plantation of Providence ſhall come within this juriſdiction, they ſhall be apprehended and brought before ſome of the magiſtrates; and if they will not diſclaime the ſaid corrupt opinion and cenſure, they ſhall be commanded preſently to depart," etc.—*Maſs. Col. Rec.* vol. i. p. 224; ſee alſo WINTHROP, *Journal*, vol. i. p. 307; ſee alſo note to letter of July 31, 1637.

12

fmall grief that I am otherwife perfuaded, and that fometimes you fay (and I can fay no lefs) that we differ: the
fire will try your works and mine: the Lord Jefus help
us to make fure of our perfons that we feek Jefus that was
crucified: however it is and ever fhall be (the Lord affifting) my endeavor to pacify and allay, where I meet with
rigid and cenforious fpirits, who not only blame your
actions but doom your perfons: and indeed it was one of
the firft grounds of my diflike of John Smith[1] the miller,
and efpecially of his wife, viz.: their judging of your perfons as [devel's][2] &c.

I alfo humbly thank you for that fad relation of the
monfter,[3] &c.   The Lord fpeaks once and twice: he be
pleafed to open all our ears to his difcipline.

[1] John Smith one of the earlieft fettlers in Providence.   He is on the lift of
thofe who received a "home lot" in 1638,
and was one of the committee, with Roger Williams and others, appointed May
16, 1647, to organize a government.—
R. I. Col. Records, vol. i, pp. 24 and 42.
He was one of the moft prominent men
in the colony for many years; but it
feems that he incurred the diflike of
Williams.

[2] The word in brackets is expunged in
the original manufcript.

[3] This "monfter" was the deformed
child of the wife of William Dyer, "a
very proper and fair woman.   The child
was buried, (being ftill-born) and viewed
of none but Mrs Hutchinfon and the
midwife."   A particular account of this
"monfter" is given by Winthrop under
date of March 27, 1638.—*Journal*, vol.
i. p. 226.

Winthrop fays that Dyer and his wife

"were notorioufly infected with Mrs.
Hutchinfon's errors, (fhe being much
addicted to revelations.)"   Mrs. Hutchinfon endeavored to conceal the fact of
the birth of the child, by advice, as fhe
faid of Mr. Cotton.   "The Governour,
fpeaking with Mr. Cotton about it, told
him the reafon why he advifed them to
conceal it: 1. Becaufe he faw a providence of God in it," etc., which apology
was accepted.—*Hift. of N. Eng.* vol. i.
p. 313.

This ftrange affair feems to have created a fenfation in the colony, and the
midwife fufpected of being a witch, was
obliged to leave the jurifdiction.

Gov. Bradford, of Plymouth, in a letter to Winthrop, fays "I thank you for
your letter touching Mrs. Hutchinfon:
I heard fince of a monftrous and pro-
digious birth which fhe fhould difown
amongft you.—*Winthrop Papers*, 4 *Mafs.
Hift. Coll.* vol. vi. p. 156.

Mrs. Hutchinſon[1] (with whom and others of them I have had much diſcourſe) makes her apology for the concealment of the monſter, that ſhe did nothing in it without Mr. Cotton's[2] advice, though I cannot believe that he

[1] Anne Hutchinſon, founder of the Antinomian party in New England. Being intereſted in the preachings of John Cotton, came to Boſton in 1634. " She ſoon acquired eſteem and influence. She inſtituted meetings of the women of the Church to diſcuſs ſermons and doctrines, in which ſhe diſplayed great familiarity with ſcripture, but made enemies by her nnovating theories. Two years after her arrival, the ſtrife between her ſupporters and opponents broke out into public action. ' The diſpute' ſays Bancroft, ' infuſed its ſpirit into every thing ; it interfered with the levy of troops for the Pequot war ; it influenced the reſpect ſhown to the magiſtrates, the diſtribution of town lots, the aſſeſſment of taxes, and at laſt the continued exiſtence of the two oppoſing parties was conſidered inconſiſtent with the public peace.' Her peculiar tenents were condemned by the eccleſiaſtical ſynod in 1637, and after a two days trial before the General Court, ſhe was ſentenced to baniſhment. She joined her friends, who, under John Clarke and Wm. Coddington, ſettled in Rhode Iſland."—DRAKE, *Biog. Dict.* Mrs. Hutchinſon " was a woman of rare endowments of intellect, and brilliant qualities of both perſon and character. Her mind, tinged with a ſhade of fanaticiſm, was of that impaſſioned and fervid caſt, which enabled her to clothe her peculiar doctrines in the charms of a faſcinating eloquence, and eaſily to ſubject to her ſway the opinions of thoſe, who were not entirely quieſcent beneath the deſpotiſm of the prevailing theology of the times. . . . . The queſtions at iſſue were, in moſt reſpects, the ſame as have perplexed the minds and divided the opinions of Chriſtians in every age of the church, and about which uniformity of ſentiment is never to be hoped for."—GAMMELL, *Life of Roger Williams,* p. 96.

In 1642, on the death of her huſband, Mrs. Hutchinſon removed to Weſtcheſter County, New York, and took up her reſidence near Hell Gate. The following year her houſe was attacked by the Indians, who ſet it on fire, and murdered her whole family, compriſing ſixteen perſons, with the exception of one daughter who was carried away into an unknown captivity. "Her tragical death and the extinction of her family," writes Profeſſor GAMMELL, "ſerved but to confirm her enemies in Maſſachuſetts in their convictions of her wickedneſs, and the juſtice of their proceedings againſt her. They were confidently regarded as a revelation of the judgment of God.

[2] John Cotton, with whom Williams afterwards had a controverſy upon theological matters. For the voluminous writings of theſe eminent men, ſee the *" Bloody Tenent"* and other works, in the third and fourth volumes of the publications of the Narraganſett Club.

subfcribes to her applications of the parts of it. The Lord
mercifully redeem them, and all of us from all our delufions, and pity the defolations of Zion and the ftones
thereof.

I find their longings great after Mr. Vane,[1] although
they think he can not return this year: the eyes of fome
are fo earneftly fixed upon him that Mrs. Hutchinfon
profeffeth if he come not to New, fhe muft to Old
England.

I have endeavored by many arguments to beat off their
defires of Mr. Vane as G. G. and the chief are fatisfied
unlefs he come fo for his life, but I have endeavored to
difcover the fnare in that alfo.

Sir, concerning your intended meeting for reconciling
of thefe natives our friends, and dividing of the Pequots
our enemies, I have engaged your name, and mine own;
and if no courfe be taken, the name of that God of Truth
whom we all profefs to honor will fuffer not a little, it being an ordinary and common thing with our neighbors,
if they apprehend any fhow of breach of promife in
myfelf, thus to objeć: do you know God, and will you
lie? &c.

The Pequots are gathered into one, and plant their
old fields, Wequafh and Uncas carrying away the people
and their treafure, which belong to yourfelves: I fhould
be bold to prefs my former motion, or elfe that with the
next convenience they might be fent for other parts, &c.

---

[1] Sir Henry Vane, Governor of Maffachufetts the previous year, had juft returned to England. While in Bofton,
he had befriended Mrs. Hutchinfon,
having no fympathy with the clergy and
other Maffachufetts people who were
perfecuting her. She and her followers,
therefore, looked to him for protećion.
See an extended note to letter of Oćto-
ber 25, 1649, on Sir Henry Vane.

I hope it will never be interpreted that I prefs this out of fear of any revenge upon myfelf by any of them. I ever yet (in point of reafon to fay no more) conceived this place the fafeft of the land, and can make it appear, &c., but out of defire to clear your names and the name of the moft High, which will be ill reported of in cafe (according to fo many promifes) an honorable and peaceable iffue of the Pequot war be not eftablifhed.

Sir, the bearer hereof (not daring either to bring my letter or attend for an anfwer) I muft requeft you to fend your letter to Richard Collicut's, that fo a native may convey it, or elfe to Nicholas Upfhall's: and I fhould be bold humbly to propound to the country whether in cafe there be a neceffity of keeping league with the natives, and fo confequently many occafions incident, (and fome which I will not write of) as alfo a conveniency of information this way, how matters may ftand with you on the fea-fhore, as I fay,, whither it be not requifite fo far to difpenfe with the late order of reftraint as to permit a meffenger freely.

'Tis true I may hire an Indian: yet not always, nor fure, for thefe two things I have found in them: fometimes long keeping of a letter: fecondly, if a fear take them that the letter concerns themfelves they fupprefs it, as they did with one of fpecial information which I fent to Mr. Vane.

Sir, there will be new Heavens and a new Earth fhortly but no more Sea. (Revel. 21. 2.) the moft holy God be pleafed to make us willing now to bear the toffings, dangers and calamities of this fea, and to feal up to ufe upon his own grounds, a great lot in the glorious ftate approaching. So craving pardon for prolixity, with mine

and wife's due refpect to Mrs. Winthrop, Mr. Deputy,
Mr. Bellingham, &c., I reft

Your worfhip's defirous to be ever yours unfeigned

ROGER WILLIAMS.

Endorfed by Gov. Winthrop, "2. 16. 1638."

To his much honored Governor John Winthrop.[1]

PROVIDENCE, the 22 of 3d mon. [May 22, 1638.]

SIR, — Bleffed be the Father of Spirits, in whofe hand
our breath and ways are, that once more I may be bold
to falute you and congratulate your return from the brink
of the pit of rottennefs.[2]

What is man that thou fhouldeft vifit him and try
him? &c.   Job 7th.   You are put off to this tempeftuous
fea again, more ftorms await you, the good Lord repair our
leaks, frefhen up the gales of his bleffed Spirit, fteady our
courfe by the compafs of his own truth, refcue us from all
our fpiritual adverfaries, not only men, but fiends of war,
and affure us of an harbor at laft, even the bofom of the
Lord Jefus.

Sir, you have many an eye (I prefume) lifted up to the
hills of mercy for you: mine might feem fuperfluous: yet
privately and publicly you have not been forgotten, and I
hope fhall not while thefe eyes have fight.

[1] 4 *Mafs. Hift. Coll.* vol. vi. p. 244.   which brought him near death.—*Hift.*
[2] Alluding to the illnefs of Winthrop, *of New England*, vol. i. p. 318.

Sir, this laſt night Mr. Allen of Hartford, and Lieutenant Holmes lodged with me, and relate that Mr. Haynes[1] or ſome chief reſolved to be with you this week. So that you may pleaſe a little ſtop till their coming. Lieutenant Holmes relates that William Baker, who lay hid ſo long among the Mohegans and Pequots, for whom he gave bail, &c., was hid again the ſecond time among the ſame by Uncas, but the Lieutenant, by a Providence, heard of him and returned him to Hartford, where he hath ſuffered for his much uncleanneſs two ſeveral whippings. This fellow, notorious in villiany, and ſtrongly affected by thoſe wretches, both ſtudying revenge, is worthy to be watched even by the whole country, and to be diſperſed from the Pe- quots, and they each from other, according as I have been bold to motion formerly.

Sir, we have been long afflicted by a young man boiſte- rous and deſperate, Philip Verin's ſon of Salem,[2] who as he hath refuſed to hear the word with us (which we mo- leſted him not for) this twelve month, ſo becauſe he could not draw his wife, a gracious and modeſt woman, to the ſame ungodlineſs with him, he hath trodden her under foot

---

[1] John Haynes, Governor of Connec- ticut. He came from England with Thomas Hooker in 1633. In 1637 he was prominent among the founders of Connecticut, and was choſen its firſt Governor in 1639, and every alternate year afterward till his death. He was one of the five who, in 1638, drew up a written conſtitution for the colony. BAN- CROFT ſpeaks of him as a man "of large eſtate, and larger affections : of heavenly mind, and ſpotleſs life ; of rare ſagacity, and accurate but unaſſuming judgment ; by nature tolerant and a friend to free- dom." He was one of the beſt educated of the early ſettlers of this country.— DRAKE, *Biog. Dictionary.*

[2] Philip Verin's ſon, of Salem. Proba- bly one of the family of Joſhua Verin, one of the firſt ſettlers of Providence, who accompanied Roger Williams when he paddled acroſs Seekonk River in his log canoe, but who ſoon after removed to Salem. See letter following that of October 10th, for a note on Joſhua Verin.

tyrannically and brutifhly : which fhe and we long bearing, though with his furious blows fhe went in danger of
life, at the laft the major vote of us difcard him from our
civil freedom, or disfranchife, &c. : he will have juftice (as
he clamors) at other Courts : I wifh he might, for a foul
and flanderous and brutifh carriage, which God hath delivered him up unto; he will [haul] his wife with ropes to
Salem, where fhe muft needs be troubled and troublefome,
as differences yet ftand. She is willing to ftay and live
with him or elfewhere, where fhe may not offend, &c.   I
fhall humbly requeft that this item be accepted, and he no
way countenanced, until (if need be) I further trouble
you :   So with due refpecls to Mrs. Winthrop, Mr. Deputy, Mr. Bellingham, &c., I reft,

Your worfhip's unfeigned

Roger Williams.

To his much honored Governor John Winthrop.[1]

Providence, 27th of 3d. [May 27, 1638.]

Much honored Sir, — I have prefumed to fend this
Narraganfett man, to attend your pleafure concerning the
Pequots, and Canonicus and Miantunnomue's complaint
againft them and their protectors.

  The fum of their defire I lately acquainted you with,
viz. : that you would pleafe (even all the Englifh) to fit
ftill and let themfelves alone with them according to con-

------

[1] 4 *Mafs. Hift. Coll.* vol. vi. p. 246.

fent, when Miantunnomu was laſt with you, who coming
home, fell upon Nayantick men who ſheltered the Pequots,
but was ſtopped by our friends of Connecticut.

Or, ſecondly, that ſome other courſe (in conſultation)
might be taken for diſperſion of them : even as far as Old
England or elſewhere, as they ſpeak.

Sir, I do conceive either courſe will be difficult, becauſe
our friends at Connecticut are ſtrangely bewitched with
the ſubjection of theſe Pequots to themſelves, and are alſo
as ſtrangely reſolved upon fighting and violent courſes, (as I
underſtand by letters, and otherwiſe by ſpeech) unleſs Miantunnomu come over perſonally to them to anſwer for
proud ſpeeches which they hear of.

Miantunnomu hath long ſince promiſed, and ſtill waits
to go any whither you ſhall pleaſe to make anſwer, to
meet, &c.

Some from Connecticut write me word, that Indians
will teſtify ſuch ſpeeches to Miantunnomu's teeth : and it
may be ſo whether true or falſe.

I alſo, in caſe I ſhould liſten to Indian reports, ſhall bring
many who will affirm that Tho : Stanton hath received
mighty bribes (whence *origo mali*) that Uncas the Mohegan hath received little leſs than a thouſand fathom of
beads, whence he carries out ſome preſent to our friends at
Connecticut, but I ſay I will not believe it.

But this I know, that according to league in two articles,
that the Pequots ſhall not be ſheltered nor diſpoſed of
without mutual conſent of the Engliſh and the two Narraganſett Sachems.

Secondly, that if the Pequots be ſuffered in the land to
congregate and unite into four or five hundred together
(as Lieutenant Howe confeſt to me) it will coſt more blood

13

on all fides then yet hath been fpilt; for on the one part, the Narraganfetts can no more forbear them than a wolf his prey, and on the other fide for the Pequots upon all advantage the Englifh fhall find, that *Vindicta levis vitâ incandior ipfâ eft.*

Thirdly, that our friends at Connecticut are marvelloufly deluded by the Mohegans, as to be fo confident of them, that Mr. Hooker writes no proof can be brought againft them for word or deed: when it is clear they were Pequots, and lately hid, (once and the fecond time) William Baker from the Englifh, and that upon pain of death to any that fhould reveal him, as Lieutenant Holmes told me. Sir, my defire is that it would therefore pleafe the Lord to guide you all to make a prudent difpofal and difperfion of the Pequots, which the Narraganfetts will further by peace or war. So with all due falutations I humbly reft, unfeigned in all defire of your prefent and eternal peace.

ROGER WILLIAMS.

Mr. Allen told me that there were numbers of the Pequots at Narraganfett, but I fatisfied him that they were at Nayantick, (whence if themfelves had not ftopped) they had long fince been removed.

For his much honored Mr. Governor, John Winthrop.

PROVIDENCE, [June, 1638.][1]

SIR,—I fometimes fear that my lines are as thick and over bufy as the mufketoes, &c., but your wifdom will connive, and your love will cover, &c.

Two things at prefent for information.

Firft in the affairs of the Moft High; his late dreadful voice and hand: that audible and fenfible voice, the Earthquake.[2]

All thefe parts felt it, (whether beyond the Narraganfett I yet learn not), for myfelf I fcarce perceived ought but a kind of thunder and a gentle moving, &c., and yet it was no more this way to many of our own and the natives apprehenfions, and but one fudden fhort motion.

The younger natives are ignorant of the like: but the elder inform me that this is the fifth within thefe four fcore years in the land: the firft about three fcore and ten years fince: the fecond fome three fcore and four years fince, the third fome fifty-four years fince, the fourth fome forty-fix fince: and they always obferved either plague or pox or fome other epidemical difeafe followed; three, four or five years after the Earthquake, (or Naunaumemoauke, as they fpeak).

He be mercifully pleafed himfelf to interpret and open

---

[1] 4 *Mafs. Hift. Coll.* vol. vi. p. 229.

[2] WINTHROP, under date of June 1, thus records this event: "Between three and four in the afternoon, being clear, and warm weather, the wind wefterly, there was a great earthquake. It came with a noife like a continued thunder or the rattling of coaches in London, but was prefently gone. It was at Connecticut, at Narraganfett, at Pifcataquack, and all parts round about. It fhook the fhips, which rode in the harbour, and all the iflands, etc. The noife and the fhakings continued about four minutes. The earth was unquiet twenty days after, by times.—*Hift. of New England*, vol. i. p. 319.

his own riddles, and grant if it be pleafing in his eyes) it may not be for deftruction, and but (as the Earthquake before the Jailor's converfion) a means of fhaking and turning of all hearts, (which are his,) Englifh or Indian, to him. To further this (if the Lord pleafe) the Earthquake fenfibly took about a thoufand of the natives in a moft folemn meeting for play, &c.

Secondly, a word in mine own particular, only for information. I owe between 50 and 60*li* to Mr. Cradock[1] for commodities received from Mr. Mayhew.[2] Mr. Mayhew will teftify that (being Mr. Cradock's agent) he was content to take payment, what (and when) my houfe at Salem yielded: accordingly I long fince put it into his hand, and he into Mr. Jollies',[3] who befide my voluntary act and his attachment fince, fues as I hear for damages, which I queftion: fince I have not failed againft contract and content of the firft agent, but the holy pleafure of the Lord be done: unto whofe merciful arms (with all due refpects) I leave you, wifhing heartily that mercy and goodnefs may ever follow you and yours.

Roger Williams.

Sir, to your dear companion, Mr. Deputy, Mr. Bellingham, and theirs, all refpective falutes, &c.

[1] Mathew Cradock, Governor of the Maffachufetts Company.

[2] Thomas Mayhew was a member of the General Court of Maffachufetts, and probably a merchant. Others befides Williams feem to have had trouble with him, for Cradock, whofe agent he was, in a letter to Winthrop, January 13th, 1636, fays "The greyffe I have been put to by the moft vyle bad dealing of Thomas Mayhew hath and doth fo much difquiet my mind, as I thank God never any thing did in the lyke manner. The Lord in mercy free me from this, I abfolutely forbad charging moneys from thence, or buying any goods there."—*Winthrop Papers: 4 Mafs. Hift. Coll.* vol. vi. p. 122.

[3] Jollies or, Joliffe, an agent of Mr. Cradock, fee previous letter.

To his much honored Governor John Winthrop.

[No date; June, 1638.]

SIR,— I perceive by thefe your laft thoughts, that you have received many accufations and hard conceits of this poor native Miantunnomu, wherein I fee the vain and empty puff of all terrene promotions, his barbarous birth or greatnefs being much honored, confirmed and augmented (in his own conceit) by the folemnity of his league with the Englifh and his more than ordinary entertainment, &c., now all dafhed in a moment in the frowns of fuch in whofe friendfhip and love lay his chief advancement.

Sir, of the particulars, fome concern him only, fome Canonicus and the reft of the Sachems, fome all the natives, fome myfelf.

For the Sachems, I fhall go over fpeedily, and acquaint them with particulars. At prefent, let me ftill find this favor in your eyes, as to obtain an hearing, for that your love hath never denied me, which way foever your judgment hath been (I hope and I know you will one day fee it) and been carried.

Sir, let this barbarian be proud and angry and covetous and filthy, hating and hateful, (as we ourfelves have been till kindnefs from heaven pitied us, &c.,) yet let me humbly beg relief, that for myfelf, I am not yet turned Indian, to believe all barbarians tell me, nor fo bafely prefumptuous as to trouble the eyes and hands of fuch (and fo honored and dear) with fhadows and fables. I commonly guefs fhrewdly at what a native utters, and, to my remem-

---

[1] 3 *Maff. Hiff. Coll.* vol. i. p. 166. KNOWLES's *Mem. of Roger Williams*, p. 149.

brance, never wrote particular, but either I know the bottom of it, or elfe I am bold to give a hint of my fufpenfe.

Sir, therefore in fome things at prefent (begging your wonted gentlenefs toward my folly) give me leave to fhow you how I clear myfelf from fuch a lightnefs.

I wrote lately (for that you pleafe to begin with) that fome Pequots, (and fome of them actual murderers of the Englifh, and that alfo after the fort cut off) were now in your hands. Not only love, but confcience, forced me to fend, and fpeedily, on purpofe, by a native, mine own fervant. I faw not, fpake not with Miantunnomu, nor any from him. I write before the All-feeing Eye. But thus it was. A Narraganfett man (Awetipimo) coming from the bay with cloth, turned in (as they ufed to do) to me for lodging. I queftioned of Indian paffages, &c. He tells me Uncas was come with near upon forty natives. I afked what prefent he brought. He told me, that Cut-fhamoquene had four fathom and odd[1] of him, and forty was for Mr. Governor. I afked him, how many Pequots. He told me fix. I afked him, if they were known. He faid Uncas denied that there were any Pequots, and faid they were Mohegans all. I afked, if himfelf knew any of them. He anfwered, he did, and fo did other Indians of Narraganfett. I afked, if the murderer of whom I wrote, Pametefick, were there. He anfwered, he was, and (I further enquiring) he was confident it was he, for he knew him as well as me, &c.

All this news (by this providence) I knew before it came to Narraganfett. Upon this I fent, indeed fearing guilt to

[1] "Four fathom and odd" of wampum, or peage, which in ftrings, was meafured by the yard or fathom. See note on wampum.

mine own foul, both againft the Lord and my countrymen. But fee a ftranger hand of the Moft and Only Wife. Two days after, Uncas paffeth by within a mile of me (though he fhould have been kindly welcome) One of his company (Wequaumugs) having hurt his foot, and difabled from travel, turns into me; whom lodging, I queftioned, and find him by father a Narraganfett, by mother a Mohegan, and fo freely entertained by both. I, further enquiring, he told me he went from Mohegan to the Bay with Uncas. He told me how he had prefented forty fathom to (my remembrance) to Mr. Governor, (four and upwards to Cutfhamoquene,) who would not receive them, but afked twice for Pequots. At laft, at Newtown, Mr. Governor received them, and was willing that the Pequots fhould live, fuch as were at Mohegan, fubject to the Englifh Sachems at Connecticut, to whom they fhould carry tribute, and fuch Pequots as were at Narraganfett to Mr. Governor, and all the runaways at Mohegan to be fent back. I afked him, how many Pequots were at Narraganfett. He faid, but two, who were Miantunnomue's captives, and that at Nayantick with Wequafh Cook were about three fcore. I afked, why he faid the Indians at Narraganfett were to be the Governor's fubjects. He faid, becaufe Nayantick was fometimes fo called, although there had been of late no coming of Narraganfett men thither. I afked him, if he heard all this. He faid, that himfelf and the body of the company ftaid about Cutfhamoquene's. I afked, how many Pequots were amongft them. He faid fix. I defired him to name them, which he did thus : Pametefick, Weeaugonhick, (another of thofe murderers) Makunnete, Kifhkontuckqua, Saufawpona, Quffaumpowan, which names I prefently wrote down, and (*pace veftra dixerim*) I am as confident of the truth, as that I breathe. Again, (not to be too bold in all the particulars at this time,) what a grofs and monftrous untruth is that concerning myfelf, which your love and wifdom to myfelf a little efpy, and I hope fee malice and falfehood (far from the fear of God) whifpering together? I have long held it will-worfhip to doff and don to the Moft High in worfhip; and I wifh alfo that, in civil worfhip, others were as far from fuch a vanity, though I hold it not utterly unlawful in fome places. Yet furely, amongft the barbarians, (the higheft in the world,) I would rather lofe my head than fo practice, becaufe I judge it my duty to fet them better copies, and fhould fin againft mine own perfuafions and refolutions.

Sir, concerning the iflands Prudence and (Patmos, if fome had not hindered) Aquednick,[1] be pleafed to underftand your great miftake : neither of them were fold properly, for a thoufand fathom would not have bought either, by ftrangers. The truth is, not a penny was demanded for either, and what was paid was only gratuity, though I choofe, for better affurance and form, to call it fale.

And, alas! (though I cannot conceive you can aim at the Sachems) they have ever conceived, that myfelf and Mr. Coddington[2] (whom they knew fo many years a Sachem

---

[1] *Aquetneck, Aquidneck,* the Ifland of Rhode Ifland.

[2] William Coddington was a native of Lincolnfhire, England, and was there appointed an affiftant judge for the colony of Maffachufetts Bay, in 1629. He came over with the Governor and the Charter in 1630, and was feveral times re-elected to that office. He was alfo, for fome time, treafurer of that colony, as was alfo, fays CALLENDER, "the chief-eft in all the public charges and a principal merchant in Bofton, where he built the firft brick houfe." He came to Rhode Ifland with a few friends, and his name ftands firft among thofe who incorporated themfelves into a body politic in the year 1638. They choofe him to be their judge, or chief ruler, and continued to elect him Governor until the patent was received, and the ifland incorporated with Providence Plantations. In

at Bofton), were far from being rejected by yourfelves, as
you pleafe to write, for if the Lord had not hid it from
their eyes, I am fure you had not been thus troubled by
myfelf at prefent. Yet the earth is the Lord's and the fullnefs thereof. His infinite wifdom and pity be pleafed to
help you all, and all that defire to fear his name and tremble at his word in this country, to remember that we all
are rejected of our native foil, and more to mind the many
ftrong bands, with which we are all tied, than any particular diftafte each againft other, and to remember that excellent precept, Prov. 25, If thine enemy hunger, feed him,
&c. ; for thou fhalt heap coals of fire upon his head, and
Jehovah fhall reward thee ; unto whofe mercy and tender
compaffions I daily commend you, defirous to be more
and ever

Your worfhip's unfeigned and faithful

ROGER WILLIAMS.

his depofition he ftates that he was one
of thofe who made a peace with Canonicus and Miantonomi in the colony's behalf with all the Narraganfett Indians,
and by order of Maffachufetts Bay, before they made war with the Pequots.
It was fubfequent to this that he removed
to Rhode Ifland.

In 1647 he affifted in framing the
body of laws which has fince been the
bafis of our conftitution and government.
In 1651 he had a commiffion from the
fupreme authority in England to be Governor of the Ifland, feparate from the
reft of the colony, purfuant to a power
referved in the patent, but the people being jealous that " the commiffion
might affect their laws and liberties, as
fecured to them by the patent,"—" he
readily laid it down " fays CALLENDER,

" on the firft notice from England that
he might do fo."

Many of the colonifts embraced the
fentiments of the Society of Friends,
among whom was Governor Coddington.
Their yearly meeting was held at his
houfe until his death.

Coddington appears to have enjoyed a
high reputation, and was ever active in
promoting the welfare of the commonwealth which he had affifted in founding.
He was a warm advocate for liberty of
confcience, as was fhown in his acts, and
as may be feen from his writings. Two
lay letters from him on religious matters
as preferved in BESSE's *Sufferings of the
Quakers,* London, 1753: 2 vols. folio;
and in a tract entitled " *Demonftration of
True Love unto You the rulers of the
colony of Maffachufetts* " in *New England.*
London, 1674.

14

Sir, mine own and wife's refpective falutes to your dear companion and all yours; as alfo to Mr. Deputy, Mr. Bellingham, and other loving friends.

I am bold to enclofe this paper, although the paffages may not be new, yet they may refrefh your memories in thefe Englifh-Scotch diftractions,[1] &c.

To his much honored Governor John Winthrop.

PROVIDENCE, this 5th of the prefent weeke.   [June, 1638.][2]

MUCH HONORED SIR,— Bleffed be the Father of mercies that once again I received your hand the laft night by the meffengers by whom I fent.

By them I underftand that according as you pleafe to intimate your expectation, Mr. Haynes is come: with Uncas, thirty-four Mohegans, and fix Pequots.[3]

One of the fix Pequots is Pametefick, who was one of the murderers that cut off the three Englifh, going in

---

[1] "Scotch diftractions." "The troubles which arofe in Scotland about the book of Common Prayer, and the canons, which the King would have forced upon the Scotch churches, did fo take up the King and council, that they had neither heart or leifure to look after the affairs of New England."—WINTHROP, *Hift. of New England*, vol. i. p. 320.

[2] 4 *Mafs. Hift. Coll.* vol. vi. p. 230.

[3] WINTHROP, under date of June 5, fays "Unkas the Monahegan Sachem in the twift of Pequot River, came to Bofton with thirty-feven men. He came from Connecticut with Mr. Haynes, and tendered the Governor a prefent of twenty fathom of wampom. This was at the Court, and it was thought fit by the council to refufe it, till he had given fatisfaction about the Pequods, etc. But two days after, having received good fatisfaction of his innocency, etc., and he promifing to fubmit to the order of the Englifh touching the Pequods he had, and the differences between the Narraganfetts and him, we accepted his prefents. . . . The Governor gave him a red coat, and defrayed his and his men's diet, and a letter of protection to all men, etc., and he departed very joyful." *Hift. of New England*, vol. i. p. 319.

a boat for clay upon Connecticut river, after the Fort was cut off. They not only fpilt their blood, but exercifed inhuman and tormenting revenge upon two of them, which cries for vengeance to heaven.

So that I refer it humbly to your wifdom whether (although I defire not the deftruction of the furviving Pequots, but a fafe difperfion of them, yet) the actual murderers be not to be furrendered up, and this Pametefick (I am partly confident this is he) at prefent apprehended: Our loving friends of Connecticut reported that fome Mohegan women were wronged (as their hair cut off, &c.,) by the Narraganfetts: but Uncas knows it was done by Wequafhcuck of Nayantick, to whom Uncas fent for a Pequot queen. They two have got in the Pequots (though Uncas have the harveft.) Againft Wequafhcuck, Canonicus or Miantunnomu had long fince proceeded, but our loving friends of Connecticut interpofed: I hope for the beft to fave blood. So befeeching the great Councillor and Prince of Peace to guide your councils, I reft your Worfhip's moft unworthy yet unfeigned

ROGER WILLIAMS.

All refpective falutes, &c.

To his much honored Governor John Winthrop.

PROVIDENCE, 23d, 5th.   [July 23, 1638.][1]

Two days since I was bold to present you with a line, and still (so it pleaseth the most High,) I am occasioned again to be a constant trouble, &c.

These your Worship's servants visiting me in their travel, I enquire after your runaways. The man saith he hath much to relate to yourself, and wanting utterance, desires me to write. He saith he hath enquired much after the runaways, and understands for certain that they are all at Mohegan.

That the flight was long since plotted, for he hath now heard by a Pequot that came from Mohegan, that the ten Mohegans which came to your Worship in the spring to buy one of the maidens, and offered ten fathom of beads, came from Uncas, who intended that maid for his wife.

That he gave order to those ten men, that, (in case they could not buy her) they should leave one man there at your house, to persuade and work their escape.

That man was the Pequot Robin, who hath effected his business, for which (as he hears) Uncas promised him and hath given him the ten fathom of Wampum.[2]

---

[1] 4 *Mass. Hist. Coll.* vol. vi. p. 231.

[2] Wampum. Strings, or strings of shells, used by the Indians as money. These, when united, formed a broad belt, which was worn as a ornament or girdle. It was sometimes called wampumpeage or peage.

"The Indians are ignorant of Europe's coin. Their own is of two sorts: one white, which they make of the stem or stock of the periwinkle, when all the shell is broken off . . . The second is black, inclining to blue, which is made of the shell of a fish; and of this sort three make a penny. Their white money they call *wampam*, which signifies white; their black, *sunkabock* signifying black."—WILLIAMS' *Key to the Indian Language*, London, 1643 : Chap. xxvi.

"A Sagamore with a humbird in his ears for a pendant, a black hawk in his occipit for a plume, good store of *wam-*

Uncas hath taken the two daughters, Marie and Jane both to wife, and fayth that now he hath done fending of prefents to Maffachufetts.

Reprive was promifed Joane by the Old Squaw for the furtherance of the bufinefs and hath her. He advifed their efcape by Neepmuck, becaufe once before, efcaping through the Narraganfett country, himfelf was fent back by the Narraganfett Sachems.

This man thinks alfo that no Indian means will be able to effect their return, but that the Englifh muft fetch them. It will be your worfhip's wifdom to forecaft fo much, and to prepare (Captain Patrick and many more may be occafioned to fetch theirs alfo.) Yet I requeft your Worfhip's patience a few days.

Sir, this young man who comes along, is this woman's nephew, an ingenious, fober fellow, one of my long acquaintance, whom I call Oldway, as his Indian name (Necawnimeyat) fignifies; he tells me he hath a good mind to abide one year with thefe his friends in your worfhip's fervice. I encourage him and prefent him to your wifdom and pity, not knowing but that the purpofe of the Only Wife and moft pityful God may be toward him for good. Unto the everflowing ftreams of the moft holy Fountain of living waters, (whofe drops are able to refrefh and fave worlds of wandering fouls), I heartily recommend your worfhip, your deareft companion, and all yours, grieving that I dare be no more your worfhip's

ROGER WILLIAMS.

pum-peage begirting his loins, his bow in hand, his quiver at his back, with fix naked fpatterlafhes at his heels for his guard, thinks he is one with King Charles."—Wood's *New England*, London, 1634, p. 66.

"And there the fallen chief is laid,
In taffell'd garb of fkins arrayed
And girdled with his *wampum*-braid."
WHITTIER, *The Funeral Tree.*

To his much honored Governor John Winthrop.[1]

[PROVIDENCE, August, 1638.][1]

MUCH HONORED SIR,—The bearer lodging with me, I am bold to write an hasty advertisement concerning late passages.   For himself, it seems he was fearful to go farther than forty miles about us, especially considering that no natives are willing to accompany him to Pequot or Mohegan, being told by two Pequots (the all of Miantunnomu's captives which are not run from him) what he might expect, &c.

Sir, Captain Mason[2] and Thomas Stanton landing at Narraganfett, and at Miantunnomu's announcing war within six days against Juanemo, for they say that Miantunnomu hath been fair in all the passages with them, Juanemo sent two messengers to myself, requesting counsel.   I advised him to go over with beads to satisfy, &c.

He sent four Indians.   By them Mr. Haynes writes me, that they confessed fifteen fathom there received at Long Island.   Thereabout they confessed to me, (four being taken of Pequots by force, and restored again,) as also that

---

[1] 3 *Mass. Hist. Coll.* vol. i. p. 170. KNOWLES' *Mem. R. Williams*, p. 153. *R. I. Hist. Coll.* vol. iii. p. 148, abridged.

[2] Capt. John Mason born in England about 1600, died at Norwich, Conn., 1672.   He was one of the first settlers of Dorchester, Mass., in 1630, but removed to Windsor, Conn., in 1635.   In the celebrated attack on the Pequot fort, (mentioned in previous letters) Mason led the force, the Indians being under the command of Uncas and Miantonomoh.   Soon after this event he was appointed Major-General of the Connecticut forces, which office he held to his death.   He was a magistrate from 1642 to 1648, and Deputy-Governor from 1660 to 1670.   In 1659 he took up his residence in Norwich.—*Mason's Life by Geo. E. Ellis*, is in SPARKS' *Amer. Biography*, vol. iii. new series.   Mason drew up a history of the Pequot war, which was printed in INCREASE MATHERS' *Relation of Troubles with the Indians*, 1677. Reprinted, with notes by T. Prince, Boston, 1736; again by J. Sabin, New York, 1869.

the iflanders fay fifty-one fathom, which fum he demanded, as alfo that the Nayantick meffengers laid down twenty-fix fathom and a half, which was received in part, with declaration that Juanemo fhould within ten days bring the reft himfelf, or elfe they were refolved for war, &c. I have therefore fent once and again to Juanemo, to perfuade himfelf to venture, &c. Canonicus fent a principal man laft night to me, in hafte and fecrecy, relating that Wequafh had fent word that, if Juanemo went over, he fhould be killed, but I affure them the contrary, and perfuade Canonicus to importune and haften Juanemo within his time, ten days, withal hoping and writing back perfuafions of better things to Mr. Haynes, proffering myfelf, (in cafe that Juanemo through fear or folly fail) to take a journey and negotiate their bufinefs, and fave blood, whether the natives' or my countrymen's.

Sir, there hath been great hubbub in all thefe parts, as a general perfuafion that the time was come of a general flaughter of natives, by reafon of a murder committed upon a native within twelve miles of us, four days fince, by four defperate Englifh. I prefume particulars have fcarce as yet been prefented to your hand. The laft fifth day, toward evening, a native, paffing through us, brought me word, that at Pawtuckqut, a river four miles from us toward the bay, four Englifhmen were almoft famifhed. I fent inftantly provifions and ftrong water, with invitation, &c. The meffengers brought word, that they were one Arthur Peach of Plymouth, an Irifhman, John Barnes, his man, and two others come from Pafcataquack, travelling to Connecticut; that they had been loft five days, and fell into our path but fix miles. Whereas they were importuned to come home, &c., they pleaded forenefs in travelling, and therefore their defire to reft there.

The next morning they came to me by break of day, relating that the old man at Pawtuckqut had put them forth the laſt night, becauſe that ſome Indians ſaid, that they had hurt an Engliſhmen, and therefore that they lay between us and Pawtuckqut.

I was buſy in writing letters and getting them a guide to Connecticut, and enquired no more, they having told me, that they came from Plymouth on the laſt of the week in the evening, and lay ſtill in the woods the Lord's day, and then loſt their way to Weymouth, from whence they loſt their way again towards us, and came in again ſix miles off Pawtuckqut.

After they were gone, an old native comes to me, and tells me; that the natives round about us were fled, relating that thoſe four had ſlain a native, who had carried three beaver ſkins and beads for Canonicus' ſon, and came home with five fathom and three coats; that three natives which came after him found him groaning in the path; that he told them that four Engliſhmen had ſlain him. They came to Pawtuckqut, and enquired after the Engliſh, which when Arthur and his company heard, they got on hoſe and ſhoes and departed in the night.

I ſent after them to Narraganſett, and went myſelf with two or three more to the wounded in the woods. The natives at firſt were ſhy of us, conceiving a general ſlaughter, but (through the Lord's mercy) I aſſured them that Mr. Governor knew nothing, &c. and that I have ſent to apprehend the men. So we found that he had been run through the leg and the belly with one thruſt. We dreſſed him and got him to town next day, where Mr. James and Mr. Greene endeavored, all they could, to ſave his life; but his wound in the belly, and blood loſt, and fever following, cut his life's thread.

Before he died, he told me that the four Englifh had flain him, and that (being faint and not able to fpeak) he had related the truth to the natives who firft came to him, viz. : that they, viz. : the Englifh, faw him in the Bay and his beads : that fitting in the fide of a fwamp a little way out of the path, (I went to fee the place, fit for an evil pur-pofe,) Arthur called him to drink tobacco, who coming and taking the pipe of Arthur, Arthur run him through the leg into the belly, when, fpringing back, he, Arthur, made the fecond thruft, but miffed him; that another of them ftruck at him, but miffed him, and his weapon run into the ground ; that getting from them a little way into the fwamp, they purfued him, till he fell down, when they miffed him, and getting up again, when he heard them clofe by him, he run to and again in the fwamp, till he fell down again, when they loft him quite ; afterwards, towards night, he came and lay in the path, that fome paf-fenger might help him as aforefaid.

Whereas they faid, they wandered Plymouth-way, Ar-thur knew the path, having gone it twice ; and befide, Mr. Throckmorton met them about Naponfet River in the path, who, riding roundly upon a fudden by them, was glad he had paft them, fufpecting them. They denied that they met Mr. Throckmorton.

The meffenger that I fent to Narraganfett, purfuing after them, returned the next day, declaring that they fhowed Miantunnomu letters to Aquednick, (which were mine to Connecticut,) and fo to Aquednick they paft, whither I fent information of them, and fo they were taken. Their fudden examination they fent me, a copy of which I am bold to fend your worfhip enclofed.

The iflanders (Mr. Coddington being abfent) refolved to

15

fend them to us, fome thought, by us to Plymouth, from whence they came. Sir, I fhall humbly crave your judgment, whether they ought not to be tried where they are taken. If they be fent any way, whether not to Plymouth.[1] In cafe Plymouth refufe, and the iflanders fend them to us, what anfwers we may give, if others unjuftly fhift them unto us. I know that every man, quatenus man, and fon of Adam, is his brother's keeper or avenger; but I defire to do bonum bene, &c.

Thus, befeeching the God of heaven, moft holy and only wife, to make the interpretation of his own holy meaning in all occurrences, to bring us all by thefe bloody paffages to an higher price of the blood of the Son of God, yea of God, by which the chofen are redeemed, with all due refpects to your dear felf and dear companion, I ceafe.

Your worfhip's moft unworthy

ROGER WILLIAMS.

This native, Will, my fervant, fhall attend your worfhip for anfwer.

My due refpect to Mr. Deputy, Mr. Bellingham, &c.

---

[1] Governor Winthrop advifed that the prifoners be fent to Plymouth; who being brought there and examined did all confefs the murder, and that they did it to get the Wampum; but all the queftion was about the death of the Indian.—*Hift. of New Eng.*, SAVAGE's ed. vol. i. p. 323.

"Conduct like this" obferves Prof. GAMMELL, "in vindication of the rights of the natives, and in promoting the peace and happinefs of all the inhabitants of the country, did not fail to fecure the abiding confidence of the Indian chiefs. In every queftion that arofe between them and the Englifh, Williams was made their advifer, and often became the mediator between the parties." *Life of Williams*, p. 106.

*To his much honored and beloved Mr. Governor of Maʃʃa-
chuʃetts.*

Providence, 14th of the 6th.　[Auguſt 14th, 1638.]¹

Sir,—Since my laſt (unto which you were pleaſed to
give anſwer with kind advice concerning the murder of
the native) I have received divers letters from Connecticut : the ſum of all is this; that it hath pleaſed the Lord
to incline all hearts to peace. Juanemo was perſuaded to
go over in perſon and give that ſatisfaction which was demanded : only concerning a mare killed by ſome Nayanticks, (others ſay by Pequots,) but as yet no proof ; our
friends have taken his promiſe to inquire and inform, and
ſo they diſmiſſed him.

It hath pleaſed the Magiſtrates at Connecticut to invite
Miantunnomu over to them to diſcover ſome Pequot paſſages and murderers, which are denied, and to enter upon
ſome Articles with themſelves :² denying themſelves to be
obliged in the Articles of the Bay.

I have conceived that all the Engliſh in the land were
wrapped up in that Agreement (a copy of which you were
pleaſed Sir, to ſend me,): nevertheleſs I perſuade him to
go over. His deſire was (which Agowaun Sachem Maſ-
quanominity had in charge to expreſs to you) that Mr.
Governor would pleaſe to ſpare four Engliſh from himſelf
as witneſſes of paſſages; as alſo myſelf with Cutſhamo-
quene and Maſquanominit.

I have formerly engaged my promiſe to Miantunnomu :
and reſolve to take two or three Engliſh from hence, and

---

4 *Maʃs. Hiʃt. Coll.* vol. iv. p. 248.
¹ This has reference to a meeting to
be held at Hartford, at which the Narraganſetts and Mohegans were to appear
to ſettle their perſonal difficulties and to
have an underſtanding regarding the Pequots.

hope (through the Lord's mercy) that the journey may be for peace.

Sir, unlefs any pafs by accident to Connecticut (if fo you fhall fee good) that defire of three or four Englifh may be denied, and yet granted in effect by the going of fome freely with myfelf.

Only fir, be pleafed to give an hint of your pleafure in any matter confiderable, which we fhall endeavor to effect.

The natives, friends of the flain had confultation to kill an Englifhman in revenge: Miantunnomu heard of it, and defired that the Englifh would be careful on the highways, and fent himfelf exprefs threatenings to them, &c., and informed them that Mr. Governor would fee juftice done. Oufamequin coming from Plymouth told me that the four men were all guilty; I anfwered, but one; he replied, true, one wounded him, but all lay in wait two days, and affifted. In conclufion: he told me that the principal muft not die, for he was Mr. Winflow's man: and alfo that the man[1] was by birth a Neepmuck man; fo not worthy another man fhould die for him: I anfwered what I thought fit, but conceive there will be need of wifdom and zeal in fome, and remembrance of that *Vox Cæli:* He that doth violence to the blood of any perfon, let him flee to the pit: let none deliver him. The Lord mercifully cleanfe the land from blood, and make the blood of his fon Jefus more precious in all our eyes. So prays

Your Worfhip's moft unworthy

ROGER WILLIAMS.

To Mrs. Winthrop, Mr. Deputie and his, all yours, beft refpects, &c.

[1] In reference to the Indian killed by the fame Englifhmen, of which mention is made in the preceding letter.

For the right Worfhipful and his much honored friend Mr. Governor of the Maffachufetts, thefe.

At NARRAGANSETT, the 10th of the 7th, early. [September 10, 1638.][1]

MUCH HONORED SIR,—Thefe Sachems with myfelf confulting the laft Lord's day as foon as I here arrived; I difpatched a letter to meet our Connecticut friends at Mohegan: defiring a fpeedy word from Captain Mafon (according as he found the bufinefs eafy or difficult) to give direction for the courfe of the Narraganfetts, either to Mohegan or Pequot. With all, the Meffenger had charge to deal with Uncas, from us all, Canonicus, Miantunnomu, &c., to be wife and faithful to us in what we fhould propofe to him.[2]

The meffenger returned the laft night (and being a difcreet man to obferve paffages) he related that coming near the town, viz.: to wit, Mohegan, he heard fix guns, which perfuaded him that Englifh were come, but

[1] 4 *Mafs. Hift. Coll.* vol. vi, p. 250. This letter chiefly relates to the difficulties between the Narraganfetts and Mohegans, growing out of the difperfion of the Pequots.

[2] From the vifit to Connecticut here alluded to, refulted " A Covenant and Agreement made between the Englifh and the Indians ;" Miantonomi reprefenting the Narraganfetts, and Uncas the Mohegans. Thefe articles were figned at Hartford, on the 21ft of September, 1638. They provide

1. That there fhall be peace between the tribes and " all former injuries and wrongs offered each other remitted and buried."

2. That if further wrongs he committed by either party, they fhall not revenge them, but fhall appeal to the Englifh, who fhall decide between them. If either party refufe to abide by the decifion, the Englifh may compel them to do fo.

3. The tribes mentioned agree to bring in the chief Sachem of the Pequots; and for the murderers known to have killed the Englifh " they fhall as foon as they can poffibly take off their heads."

4. Provides for the divifion of the Pequot prifoners, who " fhall no more be called Pequots, but Narraganfetts and Mohegans."

The agreement bears the fignatures of Miantonomi, Uncas, Gov. Haines, Roger Ludlow and Edward Hopkins.— POTTER's *Hift. of Narraganfett*, p. 177.

drawing nearer, he found they were the guns which formerly the Pequots had got from the Englifh! Entering the court, he found the houfe mingled full of Mohegans and Pequots, who defired his news, but he filent! They told him that they heard that the Englifh were coming againft them, and they had fent up two chief men who found the Englifh training. They were examined of two things, viz.: why they had lately let go two of the murderers at Nayantick, whom they had bound, and why they had feized upon all the corn at Pequot, belonging to hither Nayantick Pequots: fo they were imprifoned and bound: word whereof coming to Uncas, forty men were fent up with their bead girdles to redeem them. The meffenger got Uncas private, who would not be drawn to yield up any of his Pequots, but alledging that he had bought them with his money of the Englifh (as the Nayantick Sachems faid, for which purpofe I am bold to enclofe Mr. Haynes his anfwer) he faid they found the Englifh fo falfe, that the laft night in a general meeting they were refolved to fight it out, and for himfelf although the Englifh bound him and killed him he would not yield. He related that Mr. Haynes had given him a letter of fecurity to lie by him, in cafe that any Englifh fhould injure him, but in this purfuing his Pequots and binding his men, he had thrown away his letter, &c. Sir, your wifdom (I know) catcheth at my requeft before I make it, viz.: that in cafe I am directed from our friends of Connecticut to fend for aid, you would pleafe to caufe a readinefs at little warning. I could make true relation of the brags of the chief of thefe wretches, viz.: that the Maffachufetts Englifh did but glean after the Connecticut men, &c., in the wars: but I am confident you defire their good,

with the fafety of your own ftate : therefore I reft with a
defcription brief of the Pequot towns, now again under
Uncas and the Nayantick Sachems eftablifhed : At Pequot Nayantick are upwards of twenty houfes, up the
river at Mangunckakuck eight, up ftill at Sauquonckac-
kock ten, up ftill at Paupattokfhick fifteen, up ftill at
Tatuppequauog twenty, three or [ ] mile further with
Uncas at his town Mohegan, a great number mingled,
which are all under Uncas, befides thofe at Quinnipiuck,[1]
and others of Long Ifland, and Safacous his confederates.   At Nayantaquit[2] the hither, upwards of twenty
houfes, all under Nayantaquit Sachems, except fix or feven
men unto whom your worfhip was pleafed to give life,
upon Miantunnomue's motion, by my letter, upon their
fubmiffion.   Thefe are ftill Miantunnomue's fubjects, yet
refufing to live with him at Narraganfett, he difclaims
them, in cafe according to promife, they affift not in this
bufinefs.   The moft High gracioufly fanctify all his holy
pleafure to us, profper thefe our prefent enterprifes to his
praife, but efpecially againft thofe enemies (1. Pet. 2. 11.)
lufts which fight againft our fouls : in him I defire to be

Your worfhip's more and to eternity,

ROGER WILLIAMS.

---

[1] *Qunnepiuck.*   New Haven.   [2] *Nayantaquit, Niantic.*   Wefterly and
Charleftown.

To his much honored Governor John Winthrop.

[September or October, 1638.][1]

MUCH HONORED SIR,—Through the mercy of the Moſt High, I am newly returned from a double journey to Connecticut and Plymouth. I ſhall preſume on your wonted love and gentleneſs to preſent you with a ſhort relation of what iſſue it pleaſed the Lord to produce out of them, eſpecially ſince your worſhip's name was ſome way engaged in both.

I went up to Connecticut with Miantunnomu,[2] who had a guard of upwards of one hundred and fifty men, and many Sachems, and his wife and children, with him. By the way (lodging from his houſe three nights in the woods) we met divers Narraganſett men complaining of robbery and violence, which they had ſuſtained from the Pequots and Mohegans in their travel from Connecticut; as alſo ſome of the Wunnaſhowatuckoogs (ſubject to Canonicus) came to us and advertiſed, that two days before, about ſix hundred and ſixty Pequots, Mohegans and their confederates had robbed them, and ſpoiled about twenty-three fields of corn, and rifled four Narraganſett men amongſt them ; as alſo that they lay in way and wait to ſtop Miantunnomue's paſſage to Connecticut, and divers of them threatened to boil him in the kettle.

These tidings being many ways confirmed, my company,

---

[1] KNOWLES' *Mem. of Williams*, p. 157. 3 *Maſs. Hiſt. Coll.* vol. i. p. 173. POTTER's *Hiſt. of Narraganſett*, p. 145.

[2] It appears from this letter that Williams accompanied Miantonomo to Hartford, for the purpoſe of effecting a peace between the Narraganſetts and Mohe-

gans, and was doubtleſs inſtrumental in effecting the "Covenant and Agreement" made on the 21ſt of September, before noticed. From Hartford, he went to Plymouth to attend the trial of the four Engliſhmen for killing the Indian before mentioned.

Mr. Scott (a Suffolk man) and Mr. Cope, advifed our ftop and turn back; unto which I alfo advifed the whole company, to prevent bloodfhed, refolving to get up to Connecticut by water, hoping there to ftop fuch courfes. But Miantunnomu and his council refolved (being then about fifty miles, half-way, on our journey) that not a man fhould turn back, refolving rather all to die, keeping ftrict watch by night, and in dangerous places a guard by day about the Sachems, Miantunnomu and his wife, who kept the path, myfelf and company always firft, and on either fide of the path forty or fifty men to prevent fudden furprifals. This was their Indian march.

But it pleafed the Father of mercies, that (as we fince heard) we came not by till two days after the time given out by Miantunnomu, (by reafon of ftaying for me until the Lord's day was over,) as alfo the Lord fent a rumor of great numbers of the Englifh in company with the Narraganfetts, fo that we came fafe to Connecticut.

Being arrived, Uncas had fent meffengers that he was lame, and could not come. Mr Haynes faid, it was a lame excufe, and fent earneftly for him, who at laft came, and being charged by Mr. Haynes with the late outrages, one of his company faid, they were but an hundred men. He faid, he was with them, but did not fee all that was done, and they did but roaft corn, &c. So there being affirmations and negations concerning the numbers of men and the fpoil, not having eye-witneffes of our own, that fell, as alfo many other mutual complaints of rifling each other, which were heard at large to give vent and breathing to both parts.

At laft we drew them to fhake hands, Miantunnomu and Uncas; and Miantunnomu invited (twice earneftly)

16

Uncas to fup and dine with him, he and all his company
(his men having killed fome venifon;) but he would not
yield, although the magiftrates perfuaded him alfo to it.

In a private conference, Miantunnomu, from Canonicus
and himfelf, gave in the names of all the Pequots Sachems
and murderers of the Englifh. The names of the Sachems were acknowledged by Uncas, as alfo the places, which
only I fhall be bold to fet down:

Naufipouck, Puttaquappuonckquame his fon, now on
Long Ifland.

Nanafquiouwut, Puttaquappuonckquame his brother, at
Mohegan.

Puppompogs, Safacous his brother, at Mohegan.

Maufaumpous, at Nayantick.

Kithanfh, at Mohegan.

Attayakitch, at Pequot or Mohegan.

Thefe, with the murderers, the magiftrates defired to
cut off, the reft to divide, and to abolifh their names. An
inquifition was made; and it was affirmed from Canonicus,
that he had not one. Miantunnomu gave in the names of
ten or eleven, which were the remainders of near feventy,
which at the firft fubjected themfelves, of which I advertifed your worfhip, but all again departed, or never came
to him; fo that two or three of thefe he had with him;
the reft were at Mohegan and Pequot.

Uncas was defired to give in the names of his. He
anfwered, that he knew not their names. He faid there
were forty on Long Ifland; and that Juanemo and three
Nayantick Sachems had Pequots, and that he himfelf had
but twenty. Thomas Stanton told him and the magiftrates, that he dealt very falfely; and it was affirmed by
others, that he fetched thirty or forty from Long Ifland at

one time.   Then he acknowledged, that he had thirty, but
the names he could not give.   It pleafed the magiftrates
to requeft me to fend to Nayantick, that the names of
their Pequots might be fent to Connecticut; as alfo to give
Uncas ten days to bring in the number and names of his
Pequots and their runaways, Mr. Haynes threatening
alfo (in cafe of failing) to fetch them.

Sir, at Plymouth, it pleafed the Lord to force the prifoners to confefs, that they all complotted and intended
murder; and they were, three of them. (the fourth having
efcaped, by a pinnace, from Aquedneck,) executed in the
prefence of the natives who went with me.   Our friends
confeffed, that they received much quickening from your
own hand.   O that they might alfo in a cafe more weighty,
wherein they need much, viz.: the ftanding to their prefent government and liberties, to which I find them weakly
refolved.

They have requefted me to enquire out a murder five
years fince committed upon a Plymouth man (as they now
hear) by two Narraganfett Indians, between Plymouth and
Sowwams.   I hope (if true) the Lord will difcover it.

Sir, I underftand that there hath been fome Englifhmen
of late come over, who hath told much to Cutfhamoquene's Indians (I think Auhaudin) of a great Sachem in
England (ufing the King's name) to whom all the Sachems in this land are and fhall be nothing, and where his
fhips ere long fhall land; and this is much news at prefent
amongft natives.   I hope to enquire out the men.

Mr. Vane[1] hath alfo written to Mr. Coddington and

---

[1] Sir Henry Vane left Bofton for Eng-
and in 1637.   It would appear by this
remark of Williams's that Sir Henry
feared troubles in Bofton, and advifed
Coddington's early removal.   The latter purchafed the Ifland of Aquidneck

others on the ifland of late, to remove from Bofton as fpeedily as they might, becaufe fome evil was ripening, &c. The moft holy and mighty One blaft all mifchievous buds and bloffoms, and prepare us for tears in the valley of tears, help you and us to trample on the dunghill of this prefent world, and to fet affections and caft anchor above thefe heavens and earth, which are referved for burning.

Sir, I hear, that two malicious perfons, one I was bold to trouble your worfhip with not long fince,) Jofhua Verin,[1] and another yet with us, William Arnold, have moft falfely and flanderoufly (as I hope it fhall appear) complotted together (even as Gardiner did againft your-felves) many odious accufations in writing. It may be, they may fome way come to your loving hand. I pre-fume the end is, to render me odious both to the King's majefty, as alfo to yourfelves. I fhall requeft humbly your

---

in 1637, and in March 1638 the firft covenant was entered into by the pur-chafers, and Coddington chofen Judge.

[1] Jofhua Verin was one of the five who accompanied Williams to Providence in 1636, but removed foon after to Salem, in confequence of a vote of cenfure "for a breach of a covenant for reftraining liberty of confcience."—*R. I. Col. Re-cords*, vol. i. p. 16. He now feems to be giving Williams fome trouble, as ap-pears from this letter, which is thus men-tioned by Winthrop:

"At Providence, alfo, the devil was not idle. For whereas at their firft coming thither, Mr. Williams and the reft did make an order, that no man fhould be molefted for his confcience, now men's wives and children, claiming to go to all religious meetings, though never fo often, or though private, upon the week days; and becaufe one Verin refufed to let his wife go to Mr. Wil-liams fo oft as fhe was called for, they required to have him cenfured. But there ftood up one Arnold, a witty man of their own company and withftood it, telling them that, when he confented to that order, he never intended it fhould extend to the breach of any ordinance of God, fuch as the fubjection of wives to their hufbands. Then one Greene replied, that if they fhould reftrain their wives, all the women in the country would cry out of them, &c. . . . . In conclufion, when they would have cen-fured Verin, Arnold told them, that it was againft their own order, for Verin did that he did out of confcience; and their order was, that no man fhould be cenfured for his confcience.—Savage's Winthrop, *Hift. of New England*, vol. i. p. 340

wonted love and gentlenefs (if it come to your worfhip's hand) to help me with the fight of it, and I am confident yourfelf fhall be the judge of the notorious wickednefs and malicious falfehoods therein, and that there hath not paft aught from me, either concerning the maintaining of our liberties in this land, or any difference with yourfelves, which fhall not manifeft loyalty's reverence, modefty and tender affection.

The Lord Jefus the Son of righteoufnefs, fhine brightly and eternally on you and yours, and all that feek him that was crucified. In him, I defire ever to be

Yours worfhip's moft unfeigned

ROGER WILLIAMS.

All refpective falutations to kind Mrs. Winthrop, Mr. Deputy, Mr. Bellingham, and theirs.

For his much honored Mr. Governor, John Winthrop.

[September, 1638.][1]

MUCH HONORED SIR,—Some while fince I wrote to you a fhort narration[2] of the iffue of my voyage to Connecticut and Plymouth. I defire only to know whether it came to hand. I have been carefully fearching into that rumor of the Plymouth man flain four years fince. The perfons to whom I was directed by our Plymouth friends for information are yet abfent on hunting: and Miantunnomu is but new returned from Connecticut, yet with what inftruction I have already gotten I am this morning taking a journey to the Sachems about it.

---

[1] 4 *Mafs. Hift. Coll.* vol. vi. p. 252.
[2] The communication here referred to may be feen in 3 *Mafs. Hift. Coll.* vol. i. p. 173; of date about September, 1638.

I hear of three Cowefet[1] men in hold about Mr. Hathorne's[2] cow. The Sachems affirm they cannot difcover the party. Thefe three were three of fix then there hunting, yet they fay two things: Firft, that many Northern and Sauguft[3] Indians hunt there; alfo and fecondly, it may be that fome adverfe perfon might, out of fubtle envy, fhoot the beaft, to render them odious to the Englifh, and to caufe their deferting of the place, which they would have done but that Englifh were very defirous (efpecially Mr. Endicott) that they fhould kill and fell venifon, &c.

For myfelf, I fhall faithfully enquire and difclofe: although divers underftanding perfons of Salem have affirmed that the cow dying about three months after, when fo many head of cattle died, it is very queftionable whether the arrow occafioned the death, &c.

Sir, this is the occafion of this enclofed: I underftand that a fervant of yours, Jofhua —— is fome trouble to yourfelf, as alfo to others, and confequently cannot (if he defire to fear the Lord) but himfelf be troubled and grieved in his condition, though otherwife I know not where under Heaven he could be better.

If it may feem good in your eyes (wanting a fervant) I fhall defire him (not fimply from you) but for your peace and his. I fhall defire your beft and full fatisfaction in payment, and what fum you pitch on, to accept it either from this bill, or if you better like from that debt of Mr. Ludlow, for which he promifed your worfhip to pay me eight hundred weight of tobacco but did not, and I prefume your worfhip may with eafe procure it; but I fub-

---

[1] Cowefet. Eaft Greenwich.   [2] Mr. Hathorne, of Salem.
[3] *Saugus.* Lynn, Maffachfuetts.

fcribe *ex animo* to your choice, and with refpective falutations and continued fighs to Heaven for you and yours, reft defirous to be

Your worfhip's unfeigned though unworthy

ROGER WILLIAMS.

Sir, I am loath, but I prefume once more to trouble you with that deceitful man James Hawkings, craving that you would pleafe to lend a hand that by yourfelf or the Court at Bofton, I may find mercy againft fuch injuftice.

Sir, my wife (together with her beft refpects) to Mrs. Winthrop, requefts her acceptance of an handfull of chefnuts, intending her (if Mrs. Winthrop love them) a bigger bafket of them at the return of Jigles.

For his much honored and beloved Mr. John Winthrop at his houfe at Bofton.

PROVIDENCE, 10th, 30. [December 30, 1638.][1]

SIR,—Hoping of your health this dead feafon, with refpective falutations: I am bold to requeft a little help, and I hope the laft, concerning mine old and bad debtor about whom I have formerly troubled your worfhip, Mr. George Ludlow.

I hear of a pinnace to put into Newport, bound for Virginia, and I underftand that if you pleafe to teftify what you remember in the cafe, I may have fome hope at laft to get fomething.

[1] *4 Mafs. Hift. Coll.* vol. vi. p. 256.

You were pleafed, after dealing with him at Bofton, to certify me that he had promifed to difcharge unto me 800*li* of tobacco, which you afterwards thought to have been dif-charged : but he failing, although my due came to much more, I requeft if you can remember in a line or two to teftify : and I fhall defire to blefs the Lord for you, and to beg of him a merciful requital into your bofom, even from his holy left and right hand efpecially : my writings are (from hand to hand about the bufinefs) loft ; fo that all my evidence will be from your hand, of his acknowledgment and promife.   Sir, I reft unceffantly mourning that I am no more   Your worfhip's unfeigned

ROGER WILLIAMS.

Sir, I may not omit my thankful acknowledgment of that counfel of peace you were pleafed to give to a young man who (when I was at Block Ifland) repaired to your worfhip for advice in fome jar between him and his neigh-bors : your counfel was profperous, and I defire you may have the joy of it.   For fo faith the Lord, to the counfel-lors of peace and joy.

Sir, I purpofe within twenty days (if God will) to tra-vel up to Mohegan : at my return I fhall trouble you with a line from Uncas, if I can fpeak with him about your Pequots.

Sir, I pray let your fervant direct the native with this letter to Mr. David Yale,[1] Mrs. Eaton's fon.

---

[1] David Yale of Bofton, fon-in-law of Governor Eaton of New Haven, men-tioned in the will of Edward Hopkins. SAVAGE's WINTHROP, *Hiſt. of New Eng-* *land*, vol. i. p. 273.   NOTE.—He was the anceftor of Elihu Yale from whom Yale College takes its name.—SAVAGE, *Genealogical Diɑ.* vol. iv. p. 666.

*For the right Worſhipful and his much honored friend Mr.
Governor of the Maſſachuſetts, theſe.*

Sir,—Upon the receipt of your laſt (anſwering my queries) I have acquainted the Sachems with the buſineſs: I
am not yet furniſhed with anſwer ſufficient: what I have
at preſent I ſhall humbly and faithfully ſubmit to conſideration: one from them, two from myſelf.

From them: upon ſolemn conſultation with them about
the 100*li* demanded of themſelves, they ſay—

Firſt, that they remember not that either in the firſt
Agreement and League (in the beginning of the Pequot
wars) or ſince, in any expreſſion, that ever they undertook
to anſwer in their own perſons or purſes what their ſubjects ſhould fail in.

Second. Nor do they believe that the Engliſh Magiſtrates do ſo practice, and therefore they hope that what is
righteous amongſt ourſelves we will accept of from them.

Third. Therefore they profeſs that what evil ſoever ſhall
appear to be done by any (ſubject to them) againſt the
bodies or goods of the Engliſh, ſatisfaction ſhall readily be
made out of the bodies or goods of the delinquents.

For the 100*li* demanded, they ſay concerning the Salem
cow, they have to this day enquired, and can diſcover no
guilt either in the perſons impriſoned or the reſt, but do
believe that it was falſely laid upon them by ſuch northern
natives whoſe traps they were, who themſelves were guilty.

For the horſes, they have ſent for Wuttattaaquegin who
hath not been with them theſe three years, but keeps at

[1] 4 *Maſs. Hiſt. Coll.* vol. vi. p. 254.

17

Maffachufetts: they intend alfo to call a general meeting of the Country at his coming, within a few days, when I fhall have further anfwer from them.

Sir, a word more from myfelf: I have long fince believed that as it is with the Moft High (Prov. 21. 3.) fo with yourfelves. To do judgment and juftice is more acceptable then facrifice. And therefore that it fhall not be ungrateful in your eyes, that I humbly requeft leave to fay that I fee the bufinefs is ravelled, and needs a patient and gentle hand to rectify mifunderftanding of each other and mifprifons. The Sachems to prevent the fears of their men in hunting or traveling, &c., earneftly defired me to fatisfy the Englifh, that if the bearers of a writing from me fhould offend any ways, that they, the Sachems, would upon information from myfelf, caufe the delinquents to make fatisfaction out of their goods or bodies; to the end that the Englifh might not imprifon or tranfport away their perfons, (which the natives fufpect,) two of their men having been not long fince carried away in an Englifh fhip from the Bay, and two of their women the laft fummer from Conanicut in this Bay.

In two particulars (as I conceive) neither the natives or myfelf were rightly underftood. Firft, in the fcope of the writing, which was not to afk leave to hunt as before. Secondly, in the promife, which was not to pay off themfelves (I mean the Sachems) but to caufe their men to deal juftly and to give fatisfaction for offences committed out of their goods or bodies.

I hope it will pleafe the Lord to perfuade your hearts to believe what I affirm, and again to review the writing. However, rather than any labor or pains of mine (well meant to preferve peace) fhall caufe or occafion diffention,

I refolve to be yet poorer, and out of my poverty to endeavor and further fatisfaction. (The earth is the Lord's
and the fullnefs of it.) To the Everlafting Arms of his
mercy I daily recommend you and yours, and reft

Your Worfhip's moft unworthy

Roger Williams.

My refpective falutes to Mr. Deputy, Mr. Bellingham, &c.
Sir, I have heretofore been bold to requeft your help in
recovering an old debt from Mr. George Ludlow: and
you were pleafed after dealing with him, to fignify that
he had promifed to deliver afhore for me eight hundred
pounds weight of tobacco: I fhall now humbly requeft
that if Mr. Stratton defire it, or if he be again bound for
Virginia, that you would pleafe to teftify fo much as you
remember in a line or two, which may be of great ufe for
my recovering of the debt, and I fhall defire to be thankful.

---

*For his much honored and beloved Mr. Governor of the Maf-
fachufetts, thefe.*

PROVIDENCE, 2d, 3d. [May 3, 1639.][1]

Sir,—In my laft I gave intimation of another anfwer,
which from the Sachems is this.

Firft, that although they remember not any agreements
that have paffed about the natives yielding up their hunting
places, advantages, &c., within prefcribed limits, &c., yet,
becaufe fatisfactory agreements may have been unknown

---

[1] 4 *Mafs. Hift. Coll.* vol. vi, p. 257.

to them, between yourfelves and the natives about you, they have fent for this man, Wuttattaaguegin, (who keeps moft at Maffachufetts with Cutfhamoquene,[1] and hath not been this three years with them.)

This man Wuttattaaguegin hath promifed to fatisfy in wampam, beaver and venifon what it comes to.

But he believes not the damage can be fo great, for thus he relates : having laid his traps, intending daily to tend them, Cutfhamoquene fent for him to be a guide for him in a hunting match about the Bay, where other natives were ignorant. He went, yet fent a youth to view his traps, who faith that he faw the Englifhmen loofe three horfes out of the traps, and rode away upon two of them, the third only was lamed.

Upon this he defired liberty to return to the Bay, to inquire more perfectly the damage : and being not come back as yet, they have this prefent fent again for him.

Yet becaufe they fee not that Wuttattaaguegin broke any known covenant in laying his traps in that place, nor willingly wrought evil againft the Englifh, they conceive it would be very fair and honorable in all natives eyes, that it would pleafe the Englifh to make known as well their moderation as their juftice in the cafe.

And for themfelves they refolve if this man fhould not be faithful or able to fatisfy your demand, they promife (upon perfuafions and fome offers of mine to them) to contribute themfelves out of their own, and to draw in help, that may in wampum, beaver, and venifon make up the whole fum before the next hunting be over.

[1] Cutfhamoquene, Sagamore of Maffachufetts.

So craving humbly your loving acceptation of my poor service herein, or whatever elfe you fhall pleafe to ufe me in, I reft

Your worfhip's moft unworthy

ROGER WILLIAMS.

My due refpect to my honored friends Mr. Deputy and the reft of the Council.

For his much honored and beloved Mr. John Winthrop, Governor of Maffachufetts, thefe.

PROVIDENCE, this 9th of the 3rd. [May 9th, 1639.]¹

SIR,—I am requefted by Canonicus and Miantunnomu to prefent you with their love and refpect (which they alfo defire may be remembered to all the Englifh Sachems) as alfo with this expreffion of the continuance of their love unto you, viz.: thirty fathom of beads, (ten from Canonicus, and twenty from Miantunnomu)² and the bafket a prefent from Miantunnomu's wife to your dear companion Mrs. Winthrop: three things they requeft me to defire of you.

Firft, the continuance of your ancient and conftant friendfhip toward them, and good opinion of their fincere affection to the Englifh.

I objected againft this, that I lately heard that two boats of Englifh were cut off by Pequots, and that Miantunnomu knew of the act, &c.

₁ 4 *Mafs. Hift. Coll.* vol. vi. p. 259.
² Winthrop in his Journal of May 2, notices the reception of wampum, the annual tribute from the Indians of Block Ifland.—*Hift. of New Eng.* vol. i. p. 355.

To this they anfwered, that they have not fo much as heard of any mifcarriage of the Englifh this way of late, and that two days fince a Narraganfett man came from Long Ifland and brought no fuch tidings.

That they have always (and fhall ftill) fuccor the Englifh in any fuch diftreffes: and that if but a fingle Englifhman, woman, or child be found in the woods by any of theirs, they fhould punifh feverely that man that fhould not fafely conduct them and fuccor them, &c.

Secondly, That you would pleafe to ratify that promife made to them after the wars, viz.: the free ufe of the Pequot country for their hunting, &c.

Thirdly, That fince there are many Pequot Sachems and Captains furviving, many of whom have been actual murderers of the Englifh, and (three of them) which have flain fome of their Sachems.

And that fince the Agreement the laft year at Connecticut with Mr. Haynes and the Magiftrates, you have not yet pleafed come to action.[1]

And that the Pequots being many hundreds of them may with thefe their Sachems do more mifchief to us and them.

They therefore requeft that you would pleafe to write by them at prefent to Mr. Haynes that fo upon your joint Agreement they may themfelves freely purfue thofe Pequot Princes and Captains, whom Mr. Haynes (who had the lift of them from me the laft year) fhall name unto them.

I objected the report of great numbers of Pequots among themfelves, &c.

---

[1] The " Covenant and Agreement " entered into at Hartford, September 21, 1638. See note to Letter of the 10th September, 1638.

They anfwer as formerly, that to clear themfelves from that, and to make it appear how both the Mohegans and the Nayantick men have received the Pequots and their prefents (when they refufed them) and fo have made prefents to the Englifh with the Pequot beads, which themfelves never did nor could: they will now fall upon this fervice, and if the Mohegans and Nayantick men will not join with them in it, they will themfelves purfue the perfons that fhall be named to them wherefoever they find them, although at Mohegan or Nayantick, without touching a Mohegan or Nayantick man further than you fhall pleafe to advife them.

More they fay, but I fhould be tedious, and therefore with all due refpect to your loving felf, Mrs. Winthrop, Mr. Deputy, &c., I reft

Yours worfhip's faithful and unfeigned

ROGER WILLIAMS.

Canonicus begs of you a little fugar.

For his much honored Mr. Governor, John Winthrop.

[Auguft, 1639.][1]

MUCH HONORED SIR,—You were pleafed fome while fince to refer me to Mr. Haynes for a lift of fuch Pequots as were authors and chief actors in the late murders upon the Englifh.

Accordingly I have fent up once and again to Mr.

[1] 4 *Mafs. Hift. Coll.* vol. vi. p. 261.

Haynes, and we are come to a period: the child is come
to the birth: a little ſtrength from your loving hand (the
Lord ſo pleaſing, and bleſſing) will bring it forth.

This liſt here encloſed (which I requeſt may be returned)
was drawn by my beſt enquiry and Tho. Stanton in the
preſence of the Magiſtrates at Connecticut the laſt year.

This liſt he was pleaſed to ſend me with the addition of
ſeven more under his own hand.

Some queries I made upon ſome of the ſeven: as alſo
[*torn*] Saſacous his brother Puppompogs (now upon Long
Iſland) whom Mr. Haynes deſired might be ſpared, and I
applauded the deſire in many reſpects, only I deſired for
many other reſpects that he might be ſent to ſome other
part of the world.

Alſo ſince that the Nayantick Sachems who harbor many
of theſe, and Uncas, Canonicus and Miantunnomu requeſted that a pinnace might lie ſome few days at Pequot,
to promote and countenance the work while Miantunnomu
purſued them.

Unto all which Mr Haynes in this laſt is pleaſed to
anſwer, ſo that we are come to a period. This week I
went up to the Narraganſett about other buſineſs: there I
found a bar, which I thought good to requeſt your worſhip to remove by a word or two.

Your captive (which was Maumanadtuck's wife) now at
Pequot, preſuming upon your experimented kindneſs toward her, informs all Pequots and Nayanticks that Mr.
Governor's mind is, that no Pequot man ſhould die, that
her two ſons ſhall ere long be Sachems there, &c. Your
wiſdom (now by a freſh line or two) declaring that none
but theſe (who by the beſt of intelligence appear to be
deeply guilty,) ſhall die, may facilitate the execution, to

the honor of your mercy and juftice, and the clearing of the land from blood, either that of our countrymen already fpilt, or that may be hazarded by thefe wretches. I might but will not trouble your worfhip with fome prefumptions that way: the Lord be pleafed to further and blefs: and help your precious foul and mine to remember that vengeance, and to long and expect for it upon the enemies of Jefus, when blood fhall flow out of the wine prefs to the horfe bridles by the fpace of fixteen hundred furlongs.

Your worfhip's unfeigned hitherto

ROGER WILLIAMS.

Mine humble and true refpects to Mrs. Winthrop, Mr. Dudley,[1] Mr. Bellingham, &c.

The meffenger is ignorant of the matter, and is fatiffied.[2]

To his much honored Governor John Winthrop.

PROVIDENCE, 21. 5. [July 21, 1640.][3]

MUCH HONORED SIR,—Your runaways (as I before furmifed) are at Mohegan, and the Squa Sachem's daughter is married to the Sachem Uncas. I know the match hath been long defired (although the Sachem have five or fix wives already) which makes me fear that all Indian means will not reach your juft defires. May you pleafe to reft a

---

[1] Mr. Dudley; fee note to the following letter.

[2] Endorfed by Governor Winthrop, " Mr. Williams about the Pequods to be killed, (6), 1639." (i. e. Auguft, the 6th mo.)

[3] 4 *Mafs. Hift. Coll.* vol. vi. p. 263.

little, for Miantunnomu (as he pretends out of love and respect to your person) is very diligent about a peaceable return of them, that he may bring them with him, and as many more of the runaways as he can get. Uncas was gone to Connecticut, so that a little patience is requisite.

Sir, this you may please to signify to your much honored brother, Mr. Governor,[1] that this business only hinders Miantunnomu's coming. He is (not satisfied but) persuaded to trust to interpreters whom he fears to trust, and to come without myself.

As also may you please to understand that the Nayantick Sachems still refusing to yield up any of those Pequots to death to whom they had promised life; our friends of Connecticut (as I have heard by two letters from Tho. Stanton) intend present revenge upon them. Canonicus and Miantunnomu still persuade (to mine own knowledge) the Sachems at last to be wise, and yield up their Pequots, but in vain, for the Nayantick Sachems resolve that for so many lives as are taken away by the English, or the Mohegans and Pequots with them, they will take revenge upon Mr. Throckmorton at Prudence, or Mr. Coddington,[2] &c., or Providence, or elsewhere.

I have dealt with Canonicus and Miantunuomu to desert the Nayanticks in this business. They answer they would if they had shed the blood of the English, but as they are their brethren, so they never hurt the English, but joined with them against the Pequots, &c., only they have been greedy upon the prey against the English mind: and lastly

---

[1] Dudley, who was brother to Winthrop by the marriage of their children, was Governor in 1640; and did not hold the office again till after the death of Miantonomo, who is mentioned in this letter.—Eds. *Winthrop Papers.*

[2] William Coddington, of Newport.

they fay the Englifh partiality to all the Pequots at Mohegan is fo great, and the confequences fo grievous upon the abufe of the Englifh love, that all their arguments return back (which they ufe to the Nayantick Sachems) as arrows from a ftone wall.

Tho. Stanton informs me of another caufe of war upon the Nayanticks, viz.: Wequafh[1] affirms that one of the petty Sachems of Nayantick was aboard Mr. Oldham's pinnace, and that fome goods and gold are at Nayantick. Gold I never heard of, but the pinnace, fkiff and other luggage and fmall particulars I had word of at firft, which were (by reafon of diftance) let alone : and in cafe that any one of the Sachems or more knew of Mr. Oldham's death, and that due evidence be found, I yet doubt (now fince the coming of the Lord Jefus and the period of the National Church,) whether any other ufe of war and arms be lawful to the profeffors of the Lord Jefus, but in execution of juftice upon malefactors at home : or preferving of life and lives in defenfive war, as was upon the Pequots, &c. Ifai. 2. Mic. 4.

If the fword rage in Old or New England : I know who gives out the commiffion, and can arm frogs, flies, lice, &c. He be pleafed to give us peace which earth neither gives nor takes. In him I ever defire to be more unfeigned and faithfull   Your Worfhip's

ROGER WILLIAMS.

---

[1] This is the laft time the name of *Wequafh* appears in Williams's letters. He died in the fummer of 1642. " Two days before his death " fays Williams, " as I paffed up Connecticut River, it pleafed my worthy friend Mr. Fenwick, to tell me that my old friend *Wequafh* lay very fick : I defired to fee him, and himfelfe was pleafed to be my guide two mile where *Wequafh* lay."—*Key, Introduction.*

Wequafhcuck or *Wequafh Cook,* was another Indian, who lived many years after the death of Wequafh.

To his much honored Governor John Winthrop.

PROVIDENCE, 7. 6. (fo called) 40.   [Auguft 7, 1640.]¹

SIR,—About (from Portfmouth¹ I received yours.   As
I lately advertifed to Mr. Governor, [Dudley]² the hurries
of the natives thoughts and confultations fo continue, about
the three Nayanticks, prifoners with our friends at Connecticut; that your runaways are longer fecure in their efcape
then otherwife they fhould be.

   The Mohegan Sachem, Uncas, refufeth to part with his
prey: And whereas Miantunnomu was going up to Mohegan himfelf with a fufficient company for the runaways,
Uncas fent word that it was your worfhip's plot to bring
him into the fnare at Mohegan, that there the Connecticut Englifh might fall upon him.

   Miantunnomu ftill promifeth me to come over to you,
and his purpofe (to his utmoft) to bring them with him.
My occafions lead me within thefe four or five days to
Connecticut, when (the Lord fo permitting) I purpofe to
go up to Mohegan and try the utmoft myfelf.   The iffue
of all is in that Everlafting Hand, in which is our breath
and our ways, in whom I defire to be ftill

Your worfhip's unfeigned

ROGER WILLIAMS.

¹ 4 *Mafs. Hift. Coll.* vol. vi. p. 265.
² Dudley, Governor of Maffachufetts.
He was a principal member of the Maffachufetts Company which fettled Bofton
and its vicinity.   He came over in 1630
as Deputy Governor with his fon-in-law
Simon Bradftreet, and held that office
twelve years, and the office of Governor
in the years 1634, 1640, 1645 and 1650.
He died in 1652.

I thank your worſhip for the Scotch intelligence:[1] The iſſue (I fear) will be general and grievous perſecution of all Saints.

Mine and my poor wife's beſt ſalutes to Mrs. Winthrop and all yours.

To Mr. Winthrop concerning Samuel Gorton.

PROVIDENCE, 8th. 1ſt. 1646. [8th March.][2]

Maſter Gorton[3] having foully abuſed high and low at Aquidnick, is now bewitching and bemadding poor Providence, both with his unclean and foul cenſures of all the miniſters of this country, (for which myſelf have in Chriſt's name withſtood him), and alſo denying all viſible and external Ordinances in depth of Familiſm, againſt which I have a little diſputed and written, and ſhall (the moſt High

[1] "Scotch intelligence." This doubtleſs alludes to the rebellion in Scotland, and the defeat of the royal army by the Scots which took place in the ſummer of 1640.

[2] WINSLOW, *Hypocraſie Unmaſked.* London, 1646. pp. 55–56.

[3] In this letter is the firſt mention by Williams of Samuel Gorton. It opens a controverſy between the firſt ſettlers of Warwick, including Gordon, Williams and many others, both of the colonies of Rhode Iſland and Maſſachuſetts. It got into the Courts, and agitated both the colonial governments. The hiſtorians of the time wrote much about it, but to enter fully into a hiſtory of the quarrel would require more ſpace than is given to all theſe letters. WINSLOW, in his Dedicatory epiſtle to the Earl of Warwick, prefixed to his book entitled *Hypocriſie Unmaſked: by a true Relation of the Proeeedings of the Governor and Company of the Maſſachuſetts againſt Samuel Gorton, and his Accomplices* ; thus writes:

"And yet Right Honorable, it will and doth appear in the following Treatiſe, that Samuel Gorton was proſecuted againſt, Firſt at Plymouth as a groſs diſturber of the Civill peace and quiet of that government, in an open, factious and ſeditious manner. Secondly, he was no leſſe troubleſome, but much more at

affenting,) to death.   As Paul faid of Afia, I, of Providence, (almoft) all fuck in his poifon, as at firft they did at
Aquidnick.   Some few and myfelf withftand his inhabitation, and town privileges, without confeffion and reformation
of his uncivil and inhuman practices at Portfmouth : Yet
the tide is too ftrong againft us, and I fear (if the framer
of Hearts help not) it will force me to little Patience, a
little Ifle next to your Prudence.   Jehovah himfelf be
pleafed to be a fanctuary to all whofe hearts are perfect
with him ; in him I defire unfeignedly to be

> Your worfhip's true and affectionate

> ROGER WILLIAMS.

Rhode Ifland, having gotten a ftrong party to adhere unto him, affronting that government (as Plymouth) in their publique adminiftration of Juftice fo foully and groffely, as mine cares never heard the like of any.   Gorton being there whipt in his perfon, and thence banifhed with fome of his principal•adherents ; they went next to Providence, where Mr. Williams and fome others have built a fmall towne.   This people receiving them with all humanity in a cold feafon, when the former places could no longer beare his infolencies ; he foone under-mined their government, gained a ftrong party amongft them to his owne, to the great diftraction of Mr. Williams, and the better party there, contending againft their Laws and the execution of Juftice, to the effufion of bloud, which made Mr.

Williams and the reft fadly complaine to the Government of the Maffachufetts, and divers of them to take protection of that Government, to defend their per-fons and eftates.   But when they faw Mr. Williams refolve rather to lofe the bene-fit of his labours, than to live with fuch ill-affected people, and the neighbour governments become affected with Gor-ton's mifrule there alfo, he (and his com-panions in evill) began to think of buy-ing a place of a Sachem, or Indian Prince," &c.

See alfo GORTON's *Simplicite's Defence againft Seven-headed Policy.*   London, 1646 ; alfo in *R. I. Hift. Coll.* vol. ii. ; HUTCHINSON's *Hift. Maffachufetts Bay* ; ARNOLD, *Hift. of Rhode Ifland*, vol. 1, ch. vi. ; *R. I. Colonial Records*, vol. i. ; WINTHROP, *Hift. of New England.*

For his honored, kind friend, Mr. John Winthrop,[1] at Pequot, thefe.

Nar. 22. 4. 45, (fo called.)   [NARRAGANSETT, 22 June, 1645.][2]

SIR :—Beft falutations, &c. William Cheefbrough,[3] now come in, fhall be readily affifted, for yours and his owne fake. Major Bourne is come in. I have (by Providence,) feen divers papers, (returning now yours thankfully,) which are fnatched from me againe. I have, therefore, been bold to fend you the Medulla and the Magnalia Dei. Pardon me, if I requeft you, in my name, to transfer the paper to

---

[1] With the exception of the letter of June 25, 1645, which follows this, no others appear in this volume from Gov. Winthrop, Senior, of Maffachufetts, to whom all the previous letters are addreffed.

John Winthrop, Jr., fon of Gov. Winthrop, of Maffachufetts, followed his father to America in 1631 ; and in 1633 returned to England. In 1635 he returned to Bofton, with authority to make a fettlement in Connecticut, and foon after fent a party to build a fort at Saybrook. In 1646, he founded the city of New London ; was chofen Governor in 1657 ; again in 1659, and annually from that period until his death which took place at Bofton, in 1676. In 1661, he went to England and procured a charter, incorporating New Haven and Connecticut into one colony. He was an accomplifhed fcholar, was particularly fkilled in chemiftry and phyfics, and was one of the founders of the Royal Society, of London. He was the author of a number of papers in the " *Philofophical Tranfactions.*"

It appears from one of the letters that Mr. Williams became acquainted with Winthrop in England, and the correfpondence will fhow that the friendfhip between them was ftrong and mutual. The letters here printed, which are from the " Winthrop Papers" in the Collection of the Maffachufetts Hiftorical Society, relate to politics, literature, agriculture and other topics, through which, like thofe to the elder Winthrop, runs a religious vein.

[2] KNOWLES, *Mem. R. Williams*, p. 207. 3 *Mafs. Hift. Coll.* vol. ix. p. 268.

[8] William Chefbrough occupied certain lands in Southertown, eaft of Pawcatuck River, over which Connecticut claimed jurifdiction, as a portion of the Pequot country, and about which ferious troubles arofe in 1661. Probably he may have been in trouble at the time this letter was written, and that Winthrop had afked the good offices of Williams in Chefbrough's behalf.

Captain Mafon, who faith he loves me.   God is love; in Him only I defire to be yours ever,

ROGER WILLIAMS.

Loving falutes to your deareft and kind fifter.

I have been very fick of cold and fever, but God hath been gracious to me.   I am not yet refolved of a courfe for my daughter.   If youre powder, with directions, might be fent without trouble, I fhould firft wait upon God in that way: however 'tis beft to wait upon Him.   If the ingredients be coftly, I fhall thankfully account.   I have books that prefcribe powders, &c., but yours is probatum in this country.

For his much honored Mr. Governor, John Winthrop.

PROVIDENCE, 25th of 4th, 1645, (fo called.)   [June 25.][1]

MUCH HONORED SIR,—Though I fhould fear that all the fparks of former love are now extinct, &c., yet I am confident that your large talents of wifdom and experience of the affairs of men will not lightly condemn my endeavor to give information and fatisfaction, as now I have done in this poor apology, with all due refpects prefented to your honor, and the hands of my worthy friends with you.

[1] 4 *Mafs. Hift. Coll.* vol vi. p. 266. This is the laft letter of Williams, in the "Winthrop Papers," addreffed to Gov. Winthrop of Maffachufetts, publifhed by the Maffachufetts Hiftorical Society, and the only one preferved which was written after the return of Williams from England, in September, 1644, whither he had gone in the fummer of 1643.   The fruits of his vifit were the Charter of Rhode Ifland, bearing date of the 14th March, 1643–4. Eds. *Winthrop Papers*..

Sir, for tidings concerning the public, three days since I received a letter from the Dutch Governor reporting some new hopes of peace. For ourselves, the flame of war rageth next door unto us. The Narragansetts and Mohegans, with their respective confederates, have deeply implunged themselves in barbarous slaughters. For myself I have (to my utmost) disuaded our neighbors, high and low, from arms, &c., but there is a spirit of desperation fallen upon them, resolved to revenge the death of their prince, and recover their ransom for his life, &c., or to perish with him. Sir, I was requested by both parties, yourselves and the Narragansetts, to keep the subscribed league between yourselves and them, and yours and their posterity. Sir, that, and the common bonds of humanity move me to pray yourselves and our friends of Connecticut to improve all interests and opportunities to quench these flames. My humble requests are to the God of Peace that no English blood be further spilt in America: it is one way to prevent it by loving mediation or prudent neutrality. Sir, (excepting the matters of my soul and conscience to God, the Father of Spirits) you have not a truer friend and servant to your worthy person and yours, nor to the peace and welfare of the whole country, then the most despised and most unworthy

ROGER WILLIAMS.

19

For his Worſhipful, and his much honored, kind friend, Mr.
Jobn Winthrop, at Nameaug,[1] theſe.

CAWCAWMSQUSSICK,[2] 28. 3. 47. (ſo called) [28 May, 1647.][3]

WORTHY SIR,—Loving reſpects and ſalutations to your
kind ſelf and your kindeſt companion.   Some while ſince,
you deſired a word of direction about the hay ſeed.   I deſired my brother to collect his own and other neighbors'
obſervations about it, which (with his reſpects preſented)
amounts to this.

Firſt. Uſually three buſhels of ſeed to one acre of land.

Second. It hath been known to ſpread, to mat, &c., the
Indian hills being only ſcraped or levelled.

Third. This may be done at any time of the year, but
the ſooner the better.

Fourth. It is beſt to sow it upon a rain preceding.

Fifth. Some ſay let the ripe graſs ſtand until it ſeed,
and the wind diſperſe it (ſuſque deque) up and down, for
it is of that thriving and homogeneal nature with the
earth, that the very dung of cattle that feeds on it will
produce the grain.

[1] *Nameaug.* New London. The tract
was originally called Pequot, and com-
priſed what is now known as New London and Groton. In 1658 the Aſſembly
of Connecticut enacted that "This court,
conſidering that there hath yet no place
in any of the colonies, been named in
memory of the city of London, there
being a new plantation, in the Pequot
country, with an excellent harbour, and
the only place which the Engliſh in theſe
parts have poſſeſſed by conqueſt . . . .
that therefore they might leave to poſteri-
ty the memory of that renowned city of
London, from whence we had our tranſ-
portation, have thought fit, to call the
ſaid plantation New London. The name
of the river was alſo changed, and called
the Thames."—TRUMBULL, *Hiſt. of Con-*
necticut.

[2] *Cawcawmſquſſick, Cocumſcuſſuc.* The
country around and weſt and northweſt
of Wickford.   Williams about this time
purchaſed an eſtate and built a trading
houſe here, which he afterwards ſold
to Richard Smith in order to obtain
money for his ſecond viſit to England.—
KNOWLES.

[3] KNOWLES' *Mem. R. Williams,* p. 209.
3 *Maſſ. Hiſt. Coll.* vol. ix. p. 268.

Sixth. The offs, which can hardly be fevered from the feed, hath the fame productive faculty.

Seventh. Sow it not in an orchard, near fruit trees, for it will fteal and rob the trees, &c.

Sir: Concerning Indian affairs, reports are various; lies are frequent. Private interefts, both with Indians and Englifh, are many; yet thefe things you may and muft do. Firft, kifs truth where you evidently, upon your foul, fee it. 2. Advance juftice, though upon a child's eyes. 3. Seek and make peace, if poffible, with all men. 4. Secure your own life from a revengeful, malicious arrow or hatchet. I have been in danger of them, and delivered yet from them; bleffed be His holy name, in whom I defire to be

Your worfhip's, in all unfeigned refpects and love,

ROGER WILLIAMS.

To John Winthrop, Jr. *For the Governor I have fent thefe lines.*

CAWCAWMSQUSSICK, 20. 6. 47. (fo call'd) [Auguft 20, 1647.][1]

SIR,—Due refpects prefented, &c. I am importuned by Ninigret, in exprefs words, to prefent his refpects and love to your honored father, and to the honored Prefident of the commiffioners,[2] giving great thanks for the

---

[1] KNOWLES' *Memoir of R. Williams*, p. 210. 3 *Mafs. Hift. Coll.* vol. ix. p. 269.

This letter, probably, has reference to the collection of the wampum to be paid to the Commiffioners by the Narraganfetts, in accordance with the treaty.

[2] The Commiffioners of the United Colonies.

great favor and kindnefs fhowed him. Withal, he prays
you earneftly to prefent his humble fuit, that fince he, by
reafon of his travel and illnefs, can, as yet, get no further
towards his own home, and finds he muft have much work
with the natives of thefe parts, before he repair home, and
time to fpend exceeding faft, it may be accounted no
breach of faithfulnefs of his promife, if he finifh the con-
tribution he is now about, within a few days after the punctual time. The other Sachems, upon agitations, have
promifed their utmoft concurrence, to finifh all within a
month from the day of his promife, which time he earneftly requefts may be affented to, hoping to make payment before, but not queftioning by the expiration of that
time. By this bearer, he humbly prays a word of anfwer,
that, with the more cheerful concurrence of the other
Sachems, (who join with him in this requeft,) he may be
the more cheerful in the work. Sir, I difcern nothing but
reality and reafon in his requeft; otherwife, I fhould not
dare to moleft you, or thofe honored perfons whom it concerns; to whom, with my humble refpects, and to yourfelf prefented, befeeching the Moft High to be your portion, I reft,

Your worfhip's unworthy

Roger Willliams.

Pefickofh defired me to prefent his great thanks for his
child.

Sir: Your man is with me at prefent writing, well, this
laft of the week, and will be going inftantly. Humble
thanks for the fight of papers from England. The fea
will be the fea till it be no more. Revel. 21.

Refpects to your deareft.

To the Town of Providence.

Auguft 31, 1648.[1]

WORTHY FRIENDS, that ourfelves and all men are apt and prone to differ, it is no new thing. In all former ages, in all parts of the world, in thefe parts, and in our dear native country and mournful ftate of England, that either part or party is moft right in his own eyes, his caufe right, his carriage right, his arguments right, his anfwers right, is as woefully and conftantly true as the former. And experience tells us, that when the God of peace have taken peace from the earth, one fpark of action, word or carriage is too powerful to kindle fuch a fire as burns up towns, cities, armies, navies, nations and kingdoms. And fince, dear friends, it is an honor for men to ceafe from ftrife; fince the life of love is fweet, and union is as ftrong as fweet and fince you have been lately pleafed to call me to fome public fervice and my foul hath been long mufing how I might bring water to quench, and not oil or fluid to the flame, I am now humbly bold to befeech you, by all thofe comforts of earth and heaven which a placable and peaceable fpirit will bring to you, and by all thofe dreadful alarms and warnings, either amongft ourfelves, in deaths and ficknefles, or abroad in the raging calamities of the fword, death and peftilence; I fay, I humbly and earneftly befeech you to be willing to be pacifiable, willing to be reconcilable, willing to be fociable, and to liften to the (I hope not unreafonable) motion following: To try out matters by difputes and writngs, is fometimes endlefs; to try out arguments by arms

---

[1] KNOWLES, *Memoir of Roger Williams,* in *New England.* Bofton, 1777. vol i. p. 214. BACKUS, *Hift. of the Baptifts* p. 204.

and fwords, is cruel and mercilefs; to trouble the ftate and
Lords of England, is moft unreafonable, moft chargeable;
to trouble our neighbors of other colonies, feems neither
fafe nor honorable. Methinks, dear friends, the colony
now looks with the torn face of two parties, and that the
greater number of Portfmouth, with other loving friends
adhering to them, appear as one grieved party; the other
three towns, or greater part of them, appear to be another:
Let each party choofe and nominate three; Portsmouth
and friends adhering three, the other party three, one out
of each town; let authority be given to them to examine
every public difference, grievance and obftruction of juftice, peace and common fafety: let them, by one final
fentence of all or the greater part of them, end all, and fet
the whole into an unanimous pofture and order, and let
them fet a cenfure upon any that fhall oppofe their fentence. One log, without your gentle help, I cannot ftir;
it is this: How fhall the minds of the towns be known?
How fhall the perfons chofen be called? Time and place
appointed in any expedition? For myfelf I can thankfully embrace the help of Mr. Coddington or Mr. Clarke,[1]
joined or apart, but how many are there who will attend,
(as our diftempers are) to neither? It is, gentlemen, in
the power of the body to require the help of any of her
members, and both King and Parliament plead, that in
extraordinary cafes they have been forced to extraordinary
ways for common fafety. Let me be friendly conftrued,
if (for expedition) I am bold to be too forward in this fervice, and to fay, that if within twenty days of the date
hereof, you pleafe to fend to my houfe, at Providence, the

[1] John Clarke of Rhode Ifland.

name of him whom you pleafe to nominate, at your defire I will acquaint all the perfons chofen with place and time, unto which in your name I fhall defire their meeting within ten days, or thereabouts, after the receipt of your letter.[1] I am your mournful and unworthy

ROGER WILLIAMS.

[1] Owing to quarrels of the people of Warwick and Providenee chiefly on account of Samuel Gorton, William Coddington and Alexander Partridge propofed to the Commiffioners of the United Colonies that " the Iflanders of Rhode Ifland may be received into a combination with all the United Colonies of New England, into a firm and perpetual league of friendfhip and amity, for offence and defence," etc.

Thus under a pretence of promoting peace, thefe men would have feparated the ifland from the reft of the colony. The Commiffioners, unwilling to receive them as a diftinct colony, propofed to have the ifland annexed to Plymouth, if the majority of its inhabitants would acknowledge its jurifdiction. In this dilemma, Williams came forward to endeavor to heal up the animofities with the propofitions contained in this letter to the town of Providence. His kind offices had the defired effect; harmony was re-

ftored and Williams was authorized to act as Prefident until the election fhould take place in May, 1649.

At the General Affembly held at Newport, in May, 1650, a frefh order was fent to the towns, to collect and pay what they owed to Mr. Williams for the charter within twenty days. " William Arnold and William Carpenter, inftead of fubmitting to the government of their own colony, went again and entered complaints againft fome of their neighbors to the Maffachufetts rulers, and they fent a citation to them to come and anfwer the fame in their courts, dated from Bofton, June 20th, 1650, figned by Edward Rawfon, Secretary. Such obftacles of good government were they who have made a great noife in the world about the diforders of Rhode Ifland Colony!"—BACKUS, *Hift. of the Baptifts in N. E.* Bofton, 1777: vol i. p. 207.

For his much honored, kind friend, Mr. John Winthrop, at his houfe, in Nameag, thefe.

CAWCAWMSQUSSICK, 11. 7. 48, (fo called.) [11 Sept. 1648.][1]

DEAR AND WORTHY SIR,—Beft falutations to you both and loving fifter premifed, wifhing you eternal peace in the only Prince of it. I have longed to hear from you and to fend to you fince this ftorm arofe. The report was (as moft commonly all Indian reports are) abfolutely falfe, of my removing my goods, or the leaft rag, &c. A fortnight fince, I heard of the Mohawks coming to Pawcatuck, their rendezvous ; that they were provoked by Uncas wronging and robbing fome Pawcatuck Indians the laft year, and that he had dared the Mohawks, threatening, if they came to fet his grounds with gobbets of their flefh ; that our neighbors had given them play, (as they do every year ; yet withal I heard they were divided ; fome refolved to proceed, others pleaded their hunting feafon. We have here one Waupinhommin, a proud, defperate abufer of us, and a firebrand to ftir up the natives againft us, who makes it all his trade to run between the Mohawks and thefe, and (being a captain alfo himfelf) renders the Mohawks more terrible and powerful than the Englifh. Between him and the chief Sachems hath been great confultations, and to my knowledge, he hath perfuaded them to defert their country and become one rebellious body or rout with the Mohawk, and fo to defy the Englifh, &c.[2] I have fent alfo

---

[1] 3 *Mafs. Hift. Coll.* vol. i, p. 178.

[2] We find an explanation of this in Backus, who fays " The Indians were far from being eafy ; and in Auguft, 1648, about 1000 of them from various parts were collected in Connecticut, with 300 guns among them ; and it was reported that they were hired by the Nar- raganfetts to fight with Uncas." A deputation was fent from Plymouth to confer with the Narraganfetts. Williams fent for the Sachems, who, upon meeting him, denied their hiring the Mohawks to war againft Uncas.—*Hift. of the Baptifts*, vol. i. p. 194.

what I can inform to the commiffioners. At prefent, (through mercy) we are in peace.

Sir, I defire to be ever

Yours in Chrift Jefus,

ROGER WILLIAMS.

The letter I have fent by Warwick, twenty miles nearer than by Seekonk.

For my much honored, kind friend, Mr. John Winthrop, at his houfe, at Nameug, thefe.

CAWCAWMSQUSSICK, 23. 7. 48, (fo called.) [Sept. 23, 1648.][1]

KIND SIR,—Beft falutations to your dear felves and loving fifter. I am bold and yet glad to trouble you, that by this occafion I may hear of your welfare. Capt. Mafon lately requefted me to forbid the Narraganfetts to hunt at Pequot, and to affure them of his vifiting of them if they fo did. I have written now an anfwer, which I am bold to requeft you to fend at your next opportunity. Two days fince I was at Providence, and then Mr. Brown was not returned, only he had wrote home fome angry paffage againft the Narraganfetts, who are now in expectation of fome affault from the Englifh. Sir, whether it pleafe God to vifit us with peace or war, in life and death I defire to be

Yours ever in Chrift Jefus,

ROGER WILLIAMS.

[1] KNOWLES, *Mem. of Roger Williams,* p. 215. 3 *Mafs. Hift. Coll.* vol. ix. p. 270.
20

Sir, our neighbors, Mr. Coddington and Capt. Partridge, ten days fince, returned from Plymouth, with propofitions for Rhode Ifland to fubject to Plymouth;[1] to which himfelf and Portfmouth incline; our other three towns decline, and Mr. Holden and Mr. Warner, of Warwick,[2] came from thence alfo, and they fay, gave fatisfaction why they dare not (the other three towns) depart from the charter. Sir, in this divifion of our neighbors, I have kept myfelf unengaged, and prefented motions of pacification, amongft which I was bold to propofe a reference to your worthy felf and fome other friend to be chofen; our town yields to it, and Mr. Bofton (though oppofite) and poffibly you may have the trouble and honor of a peace-maker.

Sir, pray feal the enclofed.

[1] See note to previous letter for the propofition to fubject the ifland of Rhode Ifland to Plymouth. Three years before the propofal was made by Coddington and Partridge, Maffachufetts fet up a title to Rhode Ifland, and claimed allegiance from its inhabitants. WINTHROP, under date of May——1645, fays "The government of Plymouth fent one of their magiftrates, Mr. Brown,* to Aquetneck ifland, to forbid Mr. Williams and others to exercife any of their pretended authority upon the ifland, claiming it to be within their jurifdiction. Our Court alfo fent to forbid them to exercife any authority within that part of our jurifdiction at Pawtuxet and Shawomet, and although they had boafted to do great matters there, by virtue of their charter, yet they dared not to attempt anything." SAVAGE's *Winthrop*, vol. ii. p. 270.

In Auguft, 1645, Williams received an official notice from Increafe Nowell, Secretary, afferting that Maffachufetts held "a charter whereby the Narraganfett Bay, and a certaine tract of land wherein Providence and the Ifland of Aquidnay are included," and giving him notice to "forbeare any jurifdiction therein."—See *Mafs. Col. Records*, vol. iii. p. 49; alfo *R. I. Col. Records*, vol. i. p. 133.

[2] Randall Holden and John Warner two of the leading men of Warwick.

*"John Brown," here referred to, fays SAVAGE, "is honorably mentioned in MORTON's *Memorial*, as having been acquainted with the defert of the pilgrims before they left Leyden. He became Affiftant in 1636, and was afterwards a Commiffioner of the United Colonies from 1644 to 1655, and died in 1662. A fon, James, who lived at Swanzea, was an affiftant in 1665."— *Note to Winthrop*, p. 270.

For his much honored and beloved Mr. John Winthrop, at Nameug.

CAWCAWMSQUSSICK, 10. 8. 48, (fo called.) [10th Oct. 1648.][1]

SIR,—Beft falutations to your dear felves and loving fifter. In my laft I intimated a promife of prefenting you with what here paffeth. Captain Atherton,[2] Captain Prichard, Richard Wood and Strong Tuchell, have been with me (as alfo Wm. Arnold, inftead of his fon Benedict, who withdrew himfelf, though fent unto,) thefe fix or feven days. They were at Niantick two nights. Captain Atherton purpofed to vifit you, but they appointing their meeting with all the Sachems at my houfe, they came back; and this morning, (the fourth day of the week,) they are departed with good content toward the Bay. From the commiffioners they brought feveral articles, but the main were three; concerning the Mohawks, &c.; 2d, the payment; 3d, Uncas' future fafety. To the firft, they fent anfwer (and that they confirmed with many affervations, and one of them voluntarily took the Englifhmen's God to witnefs) that they gave not a penny to hire the Mohawks againft the Mohegans, but that it was wholly wrought by Wuffoonkquaffin, (which they difcovered as a fecret) who being bound by Uncas, and Wuttouwuttauoum, Uncas his coufin, having attempted to fhoot a Mohawk Sachem at that time, refolved with the Mohawks (to

---

[1] 3 *Mafs. Hift. Coll.* vol. ix. p. 271. KNOWLES' *Mem. Roger Williams* p. 218.

[2] Humphrey Atherton, Major-General and a diftinguifhed Maffachufetts foldier. He was Speaker of the General Court in 1653, and was much employed in negotiations with the Indians. He was killed by a fall from his horfe in 1661. Atherton and Pritchard were the agents fent from Plymouth to Narraganfett to enquire into the reported league with the Mohawks, mentioned in letter of September 11th.

whom he alfo gave peag) to take revenge upon Uncas;
Wuffoonkquaffin fent them word and defired peag of them
in the fpring, but they profefs they confented not, nor fent
not a penny, afterwards they fent Waupinhommin up to
inquire to Pawcatuck and however they have given fome
of the Mohegans peag this year, (as they have always done)
yet they fay they are clear from giving a penny in hire,
&c.   They confefs their enmity againft Uncas, and they
(to the 2d) will not reft until they have finifhed their payments, that they may prefent their complaints againft Uncas, who (they fay) and other Indians, within thefe three
years, have committed thirteen murders with impunity,
being out of their reach in the Englifh protection.   This
laft year they pleaded they were near ftarved, and, therefore,
fent but a fmall quantity.   Now they promife, upon return
of their men from hunting this winter, to make a contri-
bution, the next fpring another, and fo according as they
can draw the people to it, will not ceafe to furnifh, and if
they die, their children fhall fulfil, and that it is their fore
grief, &c., with much to this purpofe.   For Uncas they
profefs neither directly nor indirectly, to have to do with
him, yet hope the Englifh will not deal partially with him.
They defired the Englifh receipt of their peag; I produced the note you fent me, which, becaufe it was not
figned with your father's hand or the Treafurer's, &c., the
meffengers promifed to fend them one from the Bay, Ninigret, made great lamentation that you had entertained hard
thoughts of him in this bufinefs, and all the Sachems here
profeffed their forrow and that you had hearkened to Wequafhcook, who they fay never contributed nor joined in
the Pequot wars, and now flatters to draw his neck out of
the payments to the Englifh.   They hope you will not

countenance him to rob Ninigret of those hunting places which the commissioners gave him leave to make use of, and he with the English had fought for with the expense of much treasure and hazard of his life. They desire that he may and Causasenamon and the rest of the Pequots, be as your little dogs, but not as your confederates, which they say is unworthy yourself, &c. Sir, I perceive the English about the Bay enquire after new places. Captain Atherton prays me shortly to convey a letter to you. I forgot one passage that the Sachems discovered, that Wussoonkquassin gave peag to the Mohawks to retreat. It seems they are (Switzer like) mercenary, and were hired on and off; these Sachems I believe desire cordially to hold friendship with both the English and the Mohawks together; I am confident (whether they lie or not, about Wussoonkquassin) that they never intended hurt against the English nor yourself and yours especially, to whom they profess great respect, and jointly they desire that Wequashcook may come back to Connecticut from whence he went, for if he join with Uncas they suspect he will secretly be a means of some of their deaths. Lastly, whereas they heard that the women with you were something fearful, Ninigret prays Mrs. Winthrop to be assured, that there never was, nor never shall be, to his knowledge, the least offence given to her or her neighbors, by any of his (though he hath learnt it partly by your just abhoring of Uncas his outrageous carriage among you, and of which I have not softly told these messengers and the admired partiality in the case.) For a token of his fidelity to Mrs. Winthrop, Ninigret, he prays me to write, that all the women of his town shall present Mrs. Winthrop with a present of corn at Pawcatuck, if she please to send in any conveyance to Pawcatuck for it.

Sir, to gratify them, I am thus bold with you, and de-firing your eternal peace, I reft

Your worſhip's unworthy

ROGER WILLIAMS.

Sir, I formerly wrote to you and now ſtill crave your help with Wequaſhcook, who keeps baſely from me for five or ſix coats, and can neither get peag[1] or cloth.

———————

For his much honored and beloved Mr. John Winthrop, at Nameug.

CAWCAWMSQUSSICK, 7. 9. 48, (ſo called)   [Nov. 7th, 1648.][2]

KIND SIR,— Beft ſalutations, &c.   I am requeſted by letter of Capt. Atherton, to certify what I can adviſe about Block Iſland, whether it might be had of the natives, for divers of the Engliſh (it ſeems to my conjecture) upon ſome agitations at the laſt Court, have thoughts this way.   Sir, becauſe God hath pitched your tent theſe ways, and you know much among the natives of theſe parts, I judged it not unfit to pray you help me with a word of your information, before I write what otherwiſe I can, from the barbarians.   The counſels of the Moſt High are deep con-

[1] *Peag.*   Shells or ſtrings of ſhells uſed by the Indians from New England to the Carolinas, as well as among the early ſettlers as money ; alſo called *wampum.*

   " The Indians of Virginia had nothing which they reckoned riches before the English went among them except *peak,* made out of the cong ſhell.—BEVERLY'S *Hiſt. of Virginia,* 1705.

[2] KNOWLES, *Mem. R. Williams,* p. 221. 3 *Maſſ. Hiſt. Coll.* vol. ix. p. 274.

cerning us poor grafshoppers, hopping and fkipping from branch to twig in this vale of tears. Wm. Peacock hath had a very heavy tafk in carrying Jofeph with cattle from you; fix or feven days and nights the poor fellow was feeking them (being loft and fcattered from Niantick.) Then he brought fix to my houfe, four being finally loft; I took what pains I could to get them fought again, and three I hear are found, after which Wm. Peacock is now out, and I look for him this night with thofe three : Ninigret did his part honeftly, but the youths and boys thereabouts (by fome occafion hallooing) the cattle thence took the woods. Jofeph Wild hath written to me, and I acquaint him with the caufe, that one man alone cannot well drive cattle amongft barbarians, efpecially without an Indian guide. It were exceeding well that three or four poles were enclofed at Niantick, to keep cattle there at night, for if God vouchfafe peace and plantations (profperity) there is needs of it,

Sir, I defire to be your worfhip's unfeigned,

ROGER WILLIAMS.

For Mr. John Winthrop, at Naumeug.

NAR : [1]

SIR,—Loving refpects to yourfelf and deareft, and Mrs. Lake, premifed. Two days fince, Ninigret came to me and requefted me to write two letters ; the one, in anfwer

---

[1] *R. I. Hift. Coll.* vol. iii. p. 151 ; KNOWLES' *Mem. of Roger Williams,* p. 222 ; 3 *Maſſ. Hift. Coll.* vol. ix. p. 275. This letter has no date, nor direction ; but it was evidently written to Mr. Winthrop, not long after the preceding letter.

to Captain Atherton's motion for some English planting
on Block Ifland, and on a neck at Niantick: the other,
to yourself, in which protefting his innocence as to the
death of his fon-in-law, with which Uncas and the Pequots charge him.   He prays you (as of yourfelf) to fignify
(as much as you can) items to the Pequots, that they be
quiet and attempt nothing (at leaft, treacheroufly,) againft
him, which he fufpects, from words from Uncas, that it will
be pleafing to the Englifh.   He prays you alfo to be mind-
ful of endeavoring to remove Wequafhcook, fo conftant a
provocation before him; and, at prefent, he prays you to
fend for fome fkins, which lately, as lord of the place, he
hath received.   I hope the Englifh Sachems, as I tell him,
in the fpring will hear and gratify him in his juft defires,
the want of which, I guefs, is the caufe that he is not free,
as yet, for Block Ifland, &c.; but expreffeth much, if the
Englifh do him juftice againft his enemies.   Oh, fir, how
far from nature if the fpirit of Chrift Jefus, that loves and
pities, prays for and doth good to enemies?   Sir, it is like
he will requeft a line of anfwer, which, if you pleafe to
give, I pray, fir, write when either of thofe fhips you
write of are for England, and by which you write yourfelf; alfo where Mr. Throckmorton is, and whether he
defires I fhould trouble you with the peag of which I
wrote, which I propofe, if God pleafe, (unlefs countermanded by either of you) to fend immediately upon hearing from you.

Sir, yours,

ROGER WILLIAMS.

Sir, fince I wrote this, it pleafed God to fend a Dutchman for an old debt, and the fame night Mr. Goodyear

alfo, to whom and his wife (for her former hufband) I am indebted, and fo was neceffitated to make fatisfaction to Mr. Goodyear alfo. Thefe providences of God fo falling will neceffarily caufe me to be preparing fome few days more that peag for Mr. Throckmorton. But moft certainly it, (God pleafe I live,) notwithftanding ways and weather, fhall be fent; this I write, that although Mr. Throckmorton fhould depart, or come home, yet he may prefume on your faithfulnefs and love to difpofe of it, as he requefteth.

Sir, your unworthy,

R. W.

Captain Underhill,[1] now here in a Dutch veffel, prefents loving refpects.

For the Worfhipful Mr. John Winthrop, at Nameug, thefe.

[Probably December, 1648.][2]

SIR,—Refpective falutations to you both, and fifter Lake. At this inftant (the firft of the week, toward noon,) I received yours, and fhall be glad, (if God will,) you may gain a feafonable paffage by us, before the hardeft of winter, although I cannot advife you (but to pray againft winter flights and journeys,) yet if the neceffity of God's providence fo caft it, I fhall be glad that we might have you prifoner in thefe parts, yet once in a few days (though in deep fnow) here is a beaten path, &c. Sir, Ninigret again

---

[1] Capt. Underhill, one of the prominent officers in the attack of the Pequot fort.

[2] KNOWLES' *Memoir of R. Williams*, p.

223; 3 *Mafs. Hift. Coll.* vol. xi. p. 276. This letter has no date, but is endorfed by Mr. Winthrop, 'rec'd December.'

importunes me to write to your father and yourfelf, about his hunting at Pequot, and that you would alfo be pleafed to write to your father.   I have endeavored to fatisfy him what I can, and fhall, yet I am willing at prefent to write to you, not fo much concerning that you can further gratify him at this time, but that I may by this opportunity, falute you with the tidings from the Bay the laft night. Skipper Ifaack and Moline, are come into the Bay with a Dutch fhip, and (as it is faid) have brought letters from the States to call home this prefent Dutch Governor,[1] to anfwer many complaints, both from Dutch and Englifh, againft him.   In this fhip are come Englifh paffengers, and they bring word of the great trials it pleafeth the Moft High and Only Wife, to exercife both our native England and thefe parts alfo.   '

The Prince is faid to be ftrong at fea, and among other mifchiefs hath taken Mr. Trevice his fhip which went from hence, and fent it for France, it feems their rendezvous.

It is faid that after Cromwell had difcomfited the Welch, with fix thoufand, he was forced to encounter nineteen thoufand Scots, of whom he took nine hundred prifoners, &c.   Great ftore of Scots and Welfh are fent and fold as flaves into other parts.   Cromwell wrote to the Parliament that he hoped to be at Edinburgh in a few days.   A commiffion was fent from the Parliament, to try the King in the Ifle of Wight, lately prevented from efcape.[2]

The Prince of Orange and the States are falling, if not

---

[1] The fhip in which Governor Peter Kieft, of New Amfterdam, returned to Holland, was wrecked on the coaft of Wales; and Kieft with about fixty others were drowned.—HUBBARD.   He was fucceeded by Peter Stuyvefant.

[2] After a feries of difafters Charles I. threw himfelf into the hands of the Scot-

already fallen, into wars, which makes fome of the States
to tender Manhattoes,[1] as place of retreat.

· Sir, to Him in whofe favor is life, I leave you, defiring
in Him to be

Your worfhip's unworthy

ROGER WILLIAMS.

John prays you to be in earneft with Mr. Hollett about
his houfe, hoping to be back in a fortnight.

[*To Mr. John Winthrop, at Naumeug.*]

Nar : [NARRAGANSETT, probably February, 1648-9.][2]

SIR,—Beft falutations to your worthy felf and yours, premifed.   I am glad for your fake, that it hath pleafed God to
prevent your winter travel ; though I gladly, alfo, this laft
week, expected your paffage, and being at Providence, haftened purpofely to attend you here.   Our candle burns out
day and night, we need not haften its end (by fwaling) in
unneceffary miferies, unlefs God call us for him to fuffer,
whofe our breath is, and hath promifed to fuch as hate life

---

tifh army, which furrendered him to the
Parliament's commiffioners appointed to
receive him.   Attempting to make his
efcape to the continent, he was arrefted
by the Governor of the Ifle of Wight,
into whofe hands he had placed himfelf,
and by whom he was lodged in Carifbrook Caftle.   In the following month
of January, 1648, he had his trial.

[1]Manhattan.   Manhadoes.   New Amfterdam, now New York.
   [2] KNOWLES, *Memoir of Roger Williams*,
p. 224; 3 *Mafs. Hift. Coll.* vol. ix. p. 280.
   This letter has no date.   Mr. Knowles
thinks it was written towards the clofe
of December, 1648; the editor of the
Wintbrop Papers fuggefts February, or
early in March of 1648-49.

for him, an eternal. Sir, this laft week, I read an ordinance of both houfes, (dated third month, May laft,) decreeing death to fome conciences, but imprifonment to far more, ever (upon the point) to all but Prefbyterians.[1] We have a found, that Fairfax and Cromwell are proclaimed traitors, but I rather credit that report, that Cromwell only was fent for by the Parliament, which, it feems, inclines with the King, and the city all againft the army. The Earl of Warwick was gone for Holland with twenty-two fhips purfuing the Prince. Mr. Foot and others went to Holland, (whither Mr. Trevice his fhip was carried) and were offered the fhip for two thoufand pounds, but I cannot hear of their agreement. About forty from the Parliament went to the King, to the Ifle of Wight, (who was lately and ftrangely prevented of efcape,) to treat, but could not agree upon the firft, viz.: that the King fhould acknowledge the beginning of the war to be his. Sir, this is the chief of matters told me few days fince, by Mr. Throckmorton, who came ten days fince from the Bay, and came well in a full laden veffel to anchor by Saconet rocks, but it pleafed God his new cable was cut by the rocks, and he drove upon Rhode Ifland fhore, where it is feared the veffel is fpoiled, but (through God's mercy) he faved his goods. Sir, Mr. Brewfter, (by letter) requefts me to convey three letters and bags of metal to you. I wifh they may have

[1] The Prefbyterians of England and the Scots, who were always haunted by the idea that there was fomething facred and inviolable in monarchy thought to refcue the King from the hands of the Independents, but were defeated, and all the Prefbyterians were forcibly expelled from the Englifh Houfe of Commons, which now confifting only of about fixty members—the *Rump Parliament*—appointed a court, compofed of perfons from the army, the Houfe of Commons and the city of London, to try the King. The court was opened at Weftminfter Hall, on the 20th of January, 1649; on the 27th, Charles was condemned to death, and on the 30th of the fame month was beheaded in front of the palace at Whitehall.—HUME, *Hift. of Eng'd.*

worth in them, efpecially to draw us up to dig into the heavens for true treafure. Sir, (though Mr. Brewfter wrote me not word of it) yet in private, I am bold to tell you, that I hear it hath pleafed God greatly to afflict him in the thorns of this life. He was intended for Virginia; his creditors in the Bay came to Portfmouth and unhung his rudder, carried him to the Bay, where he was forced to make over all, houfe, land, cattle, and part with all to his cheft. Oh how fweet is a dry morfel and a handful, with quietnefs from earth and heaven. *Sane nefcio de quo fcribis furti fufpecto.* John Jones is thought here to be falfe or faulty. He faid he was your fervant, that you gave him 10*s.* in peag to bear his charges, which being ftolen out of his pocket, he borrowed fo much of me here in your name, promifing to pay me at his return, being to receive money for you in the Bay; he had, alfo, 10*s.* more, to buy, for me, two or three neceffaries. He took 27*s.* 6*d.* of Valentine, Mr. Smith's man, my neighbor at the trading houfe, for a drum, which he faid he left at my house at Providence, which drum coft him 48*s.* and he promifed to fend it by an Indian, but refufed, and offered to fell it again at Providence; it is now attached.

Mr. Brewfter requefted me to pay the Bay carriers, which I have thus ordered, that fix awl blades I pay to a native to carry to Ninigret, and pray you to pay fix more to him that brings them to you. I am forry you had no more corn from Ninigret, yet glad you had fo much, for I am forced to pay 4*s.* the bufhel for all I fpend. Sir, I have not known the like of Indian madnefs. The Father of Lights caufe us to blefs him for and with our reason, remembering Nebuchadnezzar.

Sir, I defire to be yours ever in Chrift Jefus,

ROGER WILLIAMS.

For his much honored, kind friend, Mr. John Winthrop, at his house at Nameug, these.

CAWCAWMSQUSSICK, [probably January, 1648–49.][1]

SIR,—Best salutations presented to you both, with humble desires, that, since it pleaseth God to hinder your presence this way, he may please, for His infinite mercy's sake, in his Son's blood, to further our eternal meeting in the presence of Him that sits upon the throne, and the Lamb forever; and that the hope thereof may be living, and bring forth the fruits of love where it is possible, and of lamenting for instructions. Sir, the affairs of our country (Vaderland, as the Dutch speak) would have afforded us much conference. The merciful Lord help us to make up in prayer to his holy majesty, &c. Sir, for this land, our poor colony is in civil dissension.[2] Their last meetings, at which I have not been, have fallen into factions; Mr. Coddington and Captain Partridge, &c., are the heads of the one, and Captain Clarke, Mr. Easton, &c., the heads of the other faction. I receive letters from both, inviting me, &c., but I resolve (if the Lord please) not to engage,

---

[1] KNOWLES' *Memoir of R. Williams*, p. 227; 3 *Mass. Hist. Coll.* vol. ix. p. 278.
     This letter is without date; but from its contents, was probably written shortly before that which follows.

[2] "One of the principal difficulties, which, at this time, disturbed the peace of the colony, arose from the extraordinary proceedings of Mr. Coddington, the leading inhabitant of the Island of Rhode Island. From the very organization of the government under the charter, he arrayed himself in the opposition and seems to have left no effort untried to overturn and destroy it. Uniting with himself a faction composed probably of persons accustomed to take their opions from him, he first petitioned the colony of Plymouth to take the island under its jurisdiction; and when this application failed, notwithstanding he had been elected President, in the meantime he went to England, to endeavor to set aside the charter which Mr. Williams had procured, and destroy the union of the towns which had been organized by its provisions."—GAMMELL, *Life of Roger Williams*, p. 133.

unlefs with great hopes of peace-making. The peace makers are fons of God. Our neighbors, the Narragan-fetts, are now confulting, and making peag, to carry, with-in a few weeks, another payment. Sir, about a month fince, one William Badger, a feaman, and now a planter at William Field's farm,[1] near Providence, paffed by me, trav-eling to the Seabrook. I have received letters fince from Captain Mafon, to whom I wrote by him, and hear nothing of him. I fear he mifcarried, for he was alone, without a guide. And, fince I mention Captain Mafon, worthy Sir, I humbly beg of the Father of Lights to guide you, in your converfe and neighborhood with him. In his letters to me, he tells me of fome extraordinary lifts againft Un-cas, and that he will favor him, but no more than religion and reafon bid him. He promifeth to vifit me, in his paf-fage, this fummer, eaftward, (I guefs he means towards Plymouth.) I fhall then argue, if God will, many things, and how it ftands with religion and reafon, that fuch a monftrous hurry and affrightment fhould be offered to an Englifh town, either by Indians or Englifh, unpunifhed. Sir, you have feen many parts of this world's fnowball, and never found aught but vanity and vexation At Nameug fhall you find no more, except in the fountain of living waters. Sir, heap coals of fire on Captain Mafon's head; conquer evil and good, but be not cowardly, and overcome with any evil.

If you have by you the Trial of Wits,[2] at convenience,

---

[1] The farm adjoining Field's Point, three miles from Providence.

[2] "*Triall of wits.*" We have fought in vain, for a book bearing this title, and think a work of humor or wit could not have been meant, fuch not being in cha-racter with the ftudies of Williams. With his practice of abbreviating words, Mr. Williams may have meant '*Trial of Witneffes*,' fimilar to a popular book of Bifhop Shirley's entitled '*Trial of Wit-neffes, of the Refurrection.*'

fpare it me a few days.   However, ftudy, as the Lord commands, your quietnefs, for which I fhall ever pray and endeavor.

Your worfhip's unfeigned

ROGER WILLIAMS.

For his honored, kind friend, Mr. John Winthrop, at Nameug.

CAWCAWMSQUSSICK, 29. 11. 48. (fo called) [29th January, 1648–49.][1]

SIR,—Beft falutations and wifhes to the Father of mercies for your worthy felf, yoke-fellow, fifter, &c.   It muft
be fo in this world's fea.   *Sicut fluctus fluctum, fic luctus
luctum fequitur.*   And every day hath his fufficiency or
fullnefs of evil to all the children of the firft finful man ;
no perfons, no places, exempted from the reach of the firft
curfe.   My humble defire is to the moft righteous and only
wife Judge, that the wood of Chrift's gallows (as in Mofes' act) may be caft into all your and our bitter waters,
that they be fweet and wholefome inftructors of the fruits
of fin, the forrows of others abroad, (in our England's
Aceldama,) our own defervings to feel upon ourfelves, bodies and fouls, (wives and children alfo) not by barbarians,
but devils, and that enternally, forrows inexpreffible, in-
conceivable, and yet, if Chrift's religion be true, unavoida-
ble, but by the blood of a Saviour, &c.   Sir, pardon me,
this is not the matter.   Sir, your letters I fpeedily defpatched by a meffenger on purpofe.   For a place, I know
indeed of one in Plymouth claim, and would fpecify, but

---

[1] KNOWLES' *Mem. R. Williams*, p. 228.   3 *Mafs. Hift. Coll.* vol. ix. p. 279.

that your fpirit being troubled, countermanded it again, in your poftfcript concerning Elderkin, whom I will, if God will, effectually labor with, and write the iffue with fpeed. All our neighbors, the barbarians, run up and down, and confult; partly fufpecting like dealings; partly ready to fall upon the Mohegans, at your word, and a world of foolifh agitations, I could trouble you with, but I told the chiefeft yefterday, that it is not our manner to be rafh, and that you will be filent till your father and other ancient Sachems fpeak firft, &c. Sir, concerning the bags of ore, it is of Rhode Ifland, where it is certainly affirmed to be both gold and filver[1] ore, upon trial. Mr. Coddington went to the Bay, with his daughter, for England,[2] and left Captain Partridge in truft with all, the laft week, at Newport. George Wright alias Captain Wright, ftabbed with a pike, Walter Lettice at Newport, and is in prifon; the other, if not dead, is not like to live.

Sir, yours ever, in all unfeigned refpect, &c.

ROGER WILLIAMS.

I want wax to feal, otherwife I would have expreffed fomething, which I referve till another feafon, if the Lord will.

---

[1] " The colony was thrown into great excitement, by the difcovery of a gold mine on the Ifland. Mr. Williams fent fome bags of the ore to Mr. Winthrop, and writes ' it is certainly affirmed to be both gold and filver ore, upon trial.' The Affembly paffed an act, taking poffeffion of the mine in the name of the State of England, and iffued a proclamation forbidding all perfons to intermeddle with any of the ore. This was publifhed by William Dyre, appointed for that purpofe, for want of a Herald-at-arms, and the arms of England, and of the Lord High Admiral, were fet up at the mine. Fortunately a more accurate examination diffipated the golden dreams of the colonifts by proving the report unfounded."—STAPLES, *Annals of Providence*, p. 72.

[2] The purpofe for which Coddington went to England is ftated in a note to the preceding letter.

22

*For the worſhipful, and kind friend, Mr. John Winthrop, at
Nameug.*

CAWCAWMSQUSSICK, I. 48. (ſo called.)   [March, 1648–9.][1]

SIR,—Beſt reſpeĉts and love preſented, and thanks hearty
for your letters, former and latter, all now received.   I am
again importuned by our neighbor Sachems, having heard
of Wequaſhcook's carrying off peag to Captain Maſon, to
pray you to inform them whether that peag be part of the
payment ; becauſe Wequaſhcook and his company refuſe
to pay.   They deſire me alſo to write to the Bay about it,
which I defer to do until their payments go, which are
ſomething delayed becauſe of the death of Ninigret's wife's
mother, which is the ſame you write of, Wequaſhcook's
mother, and it is now *qunnantacaun*, that is, lamentation.
Sir, ſince I wrote to you, our four towns met by deputies,
ſix out of a town.   This Court laſt week wrote to me information of their choice of myſelf as Deputy Preſident,[2] in
the abſence of the Preſident, who, whether they have fixed
on yourſelf, or Mr. Coddington's faĉtion prevail to keep
his name in, now gone for England, I cannot yet learn, but
I have excuſed myſelf for ſome reaſons, and I hope they
have choſen better.   I wrote to them about an act of oblivion, which, bleſſed be the God of peace, they have paſt,
and have appointed a Court of eleĉtion in the third month,
at Warwick.   Sir, I am exceeding glad of your beginnings at
Pawcatuck.   I pray fail not to enquire whether from there,
or from Mohegan or Conneĉticut, you can help me to one

[1] 3 *Maſs. Hiſt. Coll.* vol. ix. p. 282 ;
KNOWLES, *Mem. of Roger Williams*, p.
230.
[2] This appointment of Williams as

Preſident of the colony was the reſult
of his letter to the town of Providence.
See note to Letter of Auguſt 31, pre
ceding.

hundred bufhels of Indian corn. To your dear yokefel-
low and fifter refpective falutation. The fun of righteoufnefs gracioufly fhine on you. I defire, unfeignedly, to be
your worfhip's unfeigned in love.

ROGER WILLIAMS.

The Sachems pray you to tell them whether their
peag[1] will be fold at under rates, as Punhommin, coming
two days fince from the Bay, informs them, viz. : that they
muft pay great black at thirteen to the penny, and fmall
black at fifteen, and white eight to the penny. I tell them
the laft year it was meafured, and fo word was fent to me
they fhould pay it by meafure.

For his honored, kind friend, Mr. John Winthrop, at Pequot.

[Probably March or April, 1649.][2]

SIR,—I am the more eafily perfuaded by this barbarian
prince, Ninigret, to trouble you fo often, that I may the
oftener hear of your welfare, and at prefent how it pleafed
God to bring you home to yours again. Upon your word,

[1] *Peag* paffed among the early fettlers as money. There was a law of the colony regulating its value. "No one fhall take any black peage of the Indians, but at four a penny ; and if any fhall take black peage under four a penny, he fhall forfeit faid peage, one-half to the informer, the other half to the State."—*Laws of Rhode Ifland,* 1648.
The frequent mention in thefe letters of peag carried to Bofton by the Narra-ganfetts, Niantics and Mohegans, has reference to the debt or tribute, which, by an agreement entered into at Bofton, they were required to deliver.

[2] 3 *Mafs. Hift. Coll.* vol. ix. p. 283; KNOWLES' *Mem. of Roger Williams,* p. 231.
This letter is without date. It was probably written in March, or early in April, 1649.

Ninigret prays you to fend him word, whether within ten days, of this 5th of the week prefent, you will pleafe to meet him at Wequatucket, fo it be when Mr. Stanton is prefent.   He would confer about Mr. Eliot's[1] letter and coat, about Wequafhcook's ufurping at Pawcatuck, about his prefent hunting, about the prefent difpofal of the Pequot fields, about his letters to the Bay, which, in your name, I have almoft perfuaded to fufpend until the meeting of the commiffioners[2] at Bofton.   Here is now a great hurry made by Anquontis, one of thofe petty Sachems, of whom Mr. Eliot wrote to you and me   He hath offered great abufe to one of the chiefs, and Ninigret is now going to Conanicut about him.   I perfuade not to engage themfelves, but to fend him to the Bay with my letter·   Sir, loving refpects to Mrs. Winthrop, Mrs. Lake, whom God gracioufly, with your loving felf and yours, bind up in the bundle of that life, which is eternal in Chrift Jefus, in whom I defire to be,

Yours ever,

Roger Williams.

[1] John Eliot, commonly called the Apoftle of the Indians ; the tranflator of the Old and New Teftament in the Indian language and of various works relating to the Indians.

[2] Mention has before been made of the "Commiffioners of the United Colonies," fome notice of which feems neceffary.   The colonies fo united confifted of Plymouth, Maffachufetts Bay, Connecticut and New Haven, and was the earlieft confederacy among the New England colonies.   " It was " fays Profeffor Gammell, " a union of great importance to the interefts of thofe embraced in it, and may be regarded as in fome fort, the germ of the fubfequent confederations which have marked the hiftory of the American people.   The objects which were propofed in its formation were neutral protection againft the depredations of the Indian tribes, who were now becoming more formidable by the acquifition of fire-arms, and againft the encroachments of the Dutch and French, together with the prefervation of the liberty and peace of the gofpel, and the advancement of the Kingdom of Chrift.

For my honored kind friend Mr. John Winthrop, at Pequot.

NAR. 15. z. 49. (fo called.) [NARRAGANSETT, April 15, 1649.]¹

SIR,—Beſt reſpeéts and love to you both. By this bearer (Nath. Waller) I received your book,² and had by the
ſame returned it, but that I deſire to read it over once more,
finding it pleaſant and profitable, and crave the ſight of any
other of that ſubjeét at your leiſure, kindly thanking you
for this encloſed. As yet no tidings further from England. Here the Dutch Governor threatens ſome trouble
about the Dutch prize³ which Captain Clarke, Bened and
others bought, which he deſires to be reſtored, as being no
prize, as taken contrary to the peace with Spain. If not
reſtored he threatens to take all veſſels from hence, to
which end it may be it is, that Jacob Curlow (whom
the Indians call Yaupuck) have lately bought of ſome of
the Narraganſett Sachems the little Iſland⁴ in the mouth of
this Bay (called Aquedeneſick and Dutch Iſland), intending to build and trade there, contrary to an order of this
Colony againſt foreigners, as alſo againſt the agreement
between the Commiſſioners and the Sachems, not to ſell
any land without their conſent. We are borne to trouble

. . . The colony at Providence, formed
as it had been, principally of the outcaſt
and baniſhed from the ſettlements of
New England, was not invited to join
the confederacy ; and her ſubſequent application for admiſſion, like that of the
ſettlers on Rhode Iſland was ſternly refuſed.—*Life of Roger Williams*, p. 114.

¹ 4 *Maſs. Hiſt. Coll.* vol. vi. p. 267.

² Probably the book called " Triall of
Wits " ſent for in a preceding letter,
page 167, ſee note.

³ The Dutch were, by law, forbidden
to trade with the Indians within the juriſdiétion of the colony upon pain of
forfeiture of ſhip and goods. Probably
one of their veſſels engaged in trade had
been captured.

⁴ The ſmall iſland weſt of the iſland of
Conanicut at the entrance to Narraganſett
Bay, now under the juriſdiétion of the
government of the United States, and
upon which a fortification has recently
been eréted.

as the fparks fly upward.   Above the fun is our reft, in the
Alpha and Omega of all blefTednefs, unto whofe arms of
everlafting mercy I commend you, defirous to be yours
even in him.

ROGER WILLIAMS.

My loving refpect to your loving fifter.   I hope it will
pleafe God to fend you a mill.

---

*For the Worfhipful his very loving friend Mr. John Win-
throp, at Bofton, or elfewhere.*

[No date ; probably April or May, 1649.][1]

SIR,—Beft falutes, &c.   I long to hear of your refrefh-
ing after fo much fighing, &c.   Our neighbor Sachems
(having fent two natives this morning to my houfe inftead
of Caufafenamont, to attend your coming,) are importu-
nate with me to write to you, and to pray you (if this
meffenger Safepunnuit meet you on the way) to write a
word to the Bay, concerning the late bufinefs of Uncas'
pretended death at Mohegan.   For preface, this Mr.
Smith's pinnace (that rode here at your being with us)
went forth the fame morning to Newport, bound for Block
Ifland, and Long Ifland, and Nayantick for corn : with
them went a Narraganfett man, Cuttaquene, an ufual trader for Mr. Smith : the wind being (after three or four

---

[1] 4 *Mafs. Hift. Coll.* vol. vi. p. 268.
Probably written in the Spring of
1649, before May 10, at which time
Governor Endicot was elected Gover-
nor of Maffachufetts in place of Gover-
nor Winthrop, who died on the 26th of
March of this year.—Note by SAVAGE to
Winthrop Papers.

days ſtay at Newport,) northeaſt and ſtrong, they put into your river and ſo to Mohegan. Uncas came aboard, *on a ſudden groaned and cried out that the Narraganſett had killed him: the Narraganſett man denied it, and Uncas ſhowed a wound on his breaſt which bled afreſh, &c.*[1] Many circumſtances paſſed. In fine Uncas cauſed the man's two forefingers to be cut off and ſent to Capt. Maſon, who being come, cauſed the man to be unbound, and took him along with himſelf to Hartford. Our neighbor Sachems now pray you and the Magiſtrates of the Bay, and of the whole country, that the matter may be thoroughly ſearched out with all diligence, for two cauſes: Firſt, for the clearing of themſelves, who all profeſs moſt ſolemnly to be altogether innocent, &c., and they ſay it had been childiſh, now they are ſo near finiſhing their payment, to have prevented the Engliſh juſtice againſt Uncas, which they are in great hopes of when matters ſhall be heard, &c. They hear that Cuttaquene, the man in hold, being threatened death by a hatchet over his head, to confeſs his complotters, authors, &c., he named (as they ſay) themſelves to ſave his own life. The ſecond cauſe, that Uncas might be diſcovered, for they ſuppoſe he (knowing how near he is to a trial (after the payment finiſhed) according to the Engliſh Sachems promiſe,) projected this vilainy, &c., to render the Narraganſetts ſtill odious to the Engliſh, and prevent his trial. I was bold to write your deareſt for a word of Engliſh information; which I think will come by the Engliſh (who went to ſee your parts.) By natives I hear *that your James went to Uncas and charged him with project-*

---

[1] "The complaint of Uncas againſt the Narraganſett man, here related, was conſidered by the Commiſſioners of the United Colonies, at their ſeſſion, at Boſton, in July, 1649."—See HAZARD, ii. p. 130. Note to *Winthrop Papers.*

ing *himself and acting himself a small stab on his breast in a safe place, &c. Many circumstances look earnestly toward a plot of Uncas, both at this time, and in the manner,*[1] of the fact of which you will hear more. He that is the Father of Lights, and Judge of the whole world will shortly bring all secret things to light. At present two things make me (if all things else were clear) to suspend belief to Uncas' words: First, that the going forth of Cuttaquene in Mr. Smith's vessel was on an instant, and accidental, and never intended (that I can hear yet of) for Mohegan; however if the English had thoughts of it (which will be known upon their landing) yet they never mentioned it to the native, who, it is like, would never have consented, for this second consideration. This man Cuttaquene (without a miracle) could not attempt this thing, for I know him, and all men know him, to be of a gentle and peaceable spirit, and was never forth with them in their wars; and no way like to stop such a man at noonday, in the midst of his own, &c. Sir, I am sorry I have no horse, nor boat fit to serve you at this time. My canoe with a wind fair would quickly set you here with ease: I have writ to my wife that it may attend you: and I humble beg of the God of Heaven that his holy Angels may attend you in all his ways, in whom I desire to be your worship's respective and affectionate

ROGER WILLIAMS.

Sir, if this meet you at Providence, I pray impart it to my brother and friends to whom I cannot now write.

---

[1] This paragraph is somewhat obscured, by an attempted erasure, by an another hand. See *note to Winthrop Papers.*

To Mrs. John Winthrop, Jr.

NARRAGANSETT, [no date, probably April, 1649.][1]

MRS. WINTHROP,—Loving refpects to your kind felf and dear fifter. I am importuned by our neighbor Sachems to write to your dear hufband in the Bay, that whereas they hear that Uncas is hurt by a Narraganfett man, that went in Richard Smith's[2] pinnace, they pray him to be affured that whatever is done, more or lefs, they are ignorant of it, and will ufe no other means againft him than the Englifh juftice in a legal way. They pray me alfo to write to you, that by yourfelf or fome of our loving friends with you, this meffenger may bring word of the truth of matters among them : I believe nothing of any of the barbarians on either fide, but what I have eye fight for, or Englifh teftimony. I am the more willing to write, becaufe I might hereby hear of your health, and of your children and neigbors, to whom I wifh eternal peace in the Son of God, in whom I defire to be

Your loving friend,

ROGER WILLIAMS.

I pray caufe a line to be fent back by this bearer, what the matter is.

---

[1] 4 *Mafs. Hift. Coll.* vol. vi. p. 270.

[2] "Richard Smith, fen'r," fays Williams in his letter of 21ft July, 1679, "for his confcience to God left fair poffeffions in Glocefterfhire, and adventured with his relations ana eftate to New England, and was a moft acceptable inhabitant, and a prime leading man in Taunton and Plymouth colony." He was one of the party with Gov. Winthrop, of Connecticut, and .others to whom the Narraganfett Sachem Coginaquon, granted the " Northern Tract " in the Narraganfett country. The title to this land was afterwards confirmed to Smith and his affociates by an order from King Charles 2d.—*R. I. Col. Rec.* vol. i. pp. 464–466. Richard Smith, in

23

To the Worſhipful Mr. John Winthrop, at Pequot.

NARRAGANSETT, 9. 3. 49, (ſo called.)   [May 9, 1649.][1]

SIR,—Beſt ſalutations and wiſhes preſented to your deareſt with yourſelf, &c.   Theſe encloſed came to my hand
in two ſeveral letters from the Bay encloſed, your brother
in a letter from him, requeſting my help, &c.   I have
therefore, ſpeeded them by the Sachems, who will, therefore, expeᴄt ſome word of tiding from the Bay, which you
may pleaſe to ſignify, in one line to me.   Whatever you
hear, or can well colleᴄt, will be any word of tidings, &c.,
by which occaſion (if you have occaſion) you may well
reſcribe.   Benediᴄt was deſired by the magiſtrates in the
Bay to take ſpecial care to charge Wequaſhcook, concerning[2]   .   He hath requeſted this taſk from me, which
this morning I purpoſe to do (with God's help) carefully.
Sir, two days ſince, my boat not being fitted, coming from
Providence, I was (in *articulo temporis*) ſnatched by a merciful, and, ſome ſay, a miraculous hand, from the jaws of
death.   The canoe being overſet, ſome goods, to ſome value, were ſunk, ſome whereof I hope, if God pleaſe, to recover.   However, bleſſed be God, and bleſſed are ſuch
whom he correᴄteth and teacheth in him.   Yours he graciouſly make me, though unworthy.

ROGER WILLIAMS.

the autumn of 1651, purchaſed of Roger
Williams his eſtate at Cawcumquffick,
(now Wickford), from which place ſo
many of theſe letters were written.   In
his teſtimony in favor of Smith's title to
the Wickford lands, dated July 21, 1679,
Williams ſays, that forty years from this
date, Smith "put up in the thickeſt of
the barbarians the firſt Engliſh houſe
among them."   This would carry the
ſettlement back to 1639.

[1] KNOWLES' *Mem. Roger Williams* p.
232; 3 *Maſſ. Hiſt. Coll.* vol. ix. p. 284.

[2] "Concerning."   Though the original of this letter is much torn, the blank
following the above word is the only one

To my much refpected friend Mr. John Winthrop, at Pequot.

13. 3. 49, (fo called.)   [May 9th, 1649.][1]

SIR,—Salutations, &c.   Your laft letter, which you mention, I fent by way of the Englifh, fince I came hither from Providence.   I know of no letter of yours, that came back, as you write.   One of mine to yourfelf, when you were in the Bay, was met by the peag meffengers from the Bay, and brought by them again to my hand, becaufe, as they conceived, the whole about Uncas, his wounding, was not yet, as then, known, which, at your coming hither, by the Englifh relation was perfected.   Tidings from Uncas are, that the Englifh come from the Bay to Hartford about Uncas, and are appointed to take this way, and to take Ninigret with them.   Aquawoce (Wepiteammock) is at the point of death.   *Expectat nos mors ubique; cur non nos mortem?*   In life and death the Son of God fhine on us.   In him,

Yours I defire to be, ever unfeigned,

ROGER WILLIAMS.

which I was not able fatisfactorily to make out or fupply.   The fragments of a few letters look more like parts of the word "Nenekunat" (Ninigret) than any other.   Between that Sachem and Wequafhcook, as appears from another letter of Roger Williams, there was a mifunderftanding.—*Note by Prof. Knowles.*

[1] KNOWLES, *Mem. R. Williams*, p. 233; 3 *Mafs Hift. Coll.* vol. ix. p. 285.

"This letter is worthy of notice, as affording a flight intimation of that deficiency of paper and other articles, which the exclufion from intercoufe with Bofton occafioned.   This letter was written on the envelope, or blank fide of one addreffed to the writer, as is evident from the direction, which ftood originally thus: "To my much refpected friend, Mr. Roger Williams."   Mr. Williams ftruck out his own name, and put in the place of it, "John Winthrop, at Pequot," in a blacker ink.—*Note by Prof. Knowles.*

For his honored, kind friend, Mr. John Winthrop, at Nameug, these.

NAR. 26. 3. 49. (fo called) [May 26th, 1649.][1]

SIR,—Loving refpects to your dear felf, and deareft, &c. This laft of the week, in the morning, your man and all his charge are come juft now to me in fafety. I, myfelf, alfo came hither late laft night, and wet, from Warwick, where this colony met and upon difcharge of my service, we chofe Mr. Jofeph Smith,[2] of Warwick, (the merchant or fhop-keeper that lived at Bofton) for this year, Prefident. Some were bold (though Captain Clarke was gone to the Bay and abfent) to ufe your name, and generally applauded and earneftly defired, in cafe of any poffible ftretching our bounds to you, or your drawing near to us, though but to Pawcatuck. One law paffed, that the natives fhould no longer abufe us, but that their black[3] fhould go with us, as with themfelves, at four per penny. All wines and ftrong waters forbidden the natives throughout the colony, only a privilege betrufted in my hand, to fpare a little for neceffities, &c.[4]

Sir, tidings are high from England; many fhips from

---

[1] KNOWLES' *Mem. R. Williams*, p. 234; 3 *Mafs. Hift. Coll.* vol. ix. p. 286.

[2] In May, 1649, the General Affembly met at Warwick, when Mr. Williams having declined a reelection, Mr. Jofeph Smith was chofen Prefident. Among the affiftants chofen was Samuel Gorton. Mr. Williams was chofen "to take a view of the records delivered unto the Court by William Dyre," referring, probably, to his complaints againft Coddington. Thefe complaints were again prefented to the General Affembly, but were deferred, probably, in confequence of the abfence of Mr. Coddington.

[3] Black, i. e. black peage.

[4] The law regarding the fale of intoxicating liquors was as rigid at this period as it is now among the prohibitionifts. At the May feffion of the General Affembly, 1650. a refolution was paffed in which it was "granted unto Mr. Roger Williams to have leave to fell a little wine or ftrong water to the natives in their ficknefs."—*R. I. Col. Records*, vol. i. p. 219.

many parts fay, and a Briftol fhip, come to the Ifle of
Shoals within a few days, confirms, that the King and
many great Lords and Parliament men are beheaded. London was fhut up on the day of execution, not a door to be
opened, &c. The States of Holland and the Prince of
Orange (forced by them) confented to proceedings. It is
faid Mr. Peters[1] preached (after the fafhion of England)
the funeral fermon to the King, after fentence, out of the
terrible denunciation to the King of Babylon. Efa. 14:
18, &c.

Your letter to your brother I delivered to Mr. Gold,
(going to Bofton;) this weather, I prefume hinders. Mr.
Andrews,[2] a gentleman of Warwick, told me, that he came
from the Bay, where he heard that the Bay had proclaimed
war with the Narraganfetts. I hope it is but miftaken;
and yet all under, and while we are under the fun, nothing
but vanity and vexation.

The moft glorious Sun of Righteoufnefs fhine gracioufly
on us. In him I defire to be, Sir, ever yours,

ROGER WILLIAMS.

To his honored friend, Mr. John Winthrop.

CAWCAWMSQUSSICK, 13. 4. 49, (fo called) [June 13th, 1649.][3]

SIR,—Beft falutations, &c. The laft night one of Wequafhcook's Pequots brought me, very privately, letters
from Capt. Mafon, (and as he faid, from Uncas and We-

----

[1] Hugh Peters ; fee note to letter of
July 21, 1637.

[2] Edward Andrews, a freeman of War-

wick.—*R. I. Col. Records,* vol. i. p. 302.

[3] 3 *Mafs. Hift. Coll.* vol. xi. p. 287 ;
KNOWLES' *Memoir of R. Williams,* p. 235.

quafhcook.) The letters are kind to myfelf, acknowledging loving letters (and tokens, which upon burning of his houfe,) he had received from me, &c.; but terrible to all thefe natives, efpecially to the Sachems, and moft of all, to Ninigret. The purport of the letters and concurrence of circumftances, feem to me to imply fome prefent conclufions (from Conneΰicut) of hoftility,[1] and I queftion whether or no prefent and fpeedy, before the meeting of commiffioners, which I faw lately from the court, under Mr. Nowell's hand, was not to be till the feventh month. The murdering of Uncas is alleged by ftabbing, and fince attempted by witches, &c. The conclufion is therefore ruin. The words of the letter are: " If nothing but blood will fatisfy them, I doubt not but they may have their fill; and again I perceive fuch an obftinate willfullnefs, joined with defperate malicious praΰices, that I think and believe *they are fealed to deftruΰion.*" Sir, there are many devices in a man's heart, but the counfel of Jehovah fhall ftand. If he have

[1] " The hoftile attitude of the Indians, occafioned by the determination of the United Colonies to proteΰ Uncas at every hazard, from the punifhment due to his crime at the hands of the Narraganfetts, caufed more ferious alarm than ever before. The diffentions prevailing among them thofe of Shawomet and Pawtuxet owing allegiance to Maffachufetts, and viewing as enemies all Englifhmen whom fhe denounced, while the Niantics and Nipmucks remained true to their proper princes, made the fituation of Rhode If-land, furrounded as fhe was by thefe diftraΰed and exafperated tribes extremely perilous. The inhabitants of Warwick fuffered from this caufe. They complained that the Indians had killed their cattle, abufed their fervants, entered their houfes by force, maltreating the occupants, and ftealing their goods, and defired advice on the fubjeΰ." * * * The Commiffioners wrote a letter to the Sachems, advifing them to abftain from fuch conduΰ in future, and telling them that, if they received any injury from the Englifh, fatisfaΰion fhould be given them, as the like would be expeΰed from them. Scarcely had this miffive been fent, when letters were received from Roger Williams and others, warning the United Colonies of preparations making by the Narraganfetts to renew the war on Uncas."—ARNOLD, *Hift. of Rhode Ifland*, vol. i. p. 222–23.

a holy and righteous purpofe to make us drink of our mother's cup, the holinefs nor power, nor policy of New England, can ftop his hand : He be pleafed to prevent it, if not to fweeten it.

Sir, I pray, if you have aught, fignify in a line, and you fhall not fail of my poor papers and prayers.

Your unfeigned,

ROGER WILLIAMS.

Your letters and friends were here fome days with me. This laft choice at Warwick (according to my foul's wifh and endeavor) hath given me reft. Others are chofen, Mr. John Clarke,[1] at Newport, to whom, and all my friends on the ifland, I wrote effectually. Thither they went. I have heard nothing fince. If power had been with me, fuch a work of mercy, (although to ftrangers) I hope, by the Lord's affiftance, fhall not efcape me ; and I

---

[1] John Clarke, the founder and paftor of the firft Baptift Church in Newport, was one of the moft prominent men in the colony. In 1651, he was fent to England with Roger Williams, to promote the interefts of the colony. He remained there, until he procured the charter of 1663. After his return, he was elected three years, fucceffively, Deputy Governor. He died April 26, 1676, in the 67th year of his age. Having no children, he gave moft of his property to charitable purpofes.— While in London, he publifhed a book, entitled, "*Ill News from New England, or a narrative of New England's Perfecution ; wherein it is declared, that while*

Old England is becoming New, New England is becoming Old ; &c., &c. London, 1652. To no man, except Roger Williams, is Rhode Ifland more indebted than to him. He was the original projector of the fettlement on the Ifland, and one of its ableft legiflators. Dr. Elton, in fpeaking of Clarke, fays "He was a faithful and ufeful minifter, courteous and amiable in all relations of life, and an ornament to his profeffion and to the feveral offices which he fuftained. His memory is deferving of lafting honor for his efforts towards eftablifhing the firft goverment in the world which gave to all equal, civil and religious liberty." Note to CALLENDER's *Hift. Dift.* p. 212.

have promifed my affiftance to Mr. Clarke and others, at
Newport, if any blame or damage befall them from the
colony or elfewhere.

Sir, I forgot to thank you for the pamphlets, although
(not having been lately at Providence) I have them not;
but I have fent for them.   I have here now with me, my
eldeft daughter, of feventeen.   Her younger fifter of fifteen, hath had nature's courfe before her, which fhe wanting, a flux of rheum hath much affeſted her head and right
eye ; fhe hath taken much phyfic, and been let blood, but
yet no change.   She is advifed by fome to the Bay.   I
pray advife me to whom you judge fitteft to addrefs unto
of the Bay phyficians.

Sir, I hear a fmith of your town hath left you, and faith
I fent for him.   It is moft untrue, though we want one
at Providence, yet I fhould condemn in myfelf, or any, to
invite any convenience or commodity from our friends.   I
know him not, nor ever fpake (to my knowledge) about
him.   Mr. Throckmorton hath lately brought in fome
corn from Heinftead and thofe parts, but extraordinary
dear.   I pay him 6s. for Indian, and 8s. for wheat.   Thefe
rains if God pleafe to give peace, promife hopes of plenty.

Two days fince, letters from my brother.   He faith a
a fhip was come to the Bay from England.   She was not
come yet in the river.   A lighter went aboard, and brought
the confirmation of the King's death, but no other particulars.   The everlafting King of kings fhine on us, &c.

*To the Worſhipful his kind friend Mr. John Winthrop, Eſq.,
at Pequot.*

Nar. 26, 6, 49. (ſo called.)   [Narragansett, Auguſt 26th, 1649.][1]

Sir,—Beſt reſpects to you both, with hearty deſires of
your peace and ours, if the God of Peace ſo mercifully
pleaſe. Upon this late hubbub, (of an aſſault upon the
Pequots by the Mohegans, and one of thoſe Mohegans
purſued and ſlain by the Pequots,) the Sachems have ſent
to me for my thoughts, their men being impatient of making an aſſault alſo upon the Mohegans. I tell them the
Engliſh will not regard their complaints until the debt is
paid. But that (at this time) will not ſtop them : I tell
them the Mohegans have now killed but an old woman
(if dead) : they have killed a Captain, that makes them
conſider. Further, whereas they deſire I would write to the
Bay, I anſwer, it is better firſt that I write to you to pray you
to ſend to Hartford, to know whether the Magiſtrates and
Engliſh have ſet on Uncas, and what their reſolution is,
then upon receipt of their mind ſhall yourſelf and I know
better what to write to the Bay for them. With this I have
ſatisfied them, and conceive it very requiſite that (if you
have not already) you would pleaſe to requeſt a word from
honored friends of Hartford. If God pleaſe, this fire may
yet be quenched, which humbly deſires

Your worſhip's unworthy

Roger Williams.

Sir, I pray ſeal and ſend this to Eſq. Maſon.

---

[1] 4 *Maſs. Hiſt. Coll.* vol. vi. p. 271.

24

For his honored, kind friend, Mr. John Winthrop, at Pequot.

NAR: 25, 8, 49, (fo called,) [October 25, 1649.][1]

LOVING SIR,—To yourfelf and your dear companion beft falutation and defires of your hearts defire, and more then your hearts can defire in the knowledge and love of the Son of the living God: This paffing hand calls for this line only of neighborly falutation and information. Our neighbors meffengers are gone to (not returned from) Maffachufetts, with about 20*li* or upwards of peag. I had promifed to write for them, but the peag being brought me, and fo little, and they quarrelling amongft themfelves, and foolifhly charging inferior Sachems of non-payment, I was not free. I advifed them (according to your advice) to compell Wequafhcook to contribute, as alfo the Block Iflanders and fome petty Sachems about the great pond (who follow Wequafhcook to fave their money) but they fay it is a new thing fo to do, &c., and they defire rather the Englifh would do it, which difcovery of their weaknefs, Sir, in my poor thoughts, holds out a great Providence of God for the onenefs and fecurity of the Eng-lifh (while the barbarians are in their fractions) and fome door of hope to me of fome preparations to draw them nearer to civility, and that according to your own dear father's opinion and defire. Our natives fay the Mauqua-wogs have defired the Englifh to ftay from going to war againft the Dutch Indians, but a Dutchman tells me he heard (at Munnadoes) of five hundred Englifh coming againft them. If the Father of Mercies mercifully pre-vent not, it may prove a devouring fire. Bluefield is come to Newport and is carrying the fhip (his prize) to Munna-

---

[1] 4 *Maff. Hift. Coll.* vol. vi. p. 272.

does, having promifed the Governor to anfwer it to the
Spaniard if demanded, becaufe fhe is taken againft the
Treves.[1]   Only the feamen (being of feveral nations) are
divided and quarrel, and will hardly be pacified but by the
weak power of the Ifland, where a General Court is fuddenly called this next (2d) day at Portfmouth.   If you
have any printed relations from England, I fhall thank you
for the fight.   I have received a large and pious letter
from the Lady Vane, (which I will fhortly prefent you
with).   Sir Henry's opinion is, perfecution approaching.
Tis the portion of Chrift Jefus and his to pafs through fuffering to Glory: In Him defirous to be ever yours,

ROGER WILLIAMS.

For Mr. John Winthrop, thefe.

NAR. 9, 10, 49, (fo called,) [NARRAGANSETT, Dec. 10, 1649.][2]

SIR,—Praifed be God for your healths and peace, which
I humbly defire he may pleafe to continue and fanctify to
Himfelf.   Thefe letters Mr. Arnold importuned me to
fend, although by an hired meffenger.   This bearer (although a thief and muft be looked to) is careful, and I
have promifed, upon a note received from you, a pair of

[1] *Treve*, a "truce," or "armiflice." It may be conjectured that the writer refers to the Treaty of Munfter, concluded between Spain and the States-General in 1648.   This Bluefield is probably the Capt. "Blauvelt," a Dutchman, mentioned in O'Callaghan's Hiftory of New Netherland, i. 296, as commander of a privateer upon our coaft a few years before.   See alfo Documents relative to the Colonial Hiftory of the State of New York, i. 397–399.—Ed. *Winthrop Papers.*

[2] 4 *Mafs. Hift. Coll.* vol. vi, p. 273.

breeches. We have here notice of conclufions for the war from Bofton, and preparations of a fet number in each town. Truely, Sir, I have heard little concerning thofe murders by Englifh or natives, but fear that the Lord is kindling fires amongft us. I humbly conceive the cafe of a man murdered need not hazard the Englifh in winter hoftilities, nor the plantations, by the certain and experienced revenges of thofe Dutch Indians, and am confident that within a year's compafs, &c., by filent and watchful courfes, the murderer or murderers may be taken in Englifh towns However, David would rather wink at murderous Joab all his days, then hazard the lofs of more blood for the revenging of fome. At Seekonk a great many have lately concurred with Mr. John Clarke and our Providence men about the point of a new Baptifm, and the manner by dipping: and Mr. John Clarke hath been there lately (and Mr. Lucar) and hath dipped them. I believe their practice comes nearer the firft practice of our great Founder Chrift Jefus, then other practices of religion do, and yet I have not fatisfaction neither in the authority by which it is done, nor in the manner; nor in the prophecies concerning the rifing of Chrift's Kingdom after the defolations by Rome, &c. It is here faid that the Bay hath lately decreed to profecute fuch, and hath writ to Plymouth to profecute at Seekonk, with overtures that if Plymouth do not, &c. Here hath been great bickerings about Bluefield's fhip at Newport, there arrefted by fome of his company, and ordered to be fold and payments made, although he ftand deeply bound to repay all to the Spaniard upon demand, becaufe taken againft the Treves. This fhip and other veffels, and great and fmall ordinance going off, caufed high reports (almoft to my belief as I wrote to you) of some Irish pirates, whom we have cause to fear, and (seeking to God) prepare also for. I have heard of a book from England importing another high case on foot touching a more equal division of lands among brethren, and provision for the younger brethren. I thankfully acknowledge your love concerning my daughter.[1] My wife (here with me) informs me of a course of physic she has entered into with Mr. Clarke[2] of Boston, where she hath been lately, and is better. We are encompassed with motions about her; but neither I nor she can entertain thoughts of so early a marriage. She, as my wife tells me, desires to spend some time in service, and liked much Mrs. Brenton, (who wanted); but I trouble you with such passages, &c. My wife prays a little of your powder for Mrs. Weekes' daughter, of Warwick, who is every winter greatly afflicted by occasion of such obstructions, and breaks forth to lamentable effects. The condition (although the parents offer payment with thanks,) I question not but will prevail with your loving breast, wherein God graciously dwell, as in a palace of his delights. In him I desire to be   Ever yours unfeigned

ROGER WILLIAMS.

Your servant, Post, lay with me two nights, earnestly importuning me to send his thankful remembrance and service.

I am troubled about Nenekunat's hunting, to whom

---

[1] Probably his daughter Mary, who is said to have been born at Plymouth, in August, in 1633, now sixteen years of age.—Eds. *Winthrop Papers.*

[2] Dr. John Clarke, physician of Newbury and Boston, who died in January, 1664–5. A good portrait of him is in the cabinet of the Massachusetts Historical Society.—Eds. *Winthrop Papers.*

Wequafhcook fends threatening of Captain Mafon's vifit. They have importuned me to write to Captain Mafon, which I have done.

On the laft firft day was a great fray between Warwick men and thofe Indians, and blood fpilt, and many cuts and hurts on both fides : who both on the third day fent for me, who went, and (by God's mercy) compofed not only the prefent, but have begun a treaty of full agreement with the natives about their land, if the Bay pleafe.

Sir, my love to Mr. Brewfter,[1] to whom I thought now to write; but by the next if God pleafe.

For the Worfhipful his kind friend Mr. John Winthrop, Efq. at Pequot.

NAR. 16, 12, 49, (fo called.)   [NARRAGANSETT, 16th February, 1649–50.][2]

SIR,—I rejoiced exceedingly from your own loving hand (by Robin Caufafenamont) to receive tidings of your healths after this fharp time. Bleffed be God, who hath provided warm lodging, food, and clothing, and fo feafonable and admirable an element of fire for his poor creatures againft fuch times; the fame bleffed Lord make us learn of his little ants, (Prov. 6.) to provide timely againft eternal bitternefs. *Hoc momentum vnde pendet æternitas.* For expedition I advifed Robin to get over to Rhode Ifland himfelf, which I think he did, but I have not fince heard

---

[1] Jonathan Brewfter, was the eldeft fon of Elder William Brewfter, the diftinguifhed Puritan, who came over in the Mayflower, in 1620.

[2] 4 *Mafs. Hift. Coll.* vol. vi. p. 276.

of him. I am forry for this affliction to Mr. Smith in his daughter's hufband, and we fear Richard Smith his fon, alfo, but hope it will pleafe God to give us tidings of deliverance: however, it is not fafe for duft and afhes to tempt the Moft High in fighting with his winter ftorms without neceffity. I grieve that my dear countrymen of Connecticut are fo troubled with that filthy devil of whorifh practices, and more that yet they are perfuaded of fuch courfes to caft him out. Adultery is a fire which will root out, but the gentiles, the nations of the world, will never be proved capable of fuch laws and punifhments as that holy nation, bred up and fed with miraculous difpenfations, were fit for. Sir, I humbly blefs God that hath vouchfafed you light and power to witnefs againft many evils of your countrymen, to His Honor and yours. As yet we have not tidings from our mother. God mercifully fit us for his holy pleafure in hearing, doing, fuffering, living, dying: He gracioufly guide you and your deareft by his counfel to his glory : So prays

Your unfeigned,

ROGER WILLIAMS.

Mr. Throckmorton is preparing and waiting daily for a reafon to vifit you.

Roger Williams to John Winthrop, Jr.

NAR. 24, 12, 49, (fo called.) [NARRAGANSETT, 24th February, 1649–50.][1]

KIND SIR,—Beſt ſalutations, &c. In my laſt, by Conſider, I forgot a paſſage about that letter to the Commiſſioners which you were pleaſed to take from me. Mr.
Browńe lately told me that he cannot call to mind that
ever it was produced; he conceives, if you forgot not,
that the Preſident did, or that it was ſuppreſſed. I crave
one line about it. Mr. Browne hath often profeſſed liberty
of conſcience, but now the way of new baptiſm ſpreads
at Seekonk as well as at Providence and the Iſland. I
have been ſo bold as to tell him that he perſecutes his ſon
and the people, and on the other ſide Mr. Newman[2] alſo.
Sir, if you have Carpenter's Geography,[3] or other diſcourſe
about the Earth's diurnal motion, ſpare it a little to

Yours moſt unworthy

ROGER WILLIAMS.

Sir, I pray if the Long Iſland man be not gone, aſk for
a book I lent him.

---

[1] 4 *Maſs. Hiſt. Coll.* vol. vi. p. 277.

[2] Samuel Newman, born in England
in 1600, and educated at Oxford. Emigrated to Maſſachuſetts in 1638, and after ſpending ſeveral years at Dorcheſter
and Weymouth, ſettled at Rehoboth,
where he reſided till his death in 1663,
greatly eſteemed for his talents and piety. He compiled a Concordance of the
Bible, which was ſuperior to any that
had before appeared. It was printed in
London in 1643.—BLAKE, *Biog. Dict.*

His deſcendants are ſtill found in Rehoboth and Seekonk.

[3] "Carpenter's Geography." Nathaniel Carpenter born 1588 died 1635,
was an Engliſh clergyman. He wrote
ſeveral volumes conſiſting of ſermons,
philoſophical works and a *Geography De-
lineated*, Oxford, 1625. 4to. 2d edition,
1635.—WATTS, *Bio. Britannica.*

For his honored, kind friend, Mr. John Winthrop, at Pequot.[1]

Sir,—Yours received and sent. I pray in your next a word about Earle's paper; a word of the war againft the natives. I cannot yet get particulars touching Cromwell in Ireland,[2] yet hope ftill that God will honor him, whom I hope he truly defires to honor. I grieve to underftand from your former that Mofes is not underftood in New England, touching what he did to that one nonefuch typical and miraculous people of Ifrael; yet furely, licentioufnefs of all forts needs a fharpe [*torn*] though too fharp, and more then God requires or ever did in all nations equal to Ifrael, is deftrudive, &c. Sir, in hafte

Yours ever unfeigned

ROGER WILLIAMS.

Sir, if you have occafion to deal with Thomas Stanton, or any up to Connedicut for corn of any fort, I pray remember me if it were 500*bll:* I purpofe to write to my old friend Pynchon,[3] and pray you if you have occafion, intimate a word to him.

---

[1] 4 *Mafs. Hift. Coll.* vol. vi. p. 279.
[2] This letter has no date; but the writer, although he had not yet got the "particulars touching Cromwell in Ireland," poffibly had heard rumors of his doings at Drogheda and Wexford, in September and Odober of 1649.—Eds. *Winthrop Papers.*
[3] William Pynchon. See note to letter of Odober 17, 1650.

25

For the worfhipful, his kind friend, Mr. John Winthrop, at Nameug.

NAR. 20, 1, 49. (fo called.)   [20th March, 1649.][1]

SIR,—Loving refpects and beft wifhes to you both, &c.
By Nenekunat I received your laft, relating a found of
more bloody fhowers about Old, and faid trials at our
doors in New. 'Tis mercy that we have not our perfonal
fhares in them, 'tis mercy we are not confumed. The
Father of Lights vouchfafe us fympathifing hearts and prepared to follow the Lamb through all tribulations into
Glory. Nenekunat now with me importunes me to write
this to you, to pray you to take notice of a meffage that
Kaufa Senamon (your Robin lately brought to him from
Connecticut, viz.: that he fhould difcharge and fend to
Long Ifland that young Sachem Taufaquonawhut, who
hath lately married his eldeft daughter, becaufe as Captain
Mafon and the Magiftrates fay, he is a Pequot. He prefents this anfwer to yourfelf, and prays you to prefent it to
the Englifh Sachems as you find occafion. He faith that
this Taufaquonawhut was fought to by Uncas to marry his
daughter, but he not affecting her (becaufe of her fore
eyes) came to his daughter, who falling in love, he, and
the mother, and daughter, and himfelf (Nenekunat) defire
they might live near together, which they do a fmall diftance off. He fays fome bring him word that the Englifh
will divorce them: others that his daughter may follow
him to Long Ifland if fhe will.

He fays that the young man was a child when the Pequot wars were, and had no hand in oppofition, &c. That
he was not the fon of any of thofe Sachems who fought

[1] 4 *Mafs. Hift. Coll.* vol. vi. p. 277.

againft the Englifh, but of Tattaopame, whom the Dutch flew. That his mother alfo is Wequafhcook's wife. That there is no other color of his being hurtful to the Englifh, but by fhowing them kindnefs as they travel by his houfe: which to my knowledge he is free to.

He prays you not to lofe your right, but fend for a fkin of a moofe which was killed upon one of your hummocks by Fifher's Ifland, lately, and carried to Wequafhcook, as the lord.

Sir, I gladly expeft your book, and one of the Parliament's Declarations which I lent the Long Ifland Englifhman who paft hereby in winter.

Sir, I defire to be ever yours unfeigned

ROGER WILLIAMS.

For the worfhipful kind friend Mr. Winthrop, at Pequot.[1]

[No date; probably May, 1650.]

SIR,—Loving refpeEts, &c. Thefe inclofed Mr. Throckmorton yefterday delivered to Mr. He: and Thomas Doxey, two days fince put forth from Newport, but Mɪ. Throckmorton being a league the foremoft, met upon Point Judith with a guft from the fouthweft, which brought

---

[1] 4 *Mafs. Hift. Coll.* vol. vi. p. 279.

The following note from John Elderkin is written upon the fame page, and preceding this letter of Williams, in the original.—Eds. *Wintbrop Papers.*

MR. WILLIAMS,—After my love remembered to you, being thankful to you for your kindnefs to me, when I was with you, this is to entreat you to fend me this letter to Pequot, as fpeedily as you can, and if you be at charges about the fending of it, I willingly will pay you. Your fervant to my power.

JOHN ELDERKIN.

Prov. 12th May, 1650.

him on backſtays, laid his veſſel on one ſide, in much danger, his canoe fell over from him, and was loſt, his oars, &c., but God brought him mercifully ſafe in hither, and Thomas Doxey back to Newport, whither he hath now ſent for his wife and Mrs. Arnold : Benedict[1] having now bought houſe and land at Newport, propoſing thither to remove. Sir, Thomas Doxey told me of your thoughts for England : this bearer, Mr. Thatcher, tells me he ſpake with ſome of the Briſtol ſhips, which ſay that twenty to one are for the Prince throughout the land, and wait for a change of wind, which (if God pleaſe to alter) is doubtleſs like to be very dreadful, yet would I not diſcourage you from liſtening to any evident call of that God who is able to carry whom he ſends, through men and devils. Our Colonies General Court is now at Newport, where (upon a freſh report of wars with France) our Engliſh is in demur of ſuffering the Frenchmen (who came in Bluefield's prize, fluſhed with blood, and have bought a Frigate of Capt. Clarke,) to go out upon their voyage to the Weſt Indies, leaſt they practice their trade upon their own coaſt. Yet one of them having lain with Mr. Amies' daughter, (of Portſmouth,) is like now to marry her. The parents of the Engliſh are troubled greatly. God mercifully bring good out of theſe evils.

Sir, it hath pleaſed God to quicken (by a Dutchman

[1] Benedict Arnold, one of the founders of Providence. His name appears in the town records under date of Auguſt, 1636. The following year he was aſſociated with William Coddington in the purchaſe of the Iſland of Conanicut, and ſigned the firſt compact in 1640. He removed to Newport in 1653, and the following year was choſen an "Aſſiſtant." At the General Election in 1657, he was choſen Preſident, and in 1663 Governor of the Colony, to which office he was annually elected to 1666; again from 1669 to 1672, and from 1677 to 1678. He died on the 20th of June of the latter year. He filled many offices of truſt at various periods, and was one of the moſt prominent men in the colony.

skipper, Lorence, now following fishing here about us,) some English that way, and Bened:[1] desires to buy my shallop and further that work, which I heartily desire (if God so please to favor us) may prosper with you and us. The Natives have taken abundance of sturgeon, and cod, and bass this year. Nawset English (where Mr. Prince is) putting forth seven or eight boats to fish this Spring, by the oversetting of one boat, and loss of two men in the going out of the harbor's mouth, were for the present discouraged. The Lord useth to temper great desires and hopes with such sharps, I hope they will on again. Sir, I want paper, rest yours,

ROGER WILLIAMS.

There is a sound of the Narragansetts warring upon Rhode Island (which thereupon keep watch,) but it is founded on a lie, as I shall inform you.

To Mr. John Winthrop, at Pequot.

[No date. June, 1650.][2]

SIR,—Dear respects to your dear selves and loving sister, rejoicing in your peace, which may well with us (after the Hebrew idiom) comprise the rest, &c. The messenger tells me you have that tidings about Prince Rupert,[3] whose

[1] Probably, Benedict Arnold.
[2] 4 *Mass. Hist. Coll.* vol. vi. p. 281.
[3] Prince Rupert, nephew of Charles I. having been unsuccessful as an officer in the Royal Army, was appointed to the command of the fleet, in which capacity for three years he acquitted himself with honor. In 1651, the great parliamentarian Admiral Blake, attacked the Prince's squadron and sunk or destroyed it. It is doubtless to this reverse in the fortunes of Prince Rupert that Williams refers.

name in thefe parts found as a north-eaft ftorm of fnow.
The Father of Mercies gracioufly avert, or (if he fees
good for us to bring it) fhelter us under the wings of his
mercies, and gather us under them by true humiliation.
Our peace here this laft night founds very uncertain. Indian news have doubtlefs fomething in it, of a hundred
Englifh from the Bay coming to Warwick and the Narraganfett: to Warwick about controverfies between Warwick
men and Mr. Arnold: to Narraganfett for peag. They
tell of their inftant approach. Mr. Throckmorton laft
night from Providence writes that Plymouth men were
lately in great and hot debates about yielding their claim
of thefe parts to the Bay, which, after much heat in vot-
ing, was by a committee caft to the Bay, whence I conjecture they now act.[1] God gracioufly turn it to his praife
however, whatever becomes of our peace. Sir, we have
great caufe to figh at the filthinefs in this land, and alfo at
the unchriftian ways of punifhments. You may pleafe to
remember that I have been large (in the Bloodie Tenent),[2] in the difference between that land of Ifrael and all
others. It is in difcuffing of the model. Mr. Cotton refers the anfwer to the reft of the elders, whofe anfwer or
reply I yet hear not of, and pray you if you do, to intimate. 'Tis a controverfy wherein I am deeply engaged,
of which you will (if God pleafe) fee more. For your-

[1] At the General Court held at Bofton, June 10th, 1650, the commiffioners on the controverfy concerning the title to and jurifdiction of lands on Shawomet, (Warwick) and Pawtuxet made their report. The refult was, that Plymouth relinquifhed to Maffachufetts all claims to the jurifdiction of thefe lands.—*Plymouth Records*, vol. ii. p. 158–159.

[2] Williams's well-known book entitled "*The Bloody Tenent of Perfecution, for the caufe of Confcience, difcuffed, in a conference betweene Truth and Peace*, etc., London, 1644:" and COTTON's "*Reply to Williams's Examination*," etc.—*Pub. Narraganfett Club*, vols. ii. and iii.

felf, dear fir, you do I prefume (as in confcience to God
and man, you can no lefs) propofe your queries to your
friends, of note for authority and ability: whofe anfwers I
fhould thank you to fee. Newton's cafe is imminent: poor
man. God gracioufly arm him againft the laft great trial
approaching, where millions of men and devils number-
lefs would joy eternally to fwone without returning. God
gracioufly fit him and us for that battle by thefe flight vifi-
tations, &c. For Saybroke, fir, you know I rejoice and
mourn: rejoice that the Lord Jefus his name is more
founded, and mourn that not after the firft pattern, in
which I find no Churches extant framed, but all (by a
dreadful fate) oppofing, diffolving, &c., and Perez Uzzah,
the breaches and divifions wonderful. The Portraiture,[1]
I guefs is Bifhop Hall's, the ftyle is pious and acute, very
like his, and J. H. fubfcribes the Epitaph: probably he
prefented thefe paffages to the King in the times of his
reftraint, for he was truly the Bifhop's King and breathed
from firft to laft abfolute Monarchy and Epifcopacy.
Doubtlefs (*viis* and *modis*) he was guilty of much blood.
All that feems weighty in my eye are the popular tumults

---

[1] *Eikon Bafilike. The Portraiture of his facred Majefty, King Charles I. in his Solitudes and Sufferings.* London, 1648. This remarkable book caufed a great fenfation at the time it was pub-lifhed, no lefs than fifty editions, accord-ing to Lowndes, having appeared in 1648–9; and it has been afferted that if it had appeared a week fooner, it might have faved the life of the King. Bifhop Hall was not the author, as Williams furmifes; this honor has been awarded alike to Charles I. and to Bifhop Gau-den. Mr. Wordfworth wrote an elabo-rate work to prove that the King wrote it; while Sir James Mackintofh makes equal efforts to fhow that Dr. Gauden was its author. Mr. Hallam, in fpeak-ing of the Eikon Bafilike fays, "If we could truft its panegyrifts, few books in our language have done it more credit by dignity of fentiment and beauty of ftyle. It can hardly be neceffary for me to exprefs my unhefitating conviction that it was folely written by Bifhop Gau-den, who, after the Reftoration claimed it as his own."—*Literature of Europe.* London: vol. iii. p. 152.

alledged as the artifice of the Parliament : 'Tis true it is a dangerous remedy, yet that which God ufed againft Baal's priefts. The people as well as King, were ftirred up for their death. The people for Jonathan againft King Saul. The people held the Pharifees in awe, thirfting after Chrift's and the Apoftle's blood. Sir, pardon my paper in all its defects, and let me truly mourn that I am not more.

　　Yours unfeigned in Chrift Jefus,

　　　　　　　　　　Roger Williams.

Sir, I am bold to add my mite, &c., thefe enclofed.

Sir, hearing want of pins, I crave Mrs. Winthrop's acceptance of two fmall papers, that if fhe want not herfelf, yet fhe may pleafure a neighbor.

Roger Williams to John Winthrop, Jr.

Nar. 9. 8. 50, (fo called.)　[Narragansett, 9th October, 1650.][1]

Sir,—Beft refpects and love prefented to yourfelf and deareft. My houfe is now filled with foldiers and therefore in hafte I write in an Indian houfe : It hath pleafed God to give me, and the Englifh, and the Natives that were met together and the whole land I believe a gracious deliverance from the plague of war : On the laft day laft came to my houfe Capt. Atherton with above twenty foldiers and three horfes : The Captain requefted me prefently to travel to the Sachems (met together in mourning for Wepiteammock's dead fon within three or four miles of my houfe)

----

[1] 3 *Maſſ. Hiſt. Coll.* vol. ix. p. 289.

and to demand the reft of the pay three hundred and eight fathom :[1] and two hundred more for thefe charges, &c. I went alone and drew them out of the mourning houfe, who anfwered they were ever refolved to pay, but they were diftracted by that peace broke by the Mohegans in that Hoftility begun upon them at Pequot which they anfwered not becaufe of the Englifh ; but expected fatisfaction, but receive none, &c. Yet they refufed not to pay : I returned and the Captain with me went to them and two or three foldiers as was agreed, and after a little difcourfe we agreed in the fame place to meet on the fecond day : We did and all day till night, the Captain demanded the peag or two Sachems, the natives promifed peag within a little time : the Captain would have one or two prefent, and in the evening drew up his men (unknown to me fent for) round about the Sachems in a hole, and the Indians (twenty for one of us) armed and ready with guns and bows about us, the Captain defired me to tell the Sachems he would take by force Nenekunat and Peficcofh ; then I protefted to the Captain before Indians and Englifh, I was betrayed for firft I would not have hazarded life or blood for a little money ; fecond, if my caufe and call were right, I would not be defperate with fo few men to affault Kings in the midft of fuch guards about us, and I had not fo much as knife or ftick about me : After long Agitations upon the ticklifh point of a great flaughter (as all the foldiers now confefs,) the God of mercy appeared. I perfuaded the Captain to ftay at my houfe four days, and the natives within four days to bring in the peag and I would lay down ten fathom : (as formerly I had done twenty (God knows beyond my ability.)

[1]Fathoms of peage.

26

Sir, to-morrow the peag is to come, I hope fuch a quantity as will ftop proceedings: I told the Captain he had defperately betrayed me and himfelf: he tells me he will give me good fatisfaction before he depart: I prefume he fears God in the main, but fear he can never fatisfy me nor his own confcience, which I hope the Lord will fhow him, and fhow the Country what dangerous Councils the Commiffioners produce: which makes me fear God is preparing a War in the Country. Juft now a letter from Rhode Ifland comes for my voyage for England: but as yet I refolve not. God gracioufly be pleafed to fet our affections on another Country and himfelf above in his dear Son.

    Sir, yours in him I defire to be unfeigned

                                    ROGER WILLIAMS.

John Winthrop, Jr., to Roger Williams, in reply to the foregoing.

                                    PEQUOT, November 10, 1650.

    SIR,—I received your letter this morning, and muft write back in hafte, the meffengers being haftily to return, thanking you for the intelligence of this matter, which neither from the Commiffioners or from any of the Government or any other way I have had the leaft intimatiom either by meffage, or letter. I thank you chiefly for your endeavors of bringing the Indians to a peaceable conclufion of matters. The whole country are much obliged to you for your care herein, as formerly for your labors and travails in this kind which they cannot be fo fenfible of, who do not fully underftand the nature and manner of the Indians who are brought to a right [*cet. defunt.*]

    [This fragment feems to be the anfwer of Governor Winthrop to the preceding letter. Upon the back in Governor's W.'s hand,—"Copy of my letter to Mr. Williams in anfwer to his of 8. 9. 49."]

    Gov. Winthrop makes a miftake in the year, which fhould be 1650.—*Ed. Winbrop Papers.*

For his honored, kind friend, Mr. John Winthrop, at Pequot.

Nar. 17. 8. 50. (fo called.) [Narragansett, October 17, 1650.]¹

Kind Sir,—Loving refpects, &c. The Captain's demand was three hundred and eight fathom for the debt, and
two hundred for this expedition. They paid one hundred
and forty, and faid it was the whole, and that the difference
was made by the meafure. They alfo brought two hundred and forty for this Expedition: and upon the Captain's
motion I prevailed with them to fend two natives, with a
petition writ by myfelf to have all cancelled. The Captain promifed to fecond the petition, which they faid your
loving felf and Captain Gibbons and Mr. Stanton had formerly prefented in their behalf.

I was (if not too) warm, infifting on the partiality againft
the Narraganfetts and towards Uncas, and affirmed that Uncas might better fteal many horfes then Wenekunat look
over the hedge. I urged Uncas his villainous dealing
againft your poor town, yourfelf, &c. There is a myftery
in it, of which formerly, Sir, yourfelf and I had fome
hints, and may, if it pleafe the Lord to bring us together
before winter. The Captain told me the bufinefs was defigned by the Commiffioners, and that (as he perceived)
they were refolved to hazard a war upon it, &c. But
praifed be the moft holy, gracious, and only wife, who not
only watched over you and us; but if I miftake not over the
whole country, while the watchmen flept; for to me it is
certain, a war between the Englifh and the Mauquawogs,
or between the Englifh and the Narraganfetts, will, if not
difpoffefs many a planter and difplant plantations; yet haz-

¹ *4 Mafs. Hift. Coll.* vol. vi. p. 283.

ard much blood, and flaughter, and ruin to both Englifh
and Indian ; and when foever this fore plague of God
comes, though upon never fo juft a caufe in the laft way
of remedy and extremity, yet it is one of his three moft
dreadful earthly and temporal judgments upon the children
of men.

Sir, Thomas Doxie came in almoft three weeks fince, he
had no mind for Providence, but ftood away for Martin's
Vineyard, and left a letter for his wife here to meet him, who
came here this day, fome few hours fince from Providence,
but we hear not of Thomas ; fo that the poor woman is
much difconfolate, for to get from Providence fhe was
forced to promife to come back, if Thomas would not
come up ; yet Benedict writes to me and to her here exceeding lovingly. I fear he has gone to Munnadoes to
finifh this voyage with the two Dutchmen with him.
Katherine prefents fervice and prays advice. The Father
of mercies gracioufly blefs thefe trials to her, that it
may be for her good in the latter end, which I fhall (through
his grace) endeavor to further.

Sir, I am your unworthy

ROGER WILLIAMS.

For his honored kind friend Mr. Winthrop, at Pequot, thefe.

[No date; October, 1650.]¹

Sir,—Beft falutation, &c. Yours by Elderkin (who predicates your juft praife in many refpects, &c.,) common, philofophical modern virtue, *laudata crefcit*,—how much more fhould true, heavenly, and eternal? I wrote you largely the iffue of things, and hope you have received, &c. In fum, that the Captain had one hundred and forty fathom for the debt, (which was all, fay the Indians, but three hundred and eight fay the Englifh) alfo two hundred and forty for this charge. A petition I wrote to the Court for the Natives touching the difference, and this bearer, Mr. Caukin, tells me it was accepted in the Court of Deputies (of which he was one). He tells me of a book lately come over in Mr. Pynchon's name,² wherein is fome derogation to the blood of Chrift. The book was therefore burnt in the Market place at Bofton, and Mr. Pynchon to be cited to the Court. If it come to your hand, I may hope to fee it; however the Moft High and only Wife will by this cafe difcover what liberty confcience hath in this land. Sir, as I wrote, Katherine came in hither the day I wrote to feek Thomas Doxey, and he came in the next day after, and the next day to Providence together. She tells me (to give Benedict³ content) fhe let Bened:

¹ 4 *Mafs. Hift. Coll.* vol. vi. p. 284. This letter is without date; but from Mr. Winthrop's endorfement of "Octo. 23," it may be inferred that it was written a few days before.

² William Pynchon fettled at Roxbury, Mafs., in 1630; at Springfield, about 1637, and returned to England in 1652. He was the author of feveral books. The one here alluded to is probably "*The Meritorious Price of Man's Redemption*, etc. London: 1650. It was received in Bofton during the feffion of the General Court in October following, which body ordered the book to be burnt the next day "after the Lecture." A fecond edition was printed in 1655.

³ Benedict Arnold.

write to her uncle: but fhe herfelf writ privately that if anything were fent, it might be in houfehold ftuff. I hope (yet fear) thofe trials may take off Thomas from company, fpending, &c., unto which your help will not be wanting. I think he will bring her to Pequot or Long Ifland. Your tidings of God's renewed mercy again to Cromwell is confirmed: Sir, in his mercy reft you and yours, and in him I defire to be ever yours

ROGER WILLIAMS.

Endorfed by John Winthrop, jr., "Mr. Williams, Octo: 23 :"

For my well-beloved and much refpected, the inhabitants of the Town of Providence.

To Mr. Robert Williams and Mr. Thomas Harris, or either of them.

NAR. 22, 11, 50. (fo called.) [NARRAGANSETT, 22d February, 1651.][1]

WELL BELOVED FRIENDS,—Loving refpects to each of you prefented, with hearty defires of your prefent and eternal peace. I am forry that I am occafioned to trouble you in the midft of many your other troubles, yet upon the experience of your wanted loving-kindnefs and gentlenefs toward all men and myfelf alfo, I pray you hear me patiently. I had propofed to have perfonally attended this Court, and to have prefented, myfelf, thefe few requefts following, but being much lamed and broken with fuch

[1]KNOWLES, *Mem. R. Williams*, p. 402.

travels, I am forced to prefent you in writing thefe five requefts. The firft four concern others living and dead
amongft us; the fifth, concerns myfelf.

Firft, then, I pray be pleafed to review the propofitions
between us and our dead friend, John Smith; and fince it
hath pleafed the God of all mercies, to vouchfafe this town
and others fuch a mercy, by his means, I befeech you uftdy
how to put an end to that controverfy depending between
us and him, (as I may fo fpeak) and his; 'tis true, you
have referred that bufinefs to fome of our loving neighbors
amongft you; but fince there are fome obftruflions, I befeech you put forth your wifdoms, who know more ways
to the wood than one. Eafe the firft, and appoint others,
or fome other courfe, than the dead clamor not from his
grave againft us, but that the country about us may fay,
that Providence is not only a wife, but a grateful people to
the God of mercies, and all his inftruments of mercy towards us.

My fecond requeft concerns the dead ftill. I underftand,
that one of the orphans of our dead friend, Daniel Abbott,[1] is likely (as fhe herfelf told me) to be difpofed of in
marriage. 'Tis true fhe is now come to fome years, but
who knows not what need the poor maid hath of your
fatherly care, counfel and direftion. I would not difpar-
age the young man (for I hear he hath been laborious) yet
with your leave, I might fay, I doubt not you will not give
your daughters in marriage to fuch, whofe lives have been
in fuch a courfe, without fome good affurance and certifi-
cate of his not being engaged to other women, or other-

---

[1] Daniel Abbott, one of the early fet- the firft divifion of lands purchafed by
lers of Providence, whofe name is found Williams from Canonicus and Mianto-
among thofe who received a town lot in nomi.

ways criminous, as alfo of his refolution to forfake his former courfe, left (this enquiry being neglected) the maid and ourfelves repent when mifery hath befallen her, and a juft reproof and charges befall ourfelves, of which we have no need.

For, thirdly, I crave your confideration of that lamentable object (what fhall I fay, of all our cenfure or pity, I am fure) of all our wonder and aftonifhment, Mrs. Wefton.[1] My experience of the diftempers of perfons elfewhere, makes me confident, that although not in all things, yet in a great meafure, fhe is a diftracted woman. My requeft is, that you would be pleafed to take what is left of hers into your own hands, and appoint fome to order it for her fupply, and if it may be, let fome public act of mercy to her neceffities, ftand upon record amongft the merciful acts of a merciful town, that hath received many mercies from heaven, and remember that we know not how foon our wives may be widows, and our children orphans, yea, and ourfelves be deprived of all or moft of our reafon, before we go from hence, except mercy from the God of mercies prevent it.

Fourthly. Let me crave your patience, while once more I lead your confideration to the grave, amongft the dead, the widows and the fatherlefs. From fome neighbors and the widow Mann[2] herfelf, I underftand, that notwithftanding her motherly affection, which will make all burthens lighter for her children's good, yet fhe is not without fears, that if the town be not favorable to her in after times, fome

---

[1] Mrs. Wefton, probably the widow of Francis or Mathew Wefton, both of whom received original town lots as above.

[2] Widow Man, whofe hufband William Man received one of the original town lots.

hard meafure and preffures may befall her. My requeft is, therefore, that it would pleafe you to appoint fome of your-felves to review the will, and to confider whether the pains of the father, deceafed, or want of time, hath not occa-fioned him to leave fome of his purpofes and defires im-perfect, as alfo to propofe to the town wherein, according to the rules of juftice and mercy, what the deceafed in-tended, may be perfected, for the greater comfort both of his widow and orphans.

Fifth. My laft requeft concerns myfelf. I cannot be fo unthankful to you, and fo infenfible of mine own and fami-ly's comfort, as not to take notice of your continued and conftant love and care in your many public and folemn or-ders for the payment of that money due unto me about the charter : 'tis true I have never demanded it ; yea, I have been truly defirous that it might have been laid out for fome further public benefit in each town, but obferving your loving refolution to the contrary, I have at laft re-folved to write unto you (as I have alfo lately done to Portfmouth and Newport) about the better ordering it to my advantage. I have here (through God's providence) convenience of improving fome goats; my requeft is, therefore, that if it may be without much trouble, you would pleafe to order the payment of it in cattle of that kind. I have been folicited and have promifed my help, about iron works, when the matter is ripe, earneftly de-firous every way to further the good of the town of Provi-dence, to which I am fo much engaged, and to yourfelves the loving inhabitants thereof, to whom I defire to be

Your truly loving and ever faithful,

ROGER WILLIAMS.

27

To Mr. John Winthrop, Jr.

[Auguſt, 1651.][1]

SIR,—Loving reſpects to you both, with Mrs. Lake and yours   By this opportunity I am bold to inform you, that from the Bay I hear of the ſentence on Mr. Clarke,[2] to be whipt or pay twenty pounds, Obadiah Holmes whipt or

---

[1] 3 *Maſs. Hiſt. Coll.* vol. ix. p. 291; KNOWLES' *Mem. R. Williams*, p. 241.

[2] The tranſaction here referred to, ſhowing the vigor with which the famous law of 1644, levelled oſtenſibly againſt Ana-baptiſts, was executed, is ſo remarkable, that it deſerves more than a paſſing notice.

It appears that the Rev. John Clarke, one of Rhode Iſland's moſt diſtinguiſhed men, with Obadiah Holmes and John Crandall were deputed by the Baptiſt Church in Newport, to viſit William Witter, an aged member of that church, living at Lynn, at his requeſt   The next day being Sunday, it was thought proper to ſpend it in religious worſhip at Mr. Witter's houſe, about two miles from the town.   In the midſt of Mr. Clarke's ſermon, "two conſtables entered, who, by their clamorous tongues" writes Mr. Clarke, "made an interruption in my diſcourſe, and more uncivilly diſturbed us than the purſuivants of the old Engliſh biſhops were wont to do, telling us they were come with authority from the magiſtrate to apprehend us.   I deſired to ſee the authority by which they proceeded, whereupon they plucked forth their warrant and read it to us: the ſubſtance whereof was as followeth :"

"By virtue hereof you are required to go to the houſe of William Witter, and ſo ſearch from houſe to houſe, for

certain erroneous perſons, being ſtrangers, and them to apprehend, and in ſafe cuſtody to keep, and to-morrow morning bring them before me." ROBERT BRIDGES.

The conſtables carried Mr. Clarke and his companions to the Congregational meeting.   At the cloſe of the ſervice Mr Clarke roſe and addreſſed the aſſembly, but was ſpeedily ſilenced, and the next day the three "heretics" were committed to priſon in Boſton.   A few days after they were tried before a Court of Aſſiſtants, and Mr. Clarke was ſentenced to pay a fine of £20, Mr. Holmes £30, and Mr. Crandall £5 ; or, in default of payment, each was to be whipped. They refuſed to pay the fine, as it would be an acknowledgment of guilt, and were accordingly committed to priſon.

On the trial Mr. Clarke defended himſelf and his companions ſo ably, that the Court were ſomewhat embarraſſed. "At length," ſays Mr. Clarke "the Governor [John Endicott] ſtepped up and told us we had denied infant baptiſm, and being ſomewhat tranſported, told me I had deſerved death, and ſaid he would not have ſuch traſh brought into their juriſdiction."

From the priſon Mr. Clarke ſent to the Court a propoſition to meet with any of the miniſters, and hold a public diſcuſſion.   This propoſal was at firſt accepted and a day fixed ; but the clergy probably thought that a public debate

thirty pounds, on John Crandall, whipt or five pounds. This bearer hears of no payment nor execution, but rather a demur, and fome kind of conference. The Father of Lights gracioufly guide them and us in fuch paths; for other fuccor than that (in his mouth) Chrift Jefus walks not among the churches, (Rev. 1.) Sir, upon thofe provocations that lately (as in my laft I hinted) Auguontis gave the Sachems, Ninigret, Pitammock and Peficcofh, went in perfon to their town, (Chaubutick) and upon Pummakommins telling the Sachems that he was as great a Sachem as they, they all fell together

about infant baptifm with fo able an antagonift would be inexpedient. Mr. Clarke's fine was paid without his knowledge or confent, and he was releafed from prifon. Mr. Crandall was alfo releafed on condition of appearing at the next Court. Before leaving, Mr. Clarke left a declaration with the magiftrates, that he would be ready at any time, to vifit Bofton and maintain his fentiments.

Mr. Holmes was kept in prifon till the Court met in September, and then, after their public lecture in Bofton, the fentence of the Court was executed on him with fuch feverity that for a confiderable time, he could take no reft, except by fupporting himfelf on his knees and elbows.

Backus, prints a letter from Holmes giving a full account of his cafe, and the particulars of the manner in which the whipping was inflicted upon him. He alfo gives the propofitions which Clarke fubmitted to the Court for difcuffion, with the reply of the Governor and Council.—*Hiftory of the Baptifts*, vol. i. pp. 229–238.

John Spur and John Hazel, the latter an aged man, a friend and neighbor of Holmes, from Rehoboth, who had travelled fifty miles to fee him, were arrefted, imprifoned and fined for expreffing fympathy for Clarke and his affociates.

"The recital of thefe tranfactions" writes Knowles "is painful, but we muft compel ourfelves to contemplate fuch fcenes, if we would fuitably feel the contraft between the policy of Maffachufetts at that day, and the tolerant principles of Roger Williams. To that policy it muft be afcribed, that wife and good men could thus treat their fellow Chriftians." *Memoir of Roger Williams*, p. 244.

Much more might be faid of thefe ftrange tranfactions, did fpace admit. They are fully treated of by BACKUS in his *Hiftory of the Baptifts*, and by KNOWLES in his *Memoir of Williams*; alfo by John Clarke himfelf in his "*Ill Newes from New England; or, a Narrative of New England's Perfecution*." London: 1652.

by the ears; yet no blood fpilt.   The Chaubatick Indians fend to the Bay; they fay Auguontis is fent for and
Ninigret, but I know no certain other than meffengers
paffing to and again from Chaubatick to the Bay.   Here
was laft week Mr. Sellick, of Bofton, and Mr. Gardiner,
a young merchant, to fetch my corn, and more, from Mr.
Paine, of Seekonk; they are bound to the French, unlefs
diverted.   They tell me of a fhip of three hundred, come
from Barbadoes.   Mr. Wall, the mafter, ftood upon his
guard while he ftaid there; he brought fome paffengers,
former inhabitants from London, whofe cafe was fad there,
becaufe of the pofture of the ifland (where as I have by
letter from a godly friend there) they force all to fwear
to religion and laws.   This Mr. Wall hath a new and
great defign, viz.: from hence to the Eaft Indies.   The
frigates defigned for Barbadoes were ordered for Scilly,
which they affaulted, and took forts and ordnance and frigates, and drove the Governor into his laft fort.   It hath
pleafed God to bring your ancient acquaintance and mine,
Mr. Coddington, in Mr. Carwithy his fhip of five hundred; he is made Governor of this colony for his life.
General Cromwell was not wounded nor defeated, (as is
faid) but fick of flux and fever, and mending, and had a
victory over the Scots.   Sir, this world paffeth away and
the (σχημα) fafhion, fhape and form of it, only the word of
Jehovah remains   That word literal is fweet, as it is the
field where the myftical word or treafure, Chrift Jefus, lies
hid.   HIn im I hope to be yours,

ROGER WILLIAMS.

Sir, to Mr. Blindman loving falutations.

For his honored, kind friend, Mr. John Winthrop, at Pequot.

[No date; probably August 1651.][1]

Sir,—Loving refpects, &c. Yours received and the 10*s.* from your neighbor Elderkin, and letters, which fhall carefully be fent. I came from Providence laft night, and was able, by God's merciful providence, fo to order it, that I was their pilot to my houfe here, from whence I have provided a native, who, with Jofeph Foffeker, I hope will bring them fafe to you. The merciful Lord help you and me to fay, as Solomon, all that comes is vanity : all cattle, all goods, all friends, all children, &c. I met Mr. John Clarke, at Providence, *recens. e carcere.* There was great hammering about the difputation, but they could not hit, and although (my much lamented friend) the Governor told him, that he was worthy to be hanged, &c., yet he was as good as thruft out without pay or whipping, &c. ; but Obadiah Holmes remains. Mr. Carwithy is gone with his fhip to the eaftward for mafts, and returns, three weeks hence, to fet fail for England, Sir, I have a great fuit to you, that at your leifure you would fit and fend fomething that you find fuitable to thefe Indian bodies, in way of purge or vomit ; as alfo, fome drawing plafter, and if the charge rife to one or two crowns, I fhall thankfully fend it ; and commending you and yours to the only great and good Phyfician,[2] defire, Sir, to be ever

Yours in Him,

Roger Williams.

---

[1] Knowles' *Mem. Roger Williams,* p. 243 ; 3 *Mafs. Hift. Coll.* vol. xi. 293. [2] Mr. Winthrop had confiderable fkill in medicine. The benevolent zeal of Mr. Williams for the welfare of the Indians, fhows itfelf on all occafions.

*The copy of a letter of Roger Williams, of Providence, in New
   England, to Major Endicot, Governor of the Maffachufetts,
   upon occafion of the late perfecution againft Mr. Clarke and
   Obadiah Holmes, and others, at Bofton, the chief town of the
   Maffachufetts in New England.*

Auguft, 1651.[1]

SIR,—Having done with our tranfitory earthly affairs
(as touching the Englifh and the Indians) which in com-
parifon of heavenly and eternal, you will fay are but as
dung and drofs, &c.   Let me now be humbly bold to remember that humanity and piety, which I and others have
formerly obferved in you, and in that hopeful remembrance to crave your gentle audience with patience and
mildnefs, with ingenuity, equanimity and candor, to him
that ever truly and deeply loved you and yours, and as in
the awful prefence of His holy eye, whofe dreadful hand
hath formed us to the praife of His mercy or juftice to all
eternity.

Sir, I have often feared and faid within my foul, have I
fo deeply loved and refpected?   Was I alfo fo well beloved?   Or was all counterfeit, and but gilded o'er with
earthly refpects, wordly ends, &c.   Why am I filent? my
letters are not banifhed! may be welcome, may be feen
and heard, and if neither, yet will back again (together
with my prayers and cries) into my bofom·

Thus while I have fometimes mufed and refolved! objections, obftructions, and a thoufand hindrances (I fear
from Satan as Paul faid) hath preffed in, held my hand, &c.

Sir, it hath pleafed the Father of Spirits at this prefent

---

[1] ROGER WILLIAMS. *The Bloody Tenent yet More Bloody.* London, 1652, p. 303.

to fmite my heart in the very breaking up of your letter : This Death's Head[1] tells that loving hand that fealed it, and mine that opens your letter, that our eyes, our hands, our tongues, our brains are flying hence to the hole or pit of rottennefs : Why fhould not therefore fuch our letters, fuch our fpeeches, fuch our actings be, as may become our laft minutes, our death-beds, &c.

If fo, how meek and humble, how plain and ferious, how faithful and zealous, and yet how tender and loving fhould the fpirits and fpeeches be of dying and departing men?

Sir, while fomething of this nature I mufe over your Death's head, I meet (in the entrance of your letter) with this paffage, " *Were I as free in my fpirit as formerly I have been to write unto you, you fhould have received another manner of Salutation then now with a good Confcience I can Exprefs ; However God knoweth who are his, and what he is pleafea to hide from finful man in this life, fhall in that great Day be manifefted to All.*"

Sir, at the reading of this line, (I cannot but hope I have your leave to tell you.) The fpeech of that wife woman of Tekoah unto David came frefh unto my thoughts : Speaks not the King this thing as one that is guilty? For will my honored and beloved friend not know me for fear of being difowned by his confcience? Shall the goodnefs and integrity of his confcience to God caufe him to forget me? Doth he quiet his mind with this; [*God* knoweth who are his? *God* hides from finful man, *God* will reveal before All?] Oh how comes it then that

---

[1] Endicott's feal was a death's head and crofs-bones, with the name of John Gar-vad in a circle around it. A fac-fimile is given in 4 *Mafs. Hift. Coll.* vi. Appendix ii.

I have heard fo often, and heard fo lately, and heard
fo much, that he that fpeaks fo tenderly for his own, hath
yet fo little refpect, mercy or pity to the like confcientious
perfuafions of other men?   Are all the thoufands of millions of millions of confciences, at home and abroad, fuel
only for a prifon, for a whip, for a ftake, for a gallows?
Are no confciences to breathe the air, but fuch as fuit and
fample his?   May not the moft High be pleafed to hide
from his as well as from the eyes of his fellow-fervants,
fellow-mankind, fellow-Englifh?   And if God hide from
his, from any, who can difcover?   Who can fhut when he
will open? and who can open when he that hath the key
of David will fhut?   All this and more (honored Sir) your
words will warrant me to fay, without any juft offence or
ftraining.

  Object.   But what makes this to Heretics, Blafphemers,
Seducers, to make them that fin againft their confcience (as
Mr. Cotton fayth) after conviction?   What makes this to
ftabbers of Kings and Princes, to blowers up of Parliaments out of confcience?

  Firft, I anfwer, He was a tyrant that put an innocent
man into a bear's fkin, and fo caufed him as a wild beaft
to be baited to death.

  Secondly, I fay this is the common cry of Hunters or
perfecutors [heretics, heretics, blafphemers, &c.,] and why,
but for croffing the perfecutors confciences, (it may be but
their fuperftitions, &c.,) whether Turkifh, Popifh, Proteftant, &c.

  This is the outcry of the Pope and Prelates, and of the
Scotch Prefbyterians, who would fire all the world, to be
avenged on the fectarian Heretics, the blafphemous Heretics, the feducing Heretics, &c., had it not pleafed the

God of Heaven who bounds the infolent rage of the furious ocean, to raife up a fecond Cromwell (like a mighty and merciful wall or bulwark) to ftay the fury of the oppreffor, whether Englifh, Scottifh, Popifh, Prefbyterian, Independent, &c.

Laftly, I have faid much and lately, and given particular anfwers to all fuch pleas, in my Second Reply or Anfwer to Mr. Cotton's wafhing of the Bloody Tenent in the Lamb's blood, which it may be is not yet come to your fight and hand.

'Tis true, I have to fay elfewhere about the caufes of my banifhment: as to the calling of natural men to the exercife of thofe holy Ordinances of prayers, oaths, &c. As to the frequenting of Parifh Churches, under the pretence of hearing fome Minifters: As to the matter of the Patent, and King James his Chriftianity and Title to thefe parts, and beftowing it on his fubjects by virtue of his being a Chriftian King, &c.

At prefent, let it not be offenfive in your eyes, that I fingle out another, a fourth point, a caufe of my banifhment alfo, wherein I greatly fear one or two fad evils, which hath befallen your Soul and Confcience.[1]

The point is that of the civil Magiftrates dealing in matters of Confcience and Religion, as alfo of perfecuting and hunting any for any matter merely Spiritual and Religious.

---

[1] *Mr. Cotton's Letter examined and answered*, pp. 4, 5. *Pub. Narr. Club*, i: 40, 41. Cotton gives his verfion of the caufes of Williams' banifhment in his *Anfwer* 27–31. *Pub. Narr. Club*, ii. 44–52. He fays, "It is evident the two latter caufes which he giveth of his Banifh- ment," the fecond and fourth named above, "were no caufes at all, as he expreffeth them. There are many knowne to hold both thefe opinions, and yet they are tolerated not only to live in the Commonwealth, but alfo in the fellowfhip of the Churches."

The two evils intimated are thefe : Firft, I fear you can not after fo much Light, and fo much profeffion to the contrary (not only to myfelf, and fo often in private, but) before fo many witneffes ; I fay, I fear you cannot fay and act fo much, againft fo many feveral Confciences, former and later, but with great checks, great threatenings, great blows and throws of inward confcience.

Secondly, If you fhall thank God, that it is not fo with you, but that you do what Confcience bids you in God's prefence, upon God's warrant, I muft then be humbly faithful to tell you, that I fear your underprizing of holy Light, hath put out the candle, and the eye of confcience in thefe particulars, and that delufions, ftrong delufions, and that from God (by Satan's fubtleties) hath feized upon your very Soul's belief, becaufe you prized not, loved not the endangered perfecuted Son of God in his defpifed truths and fervants.

Sir, with man (as the Lord Jefus faid of the rich man) I know it is impoffible for the (otherwife piercing eye) of your underftanding to fee into thefe things, for it is difcolored, as in fome difeafes and glaffes. It is impoffible for your Will to be willing to fee, for that's in a thoufand chains refolved (as once you fpake heroically and heavenly in a better way) to fpend your deareft heart's blood in your way, &c. Yet with God all things are poffible, and they that laughed the Lord Jefus to fcorn when he faid, the Damfel is not dead but fleepeth, were afterwards confounded, when they faw her raifed by his heavenly voice.

His holy pleafure I know not, nor do I know which way the Glory of his great Name will more appear, either in finally fuffering fo great a fall and ruin of fo ftrong a pillar, that flesh may not Glory, but that his strength and glory only may be seen in weakness. Or else in your holy rising and reviving from the bed of so much spiritual filthiness, and from so bloody a mind, and lip, and hand, against all withstanders or disturbers in it. That so the short remainder of your candle may hold out to the world, the riches of His mercy, at whose word the holiest of his servants ought to tremble, and to work out their salvation with fear and trembling : I say, I desire to say it, tremblingly and mournfully (I know not which way He will please to raise His glory) only I know my duty, my conscience, my love, all which enforce me to knock to call, to cry at the Gate of Heaven, and at yours, and to present you with this loving, though loud and faithful noise and sound of a few grounds of deeper examination of both our Souls and Consciences uprightly and impartially at the holy and dreadful tribunal of Him that is appointed the Judge of all the Living and the Dead.

Be pleased then (honored Sir) to remember that, that thing which we call Conscience is of such a nature, (especially in Englishmen) as once a Pope of Rome at the suffering of an Englishman in Rome, himself observed) that although it be groundless, false, and deluded, yet it is not by any arguments or torments easily removed.

I speak not of the stream of the multitude of all nations, which have their ebbings and flowings in religion, (as the longest sword, and strongest arm of flesh carries it.) But I speak of Conscience, a persuasion fixed in the mind and heart of a man, which enforceth him to judge (as Paul said of himself a persecutor) and to do so and so, with respect to God, his worship, &c.

This Conscience is found in all mankind, more or less,

in Jews, Turks, Papifts, Proteftants, Pagans, &c. And to this purpofe let me freely without offence remember you (as I did Mr. Clarke newly come up from his fufferings amongft you) I fay, remember you of the fame ftory I did him, 'twas that of William Hartley,[1] in Queen Elizabeth her days, who receiving the fentence of hanging, drawing, &c., fpake confidently (as afterward he fuffered) what tell you me of hanging, &c. If I had ten thoufand millions of lives, I would fpend them all for the Faith of Rome, &c.

Sir, I am far from glancing the leaft countenance on the Confciences of Papifts, yea or on fome Scotch and Eng-lifh Proteftants too, who turn up all roots, and lay all level and in blood, for exaltation of their own way and Con-fcience. All that I obferve is, that boldnefs and confidence, zeal and refolution, as it is commendable in a kind when it ferioufly refpects a Deity, fo alfo, the greateft confidence hath fometimes need of the greateft fearch and exami-nation.

I confefs, that for confidence no Romifh Prieft, hath ever exceeded the martyrs or witneffes of Jefus: Witnefs (amongft fo many) that holy Englifh woman, who cried out, that if every hair of her head were a life or man, they fhould burn for the name of the Lord Jefus: But Sir, your principles and confcience, not to refpect Romifh or Englifh, faints or finners: William Hartley, and that Wo-man, with all their lives, you are bound by your Con-

---

[1] William Hartley was of St. John's College, Oxford, and a Roman Catholic Prieft. When Champian, the Jefuit emiffary, came to England in 1580, Hart-ley engaged in diftributing one of his books. He was imprifoned, and being releafed in 1584, left the Kingdom.— Wood, *Athenæ Oxonienfis,* i. p. 474. Note by Dr. CALDWELL, *Pub. Narr. Club,* iv. p. 509.

science to punish (and it may be) to hang or burn, if they transgress against your Conscience, and that because (according to Mr. Cotton's monstrous distinction (as some of his chief brethren to my knowledge hath called it) not because they sin in matters of Conscience, (which he denies the Magistrate to deal in,) but because they sin against their Conscience.

Secondly, It is so notoriously known, that the Consciences of the most holy men, zealous for God and his Christ to death and admiration, yea, even in our own country, and in Queen Mary's days especially, have been so grossly mislead by mistaken Consciences in matters concerning the worship of God, the coming out of the Antichristian Babel, and the rebuilding of the spiritual Jerusalem that I need but hint who were they that penned the Common Prayer (in its time, as glorious an idol, and as much adored by Godly persons, as any invention now extant.) I say who they were that lived and died (five in the flames) zealous for their Bishopricks, yea, and some too too zealous for their Popish ceremonies, against the doubting Consciences of their Brethren : At which and more, we that now have risen in our Father's stead, wonder and admire how such piercing eyes could be deceived, such Watchmen blinded and deluded. But

Thirdly, We shall not so much wonder when we lift up our trembling eyes to Heaven, and remember ourselves (poor dust) that our thoughts are not as the thoughts of our Maker, that, that which in the eyes of man (as the Lord Jesus tells us, Luc. 16.) is of high and sweet esteem, it stinks and is abomination with God : Hence such Worships, such Churches, such glorious professions and practices may be, as may ravish themselves and the beholders, when with the piercing eyes of the moſt High, they may look counterfeit and ugly, and be found but (ſpiritually) Whores and Abominations.

Fourthly, Wiſe men uſed to enquire, what Motives, what Occaſions, what Snares, what Temptations were there, which moved, which drew, which allured, &c. This is the Apology which the five Apologiſts (Mr. Goodwin, Mr. Nye, &c.,) made to the Parliament, to wit, That they were not tempted with the moulding of New Commonwealths, after which they might be moved to frame their religion, &c.[1]

Surely, Sir, the baits, the temptations, the ſnares laid to catch you, were not few, nor common, nor laid to every foot. Saul pretended zeal to the name of God, and love to Iſrael in perſecuting the poor Gibeonites to death, but honor me before the people, was the main engine that turned the wheels of all his actions and devotions. What ſet Jeroboam's brains to conſult and plot the invention of a new Religion, Worſhip, Prieſts, &c., but honor, and the fear of the loſs of his gained honor? What moved Jehu to be falſe and halting with God after ſo much glorious zeal in the Reformation? Yea, I had almoſt ſaid, what moved David to ſtab Uriah (the fire of God) with his pen, but the fear of diſhonor in the diſcovery of his ſin, though doubtleſs there was ſome mixtures of the fear of his God's diſpleaſure and diſhonor, alſo?

Sir, it is no ſmall offer, the choice and applauſe and rule

---

[1] The five apologiſts, Thomas Goodwin, Philip Nye, Sidrach Simpſon, Jeremiah Burroughs and William Bridge, prepared *An Apologetical Narration* to Parliament in 1643. In 1644, Williams publiſhed his *Queries of Higheſt Conſideration*, propoſed to theſe perſons and to the Scotch Commiſſioners in the Weſtminſter Aſſembly.—Note by Dr. CALDWELL, *Pub. Narr. Club,* iv. p. 511.

over fo many towns, fo many holy, of many wife, in fuch
a holy way as you believe you are in : To fay nothing of
ftrong drinks and wines, the fat and fweet of this and other
lands : Thefe and others are fnares which without abundant ftrength from God will catch and hold the ftrongeft
feet : Sir, I have known you ftrong, in repelling ftrong
temptations, but I cannot but fear and lament, that fome
of thefe and others have been too ftrong and potent for you.

Fifthly, We not only ufed to fay proverbially, but the
Spirit of God expreffly tells. us, that there is a mind-be-
witching, a bewitching of the very confciences and fpirits
of men. That as in witchcraft, a ftronger and fupernatu-
ral power lays hold upon the powers of Nature, with a fup-
preffing or elevating of those powers beneath or above
themfelves : So is it with the very Spirits and Confciences
of the moft intelligent and confcientious, when the Father
of Spirits is pleafed in his righteous difpleafure and jealoufly, fo to fuffer it to be with ours.

Sir, I from my Soul honor and love the perfons of fuch,
whom I, you, and themfelves may fee have been inftrumental in your bewitching. Why fhould it be thought
inconfiftent with the holy wifdom of God, to permit wife
and holy and learned perfons to wander themfelves and
miflead others; when the holy Scripture and experience
tells us of the dangerous counfels and ways of as wife and
learned and holy as now breathe in either Old or New
Englifh air ?

Sir, I had thought to have named one or two, who may
juftly be fufpected (though otherwife worthily beloved) but
I have chofe rather to prefent an hint, for that is enough
for fo intelligent a breaft, if but willing to make an impartial review and examination of paffages between the moft
High and your inmoft Soul in fecret.

Therefore, sixthly, for a fixed ground of suspecting your Soul and Spirit and Conscience in this particular of persecution, which I now instance in, may you please, Sir, without offence to remember, that as it is in such as have exceeded in Wine, their speech will betray them : So is it in Spiritual cups and intoxications.

The Maker and Searcher of our hearts knows with what bitterness I write, as with bitterness of Soul I have heard such language as to proceed from yourself and others, who formerly have fled from (with crying out against persecutors ! [you will say, this is your conscience: You will say, you are persecuted, and you are persecuted for your Conscience : No you are Conventiclers, Heretics, Blasphemers, Seducers : You deserve to be hanged, rather than one shall be wanting to hang him I will hang him myself: I am resolved not to leave an heretic in the country ; I had rather so many whores and whoremongers and thieves came amongst us:] Oh Sir, you cannot forget what language and dialect this is, whether not the same unfavored, and ungodly, blasphemous and bloody, which the Gardiner's and Bonner's both former and latter used to all that bowed not to the State golden Image of what Conscience soever they were. And indeed, Sir, if the most High be pleased to awaken you to render unto his holy Majesty his due praises, in your truly broken-hearted Confessions and Supplications, you will then proclaim to all the world, that what profession soever you made of the Lamb, yet these expressions could not proceed from the Dragon's mouth.

Oh remember, and the most holy Lord, bring it to your remembrance, that you have now a great price in your hand, to bring great Glory to his holy Name, great rejoicing to so gracious a Redeemer (in whom you profess is all

your healing and Salvation) great rejoicing to the holy
Spirit of all true confolation, whom yet fo long you who have
grieved and fadded, great rejoicing to thofe bleffed Spirits
(attending upon the Lamb, and all his, and terrible to his
perfecutors) great rejoicing and inftruction to all that love
the true Lord Jefus (notwithftanding their wanderings
among fo many falfe Chrifts) mourning and lamenting
after him in all parts of the world where his name is
founded: Your Talents are great, your Fall hath been fo:
Your Eminence is great, the Glory of the moft High in
mercy or juftice toward you will be great alfo.

Oh remember it is a dangerous combat for the potfheards
of the earth to fight with their dreadful Potter: It is a
difmal battle for poor naked feet to kick againft the Pricks;
It is a dreadful voice from the King of Kings, and Lord of
Lords: Endicot, Endicot, why hunteft thou me? why im-
prifoneft thou me? why fineft, why fo bloodily whippeft,
why wouldeft thou (did not I hold thy bloody hands)
hang and burn me? Yea, Sir, I befeech you remember
that it a dangerous thing to put this to the may be, to the
venture or hazard, to the poffibility. If it poffible (may
you well fay) that fince I hunt, I hunt not the life of my
Saviour, and the blood of the Lamb of God. I have
fought againft many feveral forts of Confciences, is it beyond all poffibility and hazard, that I have not fought
againft God, that I have not perfecuted Jefus in fome of
them?

Sir, I muft be humbly bold to fay, that 'tis impoffible
for any man or men to maintain their Chrift by their
fword, and to worfhip a true Chrift! to fight againft all
Confciences oppofite to theirs, and not to fight againft God
in fome of them, and to hunt after the precious life of the

29

true Lord Jefus Chrift. Oh remember whether your Principles and Confciences muft in time and opportunity force you. 'Tis but worldly policy and compliance with men and times (God's mercy overruling) that holds your hands from murdering of thoufands and ten thoufands were your power and command as great as once the bloody Roman Emperors was.

The truth is (and yourfelf and others have faid it) by your principles fuch whom you count Heretics, Blafphemers, Seducers, to be put to death; you cannot be faithful to your principles and Confciences, if you fatisfy them with but imprifonment, fining, whipping and banifhing the Heretics, and by faying that banifhing is a kind of death, as fome chief with you (in my cafe formerly) have faid it.

Sir, 'Tis like you knew or have heard of the man that faid he would never conform publicly, although he did fubfcribe in private for his liberty fake of Preaching: That, although he did conform in fome things, yet in all he never would: That; although he did himfelf yield, yet he would not moleft and enforce others: That although he yielded, that others did moleft them, yet himfelf would never perfecute, and yet did all.

But oh poor duft and afhes, like ftones once rolling down the Alps, like the Indian canoes or Englifh boats loofe and adrift, where ftop we until infinite mercy ftop us, efpecially when a falfe fire of zeal and Confidence drives us, though againft the moft Holy and eternal himfelf?)

Oh remember the black Catalogues it hath pleafed the moft jealous and righteous God to make of his fiery Judgments and moft dreadful ftrokes on eminent and remarkable perfecutors even in this life. It hath been his way and courfe in all countries, in Germany, France and England, (efpecially) whatever their pretences have been againft Heretics, Rebels, Schifmatics, Blafphemers, Seducers, &c. How hath he left them to be their own Accufers, Judges, Executioners, fome by hanging, fome by ftabbing, fome by drowning and poifoning themfelves, fome by running mad, and fome by drinking in the very fame cup which they had filled to others?

Some may fay, fuch perfecutors hunted God and Chrift, but I, but we, &c. I anfwer, the Lord Jefus Chrift fore-told how wonderfully the wifeft of the world, fhould be miftaken in the things of Chrift, and a true vifible Chrift Jefus! When did we fee thee naked, hungry, thirfty, fick, in prifon, &c. How eafy, how common, how dreadful thefe miftakes?

Oh remember once again (as I began) and I humbly de-fire to remember with you, that every gray hair now on both our heads, is a Boanerges, a fon of Thunder, and a warning piece to prepare us, for the weighing of our laft anchors, and to be gone from hence, as if we had never been.

'Twas mercy infinite, that ftopped provoked Juftice from blowing out our Candles in our youths, but now the feed-ing Subftance of the Candles gone, and 'tis impoffible without repentance,) to recall our actions! nay with re-pentance, to recall our minutes paft us.

Sir, I know I have much prefumed upon your many weighty affairs and thoughts, I end with an humble cry to the Father of mercies, that you may take David's counfel, and filently commune with your own heart upon your bed, reflect upon your own fpirit, and believe Him that faid it to his over zealous difciples, You know not what fpirit you are of: That, no fleep may feize upon your eyes, nor flumber upon your eyelids, until your ferious thoughts have ſeriouſly, calmly, and unchangeably (through help from Chriſt Jeſus) fixed.

Firſt, On a moderation towards the Spirits and Con-ſciences of all mankind, merely differing from or oppoſing yours with only Religious and Spiritual oppoſition.

Secondly, A deep and cordial reſolution (in theſe won-derful ſearching, diſputing and diſſenting times)to ſearch, to liſten, to pray, to faſt, and more fearfully, more trembling-ly to enquire what the holy pleaſure, and the holy myſte-ries of the moſt Holy are; in whom I humbly deſire to be

  Your poor fellow-servant, unfeignedly,
    reſpective and faithful,

      Roger Williams.

For his honored, kind friend, Mr. John Winthrop, at Pequot.

  Narragansett, 6. 8. 51. (ſo called.)　[6th October, 1651.][1]

Sir,—Once more my loving and dear reſpects preſented to you both, and Mrs. Lake. Being now bound, reſolvedly, (if the Lord pleaſe) for our native country, I am not certain whether by the way of the Engliſh, (you know the reaſon)[2] or by way of the Dutch. My neighbors of Provdence and Warwick, (whom I alſo lately denied) with importunities, have overcome me to endeavor the renewing of their lib-erties, upon the occaſion of Mr. Coddington's late grant.[3]

---

[1] Knowles, *Mem. R. Williams*, p. 247; 3 *Maſs. Hiſt. Coll.* vol. ix. p. 293.
[2] This reaſon was his baniſhment from Maſſachuſetts. There was much delicacy in thus ſlightly referring to a meaſure, in which Mr Winthrop's father was, from his official relations, concerned.

[3] Mr. Coddington's late grant was the charter which he had ſucceeded in ob-taining of Rhode Iſland and Canonicut Iſland to himſelf. Information of theſe deſigns were at once ſent by William Ar-nold to the Governor of Maſſachuſetts, as appears by the following letter:

Upon this occafion, I have been advifed to fell, and have fold this houfe to Mr. Smith, my neighbor, who alfo may poffibly be yours, for I hear he like to have Mrs. Chefter.

"From PAWTUXET, this 1ft day of the 7th month, 1651.

MUCH HONORED,—I thought it my duty to give intelligence unto the much honored Court, of that which I underftand is now working here in thefe parts; fo that if it be the will of God, an evil may be prevented, before it comes to too great a head, viz.:

Whereas, Mr. Coddington has gotten a charter of Rhode Ifland and Canonicut Ifland to himfelf, he has thereby broken the force of their charter. that went under the name of Providence, becaufe he has gotten away the greater part of that colony.

Now thefe company of the Gortonifts, that live at Shawomet, and that company of Providence, are gathering of £200, to fend Mr. Roger Williams unto the Parliament, to get them a charter of thefe parts. they of Shawomet have given £100 already, and there be fome men of Providence that hath given £10 and £20 a man, to help it forward with fpeed; they fay here is a fair inlet, and I hear they have faid, that if the Parliament do take difpleafure againft Maffachufetts, or the reft of the colonies, as they have done againft Barbadoes and other places, then this will ferve for an inroad to let in forces to overrun the whole country.

It is great pity, and very unfit, that fuch a company as thefe are, they all ftand profeffed enemies againft all the united colonies, that they fhould get a charter for fo fmall a quantity of land as lieth in and about Providence, Shawomet, Pawtuxet, and Cowefet, all which, now Rhode Ifland is taken out from it, is but a ftrip of land lying in between the colonies of Maffachufetts, Plymouth and Connecticut, by which means, if they fhould get them a charter, of it there may come fome mifchief and trouble upon the whole country, if their project be not prevented in time, for under the pretence of liberty of confcience about thefe parts, there comes to live all the fcum, the runaways of the country, which, in time, for want of better order, may bring a heavy burthen upon the land, &c This I humbly commend unto the ferious confideration of the much honored Court, and reft your humble fervant to command, WILLIAM ARNOLD.

They are making hafte to fend Mr. Williams away. We that live here near them, and do know the place and hear their words, and do take notice of their proceeding, do know more and can fpeak more of what may come to the country by their means, than the Court do yet confider of. We humbly defire God their purpofe may be fruftrated, for the country's peace.

I humbly defire my name may be concealed, left they, hearing of what I have herein written, they will be enraged againft me, and fo will revenge themfelves upon me.

Some of them of Shawomet that crieth out much againft them which putteth

Sir, I humbly thank you for all your loving kindnesses to me and mine unworthy. The Father of Mercies graciously reward you, guide you, preserve you, save, sanctify and glorify you in the blood of his dear Son, in whom I mourn I am no more, and desire to be yours, unfeignedly and eternally,

ROGER WILLIAMS.

This bearer, coming now from England, will acquaint you, &c.

To all yours, and all my friends, my loving salutations. Mr. Sands, of Boston, and John Hazel,[1] of Seekonk, are gone before us.

---

people to death for witches; for, say they, there be neither witches upon earth, nor devils, but your own pastors and ministers, and such as they are, &c.

I understand that there liveth a man amongst them that broke prison, either at Connecticut or New Haven; he was apprehended for adultery; the woman, I hear, was put to death, but the man is kept here in safety, in the midst of the united colonies. It is time there were some better order taken for these parts, &c.

I have hired this messenger on purpose. I humbly desire to hear if this letter come safe to your hands."—*Hutchinson Papers*, Boston, 1769, p. 237.

[It was these proceedings of Coddington that aroused the people of the colony and induced them to send agents to England, to represent their case to the government, for even all the inhabitants of the islands of which Coddington had been made Governor, did not approve his course. Many of the inhabitants of Newport and Portsmouth, therefore joined in requesting John Clarke to proceed to England as their agent. Mr. Williams and Mr. Clarke sailed together from Boston, in November. The objects of their respective commissions were different. Clarke's object was to procure a repeal of Coddington's commission: while Williams was the sole agent of Providence and Warwick, to procure a new charter for these two towns. It seems to have been admitted that the commission of Coddington, vacated the previous charter.—STAPLES. *Annals of Providence*, p. 82.]

[1] John Hazell, was the old man who was imprisoned in Boston, for expressing sympathy for John Clarke and his associates, and who died before he had reached his home.

To the honored General Court of the Maſſachuſetts Colony now aſſembled at Boſton.

Ođober, 1651.[1]

The Humble Petition of Roger Williams.

Although it be true yet it pleaſed this honored Government, now many years ſince to paſs a ſentence of baniſhment upon me, which ſentence,and the conſequences (bitter afflićtions and miſeries, loſſes, ſorrows and hardſhips) I have humbly deſired (through the help of the moſt High) to endure with a quiet and patient mind.

Yet, may it pleaſe you favorably to remember, that at my laſt arrival from my native country, I preſented this honored Government with letters from many of your noble and honorable friends, then of the Parliament of England, lamenting differences and perſuading moderation, if not reconcilement and pacification.

Pleaſe you to remember that ever ſince the time of my exile I have been (through God's help) a profeſſed and known ſervant to this colony and all the colonies of the Engliſh in peace and war, ſo that ſcarce a week hath paſſed but ſome way or other I have been uſed as inſtrumental to the peace and ſpreading of the Engliſh plantings in this country.

In the Pequot troubles, receiving letters from this Government, I hazarded my life into extreme dangers, by laboring to prevent the league between the Pequots and the Narraganſetts, and to work a league between the Engliſh and the Narraganſetts, which work as an agent from this colony and all the Engliſh in the land, I (through help

---

[1] 4 *Maſs. Hiſt. Coll.* vol. iv. 471. Probably written ſhortly before Mr. Williams embarked for England, which was in November, 1651.

from God) effected.   The fruit thereof (as our much honored Mr. Winthrop, deceased, wrote to me) hath been peace to the English ever since.

At present let me not offend you in saying that I pass not only as a private passenger, but as a messenger and agent to the high Court of the Parliament of England in the name of my neighbors, the English, occasioned by the late grant obtained by Mr. Coddington for Rhode Island.

In all which respects I humbly pray, yet (notwithstanding the former sentence) I may find yet civility and courtesy from the English of the Massachusetts colony, yet I (inoffensively behaving myself) may inoffensively and without molestation, pass through your jurisdiction[1] as a stranger for a night, to the ship, and so (if God so please) may land again, from the land of our nativity.

But some may say, you are an opposite to the way or worship, and beside you go as an adversary, with complaints against us for the town of Warwick.

To the first, I humbly pray it may be remembered, that not only I, but the many millions of millions of our Father Adam's children, (which are as the sand upon the seashore) are not of your persuasion, yea and many thousands of the poor remnant of God's children abroad, are at lamentable difference with you and themselves as to the

---

[1] "It was not without considerable molestation and embarrassment from the authorities and people of Massachusetts, that Mr. Williams was allowed to pass through their territory for the purpose of taking ship for England. He alludes to these in his subsequent letters, though he furnishes us with no means of judging of their nature or operation. Though no longer in any degree able either to harm the orthodoxy or disturb the peace of the colony, yet the authorities were opposed to the objects of his mission, and it may be, dreaded the representations, which the envoys from Rhode Island had it in their power to make to the government of the mother country of the condition of New England."—GAMMELL, *Life of Roger Williams,* p. 143.

worfhip of God in Chrift Jefus. I add, who knows but upon humble and Chriftian debatements and agitations, not only I, but your honored felves, may yet fee caufe to put our mouths in the duft together, as touching the prefent controverfies about the Chriftian worfhip.

To the fecond, I humbly and truly anfwer, yet if it pleafe this honored Court to depute two or three of yourfelves to receive and debate mine anfwer to this objection, I hope (through God's affiftance) to make it apparent, yet I go not as an enemy to the Maffachufetts, but as a profeffed inftrument of a peaceable and honorable end of the fad controverfy, and as an humble fervant, rather than an enemy, to this honored Government of the Maffachufetts.

I am unworthy, yet defire to be your humble fervant,

ROGER WILLIAMS.

The Deputies think meet to grant this petition, viz.: liberty to Mr. Williams to pafs through our jurifdiction to England, provided he carry himfelf inoffenfively according to his promife, with reference to the confent of our honored magiftrates.

WILLIAM TORREY, *Clerk.*

30

*For my honored kind friend Mr. John Winthrop, at his house
      at Pequot, in New England.*

From Sir Henry Vane's at Whitehall,
20. 2. 52. (so called,) [20th April, 1652.][1]

KIND SIR,—'Tis near two in the morning, yet a line of
my dearest remembrance to your loving self and yours,
from whom I have received so many loving lines continually.   Our old friend Col. Humphries is gone, and lately
also Col. Cooke: yet blessed be God we live, and through
the jaws of death are landed safe, and behold the wonders,
the *Magnalia* and *Miracula Dei* in England.   I have sent
a large narration, both concerning Old England affairs and
New, to Providence.   I hope and desire you may see it.
Mr. Peters is well at Whitehall.   I have often been with
him, he tells me he hath but that 200*li* per year which
the Parliament gave him, whereof he allows four score
per annum to his wife.   Your brother Stephen is a great
man for soul liberty.   I have mentioned you to Sir Henry
Vane, who wishes you were in our colony; touching which
you will see *Vestigia Dei* in my narration.   At present I pray
your acceptance of my poor papers, and tell you that I
more and more desire to be ever

Yours, in Christ Jesus,

ROGER WILLIAMS.

My kind love to Mr. Stanton and other loving friends.

---

[1] 4 *Mass. Hist. Coll.* vol. vi. p. 286.

At Mr. Davis's his houfe, at the Checkers, in St. Martin's, or at Sir Henry }
  Vane's, at Whitehall. 8th, 7, 52. (fo called.) [September 8, 1652.][1] }

*To my dear and faithful friend, Mr. Gregory Dexter, at Provi-
dence, in New England, thefe.*

My dear and faithful friend, to whom, with the deareft,
I humbly wifh more and more of the light and love of
Him who is invifible, God bleffed for evermore in the face
of Jefus Chrift.   It hath pleafed God fo to engage me in
divers fkirmifhes againft the priefts, both of Old and New
England, fo that I have occafioned ufing the help of printer
men, unknown to me, to long for my old friend.   So it
hath pleafed God to hold open an open defire of preaching and printing wonderfully againft Romifh and Englifh
will-worfhip.   At this prefent, the devil rageth and clamors in petitions and remonftrances from the ftationers and
others to the Parliament, and all cry, "fhut up the prefs."
The ftationers and others have put forth "The Beacon
Fired," and "The Second Beacon Fired;" and fome friends
of yours have put forth "The Beacon Quenched," not yet
extant.

Sir, many friends have frequently, with much love, in-
quired after you.   Mr. Warner is not yet come with my
letters : they put into Barnftable.   She came by wagon by
land, but he goes with the fhip to Briftol, and, indeed, in
this dangerous war with the Dutch, the only fafe trading is
to Briftol, or thofe parts, for up along the channel, in London way, is the greateft danger, for although our fleets be
abroad, and take many French and Dutch, yet they fometimes catch up fome of ours.

By my public letters, you will fee how we wreftle, and

---

[1] KNOWLES' *Mem. Roger Williams*, p. 253.

how we are like yet to wreftle in the hopes of an end. Praifed be the Lord, we are preferved, the nation is preferved, the Parliament fits, God's people are fecure, too fecure. A great opinion is, that the kingdom of Chrift is rifen, and (Rev. 11 :) "the kingdoms of the earth are become the kingdoms of our Lord and of his Chrift." Others have fear of the flaughter of the witneffes yet approaching. Divers friends, of all forts, here, long to fee you, and wonder you come not over. For myfelf, I had hopes to have got away by this fhip, but I fee now the mind of the Lord to hold me here one year longer. It is God's mercy, his very great mercy, that we have obtained this interim encouragement from the Council of State, that you may cheerfully go on in the name of a colony, until the controverfy is determined. The determination of it, Sir, I fear, will be a work of time, I fear longer than we have yet been here, for our adverfaries threaten to make a laft appeal to the Parliament, in cafe we get the day before the Council.[1]

Sir, in this regard, and when my public bufinefs is over, I am refolved to begin my old law-fuit, fo that I have no thought of return until fpring come twelve months. My duty and affection hath compelled me to acquaint my poor companion with it. I confider our many children, the danger of the feas, and enemies, and therefore I write not

---

[1] The General Affembly which met in Providence, in October following, directed a letter to be fent to Mr. Williams, thanking him "for his care and diligence, to watch all opportunities to promote their peace;" and if it was the pleafure of the government to renew their charter that they would "appoint and empower yourfelf to come over as Governor of this colony, for the fpace of one year."—*R. I. Colonial Records*, vol. i. p. 248.

On the 2d of October the Council of State gave an order and wrote letters to vacate Mr. Coddington's commiffion, and to confirm their former charter, which was fent over by William Dyre.—Backus, *Hift. of the Baptifts*, vol. i. p. 277.

positively for her, only I acquaint her with our affairs. I tell her, joyful I should be of her being here with me, until our state affairs were ended, and I freely leave her to wait upon the Lord for direction, and according as she finds her spirit free and cheerful, to come or stay. If it please the Lord to give her a free spirit to cast herself upon the Lord, I doubt not of your love and faithful care, in any thing she hath occasion to use your help, concerning our children and affairs, during our absence; but I conclude, whom have I in heaven or earth but thee, and so humbly and thankfully say in the Lord's pleasure, as only and infinitely best and sweetest.

Abundance of love remembered from abundance of friends to your dear self and your dearest.

My love to your cousin Clemence, and all desire love, especially our godly friends.

ROGER WILLIAMS.

For my much honored kind friend, Mistress Sadleir, at Stondon, Puckridge, these.

From my lodgings near St. Martin's, at Mr. Davis his house, at the sign of the Swan. [No date; London, 1652.][1]

MY MUCH HONORED FRIEND, MRS. SADLEIR,[2] —The never-dying honor and respect which I owe to that dear and honorable root and his branches, and, amongst the rest, to your much honored self, have emboldened me, once

[1] ELTON, *Life of Roger Williams*, p. 96.
[2] Amidst his engrossing and important occupations, while in England, Mr Williams did not forget the family of his former benefactor, Sir Edward Coke. The above letter and the two letters which follow, to Mrs. Sadleir, the daughter of Sir Edward, were obtained by the late Rev. Dr. Elton while in England, and first appeared in his *Life of Roger Williams*.—PROVIDENCE, 1853, 12mo.

more, to enquire after your dear hufband's and your life, and health, and welfare.   This laft winter I landed, once more, in my native country, being fent over from fome parts of New England with fome addreffes to the Parliament.

My very great bufinefs, and my very great ftraits of time, and my very great journey homeward to my dear yoke-fellow and many children, I greatly fear will not permit me to prefent my ever-obliged duty and fervice to you, at Stondon, efpecially if it pleafe God that I may defpatch my affairs to depart with the fhips within this fortnight.   I am, therefore, humbly bold to crave your favorable confidera-tion, and pardon, and acceptance, of thefe my humble ref-pects and remembrances.   It hath pleafed the Moft High to carry me on eagles' wings, through mighty labors, mighty hazards, mighty fufferings, and to vouchfafe to ufe, fo bafe an inftrument—as I humbly hope—to glorify him-felf, in many of my trials and fufferings, both amongft the Englifh and barbarians.

I have been formerly, and fince I landed, occafioned to take up the two-edged fword of God's Spirit, the word of God, and to appear in public in fome contefts againft the minifters of Old and New England, as touching the true miniftry of Chrift and the foul freedoms of the people. Since I landed, I have publifhed two or three things, and have a large difcourfe at the prefs, but 'tis controverfial, with which I will not trouble your meditations; only I crave the boldnefs to fend you a plain and peaceable dif-courfe, of my own perfonal experiments, which, in a let-ter to my dear wife—upon the occafion of her great fick-nefs near death—I fent her, being abfent myfelf amongft the Indians.   And being greatly obliged to Sir Henry Vane, junior—once Governor of New England—and his lady, I was perfuaded to publifh it in her name, and humbly to prefent your honorable hands with one or two of them. I humbly pray you to caft a ferious eye on the holy Scriptures, on which the examinations are grounded. I could have dreffed forth the matter like fome fermons which, formerly, I ufed to pen. But the Father of lights hath long fince fhown me the vanity and foul-deceit of fuch points and flourifhes. I defire to know nothing, to profefs nothing, but the Son of God, the King of fouls and confciences; and I defire to be more thankful for a reproof for ought I affirm than for applaufe and commendation. I have been oft glad in the wildernefs of America, to have been reproved for going in a wrong path, and to be directed by a naked Indian boy in my travels. How much more fhould we rejoice in the wounds of fuch as we hope love us in Chrift Jefus, than in the deceitful kiffes of foul-deceiving and foul-killing friends.

My much honored friend, that man of honor, and wifdom, and piety, your dear father, was often pleafed to call me his fon; and truly it was as bitter as death to me when Bifhop Laud purfued me out of this land, and my confcience was perfuaded againft the national church and ceremonies, and bifhops, beyond the confcience of your dear Father. I fay it was as bitter as death to me, when I rode Windfor way, to take fhip at Briftow, and faw Stoke Houfe, where the bleffed man was; and I then durft not acquaint him with my confcience, and my flight. But how many thoufand times fince have I had honorable and precious remembrance of his perfon, and the life, the writings, the fpeeches, and the examples of that glorious light. And I may truly fay, that befide my natural inclination to ftudy and activity, his example, inftruction, and encouragement, have

fpurred me on to a more than ordinary, induftrious, and patient courfe in my whole courfe hitherto.

What I have done and fuffered—and I hope for the
truth of God according to my confcience—in Old and New
England, I fhould be a fool in relating, for I defire to fay, not
to King David—as once Mephibofheth—but to King Jefus,
'What is thy fervant, that thou fhouldeft look upon fuch a
dead dog?' And I would not tell yourfelf of this, but that
you may acknowledge fome beams of his holy wifdom and
goodnefs, who hath not fuffered all your own and your
dear father's fmiles to have been loft upon fo poor and def-
picable an object· I confefs I have many adverfaries, and
alfo many friends, and divers eminent. It hath pleafed the
general himfelf to fend for me, and to entertain many difcourfes with me at feveral times; which, as it magnifies
his chriftian noblenefs and courtefy, fo much more doth it
magnify *His* infinite mercy and goodnefs, and wifdom, who
hath helped me, poor worm, to fow that feed in doing and
fuffering—I hope for God—that as your honorable father
was wont to fay, he that fhall harrow what I have fown,
muft rife early. And yet I am a worm and nothing, and
defire only to find my all in the blood of an holy Savior,
in whom I defire to be

> Your honored,
> Moft thankful, and faithful fervant,
> ROGER WILLIAMS.[1]

My humble refpects prefented to Mr. Sadleir.

[1] "Mr. Williams," writes Prof. GAM-
MELL, "fpent a number of weeks at Belleau, the beautiful eftate of Sir Henry
Vane where he doubtlefs often mingled
in that company of kindred minds, who
ufed fo frequently to affemble to difcufs
with their illuftrious leader, the deep
queftions of theology, or to devife plans

From Mrs. Sadleir to Roger Williams.

MR. WILLIAMS,—Since it hath pleafed God to make the prophet David's complaint ours (Ps. lxxix.): "O God, the heathen," &c., and that the Apoftle St. Peter has fo long ago foretold, in his fecond epiftle, the fecond chapter, by whom thefe things fhould be occafioned, I have given over reading many books, and, therefore, with thanks, have returned yours. Thofe that I now read, befides the Bible, are, firft, the late King's book ; Hooker's Ecclefiaftical Polity ; Reverend Bifhop Andrew's Sermons, with his other divine meditations; Dr. Jer. Taylor's works ; and Dr. Tho. Jackfon upon the Creed. Some of thefe my dear father was a great admirer of, and would often call them the glorious lights of the church of England. Thefe lights fhall be my guide ; I wifh they may be yours : for your new lights that are fo much cried up, I believe, in the conclufion, they will prove but dark lanterns : therefore I dare not meddle with them.

Your friend in the old way,

ANNE SADLEIR.

for the happinefs nd fecurity of the perilled and diftracted commonwealth. He was in habits of intimate affociation with Cromwell, who difcuffed with him the affairs of the State, and drew forth from him his views of the Indians, and his fingular adventures among them, in the wilds of New England ; with Har- rifon, the Major-General of the army ; with Laurence, the Lord Prefident of the Council of State ; and with many others in Parliament, and at the helm of public affairs. He alfo formed an intimate acquaintance with Milton, who was then Latin Secretary of the Council."—*Life of Roger Williams*, p. 149.

For his much honored, kind friend, Mrs. Anne Sadleir, at Stondon, in Hartfordshire, near Puckridge.[1]

[No date.]

MY MUCH HONORED, KIND FRIEND, MRS. SADLEIR,—
My humble respects premised to your much honored self,
and Mr. Sadleir, humbly wishing you the saving knowledge and assurance of that life which is eternal, when this
poor minute's dream is over.   In my poor span of time,
I have been oft in the jaws of death, sickening at sea, shipwrecked on shore, in danger of arrows, swords and bullets :
and yet, methinks, the most high and most holy God hath
reserved me for some service to his most glorious and eternal majesty.

I think, sometimes, in this common shipwreck, of mankind, wherein we all are either floating or sinking, despairing or struggling for life, why should I ever faint in striving, as Paul saith, in hopes to save myself, to save others—
to call, and cry, and ask, what hope of saving, what hope
of life, and of the eternal shore of mercy ?   Your last letter, my honored friend, I received as a bitter sweeting—as
all, that is under the sun, is—sweet in that I hear from you,
and that you continue striving for life eternal ; bitter, in
that we differ about the way, in the midst of the dangers
and distresses.

O blessed be the hour that ever we saw the light, and
came into this vale of tears, if yet, at last, in any way, we
may truly see our woeful loss and shipwreck, and gain the
shore of life and mercy.   You were pleased to direct me to
divers books, for my satisfaction.   I have carefully endeavoured to get them, and some I have gotten ; and upon my

[1]ELTON, *Life of Roger Williams*, p. 99.

reading, I purpofe, with God's help, to render you an ingen-
uous and candid account of my thoughts, refult, &c. At
prefent, I am humbly bold to pray your judicious and loving eye to one of mine.

'Tis true, I cannot but expect your diftafte of it; and
yet my cordial defire of your foul's peace here, and eternal,
and of contributing the leaft mite toward it, and my humble refpects to that bleffed root of which you fpring, force
me to tender my acknowledgments, which if received or
rejected, my cries fhall never ceafe that one eternal life may
give us meeting, fince this prefent minute hath fuch bitter
partings.

For the fcope of this *rejoinder*, if it pleafe the Moft
High to direct your eye to a glance on it, pleafe you to
know, that at my laft being in England, I wrote a difcourfe
entitled, "*The Bloudy Tenent of Perfecution for Caufe of Confcience.*" I bent my charge againft Mr. Cotton efpecially,
your ftandard bearer of New Englifh minifters. That difcourfe he fince anfwered, and calls his book, "*The Bloody
Tenent made white in the Blood of the Lamb.*"[1] This rejoinder of mine, as I humbly hope, unwafheth his wafhings,
and proves that in foul matters no weapons but foul weapons are reaching and effectual.

I am your moft unworthy fervant, yet unfeignedly refpective,

ROGER WILLIAMS.

[1] On a former occafion when in Eng-
land, Mr. Williams found leifure to pre-
pare for the prefs his rejoinder to Mr.
Cotton's anfwer to his "*Bloody Tenent of
Perfecution*," which he entitled "*The
Bloody Tenent yet more Bloody, by Mr.
Cotton's Endeavour to wafh it white.*"
About the fame time he also publifhed
"*Hireling Miniftry none of Chrift's; or, a
Difcourfe touching the propagating the
Gofpel of Jefus Chrift,*" and his "*Experi-
ments of Spiritual Life and Health, and
their Prefervatives.*" The former has
been reprinted by the Narraganfett Club,
vol. iii; the latter by S. S. Rider, Provi-
dence, 1863.

Mrs. Sadleir in reply to Roger Williams.

Sir,—I thank God my bleſſed parents bred me up in the old and beſt religion, and it is my glory that I am a member of the Church of England, as it was when all the reformed churches gave her the right hand. When I caſt mine eye upon the frontiſpiece of your book, and ſaw it entitled "The Bloudy Tenent," I durſt not adventure to look into it, for fear it ſhould bring into my memory the much blood that has of late been ſhed, and which I would fain forget ; therefore I do, with thanks, return it. I cannot call to mind any blood ſhed for conſcience :—ſome few that went about to make a rent in our once well-governed church were puniſhed, but none ſuffered death. But this I know, that ſince it has been left to every man's conſcience to fancy what religion he liſt, there has more chriſtian blood been ſhed than was in the ten perſecutions. And ſome of that blood, will, I fear, cry till the day of judgment. But you know what the Scripture ſays, that when there was no king in Iſrael, every man did that which was right in his own eyes,—but what became of that, the ſacred ſtory will tell you.

Thus entreating you to trouble me no more in this kind, and wiſhing you a good journey to your charge in New Providence, I reſt

YOUR FRIEND IN THE OLD AND BEST WAY.

From Roger Williams to Mrs. Sadleir.

[No date. The winter of 1652–3.][1]

My honored, kind Friend, Mrs. Sadleir,—I greatly rejoice to hear from you, although now an oppofite to me, even in the higheft points of Heaven and eternity.

Two things your lines exprefs:—Firft, your confidence in your own old way, &c.

Second. Civility and gentlenefs in that—not being pleafed to accept my refpects and labors prefented—yet you gently, with thanks and your reafon, return them. I fhall not be fo forry you differ from me, if yet the Father of fpirits pleafe to vouchfafe you a fpirit of chriftian fearching and examination. In hope of which I fhall humbly confider of the particulars of your letter.

1. That you think an heap of timber or pile of ftones to be God's fanctuary now. (Ps. lxxix. 1.) In Chrift's efteem, and in gofpel language, that you think thofe to be falfe teachers and prophets (2 Pet. ii. 1.) who are not—after the old way—diftinguifhed by the canonical colors of white, red, black, &c.

That you admire the king's book, and Bp. Andrews his fermons, and Hooker's Polity, &c., and profefs them to be your lights and guides, and defire them mine, and believe the new lights will prove dark lanterns, &c. I am far from wondering at it, for all this have I done myfelf, until the Father of Spirits mercifully perfuaded mine to fwallow down no longer without chewing: to chew no longer without tafting; to tafte no longer without begging the Holy Spirit of God to enlighten and enliven mine againft

---

[1] Elton, *Life of Roger Williams*, p. 102.

the fear of men, tradition of fathers, or the favor or cuftom of any men or times.

2. I now find that the church and fanctuary of Chrift Jefus confifts not of dead but of living ftones. (1 Pet. ii. 3, 4.) Is not a parifh or a national church forced—to the pretended bed of Chrift's worfhip—by laws and fwords? (Cant. i. 16.)

His true lovers are volunteers, born of his Spirit, the now only nation and royal priefthood (1 Pet. ii., Ps. cx.) I find that, in refpect of minifterial function and office, fuch minifters, not only popifh but proteftant, not only epifcopal but prefbyterian, not only prefbyterian but independent alfo, are all of them, one as well as another, falfe prophets and teachers, fo far as they are hirelings, and make a trade and living of preaching (John x.), as I have lately opened in my "Difcourfe of the Hireling Miniftry none of Chrift's."

3. I have read thofe books you mention, and the king's book, which commends two of them, Bifhop Andrews's and Hooker's—yea, and a third alfo, Bifhop Laud's: and as for the king, I knew his perfon, vicious, a fwearer from his youth, and an oppreffor and perfecutor of good men (to fay nothing of his own father), and the blood of fo many hundred thoufands Englifh, Irifh, Scotch, French, lately charged upon him. Againft his and his blafphemous father's cruelties, your own dear father, and many precious men, fhall rife up fhortly and cry for vengeance.

4. But for the book itfelf—if it be his—and theirs you pleafe to mention, and thoufands more, not only proteftants of feveral fects, but of fome papifts and jefuits alfo—famous for wordly repute, &c.—I have found them fharp and witty, plaufible and delightful, devout and pathetical. And I have

been amazed to fee the whole world of our forefathers, wife and gallant, wondering after the glory of the Romifh learning and worfhip. (Rev. xiii.) But amongft them all whom I have fo diligently read and heard, how few exprefs the fimplicity, the plainnefs, the meeknefs, and true humility of the learning of the Son of God.

5. But, at laft, it pleafed the God and Father of mercies to perfuade mine heart of the merely formal, cuftomary, and traditional profeffions of Chrift Jefus, with which the world is filled. I fee that the Jews believe Chrift Jefus was a deceiver, becaufe he came not with external pomps and excellency.

The Turks—fo many millions of them—prefer their Mahomet before Chrift Jefus, even upon fuch carnal and wordly refpects, and yet avouch themfelves to be the only Mufelmanni or true believers. The catholics account us heretics, diabloes, &c.; and why? but becaufe we worfhip not fuch a golden Chrift and his glorious vicar and lieutenant. The feveral fects of common proteftants content themfelves with a traditional worfhip, and boaft they are no Jews, no Turks, (Matt. vii. 21, 22.) nor catholics, and yet forget their own formal dead faith, (2 Tim. iii. 9.) dead hope, dead joys, and yet, *nefcio vos*, I know you not, depart from me, which fhall be thundered out to many gallant profeffors and confidents, who have held out a lamp and form of religion, yea, and poffibly of godlinefs too, and yet have denied the power and life of it.

Therefore, my much-honored friend, while you believe the darknefs of the new lights, and profefs your confidence, and defire of my walking with you in the old way: I moft humbly pray fo much Berean civility at your ladyfhip's hands as to fearch and remember—

1. Firſt, the Lord Chriſt's famous reſolution of that queſtion put to him, as touching the number that ſhall be ſaved (Luke xiii. 24), "Strive to enter in at the ſtrait gate; for many ſhall ſeek to enter, and ſhall not be able."

2ndly. There is an abſolute neceſſity (not ſo of a true order of miniſtry, baptiſm, &c., but) of a true regeneration and new birth, without which it is impoſſible to enter into or to ſee the kingdom of God. (John iii. &c.)

3rdly. As to the religion and the worſhip of God, the common religion of the whole world, and the nations of it, it is but cuſtomary and traditional, from father to ſon, from which (old ways, &c.), traditions, Chriſt Jeſus, delivers his, not with gold and ſilver, but with his precious blood. (1 Pet. i. 18, 19.)

4thly. Without ſpiritual and diligent examination of our hearts, it is impoſſible that we can attain true ſolid joy and comfort, either in point of regeneration or worſhip, or whatever we do. (2 Cor. xiii. 5; Rom. xiv. 23.)

5thly. In the examination of both theſe—perſonal regeneration and worſhip—the hearts of all the children of men are moſt apt to cheat, and cozen, and deceive themſelves; yea, and the wiſer a man is, the more apt and willing he is to be deceived. (Jer. xvii.; Gal. vi.; 1 Cor. iii. 18.)

6thly. It is impoſſible there ſhould be a true ſearch, without the Holy Spirit, who ſearcheth all things, yea, the deep things of God. (Rom. viii.; Ps. cxliii. 10.)

Laſtly. God's Spirit perſuadeth the hearts of his true ſervants: Firſt, to be willing to be ſearched by him, which they exceedingly beg of him, with holy fear of ſelf-deceit and hypocriſy.

Second. To be led by him in the way everlaſting: (Ps. cxxxix.), whether it ſeem old in reſpect of inſtitution, or new in refpect of reftoration. This I humbly pray for your precious foul, of the God and Father of mercies, even your eternal joy and falvation. Earneftly defirous to be in the old way, which is the narrow way, which leads to life, which few find.

Your moft humble, though moft unworthy fervant,

ROGER WILLIAMS.

"My honored Friend, fince you pleafe not to read mine, let me pray leave to requeft your reading of one book of your own authors. I mean the "Liberty of Prophefying," penned by (fo called) Dr. Jer. Taylor. In the which is excellently afferted the toleration of different religions, yea, in a refpect, that of the papifts themfelves, which is a new way of foul freedom, and yet is the old way of Chrift Jefus, as all his holy Teftament declares.

I alfo humbly wifh that you may pleafe to read over impartially Mr. Milton's[1] anfwer to the king's book.

Mrs. Sadleir in reply to Roger Williams.

MR. WILLIAMS,—I thought my firft letter would have given you fo much fatisfaction, that, in that kind, I fhould never have heard of you any more; but it feems you have a face of brafs, fo that you cannot blufh. But fince you prefs me to it, I muft let you know, as I did before (Ps. lxxix.), that the Prophet David there complains that the heathen had defiled the holy temple, and made Jerufalem

---

[1] *Eikonoklaftes (the Image Breaker,) in Anfwer to Eikon Bafilike.* London: 1649.

32

a heap of ftones. And our blefled Saviour. when he whipped the buyers and fellers out of the temple, told them that they had made his Father's houfe a den of thieves. Thofe were but material temples, and commanded by God to be built, and his name there to be worfhipped. The living temples are thofe that the fame prophet, in the pfalm before mentioned (verfe the 2nd and 3rd), "The dead bodies of thy fervants have they given to the fowls of the air, and the flefh of thy faints to the beafts of the land. Their blood have they fhed like water," &c. And thefe were the living temples whofe lofs the prophet fo much laments; and had he lived in thefe times, he would have doubled thefe lamentations, For the foul and falfe afperfions you have caft upon that king, of ever-blefled memory, Charles, the martyr, I proteft I trembled when I read them, and none but fuch a villain as yourfelf would have wrote them.

Wife Solomon has taught me another leffon in his 24th of his Proverbs, at 21ft verfe, to fear God and the King, and not to meddle with them that are given to change. Mark well that. The 8th of Eccl., verfe the 2nd, "I counfel thee to keep the king's commandment, and that in regard to the oath of God." Verfe the 20th of the 10th chap., "Curfe not the king, no, not in thy thought;" and, if I be not miftaken, the fifth commandment is the crown commandment. Rom. xiii., the 1ft and 2nd verfes, "Let every foul be fubject unto the higher powers, for," &c.; with many more places to the fame purpofe. Thus, you fee, I have the law, with the Old and New Teftament, on my fide.

But it has been the lot of the beft kings to lie under the lafh of ill tongues. Witnefs blefled David, who was a man after God's own heart, curfed by wicked Shimei, his own fubject, and called a man of blood; and good Hezekiah was railed on by a foul-mouthed Rabfhakeh; but I do not remember that they were commended in any place of fcripture, for fo doing. For the blood you mention, which has been fhed in thefe times, which you would father upon the late king, there is a book called the Hiftory of Independency—a book worth your reading—that will tell you by whom all this chriftian blood has been fhed. If you cannot get that, there is a fermon in print of one Paul Knells, the text the firft of Amos, verfe the fecond, that will inform you.

For Milton's book, that you defire I fhould read, if I be not miftaken, that is he that has wrote a book of the lawfulnefs of divorce; and, if report fays true, he had, at that time, two or three wiv̇es living. This, perhaps, were good doctrine in New England; but it is moft abominable in Old England. For his book that he wrote againft the late king that you would have me read, you fhould have taken notice of God's judgment upon him, who ftroke him with blindnefs, and, as I have heard, he was fain to have the help of one Andrew Marvell,[1] or elfe he could not have finifhed that moft accurfed libel. God has began his judgment upon him here—his punifhment will be hereafter in hell. But have you feen the anfwer to it? If you can get it, I affure, you it is worth your reading.

[1] It has before been ftated in a note that Milton was the Latin Secretary to Cromwell. Andrew Marvell, the poet, was affiftant to Milton. He thereby enjoyed his intimate friendfhip, and was one of the firft to recognize his genius. "When Paradife Loft was publifhed, it was valued but by few, as no more than a lifelefs piece, till Mr. Marvell and Dr. Barron publickly efpoufed it, each in a judicious Poem."—COOKE's *Life of Marvell*, 1726.

Milton, it is true, repudiated his wife, (Mifs Powell) on the grounds of defertion, and in juftification of his courfe, publifhed four tracts, the firft was entitled "The Doctrine and Difcipline of Divorce." The others appertained to the fame fubject. A reconciliation fubfequently took place.

I have alſo read Taylor's book of the Liberty of Pro-phefying; though it pleaſe not me, yet I am ſure it does you, or elſe I [know]* you [would]* not have wrote to me to have read it. I ſay, it and you would make a good fire. But have you ſeen his Divine Inſtitution of the Office Min-iſterial? I aſſure that is both worth your reading and prac-tice. Biſhop Laud's book againſt Fiſher I have read long ſince; which, if you have not done, let me tell you that he has deeply wounded the pope; and, I believe, howſoever he be ſlighted, he will riſe a ſaint, when many ſeeming ones, ſuch as you are, will riſe devils.

I cannot conclude without putting you in mind how dear a lover and great an admirer my father was of the lit-urgy of the church of England, and would often ſay, no reform church had the like. He was conſtant to it, both in his life and at his death. I mean to walk in his ſteps; and, truly, when I conſider who were the compoſers of it, and how they ſealed the truth of it with their blood, I cannot but wonder why it ſhould now of late be thus con-temned. By what I have now writ, you know how I ſtand. affected. I will walk as directly to heaven as I can, in which place, if you will turn from being a rebel, and fear God and obey the king, there is hope I may meet you there; howſoever, trouble me no more with your letters, for they are very troubleſome to her that wiſhes you in the place from whence you came.[1]

ANNE SADLEIR.

Near the direction, on the outſide, of Williams's firſt letter, there is the follow-ing note by Mrs. Sadleir:—

"This Roger Williams, when he was a youth, would, in

---

* Theſe words are not in the MS.
[1] This correſpondence, between Ro-ger Williams and Mrs. Sadleir, is copied from the original manuſcripts in the li-

a fhort hand, take fermons and fpeeches in the Star Chamber and prefent them to my dear father. He, feeing fo
hopeful a youth, took fuch liking to him that he fent him
in to Sutton's Hofpital, and he was the fecond that was
placed there; full little did he think that he would have
proved fuch a rebel to God, the king, and his country. I
leave his letters, that, if ever he has the face to return into
his native country, Tyburn may give him welcome."[1]

To the Towns of Providence and Warwick.

From Sir Henry Vane's, at Balleau in
Lincolnfhire, April 1,'53. (fo called.)[2]

MY DEAR AND LOVING FRIENDS AND NEIGHBORS OF
PROVIDENCE AND WARWICK,—Our noble friend, Sir Henry Vane,[3] having the navy of England moftly depending

brary of Trinity College, Cambridge.
Like many of Williams's letters they are
without date; but the allufions to his
works, and other circumftances, clearly
fhow that they were written during his
fecond vifit, in 1652-3. The writer
has examined the originals of the letters;
and for the knowledge of their exiftence
he is indebted to the courtefy of the Hon.
George Bancroft, author of the Hiftory
of the United States, and late minifter
to Great Britain.—*Note by Dr. Elton.*

[1] "Thefe letters," writes Dr. ELTON,
"prefent a lively picture of the influence
of party fpirit upon focial intercourfe,
at that remarkable period. The gratitude and humility of Williams are finely
contrafted with the cold repulfivenefs,
and, at laft, rude infolence of his corref-

pondent, whofe final letter pours forth
as much venom as could well flow from
a lady's pen. The concentrated effence
of it, in her poftfcript, reminds us of the
mutation in human affairs. The rebel
fhe denounces has acquired a nobler fame
than even that of the acute lawyer, her
father; while, if her own name is refcued from oblivion, fhe owes it to her
accidental connexion with the man fhe
configns to Tyburn."—*Life of Roger
Williams,* p. 109.

[2] BACKUS, *Hift. of the Baptifts in New
England,* vol. i. p. 285; KNOWLES, *Memoirs of Roger Williams,* p. 258.

[3] Sir Henry Vane, fon of Sir Henry
Vane, Secretary of State under James I.,
and Charles I. Joining the Puritans, he
followed them to Bofton, where he ar-

on his care, and going down to the navy at Portſmouth, I was invited by them both to accompany his lady to Lincolnſhire, where I ſhall yet ſtay, as I fear, until the ſhip is gone. I muſt, therefore, pray your pardon, that by the poſt, I ſend this to London. I hope it may have pleaſed the Moſt High Lord of ſea and land to bring Captain Chriſten's ſhip and dear Mr. Dyre unto you, and with him the council's letters, which anſwer the petition Sir Henry Vane and myſelf drew up, and the council, by Sir Henry's mediation granted us, for the confirmation of the charter, until the determination of the controverſy. This determination you may please to underſtand, is hindered by two main obſtruction. The firſt is, the mighty war with the Dutch, which makes England and Holland, and the nations tremble. This hath made the parliament ſet Sir Henry Vane and two or three more as commiſſioners to manage the war, which they have done, with much engaging the name of God with them, who hath appeared in helping ſixty of ours againſt almoſt three hundred of their

rived in 1635 and the following year was choſen Governor. A bitter religious controverſy ſprang up during his term of office. He had a horror of all forms of bigotry, and had no ſympathy with the attacks of the clergy on Mrs. Hutchinſon. A ſtrong oppoſition under the lead of Winthrop was organized againſt him, and at the next election he was defeated. In 1637, he returned to England and was elected to parliament He was a zealous opponent of the royaliſts. In 1648 he led the minority in parliament which favored the rejection of the terms of ſettlement offered by the king. In 1649, he became a member of the council of State, under Cromwell, which was entruſted with the executive government of the nation. The diſſolution of the long parliament in 1653, brought Vane and Cromwell into open conflict. After the reſtoration he was arreſted on the charge of high treaſon and committed to the Tower. His condemnation ſoon followed and he was executed on the 14th of June, 1662. His services to New England were important, and it was in a great meaſure due to him, that the charter for Rhode Iſland was procured. Roger Williams, declared that his name ought ever to be held in honored remembrance by her people.—*Life by* Upham, *in* Sparks' *American Biography,* vol. iv.

men-of-war and, perchance, to the finking and taking, about one hundred of theirs, and but one of ours, which was funk by our own men.

Our fecond obftruction is the oppofition of our adverfaries, Sir Arthur Hafelrig, and Colonel Fenwicke—who hath married his daughter—Mr. Winflow, and Mr. Hopkins, both in great place ; and all the friends they can make in parliament and council, and all the priefts, both prefbyterian and independent ; fo that we ftand as two armies, ready to engage, obferving the motions and poftures each of the other, and yet fhy each of other. Under God, the fheet-anchor of our fhip is Sir Henry, who will do as the eye of God leads him ; and he faithfully promifed me that he would obferve the motion of our New England bufinefs, while I ftaid fome ten weeks with his lady in Lincolnfhire. Befides, here are great thoughts and preparation for a new parliament—fome of our friends are apt to think another parliament will more favor us and our caufe than this has done. You may pleafe to put my condition into your foul's cafes ; remember I am a father and a hufband. I have longed earneftly to return with the laft fhip, and with thefe ; yet I have not been willing to withdraw my fhoulders from the burthen, left it pinch others, and may fall heavy upon all ; except you are pleafed to give me a difcharge. If you conceive it neceffary for me ftill to attend this fervice, pray you to confider if it be not convenient that my poor wife be encouraged to come over to me, and to wait together, on the good pleafure of God, for the end of this matter. You know my many weights hanging on me, how my own place ftands, and how many reafons I have to caufe me to make hafte, yet I would not lofe their eftates, peace, and liberty, by leaving haftily. I write to my dear wife, my great defire of her coming while I ftay, yet left it to the freedom of her fpirit, becaufe of the many dangers.   Truly, at prefent the feas are dangerous, but not comparably fo much, nor likely to be, because of the late defeat of the Dutch, and their prefent fending to us offers of peace.

My dear friends, although it pleafed God himfelf, by many favors, to encourage me, yet pleafe you to remember, that no man can ftay here as I do, having a prefent employment there, without much felf-denial, which I befeech God for more, and for you alfo, that no private refpects, or gains, or quarrels, may caufe you to neglect the public and common fafety, peace and liberties.   I befeech the bleffed God to keep frefh in your thoughts what he hath done for Providence Plantations.

My dear refpects to yourfelves, wives, and children.   I befeech the eternal God to be feen amongft you ; fo prays your moft faithful and affectionate friend and fervant,

ROGER WILLIAMS.

P. S. My love to all my Indian friends.

[Although the objects of Mr. Williams's miffion to England, were not fully accomplifhed, he felt that his prefence was needed at home, that he might, if poffible, bring the difcordant towns into harmonious co-operation.   He accordingly left the remainder of his bufinefs in the hands of John Clarke, his friend and affociate, and early in the following fummer (1654), he returned.   He landed at Bofton, being furnifhed with an order from the Lord Protector's Council, requiring the government of Maffachufetts to allow him in future to embark or land in their territories without moleftation.   Williams brought with him a letter from Sir Henry Vane, addreffed to the inhabitants of the colony of Rhode Ifland, which, from the action of the town of Providence and the letters of Williams in relation to it is here inferted.]

From Sir Henry Vane, to the Inhabitants of the Colony of Rhode Ifland.

BELLEAU, the 8th of February, 1653-4.[1]

LOVING AND CHRISTIAN FRIENDS,—I could not refufe this bearer, Mr. Roger Williams, my kind friend and ancient acquaintance, to be accompanied with thefe few lines from myfelf to you, upon his return to Providence colony; though, perhaps, my private and retired condition, which the Lord, of his mercy, hath brought me into, might have argued ftrongly enough for my filence; but, indeed, fomething I hold myfelf bound to fay to you, out of the Chriftian love I bear you, and for his fake whofe name is called upon by you and engaged in your behalf. How is it that there are fuch divifions amongft you? Such headinefs, tumults, diforders, injuftice? The noife echoes into the ears of all, as well friends as enemies, by every return of fhips from thofe parts. Is not the fear and awe of God amongft you to reftrain? Is not the love of Chrift in you, to fill you with yearning bowels, one towards another, and conftrain you not to live to yourfelves, but to him that died for you, yea, and is rifen again? Are there no wife men amongft you? No public felf-denying fpirits, that at leaft, upon the grounds of public fafety, equity and prudence, can find out fome way or means of union and reconciliation for you amongft yourfelves, before you become a prey to common enemies, efpecially fince this ftate, by the laft letter from the Council of State, give you your freedom, as fuppofing a better ufe would have been made of it than there hath been? Surely, when kind and fimple remedies are applied and are ineffectual, it fpeaks loud and broadly the

---

[1] *Rhode Ifland Colonial Records,* vol. i. p. 285.

high and dangerous diftempers of fuch a body, as if the
wounds were incurable. But I hope better things from
you, though I thus fpeak, and fhould be apt to think, that
by commiffioners agreed on and appointed on all parts, and
on behalf of all interefts, in a general meeting, fuch a
union and common fatisfaction might arife, as, through
God's bleffing, might put a ftop to your growing breaches
and diftractions, filence your enemies, encourage your
friends, honor the name of God, (which of late hath been
much blafphemed, by reafon of you,) and in particular, refrefh and revive the fad heart of him who mourns over
your prefent evils, as being your affectionate friend, to ferve
you in the Lord.

H. VANE.

———————

*For my much honored, kind friend, Mr. John Winthrop, at
Pequot.*

PROVIDENCE, July 12, 54. (fo called,)[1]

SIR,—I was humbly bold to falute you from our native
country, and now, by the gracious hand of the Lord, once
more faluting this wildernefs, I crave your wonted patience
to my wonted boldnefs, who ever honored and loved, and
ever fhall, the root and branches of your dear name. How
joyful, therefore, was I to hear of your abode as a ftake
and pillar in thefe parts, and of your healths, your own,
Mrs. Winthrop, and your branches, although fome fad
mixtures we have had from the fad tidings (if true) of the
late lofs and cutting off of one of them.

---

[1] KNOWLES' *Life of Roger Williams,* p. 261.

Sir, I was lately upon the wing to have waited on you at your houfe. I had difpofed all for my journey, and my ftaff was in my hand, but it pleafed the Lord to interpofe fome impediments, fo that I am compelled to a fufpenfion for a feafon, and choofe at prefent thus to vifit you. I had no letters for you, but yours were well. I was at the lodgings of Major Winthrop and Mr. Peters, but I miffed them. Your brother flourifheth in good efteem, and is eminent for maintaining the freedom of the confcience as to matters of belief, religion and worfhip. Your father Peters[1] preacheth the fame doctrine, though not fo zealoufly as fome years fince, yet cries out againft New-Englifh rigidities and perfecutions, their civil injuries and wrongs to himfelf, and their unchriftian dealing with him, in excommunicating his diftracted wife. All this he told me in his lodgings, at Whitehall, thofe lodgings which I was told were Canterbury's; but he himfelf told me, that that library wherein we were together, was Canterbury's, and given him by the Parliament. His wife lives from him not wholly, but much diftracted. He tells me he had but two hundred a year, and he allowed her fourfcore per annum of it. Surely, Sir, the moft holy Lord is moft wife in all the trials he exercifeth his people with. He told me that his affliction from his wife ftirred him up to action abroad, and when fuccefs tempted him to pride, the bitternefs in his bofom comforts was a cooler and a bridle to him.

Surely, Sir, your father, and all the people of God in England, formerly called *Puritanus, Anglicanus,* of late *Roundheads,* now the *Sectarians,* (as more or lefs cut off from the parifhes) are now in the faddle and at the helm, fo high that *non datur defcenfus nifi cadendo.* Some cheer

---

[1] Mr. Winthrop had married a daughter of the Rev. Hugh Peters.

up their fpirits with the impoffibility of another fall or
turn, fo doth Major Gen. Harrifon and Mr. Feake, and Mr.
John Simfon, now in Windfor Caftle for preaching againft
this laft change, and againft the Protector, as an ufurper,
Richard III., &c.   So did many think of the laft Parliament, who were of the vote of fifty-fix againft priefts and
tithes, oppofite to the vote of the fifty-four who were for
them, at leaft for a while.   Major Gen. Harrifon was the
fecond in the nation of late, when the loving General and
himfelf joined againft the former Long Parliament and
diffolved them, but now being the head of the fifty-fix party, he was confined by the Protector and Council, within
five miles of his father's houfe, in Staffordfhire.   That fentence he not obeying, he told me (the day before my leaving London) he was to be fent prifoner into Harfordfhire.
Surely, Sir, he is a very gallant, moft deferving, heavenly
man, but moft high flown for the kingdom of the faints,
and the fifth monarchy now rifen, and their fun never to
fet again, &c.   Others, as to my knowledge, the Protector,
Lord Prefident Lawrence, and others at helm, with Sir
Henry Vane, (retired into Licolnfhire, yet daily miffed and
courted for his affiftance) are not fo full of that faith of
miracles, but ftill imagine changes and perfecutions and the
very flaughter of the witneffes, before that glorious morning
fo much defired of a worldly kingdom, if ever fuch a kingdom (as literally it is by so many expounded) be to arife in
this prefent world and difpenfation.

    Sir, I know not how far your judgment hath concurred
with the defign againft the Dutch.   I muft acknowledge
my mourning for it, and when I heard of it, at Portfmouth,
I confefs I wrote letters to the Protector and Prefident,
from thence, as againft a moft uningenuous and unchriftian

defign, at fuch a time, when the world ftood gazing at the fo famous treaty for peace, which was then between the two States, and near finifhed when we fet fail. Much I can tell you of the anfwer I had from Court, and I think of the anfwers I had from heaven, viz.: that the Lord would gracioufly retard us until the tidings of peace (from England) might quench the fire in the kindling of it.

Sir, I mourn that any of our parts were fo madly injurious to trouble yours. I pity poor Sabando. I yet have hopes in God that we fhall be more loving and peaceable neighbors. I had word from the Lord Prefident to Portfmouth, that the Council had paffed three letters as to our bufinefs. Firft, to encourage us; fecond, to our neighbor colonies not to moleft us; third, in expofition of that word dominion, in the late frame of the government of England, viz.: that liberty of confcience fhould be maintained in all American plantations, &c.

Sir, a great man in America told me, that he thought New England would not bear it. I hope better, and that not only the neceffity, but the equity, piety and Chriftanity of that freedom will more and more fhine forth, not to licentioufnefs, (as all mercies are apt to be abufed) but to the beauty of Chriftianity and the luftre of true faith in God and love to poor mankind, &c.

Sir, I have defires of keeping home. I have long had fcruples of felling the natives aught but what may bring or tend to civilizing; I therefore neither brought, nor fhall fell them, loofe coats nor breeches. It pleafed the Lord to call me for fome time, and with fome perfons, to practice the Hebrew, the Greek, Latin, French and Dutch.[1]

---

[1] It appears from this letter that Williams was ufed to practice the French and Dutch, and that he employed himfelf in the honorable office of an in-

The Secretary of the Council, (Mr. Milton) for my Dutch I read him, read me many more languages. Grammar rules begin to be efteemed a tyranny. I taught two young gentlemen, a Parliament man's fons, as we teach our children Englifh, by words, phrafes and conftant talk, &c. I have begun with mine own three boys, who labor befides; others are coming to me.

Sir, I fhall rejoice to receive a word of your healths, of the Indian wars and to be ever yours,

ROGER WILLIAMS.

Sir, I pray feal and fend the enclofed.

To the Town of Providence.

[PROVIDENCE, Auguft, 1654.] [1]

WELL-BELOVED FRIENDS AND NEIGHBORS,—I am like a man in a great fog. I know not well how to fteer. I

---

ftructor of youth. This occupation he doubtless reforted to for his own fupport. That he was preffed for money is evident from his letter to the town of Providence, written in Auguft, 1654, in which he fpeaks of the ftraits he was put to for money to pay his expenfes.

It is evident too, from the writings of Mr. Williams, that he was acquainted with the Hebrew, Greek, and Latin languages, as quotations from them are frequent in his letters. In the preface to his " Key," in fpeaking of the Indian languages, he fays, " Firft others, (and myfelf) have conceived fome of their words to hold affinity with the Hebrew." . . . " Yet again, I have found a greater affinity of their language with the Greek tongue."

[1] BACKUS, *Hift. of the Baptifts of New England*, vol. i. p. 289. *R. I. Col. Records*, vol. i. p. 351.

Upon the return of Mr. Williams with the letter of Sir Henry Vane, he found matters in the colony in a very unfettled ftate, and was received with great coldnefs. He therefore wrote the above letter to the Town of Providence, in which he alludes in the moft affecting terms to the facrifices he had made in behalf of the colony, the people of which, he thought, had not appreciated his efforts.

fear to run upon the rocks at home, having had trials abroad. I fear to run quite backward, as men in a mift do, and undo all that I have been a long time undoing myfelf to do, viz.: to keep up the name of a people, a free people, not enflaved to the bondages and iron yokes of the great (both foul and body) oppreffions of the Englifh and barbarians about us, nor to the divifions and diforders within ourfelves. Since I fet the firft ftep of any Englifh foot into thefe wild parts, and have maintained a chargeable and hazardous correfpondence with the barbarians, and fpent almoft five years' time with the ftate of England, to keep off the rage of the Englifh againft us, what have I reaped of the root of being the ftepping-ftone of fo many families and towns about us, but grief, and forrow, and bitternefs? I have been charged with folly for that freedom and liberty which I have always ftood for; I fay liberty and equality, both in land and government. I have been blamed for parting with Mofhafluck, and afterward Pawtuxet, (which were mine own as truly as any man's coat upon his back,) without referving to myfelf a foot of land, or an inch of voice in any matter, more than to my fervants and ftrangers. It hath been told me that I labored for a licentious and contentious people; that I have foolifhly parted with town and colony advantages, by which I might have preferved both town and colony in as good order as any in the country about us. This, and ten times more, I have been cenfured for, and at this prefent am called a traitor by one party, againft the ftate of England, for not maintaining the charter and the colony; and it is faid I am as good as banifhed by yourfelves, and that both fides wifhed that I might never have landed, that the fire of contention might have had no ftop in burning. Indeed, the words have been fo fharp between myfelf and fome lately, that at laft I was forced to fay, they might well filence all complaints if I once began to complain, who was unfortunately fetched and drawn from my employ-ment, and fent to fo vaft diftance from my family, to do your work of a high and coftly nature, for fo many days and weeks and months together, and there left to ftarve, or fteal, or beg or borrow. But blelfed be God, who gave me favor to borrow one while, and to work another, and there-by to pay your debts there, and to come over with your credit and honor, as an agent from you, who had, in your name, grappled with the agents and friends of all your enemies round about you. I am told that your oppofites thought on me, and provided, as I may fay, a fponge to wipe off your fcores and debts in England, but that it was obftructed by yourfelves, who rather meditated on means and new agents to be fent over, to crofs what Mr. Clarke and I obtained. But, gentlemen, blelfed be God, who faileth not, and blelfed be his name for his wonderful PROVI-DENCES, by which alone this town and colony, and that grand caufe of TRUTH AND FREEDOM OF CONSCIENCE, hath been upheld to this day. And blelfed be his name who hath again quenched fo much of our fires hitherto, and hath brought your names and his own name thus far out of the dirt and fcorn, reproach, &c. I find among yourfelves and your oppofites that of Solomon true, that the contentions of brethren (fome that lately were fo) are the bars of a caftle, and not eafily broken; and I have heard fome of both fides zealoufly talking of undoing themfelves by a trial in England. Truly, friends, I can-not but fear you loft a fair wind lately, when this town was fent to for its deputies, and you were not pleafed to give an

overture unto the reft of the inhabitants about it ; yea, and
when yourfelves thought that I invited you to fome conference tending to reconciliation, before the town fhould
act in fo fundamental a bufinefs, you were pleafed to fore-
ftall that, fo that being full of grief, fhame and aftonifhment, yea, and fear that all that is now done, efpecially in
our town of Providence, is but provoking the fpirits of
men to fury and defperation, I pray your leave to pray
you to remember (that which I lately told your oppofites)
only by pride cometh contention. If there be humility on the
one fide, yet there is pride on the other, and certainly the
eternal God will engage againft the proud. I therefore
pray you to examine, as I have done them, your proceedings in this firft particular. Secondly, Love covereth a
multitude of fins. Surely your charges and complaints
each againft other, have not hid nor covered any thing, as
we ufe to cover the nakednefs of thofe we love. If you
will now profefs not to have disfranchifed humanity and
love, but that, as David in another cafe, you will facrifice
to the common peace, and common fafety, and common
credit, that which may be faid to coft you fomething, I
pray your loving leave to tell you, that if I were in your
foul's cafe, I would fend unto your oppofites fuch a line
as this : "Neighbors, at the conftant requeft, and upon the
conftant mediation which our neighbor Roger Williams,
fince his arrival, hath ufed to us, both for pacification and
accommodation of our fad differences, and alfo upon the
late endeavors in all the other towns for an union, we are
perfuaded to remove our obftruction, viz. : that paper of
contention between us, and to deliver it into the hands of
our aforefaid neighbor and to obliterate that order, which
that paper did occafion. This removed, you may be pleafed

34

to meet with, and debate freely, and vote in all matters with us, as if ſuch grievances had not been amongſt us. Secondly, if yet aught remain grievous, which we our-ſelves, by free debate and conference, cannot compoſe we offer to be judged and cenſured by four men, which out of any part of the colony you ſhall chooſe two, and we the other.[1]

Gentlemen, I only add, that I crave your loving pardon to your bold but true friend.

ROGER WILLIAMS.

The Town of Providence to Sir Henry Vane.[2]

[PREPARED BY ROGER WILLIAMS AT THE REQUEST OF THE TOWN.]

PROVIDENCE, Auguſt 27th, 1654.

SIR,—Although we are aggrieved at your late retirement from the helm of public affairs, yet we rejoice to reap the ſweet fruits of your reſt in your pious and loving lines, moſt ſeaſonably ſent unto us. Thus the ſun, when he re-tires his brightneſs from the world, yet from under the very clouds we perceive his preſence, and enjoy ſome light and heat and ſweet refreſhings. Sir, your letters were di-rected to all and every particular town of this Providence colony. Surely, Sir, among the many Providences of the

---

[1] This letter is without date, but it was doubtleſs written juſt before the town meeting which took place late in Auguſt, 1654. It had the deſired effect, and when the meeting took place, Mr. Wil-liams had a full hearing of the caſe, when he was requeſted to write an anſwer to Sir Henry Vane's letter. This letter, which follows, dated Auguſt 27th, 1654, is preſerved among the records of the city of Providence. It is in Mr. Wil-liams's hand writing and has all the cha-racteriſtics of his ſtyle.

[2] *R. I. Colonial Records*, vol. i. p. 235.

Moſt High, towards this town of Providence, and this Providence colony, we cannot but ſee apparently his gracious hand, providing your honorable ſelf for ſo noble and true a friend to an outcaſt and deſpiſed people. From the firſt beginning of this Providence colony, occaſioned by the baniſhment of ſome in this place from the Maſſachuſetts, we ſay ever ſince to this very day, we have reaped the ſweet fruits of your conſtant loving kindneſs and favor towards us. Oh, Sir, whence, then, is it that you have bent your bow and ſhot your ſharp and bitter arrows now againſt us? Whence is it that you charge us with diviſions, diſorders, &c.? Sir, we humbly pray your gentle acceptance of our two fold anſwer.

Firſt, we have been greatly diſturbed and diſtracted by the ambition and covetouſneſs of ſome amongſt us. Sir, we were in complete order, until Mr. Coddington, wanting that public, ſelf-denying ſpirit which you commend to us in your letter, procured, by moſt untrue information, a monopoly of part of the colony, viz.: Rhode Iſland, to himſelf, and ſo occaſioned our general diſturbance and diſtractions. Secondly, Mr. Dyre, with no leſs want of a public ſpirit, being ruined by party contentions with Mr. Coddington, and being betruſted to bring from England the letters from the Council of State for our reunitings, he hopes for a recruit to himſelf by other men's goods; and, contrary to the State's intentions and expreſſions, plungeth himſelf and ſome others in moſt unneceſſary and unrighteous plundering, both of Dutch and French, and Engliſh alſo, to our great grief, who proteſted againſt ſuch abuſe of our power from England; and the end of it is to the ſhame and reproach of himſelf, and the very Engliſh name, as all theſe parts do witneſs.

Sir, our ſecond anſwer is, (that we may not lay all the

load upon other men's backs,) that poffibly a fweet cup
hath rendered many of us wanton and too active, for we
have long drunk of the cup of as great liberties as any
people that we can hear of under the whole heaven.   We
have not only been long free (together with all New England) from the iron yoke of wolfifh bifhops, and their popifh
ceremonies, (againft whofe cruel oppreffions God raifed
up your noble fpirit in Parliament,) but we have fitten quiet
and dry from the ftreams of blood fpilt by that war in
our native country.   We have not felt the new chains of
the Prefbyterian tyrants, nor in this colony have we been
confumed with the over-zealous fire of the (fo called)
godly chriftian magiftrates.   Sir, we have not known what
an excife means ; we have almoft forgotten what tithes are,
yea, or taxes either, to church or commonwealth.   We
could name other fpecial privileges, ingredients of our
fweet cup, which your great wifdom knows to be very powerful (except more than ordinary watchfulnefs) to render
the beft of men wanton and forgetful.   But, bleffed be
your love, and your loving heart and hand, awakening any
of our fleepy fpirits by your fweet alarm ; and bleffed be
your noble family, root and branch, and all your pious and
prudent engagements and retirements.   We hope you fhall
no more complain of the faddening of your loving heart
by the men of Providence town or of Providence colony,
but that when we are gone and rotten, our pofterity and
children after us fhall read in our town records your pious
and favorable letters and loving kindnefs to us, and this
our anfwer, and real endeavor after peace and righteoufnefs; and to be found, Sir, your moft obliged, and moft
humble fervants, the town of Providence, in Providence
colony, in New England.

GREGORY DEXTER, *Town Clerk.*

To the General Court of Maffachufetts Bay.

PROVIDENCE, 5, 8, 54. (fo called.) [October 5, 1654.][1]

MUCH HONORED SIRS,—I truly wifh you peace, and pray your gentle acceptance of a word, I hope not unreafonable.

We have in thefe parts a found of your meditations of war againft thefe natives, amongft whom we dwell. I confider that war is one of thofe three great, fore plagues, with which it pleafeth God to affect the fons of men. I confider, alfo, that I refufed, lately, many offers in my native country, out of a fincere defire to feek the good and peace of this.

I remember, that upon the exprefs advice of your ever honored Mr. Winthrop, deceafed, I firft adventured to begin a plantation among the thickeft of thefe barbarians.

That in the Pequot wars, it pleafed your honored government to employ me in the hazardous and weighty fervice of negotiating a league between yourfelves and the Narraganfetts, when the Pequot meffengers, who fought the Narraganfetts' league againft the Englifh, had almoft ended that my work and life together.

That at the fubfcribing of that folemn league, which, by the mercy of the Lord, I had procured with the Narraganfetts, your government was pleafed to fend unto me the copy of it, fubfcribed by all hands there, which yet I keep as a monument and a teftimony of peace and faithfulnefs between you both.

That, fince that time, it hath pleafed the Lord fo to order it, that I have been more or lefs interefted and ufed in

---

all your great tranfactions of war or peace, between the Englifh and the natives, and have not fpared purfe, nor pains, nor hazards, (very many times,) that the whole land, Englifh and natives, might fleep in peace fecurely.

That in my laft negotiations in England, with the Parliament, Council of State, and his Highnefs,[1] I have been forced to be known fo much, that if I fhould be filent, I fhould not only betray mine own peace and yours, but alfo fhould be falfe to their honorable and princely names, whofe loves and affections, as well as their fupreme authority are not a little concerned in the peace or war of this country.

At my laft departure for England, I was importuned by the Narraganfett Sachems, and efpecially by Ninigret, to prefent their petition to the high Sachems of England, that they might not be forced from their religion, and, for not changing their religion, be invaded by war; for they faid they were daily vifited with threatenings by Indians that came from about the Maffachufetts, that if they would not pray, they fhould be deftroyed by war. With this their petition I acquainted, in private difcourfes, divers of the chief of our nation, and efpecially his Highnefs, who, in many difcourfes I had with him, never expreffed the leaft tittle of difpleafure, as hath been here reported, but in the midft of difputes, ever expreffed a high fpirit of love and gentlenefs, and was often pleafed to pleafe himfelf with very many queftions, and my anfwers, about the Indian affairs of this country; and, after all hearing of yourfelf and us, it hath pleafed his Highnefs and his Council to grant, amongft other favors to this colony, fome expreffly

[1] Oliver Cromwell.

concerning the very Indians, the native inhabitants of this jurifdiction.

I, therefore, humbly offer to your prudent and impartial view, firft thefe two confiderable terms, it pleafed the Lord to ufe to all that profefs his name (Rom. 12: 18,) if it be poffible, and all men.

I never was againft the righteous ufe of the civil fword of men or nations, but yet fince all men of confcience or prudence ply to windward, to maintain their wars to be defenfive, (as did both King and Scotch, and Englifh and Irifh too, in the late wars,) I humbly pray your confideration, whether it be not only poffible, but very eafy, to live and die in peace with all the natives of this country.

For, fecondly, are not all the Englifh of this land, generally, a perfecuted people from their native foil? and hath not the God of peace and Father of mercies made thefe natives more friendly in this, than our native countrymen in our own land to us? Have they not entered leagues of love, and to this day continued peaceable commerce with us? Are not our families grown up in peace amongft them? Upon which I humbly afk, how it can fuit with Chriftian ingenuity to take hold of fome feeming occafions for their deftructions, which, though the heads be only aimed at, yet, all experience tells us, falls on the body and the innocent.

Thirdly, I pray it may be remembered how greatly the name of God is concerned in this affair, for it cannot be hid, how all England and other nations ring with the glorious converfion of the Indians of New England. You know how many books are difperfed throughout the nation, of the fubject, (in fome of them the Narraganfett chief Sachems are publicly branded, for refufing to pray and be converted ;) have all the pulpits in England been commanded to found of this glorious work, (I fpeak not ironically, but only mention what all the printed books mention,) and that by the highest command and authority of Parliament, and churchwardens went from houfe to houfe, to gather fupplies for this work.

Honored Sirs, Whether I have been and am a friend to the natives' turning to civility and Chriftianity, and whether I have been inftrumental, and defire fo to be, according to my light, I will not trouble you with; only I befeech you confider, how the name of the moft holy and jealous God may be preferved between the clafhings of thefe two, viz. : the glorious converfion of the Indians in New England, and the unneceffary wars and cruel deftructions of the Indians in New England.

Fourthly, I befeech you forget not, that although we are apt to play with this plague of war more than with the other two, famine and peftilence, yet I befeech you confider how the prefent events of all wars that ever have been in the world, have been wonderful fickle, and the future calamities and revolutions, wonderful in the latter end.

Heretofore, not having liberty of taking fhip in your jurifdiction, I was forced to repair unto the Dutch, where mine eyes did fee that firft breaking forth of that Indian war, which the Dutch begun, upon the flaughter of fome Dutch by the Indians; and they queftioned not to finifh it in a few days, infomuch that the name of peace, which fome offered to mediate, was foolifh and odious to them. But before we weighed anchor, their bowries were in flames; Dutch and Englifh were flain. Mine eyes faw their flames at their towns, and the flights and hurries of men, women and children, the prefent removal of all that could for Holland; and after vaſt expenſes, and mutual ſlaughters of Dutch, Engliſh and Indians, about four years, the Dutch were forced, to ſave their plantation from ruin, to make up a moſt unworthy and diſhonorable peace with the Indians.

How frequently is that ſaying in England, that both Scotch and Engliſh had better have borne loans, ſhip money, &c., than run upon ſuch rocks, that even ſucceſs and victory have proved, and are yet like to prove. Yea, this late war with Holland, however begun with zeal againſt God's enemies, as ſome in Parliament ſaid, yet what fruits brought it forth, but the breach of the Parliament, the en-raging of the nation by taxes, the ruin of thouſands who depended on manufactures and merchandize, the loſs of many thouſand ſeamen, and others, many of whom many worlds are not worthy?

But, laſtly, if any be yet zealous of kindling this fire for God, &c., I beſeech that gentleman, whoever he be, to lay himſelf in the oppoſite ſcale, with one of the faireſt buds that ever the ſun of righteouſneſs cheriſhed, Joſiah, that moſt zealous and melting-hearted reformer, who would to war, and againſt warnings, and fell in moſt untimely death and lamentations, and now ſtands, a pillar of ſalt to all ſucceeding generations.

Now, with your patience, a word to theſe nations at war, (occaſion of yours,) the Narraganſetts and Long Iſlanders, I know them both experimentally, and therefore pray you to remember,

Firſt, that the Narraganſetts and Mohawks are the two great bodies of Indians in this country, and they are con-federates, and long have been, and they both yet are friendly and peaceable to the Engliſh. I do humbly con-

35

ceive, that if ever God calls us to a juft war with either of them he calls us to make fure of the one to a friend. It is true fome diftafte was lately here amongft them, but they parted friends, and fome of the Narraganfetts went home with them, and I fear that both thefe and the Long Ifland-ers and Mohegans, and all the natives of the land, may, upon a found of the defeat of the Englifh, be induced eafily to join each with other, againft us.

2. The Narraganfetts, as they were the firft, fo they have been long confederates with you; they have been true, in all the Pequot wars, to you. They occafioned the Mohegans to come in, too, and fo occafioned the Pequots' downfall.

3. I cannot yet learn, that ever it pleafed the Lord, to permit the Narraganfetts to ftain their hands with any Englifh blood, neither in open hoftilities nor fecret mur-ders, as both Pequots and Long Iflanders did, and Mohe-gans alfo, in the Pequot wars. It is true, they are barba-rians, but their greateft offences againft the Englifh have been matters of money, or petty revenging of themfelves on fome Indians, upon extreme provocations, but God kept them clear of our blood.

4. For the people, many hundred Englifh have experi-mented them to be inclined to peace and love with the Englifh nation.

Their late famous long-lived Canonicus fo lived and died, and in the fame moft honorable manner and folem-nity (in their way) as you laid to fleep your prudent peace-maker, Mr. Winthrop, did they honor this, their prudent and peaceable prince. His fon, Mexham, inherits his fpirit. Yea, through all their towns and countries, how frequently do many, and oft-times one Englifhman, travel alone with fafety and loving kindnefs!

The caufe and root of all the prefent mifchief, is the pride of two barbarians, Afcaffaffotic, the Long Ifland Sachem, and Ninigret, of the Narraganfett. The former is proud and foolifh; the latter is proud and fierce. I have not feen him thefe many years, yet from their fober men I hear he pleads,

Firft, that Afcaffaffotic, a very inferior Sachem, bearing himfelf upon the Englifh, hath flain three or four of his people, and fince that, fent him challenges and darings to fight, and mend himfelf.

2. He, Ninigret, confulted, by folemn meffengers, with the chief of the Englifh Governors, Major Endicott, then Governor of the Maffachufetts, who fent him an implicit confent to right himfelf, upon which they all plead that the Englifh have juft occafion of difpleafure.

3. After he had taken revenge upon the Long Iflanders, and brought away about fourteen captives, divers of their chief women, yet he reftored them all again, upon the mediation and defire of the Englifh.

4. After this peace made, the Long Iflanders pretending to vifit Ninigret, at Block Ifland, flaughtered of his Narraganfetts near thirty perfons, at midnight, two of them of great note, efpecially Wepiteammoc's fon, to whom Ninigret was uncle.

5. In the profecution of this war, although he had drawn down the Iflanders to his affiftance, yet, upon proteftation of the Englifh againft his proceedings, he retreated and diffolved his army.

Honored Sirs,

1. I know it is faid the Long Iflanders are fubjects; but I have heard this greatly queftioned, and, indeed, I queftion whether any Indians in this country, remaining bar-

barous and pagan, may with truth or honor be called the Englifh fubjects.

2. But grant them fubjects, what capacity hath their late maffacre of the Narraganfetts, with whom they had made peace, without the Englifh content, though ftill under the Englifh name, put them into?

3. All Indians are extremely treacherous; and if to their own nation, for private ends, revolting to ftrangers, what will they do upon the found of one defeat of the Englifh, or the trade of killing Englifh cattle, and perfons, and plunder, which will, moft certainly be the trade, if any confiderable party efcape alive, as mine eyes beheld in the Dutch war.

But I befeech you, fay your thoughts and the thoughts of your wives and little ones, and the thoughts of all Englifh, and of God's people in England, and the thoughts of his Highnefs and Council, (tender of thefe parts,) if, for the fake of a few inconfiderable pagans, and beafts, wallowing in idlenefs, ftealing, lying, whoring, treacherous witchcrafts, blafphemies, and idolatries, all that the gracious hand of the Lord hath fo wonderfully planted in the wildernefs, fhould be deftroyed.

How much nobler were it, and glorious to the name of God and your own, that no pagan fhould dare to ufe the name of an Englifh fubject, who comes not out in fome degree from barbarifm to civility, in forfaking their filthy nakednefs, in keeping fome kind of cattle, which yet your councils and commands may tend to, and, as pious and prudent deceafed Mr. Winthrop faid, that civility may be a leading ftep to Chriftianity, is the humble defire of your moft unfeigned in all fervices of love,

ROGER WILLIAMS,
of Providence colony, Prefident.

For his much honored, kind friend, Mr. Winthrop, at Pequot, thefe.

PROVIDENCE, 9, 8, 54. (fo called.) [Oct. 9, 1654.][1]

SIR,—I was lately fadded to hear of fome barbarous dealings to your prejudice on your ifland. I am again fadded with the tidings of weaknefs in your family, and I hope you are fadded with me at this Fire which is now kindling, the fire of God's wrath and jealoufly, which, if God gracioufly quench not, may burn to the foundations both of Indians and Englifh together. I have (upon the firft found of this fire) prefented confiderations to the General Court of Maffachufetts; Major Willard tells me, he faw them not, (the Court not yet fetting,) therefore I have prefented him with a copy of them, which upon opportunity and defire, I prefume you may command the fight of. I have therein had occafion to mention your precious peacemaking farther.

Sir, fome of the foldiers, faid here that 'tis true the Narraganfetts had yet killed no Englifh, but they had killed two hundred of Mr. Winthrop's goats, and that it was read in the Bofton meeting houfe, that Mr. Winthrop was robbed and undone, and was flying from the place unlefs fuccor was fent him. I hope to hear otherwife, and that notwithftanding any private lofs, yet that noble fpirit of your father ftill lives in you, and will ftill work (if poffible) to quench this devouring fire in the kindling. I am not yet without hope but it may pleafe the God of peace and Father of mercies to create peace for us, and by this time to inflame our

---

[1] 3 *Mafs. Hift. Coll.* vol. x p. 4.

hearts more with love to him and felicities in him, which neither fword, nor famine, nor peftilence can take from us, which (however otherwife he may deal with us) will abundantly compenfate all their fhaking below, though (feemingly) great and fundamental to us.

Sir, with very cordial refpects to you both, I am yours in the fervice of love unfeigned.

Roger Williams.

[The letter of Mr. Williams to the Town of Providence, of Auguft preceding had a falutary effect, and harmony was once more reftored in the colony. At the General Election, which followed in September, 1654, Mr. Williams was chofen Prefident. " Thus far " fays Backus, " things appeared encouraging; but as tyranny and licentioufnefs are equally enemies, both to government and liberty, Mr. Williams often had both to contend with. Soon after this fettlement, a perfon fent a feditious paper to the town of Providence," and alfo circulated it among the citizens. " That it was blood-guiltlefs, and againft the rule of the gofpel to execute judgment upon tranfgreffors againft the public or private weal."—*Hiſt. of the Baptiſts*, vol. i. p. 296. While fuch fentiments were propagated, Williams could not remain filent, and accordingly addreffed the following letter to the town, in which he denies that he had ever given the flighteft fanction to principles fo hoftile to civil peace and the dictates of reafon and fcripture.]

To the Town of Providence.

[Providence, January, 1654–5.][1]

That ever I fhould fpeak or write a tittle, that tends to fuch an infinite liberty of confcience, is a miftake, and which I have ever difclaimed and abhorred. To prevent fuch miftakes, I fhall at prefent only propofe this cafe: There goes many a fhip to fea, with many hundred fouls in one fhip, whofe weal and woe is common, and is a true picture of a commonwealth, or a human combination or

[1] *Providence Records ;* alfo, Backus, *Hiſt. of the Baptiſts,* vol. i. p. 297.

fociety. It hath fallen out fometimes, that both papifts and proteftants, Jews and Turks, may be embarked in one fhip; upon which fuppofal I affirm, that all the liberty of confcience, that ever I pleaded for, turns upon thefe two hinges—that none of the papifts, proteftants, Jews, or Turks, be forced to come to the fhip's prayers or worfhip, nor compelled from their own particular prayers or worfhip, if they practice any. I further add, that I never denied, that notwithftanding this liberty, the commander of this fhip ought to command the fhip's courfe, yea, and alfo command that juftice, peace and fobriety, be kept and practiced, both among the feamen and all the paffengers. If any of the feamen refufe to perform their fervices, or paffengers to pay their freight; if any refufe to help, in perfon or purfe, towards the common charges or defence; if any refufe to obey the common laws and orders of the fhip, concerning their common peace or prefervation; if any fhall mutiny and rife up againft their commanders and officers; if any fhould preach or write that there ought to be no commanders or officers, becaufe all are equal in Chrift, therefore no mafters nor officers, no laws nor orders, nor corrections nor punifhments;—I fay, I never denied, but in fuch cafes, whatever is pretended, the commander or commanders may judge, refift, compel and punifh fuch tranfgreffors, according to their deferts and merits. This if ferioufly and honeftly minded, may, if it fo pleafe the Father of lights, let in fome light to fuch as willingly fhut not their eyes.

I remain ftudious of your common peace and liberty.

ROGER WILLIAMS.

Roger Williams to John Winthrop, Jr.

15, 12, 54. (fo called.) [15th February, 1654.][1]

SIR,—It hath not been this fharp and bitter feafon which could have frozen my pen from faluting you both (having received yours fome weeks fince,) but I could not get a meeting with Ninigret, and meffengers effected nothing, which I fent to him. Your great trial, lofs and hindrance I am exceedingly grieved at, and cordially wifh it were in my hand to contribute to your abundant fatisfaction and reparation. I have taken willingly any pains about it, and fhall; and beg of God himfelf to pleafe to make up thefe gaps and breaches, with the teachings and comfortings of his Eternal Spirit.

I have had a folemn debate with Ninigret and the reft of the Narraganfett Sachems, in a late great meeting at Warwick, whither they came down with four fcore armed men, to demand fatisfaction for the robbing of Peficcufh, his fifter's grave, and mangling of her flefh; againft John Garriard, a Dutchman, whofe crew, and it is feared, himfelf, committed that ghaftly and ftinking villainy againft them. In this meeting the Sachems were unanimous and (as union ftrengthens) they were fo bold as to talk often of men's lives, and of fighting with us, and demanded an Englifh child for hoftage until fatisfaction, becaufe John Garriard had lived at Warwick, and had goods and debts there ftill remaining. At laft it pleafed the Lord to pacify all with our attaching of the Dutchman's goods and debts, until he have made fatisfaction (in the Dutch jurifdiction or the Englifh) to the Sachems charge againft him. There was in his crew, one Samuel, a hat-

[1] 4 *Mafs. Hift. Coll.* vol. vi. p. 286.

ter, and one Jones, a feaman, and an Irifhman, perfons infamous, fo that we fear John Garriard was drawn in by them, at leaft to confent to fhare with them in fuch a booty.

Sir, this troublefome occafion furnifhed me with full agitations about your wrong and demands alfo. And befides this I have had both former and later difcourfings and fearchings with divers Indians, and fome that were prefent, and fome that were difaffeated to Ninigret, and all anfwers and agitations, &c., amount to, firft, an abfolute denial that either the Sachems or people know of any cattle of yours flain by themfelves or the Inlanders, excepting three or four goats, which the Pawcomtuck Indians killed in their breaking up in difpleafure, and departure from Ninigret, and in their march towards the Eaftern end of your ifland homeward.[1]

2. They affirm that fuch flaughters could not poffibly be made by any of themfelves or the ftrangers, but they fhould know of it, being intermingled with them in all their quarters: and whereas I faid they were long there, and had fpent provifions; they fay they had three canoes continually going from your ifland to Pequot for provifion; which though fometime the winds hindered fome hours, yet by day or by night they always came and brought a fupply.

[1] Troubles with Ninigret had been renewed during the paft year. That chief had carried on a war with the Indians of Long Ifland, who had put themfelves under the protection of the Englifh. The Commiffioners of the United Colonies ordered Ninigret to appear at Hartford; and upon his refufal to comply with their requeft, determined on a war againft him. An armed force was fent into the Narraganfett country, when Ninigret fled, and about one hundred Pequots who had been left with the Narraganfetts fince the war, put themfelves under the protection of the Englifh. The armed force retired without attacking the enemy.—Holmes, *Annals*, p. 301.

36

3. They fay that fome Englifh whom you trufted there, not only gave Ninigret one goat, but they have known divers given or fold to Englifh or Dutch pinnaces. I confefs, Sir, this laft came not within my thoughts to favor of truth, until conferring with fome Englifh further, I find it undeniable from many Englifh witneffes, that many goats have been fold (and fome at cheap prices,) by fome whom you have trufted, to many veffels. Some of the veffels belong to our towns, and they name your kinfman Mr. Symons. The particulars are many : one I fhall hint, that you may review whether you had account of it or no : Mr. Smith's veffel gave him an ell of holland for one goat, which in our parts would yield about 14*s* : fo that I hear fome veffels brought (more then for prefent fpending) fome live goats along with them.

Sir, this Englifh work I believe is true, although I dare not abfolve the barbarians from your charge, and therefore fhall ftill continue my utmoft care and fearch.

Sir, the tidings ftirring amongft us is (as is said) from a fhip (about four months fince arrived from England,) reporting flaughters of Scotch and Englifh in divers battles fought in Scotland ; but (as is faid) the Lord was pleafed to turn the fcales to the Englifh. It is faid alfo that the Parliament (which was to begin the 3rd of September,) was broke up in difcontent. It is faid that a fleet was defigned againft Hifpaniola, and that Mr. Winflow goes in chief command, or to be Governor.[1] Sir, I yet believe not this firft found of things, and yet I believe them to be very like to be true, and greater and greater Revolutions approach-

---

[1] Edward Winflow, was appointed by Cromwell, Commiffioner to attend the expedition againft Hifpaniola in 1655; and died on the paffage, between that ifland and Jamaica, May 8th, of that year. *Edi. Winthrop Papers.*

ing. The invifible and eternal Jehovah will make his juftice and mercy more and more vifibly glorious, in eternal
fucceffive difcoveries of himfelf to his, and to the works
and creatures of his mighty hand.

It hath pleafed God, Sir, to take away (fome few days
fince) the wife of our Jofhua Windfor (once a fervant to
your dear father). She had made a paffionate wifh that
God would part them, and take away him or her. It
pleafed his Jealoufly to hear her, and to take away a child
in her womb alfo, of which fhe could not be delivered.

We have had fome gufts amongft us as to our whole
Colony and civil order. At my coming over our neighbors were run into divifions. By the good hand of the
Lord they were perfuaded to choofe twenty-four Commiffioners (fix out of a town) to reconcile. They united and
hailed me out (fore againft my fpirit) to public fervice:
yet the fpirits of fome have not been fo reconcileable:
Tho. Olney[1] and my brother in our town, (upon private
grudges), Mr. Eafton and Mr. Dyer, at Newport, fearing
Sabaudies pinnace muft be paid for, which cafe the Court
at Maffachufetts lately would not determine, but left it to
be tried in our own Colony, which was the late anfwer of
the Court at Ipfwich to Mr. Ames, who fued Mr. Dyer
in the Bay. What plots and diggings have been ufed to
overturn all Courts, fo that there might be an efcape, and
therefore Newport is made to ftand off (except fome few)
from the reft of the Colony.

Sir, we have a found of a Gen: Governor, and that Ba-

---

[1] Thomas Olney was among the ear- lem church, from which he was expelled
lieft fettlers of Providence, and one of for uniting in the errors of Williams.
the committee in 1647 to form a gov- His name appears among the Affiftants in
ernment. He was a member of the Sa- the Charter of 1663.

ron Rigby his fon is the man : but it is time to excufe this
prolixity, and to end with humble defires to the moft Holy
and Eternal King to protect, to direct, and comfort your
fpirits in all prefent and future trials.   So prays, Sir,

Yours moft unworthy

ROGER WILLIAMS.

Sir, thefe enclofed were fent to me from Mr. White,
now wintering at Warwick. It is faid he hath fkill in moft
works; many of ours have thoughts of trying his fkill
about a new bridge at Providence, and he hath promifed
to come over to us to confult, but the weather hath hindered.

Mr. Foote hath once and again moved for Iron Works
at Providence.   He told me that you had fpeech with him
about his getting of iron men to Pequot, but he thought
yourfelf would be willing to promote the work as well
here as there, and therefore promifed me to write to you.
If I had power in my hand I would venture to fuch a public good, and however would gladly contribute all affiftance, efpecially if your loving fpirit and experience be
pleafed to give encouragement.

Sir, I have not at prefent by me a copy (fair or foul) of
my Confiderations prefented to the Gen. Court at Bofton :
fomething there is in them of paffages between the Lord
Protector and myfelf; otherways they are but known
things (efpecially to yourfelf): however, if poffible I can,
I will prefent your defire with the fight of them.

POST S.—This letter hath long lain by expecting conveyance.   Indeed Ninigret promifed to fend a meffenger
for them, but (whether the winter or other occafions hindered, ficknefs, death, &c.,) yet it hath ftuck by me as

an arrow in my fide, leaft I fhould feem to neglect fuch a friend and fuch a cafe.

For the fleet of which you pleafe a line (in this your welcome tidings of your healths) we hear of fixty or one hundred fail. I know the Protector had ftrong thoughts of Hifpaniola and Cuba. Mr. Cotton's interpreting of Euphrates to be the Weft Indies: the fupply of gold, to take off taxes), and the provifion of a warmer *Diuerticulum* and *Receptaculum* then New England is, will make a footing into thofe parts very precious, and if it fhall pleafe God to vouchfafe fuccefs to this fleet, I look to hear of an invitation at leaft to thefe parts for removal, from his Highnefs, who looks on New England only with an eye of pity, as poor, cold and ufelefs.

And furely this nonefuch winter is like to fet any wheel a going for removals of very many.

Capt. Gibbons at beginning of this winter (as I prefume you have long fince heard) made this winter his laft, and is departed.

Mr. Dunfter[1] (as is faid) expected to be oufted about his judgment of children's baptifm, withdrew himfelf, and Mr. Chauncy,[2] who was fhipped for England, is now mafter of the College.

[1] Henry Dunfter, firft Prefident of Harvard College, inducted into office Auguft 27, 1640. He was highly refpected for his learning, piety and manner of government; but having imbibed the principles of Antipedobaptifm, was induced to refign his office in 1654. He removed to Scituate, Mafs., where he paffed the remainder of his days in peace. He died in 1659.—Blake, *Biog. Dict.*

[2] Rev. Charles Chauncy, fucceeded Mr. Dunfter as Prefident of Harvard College. He was vicar of Ware, in England. Being fined and imprifoned for non-conformity, he determined to feek the enjoyment of the rights of confcience in New England, where he came in 1638. After living as a fettled minifter, chiefly at Scituate, for twelve years, he was invited to return to England. He went to Bofton to embark, but the prefidency of the College being then vacant,

We alfo hear that two of Mr. Dells[1] books were lately burnt at the Maffachufetts, (poffibly) containing fome fharp things againft the Prefbyterians and Academians, of which I brought over one called the Trial of Spirits.

I pray you to read and return this Jew. I have alfo an anfwer to him by a good plain man, expounding all which the Jew takes literally, in a fpiritual way : and I have (in a difcourfe of a Knight (L'Eftrange)[2] proving Americans no Jews) another touch againft him : however, I rejoiced to fee fuch induftrious fpirits breathing in that people toward the Meffiah or Chrift of God.

Mr. Foot is faid (at prefent) to refolve for the Dutch : upon occafion of my declaring againft his man, Mr. Fowler's diforderly marriage in Mr. Foot's houfe, without any publication, and upon that occafion my refufing to promote the Iron Works as yet; he is difpleafed, and fpeaks of departure. I truly love and pity the man, yet furely from him have the Indians been furnifhed with ftore of liquors, from his houfe have the incivilities of our town been much encouraged, and much evil report he hath incurred about this marriage. He faith he knew not of it 'till over night. But (although the pretended marriage was not,) it may be refolved on before over night, yet I am forry to hear fuch talk in the town of what he knew before. Sir, the truth is (as one faid to Queen Elizabeth)

---

he was induced to accept office, and was inducted into it in 1654. He retained the place until his death in 1672, at the age of 81. He publifhed feveral volumes of fermons and theological works. BLAKE, *Biog. Dict.*

[1] William Dell, Rector of Yelden, and Mafter of Gonvil and Caius College ; ejected 1662. He publifhed in 1663 " *The Tryall of Spirits, both in Teachers and Hearers ;*" " *The Stumbling Stone,*" together with Sermons and other Theological Treatifes.—"*Select Works.*" London, 1773.

[2] Hamon L'Eftrange was the author of a book entitled "*Americans no Jews, or Improbabilities that the Americans are of that race.*"—London, 1652.

Profecto omnes fumus licentiâ deteriores. We enjoy liberties of foul and body, but it is licenfe we defire, except the Moft Holy help us : in whom, Sir, I defire to be ever

Yours,   ROGER WILLIAMS.

Mine and my wife's true refpects to Mrs. Winthrop, &c.

For my honored, kind friend, Mr. Winthrop, at his houfe at Pequot. Leave this with Mr. White, of Warwick.

PROVIDENCE, 23, 1. [March 23,] 1655, (fo called.)[1]

SIR,—Cordial refpects prefented. Mr. White coming to you, cannot come without falutation. I have this laft week many letters from England; but all dated the firft week of the Parliament's fitting. The houfe confifted moft of Prefbyterian fautors.[2] All that are waived are ranked into Cavaliers and Levellers:[3] upon the grand queftion of the Supreme Legiflature, the Lord Bradfhaw[4] fpake openly that if a Parliament were not fupreme, then was he a murderer of King Charles. Sir Arthur Hazelrig fpake high : but the report is double : fome fay a vote paft that they would not difpute that point, fome fay they did difpute, and therefore a breach followed, and the imprifon-

----

[1] 4 *Mafs. Hift. Coll.* vol. vi. p. 292.
[2] *Fauter*, a favourer, a fupporter.
[3] *Cavaliers*. The name given to the party which adhered to King Charles I. in oppofition to the Roundheads or *Levellers*, who were the adherents of Parliament.
[4] John Bradfhaw was Prefident of the tribunal by which Charles I. was tried. In the conteft between the king and the people, Bradfhaw efpoufed the caufe of the latter. Cromwell, to whofe ufurpation he was hoftile, deprived him of office. He died in 1659; and at the Reftoration, his remains were difinterred and hanged at Tyburn.

ment of Bradſhaw and Hazelrig, &c., and it is ſaid here
(by Dutch news) two beheaded. The Protector in his
ſpeech told them he had ſettled the three Nations, had
made peace with Holland, Denmark, Sweden, Switzerland,
and entered far into a treaty with France, &c. The ſea
preparations of the Engliſh rendered others jealous: ſo
that (and the troubles of the Dutch among themſelves,
which cauſe them to keep a guard of eight hundred at
the Hague) that cauſed new orders to the Admiralty, for
careful ſtriking to the Engliſh: Gen. Blake[1] with his
fleet was bound for the Southward: Gen. Pen[2] and Mr.
Winſlow with him for the Weſt. It is feared that his
poor wife will miſs him. He writes to N. Plymouth that
(except the Parliament prohibited) they were ready to ſet
ſail: he hath new fitted himſelf and ſent over his former
apparel. The Portugal embaſſador[3] hath been beheaded
for a murder in the Exchange, and Mrs. Mohun and her
maid ſtood in the pillory before the Exchange, for attempting his eſcape by women's apparel. Mr. Marſhall, and

[1] Robert Blake a celebrated Engliſh Admiral. In the ſtruggle between King Charles I. and his people, he eſpouſed the cauſe of liberty. After diſtinguiſh-ing himſelf in the army, he was placed in command of the fleet, when he de-ſtroyed the Royal ſquadron under Prince Rupert, at Malaga. In 1653 he de-feated the Dutch fleet, under Van Tromp, and the following year gained a victory over the Spaniſh fleet in the Medite-ranean. He died in 1657 and was bu-ried with great honors in Henry VIIths chapel At the reſtoration his body was torn from its reſting place and buried in a pit in St. Martin's Church yard.—*Bio-graphia Britannica.*

[2] Admiral Wm. Penn, Commander of the Engliſh fleet in the deſtruction of Ja-maica. He was a member of Parlia-ment, and after the Reſtoration obtained a high command under the Duke of York. He was knighted by Charles II. for his ſervices. Edward Winſlow, of Plymouth, probably accompanied Admi-ral Penn, as it is ſtated in the previous letter that he had gone to the Weſt In-dies. He was one of the three Com-miſſioners appointed by Cromwell to ſu-perintend the operations there.

[3] Dom Pantaleon, brother of the Portugueſe ambaſſador, was executed Ju-ly 10, 1654, for the murder of Mr. Greenway, at the Exchange.

Viner, and Mr. Tho. Goodwin,[1] miniſter to the Parliament. Mr. Goodwin preſſed the inſtance of Pharaoh and the letting of God's people free to worſhip, leaſt the Lord ſend new plagues and breaches. Sir, your meſſenger calls: I end. Yours unworthy

ROGER WILLIAMS.

I ſhall be thankful for the Jeſuits Maxims, of which I have heard, but ſaw them not.

We hear from the Bay that Capt. Leverett[2] took a Dutch ſhip lately upon the Act for Trade: whether it be for that or words, he is bound to appear at the General Court.

For my honored kind friend Mr. John Winthrop, at Pequot, theſe.

[PROVIDENCE, 1, 1, 55. (ſo called.) [March 1, 1655.][3]

SIR,—Loving reſpeɛts and beſt wiſhes, &c. I lately preſented you with a line by Mr. White: ſince I received more letters from England, confirming the tidings of two great fleets ready to ſet ſail from England the beginning of

---

[1] Thomas Goodwin, a Puritan divine, born in 1600. In 1630, to avoid perſecution he went to Arnheim, in Holland, where he ſettled. During the civil wars he returned to London and was appointed by Cromwell, Preſident of Magdalen College, Oxford. He attended the Protector in his laſt illneſs, and was ejeɛted from Oxford after the Reſtoration. He preached to an aſſembly of Independents in London until his deceaſe in 1679.— BLAKE, *Biog. Diɛtionary.*

[2] John Leverett, a Delegate to the General Court; afterwards Speaker, and from 1673 to 1679 Governor of Maſſachuſetts.

[3] 4 *Maſs. Hiſt. Coll.* vol. vi. p. 294.

This letter was evidently written after that which next precedes it, and it is probable that the date ſhould be 1, 2, 55, i. e. April 1, 1655.

37

September.   The one with Gen. Blake for the Southward;
the other with Gen. Pen for the Weſt Indies.   To him
was joined Mr. Winſlow, as Counſellor, deſigned Governor of what part ſhould be conquered.   The Parliament
ſat, and after three days debate about the laſt change of
government, the Lord Proteƈtor ſent for the Parliament
into the Painted Chamber, and told them that there was a
reciprocation, and that the ſame power which made him
Proteƈtor had called the Parliament, and therefore before
they ſhould ſit again, he muſt require a teſt or recogni-
tion by ſubſcription to his negative voice, as to the preſent
government by a Proteƈtor and a Parliament, as to the not
ſitting of the Parliament above five months, as to the mi-
litia, and as to perſecution for religion.   To this purpoſe a
table was ſet near the Parliament door, whereon the recog-
nition was preſented in parchment, unto which Mr. Len-
thall, the Speaker, and one hundred and forty ſubſcribed
preſently and entered: ſome diſſented, among whom were
Bradſhaw and Hazelrig,[1] who, (it is ſaid) are in the Tower.   The Portugal Embaſſador's brother was beheaded for
a murder, and one Coll: whoſe name I yet know not.
One Mrs. Mohun ſtood on the pillory, for attempting the
Portugal's eſcape in woman's apparel.

The 3rd of September, the day of the Parliament's firſt ſitting, was ſeen in the heavens over Hull, two armies fighting: the one from the northweſt which worſted the other
from the eaſt, both red: then a black army from the north-

---

[1] Sir Arthur Hazelrig. An Engliſh
puritan who took a prominent part in
the oppoſition to Charles I.   He was a
member of the Long Parliament, and
one of the five members whom the king
attempted to arreſt in 1642 on a charge
of treaſon.   During the Civil War he
ſerved in the army of Parliament as
Colonel.   He was created a peer by
Cromwell, but preferred to retain his
ſeat in Parliament.   He died in 1660.—
THOMAS, *Dic. of Biography.*

weft which worfted the red from the eaft, and remained victor. Some that faw it faid they faw the like at the beginning of the late Long Parliament.

Holland had great trouble with Zealand, and the Orengian faction, fo that the Hague and Amfterdam were ftrongly guarded. New orders were fent to their Admiralty for careful ftriking to the Englifh.[1] Sir, with prayers for your health and eternal peace, I reft yours in all fervices of love.

ROGER WILLIAMS.

To my honored kind friend Mr. Winthrop, at Pequot, thefe prefent.

PROVIDENCE, the 26, 2, 55. [April 26th, 1655.][2]

SIR,—Loving refpects to you both prefented, wifhing you a joyful fpring after all your fad and gloomy, fharp and bitter winter blafts and fnows. Sir, one of your friends among the Narraganfett Sachems, Mexham, fends this meffenger unto me and prays me to write to you for your help about a gun, which Kittatteafh, Uncas his fon, hath lately taken from this bearer, Ahauanfquatuck, out of his houfe at Pawchauquet. He will not own any offence he gave him, but that he is fubject to Mexham, though poffibly Kittatteafh may allege other caufes, yea and true alfo. I doubt not of your loving eye on the matter, as God fhall pleafe

---

[1] In the treaty between Great Britain and the States-General, concluded at Weftminfter, April 5, 1654, it was agreed that the fhips of the United Provinces, meeting any Englifh fhip-of- war in the Britifh feas, fhould ftrike the flag and lower the topfail.

[2] KNOWLES' *Mem. of Roger Williams,* p. 281 ; 3 *Mafs. Hift. Coll.* vol. x. p. 10.

to give you opportunity. Sir, the laft firft day divers of Bofton merchants were with me, (about Sergeant Holfey run from Bofton hither, and a woman after him, who lays her great belly to him.) They tell me, that by a bark come from Virginia, they are informed of God's merciful hand in the fafe arrival of Major Sedgwick and that fleet in the weft of England, and that General Penn was not yet gone out, but riding (all things ready) in Torbay, waiting for the word; and by letters from good and great friends in England, I underftand there are like to be great agitations in this country, if that fleet fucceed.

Sir, a hue and cry came to my hand lately from the Governor at Bofton, after two youths, one run from Captain Oliver, whom I lighted on and have returned; another from James Bill of Bofton, who I hear paft through our town, and faid he was bound for Pequot. His name is James Pitnie; he hath on a blackifh coat and hat, and a pair of greenifh breeches and green knit ftockings. I would now (with very many thanks) have returned you your Jefuit's Maxims, but I was loth to truft them in fo wild a hand, nor fome tidings which I have from England. Thefe merchants tell me, that Blake was gone againft the Duke of Leghorn,[1] and had fent for ten frigates more.

Sir, the God of peace fill your foul with that ftrange kind of peace which paffeth all underftanding.

So prays, Sir, your unworthy

ROGER WILLIAMS.

[1]Admiral Blake was at this time in the Mediteranean making great havoc among the Spanifh veffels.

To the General Court of Magistrates and Deputies Assembled at Boston.

PROVIDENCE, 15, 9 mo. 55. (so called.) [15th Nov. 1655.][1]

MUCH HONORED SIRS,—It is my humble and earnest petition unto God and you, that you may so be pleased to exercise command over your own spirits, that you may not mind myself nor the English of these parts (unworthy with myself of your eye) but only that face of equity (English and Christian) which I humbly hope may appear in these representations following.

First, may it please you to remember, that concerning the town of Warwick, (in this colony,) there lies a suit of £2000 damages against you before his Highness and the Lords of his Council; I doubt not, if you so please, but that (as Mr. Winslow and myself had well nigh ordered it) some gentlemen from yourselves and some from Warwick, deputed, may friendly and easily determine that affair between you.

Secondly, the Indians which pretend your name at Warwick and Pawtuxet, (and yet live as barbarously, if not more than any in the country) please you to know their insolencies upon ourselves and cattle (unto £20 damages per annum) are insufferable by English spirits; and please you to give credence, that to all these they pretend your name, and affirm that they dare not (for offending you) agree with us, nor come to rules of righteous neighborhood, only they know you favor us not and therefore sent us for redress unto you.

Thirdly, concerning four English families at Pawtuxet, may it please you to remember that two controversies they

[1] Hutchinson *Papers*, Boston, 1769, p. 275.

have long (under your name) maintained with us, to a conftant obftructing of all order and authority amongft us.

To our complaint about our lands, they lately have pro-feffed a willingnefs to arbitrate, but to obey his Highnefs' authority in this charter, they fay, they dare not for your fakes, though they live not by your laws nor bear your common charges, nor ours, but evade both under color of your authority.[1]

[1] It appears by this letter that the quarrels and diforders were continued at Warwick and Pawtuxet, and that they were countenanced if not fomented by Maffachufetts.

By a letter received by Mr. Williams from Cromwell, the Protector, it appears that he had been advifed by the colony's agent in England, (John Clarke,) " of fome particulars concerning the govern-ment " This letter being prefented to the Affembly at its June feffion, at Portf-mouth, it was enacted that " Whereas, we have been rent and torn with di-vifions, and his Highnefs has fent unto us an exprefs command, to provide againft internal commotions, by which his High-nefs noteth, that not only ourfelves are difhonored and endangered, but alfo dif-honor and detriment redounds to the commonwealth of England : It is order-ed, that if any perfon be found by the examination of the General Court of Commiffioners, to be a ringleader of factions or divifions among us, he fhall be fent over at his own charges, as a prifo-ner, to receive his trial or fentence at the pleafure of his Highnefs and the Lords of the Council."—*R. I. Colonial Records,* vol. i. p. 318.

This action of the General Affembly had its effect, and appears to have re-fulted in a reconciliation between fome of the prominent men of the Colony. In a volume of Records in the office of the Secretary of State, is the following memorandum in the handwriting of Mr. Williams:

" I, William Coddington do freely fubmit to the authority of his Highnefs in the colony as it is now united, and that with all my heart.

" Whereas there have been differences depending between William Coddington, Esq., and Mr. William Dyre, both of Newport, we declare joyfully for our-felves and heirs by this prefent record, that a full agreement and conclufion is made between us, by our worthy friends Mr. Baulfton, Mr. Gorton, Mr. John Smith, of Warwick, Mr. John Greene, jun., of Warwick, and Mr. John Eafton ; and in witnefs whereof, we fubfcribe our hands, and defire this to be recorded, this prefent 14th of March, 1655–1656.

WILLIAM CODDINGTON,
WILLIAM DYRE.

In prefence of
Roger Williams, *Prefident,*
John Roome,
Benedict Arnold,
John Greene, jr.

Honored Sirs, I cordially profefs it before the Moft High, that I believe it, if not only they but ourfelves and all the whole country, by joint confent, were fubject to your government, it might be a rich mercy ; but as things yet are, and fince it pleafed firft the Parliament, and then the Lord Admiral and Committee for Foreign Plantations, and fince the Council of State, and laftly the Lord Protector and his Council, to continue us as a diftinct colony, yea, and fince it hath pleafed yourfelves, by public letters and references to us from your public courts, to own the authority of his Highnefs amongft us ; be pleafed to confider how unfuitable it is for yourfelves (if thefe families at Pawtuxet plead truth) to be the inftructors of all orderly proceedings amongft us ; for I humbly appeal to your own wifdom and experience, how unlikely it is for a people to be compelled to order and common charges, when others in their bofoms, are by fuch (feeming) partiality exempted from both.

And, therefore, (laftly) be pleafed to know, that there are (upon the point) but two families which are fo obftructive and deftructive to an equal proceeding of civil order amongft us ; for one of thefe four families, Stephen Arnold, defires to be uniform with us ; a fecond, Zacharie Rhodes,[1] being in the way of dipping is (potentially) banifhed by you. Only William Arnold and William Carpenter, (very far, alfo in religion, from you, if you knew all) they have fome color, yet in a late conference, they all plead that all the obftacle is their offending of yourfelves.

[1] Stephen Arnold and Zacharie Rhodes were admitted freemen of Providence in 1658, but had, for fome years previous, lived in Pawtuxet. The latter was the anceftor of the late Chriftopher and William Rhodes, and many others of the name in Pawtuxet ; alfo of the late James T. Rhodes of Providence. William Arnold and William Carpenter were among the earlier fettlers at Providence, and in 1638 received from Mr. Williams a transfer of land bought by him from Miantonomo and Canonicus.

Fourthly, whereas, (I humbly conceive) with the people of this colony your commerce is as great as with any in the country, and our dangers (being a frontier people to the barbarians) are greater than those of other colonies, and the ill consequences to yourselves would be not a few nor small, and to the whole land, were we first maffacred or maftered by them.   I pray your equal and favorable reflection upon that your law, which prohibits us to buy of you all means of our neceffary defence of our lives and families, (yea in this moft bloody and maffacreing time.)

We are informed that tickets have rarely been denied to any English of the country; yea, the barbarians (though notorious in lies) if they profefs fubjection, they are furnifhed; only ourfelves, by former and later denial, feem to be devoted to the Indian fhambles and maffacres.

The barbarians all the land over, are filled with artillery and ammunition from the Dutch, openly and horridly, and from all the English over the country, (by ftealth.)   I know they abound fo wonderfully, that their activity and infolence is grown fo high that they daily confult, and hope, and threaten to render us flaves, as they long fince (and now moft horribly) have made the Dutch.

For myfelf (as through God's goodnefs) I have refufed the gain of thoufands by fuch a murderous trade, and think no law yet extant, among yourfelves or us, fecure enough againft fuch villainly; fo am I loth to fee fo many hundreds (if not fome thoufands) in this colony, deftroyed like fools and beafts without refiftance.   I grieve that fo much blood fhould cry againft yourfelves, yea, and I grieve that (at this inftant by thefe fhips) this cry and the premifes fhould now trouble his Highnefs and his Council.   For the feafonable preventing of which,

is this humble addrefs prefented to your wifdom, by him
who defires to be

Your unfeigned and faithful fervant,

ROGER WILLIAMS,

Of Providence Plantations, Prefident.

Hon. Sirs, fince my letter, it comes into my heart to
pray your leave to add a word as to myfelf, viz. : at my
laft return from England I prefented your then honored
Governor, Mr. Bellingham, with an order of the Lords of
the Council for my free taking fhip or landing at your
ports, unto which it pleafed Mr. Bellingham to fend me
his affent in writing ; I humbly crave the recording of it
by yourfelves, left forgetfulnefs hereafter, again put me
upon fuch diftreffes as, God knows, I fuffered when I laft
paft through your colony to our native country.

---

*For his much honored, kind friend, Mr. John Winthrop, at
Pequot or elfewhere, thefe prefents.*

PROVIDENCE, 21, 12, 55, 56. (fo called.) [February 21, 1656.][1]

SIR,—This opportunity makes me venture this falutation,
though we hear queftion of your being at Pequot. Thefe
friends can fay more of affairs than I can write. I have
letters from England of proceedings there, which yet are
not come; fome I have received, which tell me, that the
Lord hath yet created peace, although the fword is yet

---

[1] KNOWLES, *Memoirs of Roger Williams*, p. 287; 3 *Mafs. Hift. Coll.* vol. x. p. 18.

38

forced (by garrifons) to enforce it. I cannot hear of open wars with France, but only with Spain, and that the profe-cution of that Weft India expedition is ftill with all po-ffible vigor on both fides intended. This diverfion againft the Spaniards hath turned the face and thoughts of many Englifh, fo that the faying of thoufands now is, crown the Protector with gold, though the fullen yet cry, crown him with thorns. The former two or three years with plenty unthankfully received in England; the Lord fent abund-ance of waters this laft fummer, which fpoiled their corn over moft parts of the land. Sir Henry Vane being retired to his own private, in Lincolnfhire, hath now publifhed his obfervations as to religion;[1] he hath fent me one of his books, (though yet at Bofton.) His father is dead, and the inheritance falls to him, and ten or twelve thoufand more than fhould if his father had lived but a month longer; but though his father caft him off, yet he hath not loft in tem-porals, by being caft off for God. Our acquaintance Ma-jor Sedgwick, is faid to be fucceffor to unfuccefsful Vena-bles, caft into the tower. Your brother Stephen fucceeds Major General Harrifon.[2] The Pope endeavors the uni-

---

[1] Sir H. Vane was the author of "The Retired Man's Meditations," London, 1655. Two Treatifes: I. On the Myf-tical Body of Chrift on Earth. II. The Face of the Times. London: 1662, and others. "Sir Henry Vane was one of the moft profound minds that ever ex-ifted,—not inferior perhaps to Bacon. Milton has a fine fonnet addreffed to him,—

"Vane, young in years, in fage experience old."

His works difplay aftonifhing powers. They are remarkable as containing the firft direct affertion of the liberty of confcience. He was put to death in the moft perfidious manner."—Sir J. Mack-intosh: *Converfations with A. H. Ever-ett. North American Review,* xxxv. p. 448, n.

[2] John Harrifon, a republican general ferved in the parliamentary army, and was one of the judges of the court which tried Charles I. He became a member of the council of State in 1653. Crom-well endeavored to gain his fupport by the offer of an exalted pofition, but he refufed to co-operate with the "ufurper" as he called him. In 1657 he was de-

ting of all his flaves for his guard, fearing the heretics. The Lord knows whether Archer[1] (upon the reign of Chrift) faid true, 'that yet the Pope before his downfall, muft recover England; and the proteftant countries revolted from him." Sir, we are fure all flefh is grafs, and only the word of the Lord endures forever. Sir, you once kindly intended to quench a fire between Mr. Coddington and others, but now it is come to public trial. We hear the Dutch fire is not quenched. I fear this year will be ftormy; only may the moft gracious Lord by all drive and draw us to himfelf, in whom, Sir, I defire to be ever

Yours,   ROGER WILLIAMS.

To the General Court of Maffachufetts.

PROVIDENCE, 12, 3, 56. (fo called.) [May 12th, 1656.][2]

May it pleafe this much honored Affembly to remember, that, as an officer and in the name of Providence colony, I prefented you with our humble requefts before winter, unto which not receiving anfwer, I addreffed myfelf this fpring, to your much honored Governor, who was pleafed to advife our fending of fome of Providence to your Affembly.

prived of his command and imprifoned. Three years after he was executed for his fhare in the death of the king.— THOMAS, *Dict. of Biography.*

[1] John Archer, wrote a book on the *Perfonal Reign of Chrift.* Lond: 1643.

[2] HUTCHINSON, *Maffachufetts Papers,* Bofton, 1769, p. 278; *R. I. Colonial Records,* vol. i. p. 341.

The letter of November 15th, to the General Court of Maffachufetts, did not produce any favorable change in her meafures. Mr. Williams afterwards wrote to Governor Endicott, who invited him to vifit Bofton. In the prefent letter fome of the fame topics are again referred to.

Honored Sirs, our firſt requeſt (in ſhort) was and is, for your favorable conſideration of the long and lamentable condition of the town of Warwick, which hath been thus : they are ſo dangerouſly and ſo vexatiouſly intermingled with the barbarians, that I have long admired the wonderful power of God in reſtraining and preventing very great fires of mutual ſlaughters, breaking forth between them.

Your wiſdoms know the inhuman inſultations of theſe wild creatures, and you may be pleaſed, alſo, to imagine, that they have not been ſparing of your name as the patron of all their wickedneſs againſt our Engliſh men, women and children, and cattle to the yearly damage of ſixty, eighty and one hundred pounds.

The remedy is (under God) only your pleaſure, that Pumham ſhall come to an agreement with the town or colony, and that ſome covenient way and time be ſet for their removal.[1]

And that your wiſdom may ſee juſt grounds for ſuch your willingneſs, be pleaſed to be informed of a reality of a ſolemn covenant between this town of Warwick and Pumham, unto which, notwithſtanding that he pleads his being drawn to it by the awe of his ſuperior Sachems, yet I humbly offer that what was done, was according to the law and tenor of the natives, (I take it) in all New England and America, viz. : that the inferior Sachems and ſub-

---

[1] *Pumham,* a diſtinguiſhed Narraganſett chief " was a mighty man of valor." He was the Sachem of Shawomet, or Warwick, which town he claimed. He was thus brought into conſiderable difficulty with the Engliſh as early as 1645, which continued to this time. The people of Warwick now endeavored to bring Pumham under their government. The journal of Winthrop ſhows, that before they received him and his people under their protection, the court made them promiſe to keep the ſabbath, and to obſerve other religious rules.— BACKUS, *Hiſt. of the Baptiſts,* vol. i. p. 306.

jects fhall plant and remove at the pleafure of the higheft and fupreme Sachems, and I humbly conceive that it pleafeth the Moft High and Only Wife to make ufe of fuch a bond of authority over them, without which, they could not long fubfift in human fociety, in this wild condition wherein they are.

Pleafe you not to be infenfible of the flippery and dangerous condition of this their intermingled cohabitation. I am humbly confident, that all the Englifh towns and plantations in all New England, put together, fuffer not fuch moleftation from the natives, as this one town and people. It is fo great and fo oppreffive, that I have daily feared the tidings of fome public fire and mifchief.

3. Be pleafed to review this copy from the Lord Admiral, and that this Englifh town of Warwick fhould proceed, alfo that if any of yours were there planted, they fhould, by your authority, be removed. And we humbly conceive, that if the Englifh (whofe removes are difficult and chargeable) how much more thefe wild ones, who remove with little more trouble and damage than the wild beafts of the wildernefs.

4. Pleafe you to be informed, that this fmall neck (wherein they keep and mingle fields with the Englifh) is a very den of wickednefs, where they not only practice the horrid barbarifms of all kinds of whoredoms, idolatries, conjurations, but living without all exercife of actual authority, and getting ftore of liquors (to our grief) there is a confluence and rendezvous of all the wildeft and moft licentious natives and practices of the whole country.

5. Befide fatisfaction to Pumham and the former inhabitants of this neck, there is a competitor who muft alfo be fatisfied ; another Sachem, one Nawwufhawfuck, who

(living with Oufamaquin) lays claim to this place, and are at daily feud with Pumham (to my knowledge) about the title and lordſhip of it.[1]   Hoſtility is daily threatened.

Our ſecond requeſt concerns two or three Engliſh families at Pawtuxet, who before our charter ſubjeƈted themſelves unto your juriſdiƈtion.[2]   It is true there are many grievances between many of the town of Providence and them, and theſe I humbly conceive, may beſt be ordered to be compoſed by reference.

But ſecondly, we have formerly made our addreſſes and now do, for your prudent removal of this great and long obſtruƈtion to all due order and regular proceedings among us, viz.: the refuſal of theſe families (pretending your name) to conform with us unto his Highneſs' authority amongſt us.

3. Your wiſdom experimentally knows how apt men are to ſtumble at ſuch an exemption from all duties and ſervices, from all rates and charges, either with yourſelves or us.

4. This obſtruƈtion is ſo great and conſtant, that (without your prudent removal of it, it is impoſſible that either his Highneſs or yourſelves can expeƈt ſuch ſatisfaƈtion and obſervance from us as we deſire to render.

Laſtly, as before, we promiſed ſatisfaƈtion to the natives at Warwick, (and ſhall all poſſible ways endeavor their content) ſo we humbly offer, as to theſe our countrymen, Firſt, as to grievances depending, that references may ſettle them.   Secondly, for the future, the way will be open for their enjoyment of votes and privileges of chooſing or being choſen, to any office in town or colony.

---

[1] " The Plymouth people had their ſhare in the Warwick controverſy, having cauſed *Ouſamaquin* to lay claim to the ſame place, or a Sachem, who lived with him, named *Nawwaſhawſuck.*"—DRAKE, *Book of the Indians,* p. 258.

[2] William Arnold and William Carpenter, mentioned in previous letters.

Our third requeſt is, for your favorable leave to us to buy of your merchants, four or more barrels of powder yearly, with ſome convenient proportion of artillery, con-ſidering our hazardous frontier ſituation to theſe barbarians, who, from their abundant ſupply of arms from the Dutch, (and perfidious Engliſh, all the land over) are full of our artillery, which hath rendered them exceedingly inſolent, provoking and threatening, eſpecially the inlanders, which have their ſupply from the Fort of Aurania.[1] We have been eſteemed by ſome of you, as your thorny hedge on this ſide of you ; If ſo, yet a hedge to be maintained ; if as out ſentinels, yet not to be diſcouraged. And if there be a jealouſly of the ill uſe of ſuch a favor, pleaſe you to be aſſured that a credible perſon in each town ſhall have the diſpoſal and managing of ſuch ſupplies, according to the true intent and purpoſe.

For the obtaining of theſe, our juſt and neceſſary peti-tions, we have no inducement or hope from ourſelves, only we pray you to remember, that the matters prayed, are no way diſhonorable to yourſelves, and we humbly conceive, do greatly promote the honor and pleaſure of his Highneſs, yea, of the Moſt High, alſo ; and laſtly, ſuch kindneſſes will be obligations on us to ſtudy to declare ourſelves, upon all occaſions.

Your moſt humble and faithful ſervants,

ROGER WILLIAMS, *Preſident.*

In the name, and by the appointment, of Providence Colony.

---

[1] Newport, on a former occaſion, ap-plied to the General Court of Maſſa-chuſetts for leave to purchaſe powder and ammunition at Boſton, which requeſt had been refuſed. Gov. Winthrop, in ſpeaking of it ſays "it was an error, in

HONORED GENTLEMEN,—I pray your patience to one word relating to myfelf, only. Whereas, upon an order from the Lords of his Highnefs' Council, for my future fecurity in taking fhips and landing in your ports, it pleafed your honored then Governor, Mr. Bellingham, to obey that order under his own hand, I now pray the confirmation of it, from one word of this honored Court affembled.[1]

To the General Court of the Maffachufetts Bay.

BOSTON, 17, 3, 56, (fo called.) [17th May, 1656.][2]

MAY IT PLEASE THIS MUCH HONORED ASSEMBLY,—I do humbly hope, that your own breafts and the public, fhall reap the fruit of your great gentlenefs and patience in thefe barbarous tranfactions, and I do cordially promife, for myfelf, (and all I can perfuade with) to ftudy gratitude and faithfulnefs to your fervice. I have debated with Pumham (and fome of the natives helping with me) who fhewed him the vexatious life he lives in, your great refpect and care toward him, by which he may abundantly mend himfelf and be united in fome convenience unto their neighborhood and your fervice. But I humbly con-

---

ftate policy at leaft, not to fupport them, for though they were deeply erroneous, and in fuch deftractions among themfelves as portended their ruin, yet if the Indians fhould prevail againft them, it would danger the whole country."— *Hift. of New England,* vol. ii. p. 211.

[1] It appears by a poftcript to letter of November 15th, page 297, that Mr. Williams met with "fome diftreffes"

while paffing through Bofton, when about to embark for London, notwithftanding the order from Cromwell's Council for his protection; hence he now very properly, requires the General Court to confirm this order, before venturing again within the jurifdiction of Maffachufetts.

[2] HUTCHINSON, *Maffachufetts Papers,* p. 282.

ceive, in his cafe, that *dies et quies fanant hominem*, and he muft have fome longer breathing, for he tells me that the appearance of this competitor Nawwufhawfuck, hath ftabbed him. May you, therefore, pleafe to grant him and me fome longer time of conference, either until your next general affembling, or longer, at you pleafure.[1]

My other requefts, I fhall not be importune to prefs on your great affairs, but fhall make my addrefs unto your Secretary, to receive, by him, your pleafure.

Honored gentlemen,

Your humble and thankful fervant,

ROGER WILLIAMS.

Teſtimony of Roger Williams relative to the deed of Rhode Iſland, dated Providence, 25, 6. [25th Auguſt,] 1658.[2]

I have acknowledged (and have and fhall endeavor to maintain) the rights and property of every inhabitant of Rhode Ifland in peace; yet, fince there is fo much found and noife of purchafe and purchafers, I judge it not unfea-fonable to declare the rife and bottom of the planting of Rhode Ifland in the fountain of it: It was not price nor money that could have purchafed Rhode Ifland. Rhode Ifland was purchafed by love; by the love and favor which that honorable gentleman Sir Henry Vane and myfelf had

------

[1] As this letter was written but five days after the previous one, doubtlefs the requeft made by Mr. Williams for a guarrantee of protection was given him.

[2] Providence Records in the hand-writing of Mr. Williams.—BACKUS, *Hiſt. of the Baptiſts*, vol. p. 91.

with that great Sachem, Miantonomo, about the league which I procured between the Maſſachuſetts Engliſh, &c., and the Narraganſetts in the Pequod war.   It is true I ad-viſed a gratuity to be preſented to the Sachem and the na-tives, and becauſe Mr. Coddington and the reſt of my loving countrymen were to inhabit the place, and to be at the charge of the gratuities, I drew up a writing in Mr. Coddington's name, and in the names of ſuch of my loving countrymen as came up with him, and put it into as ſure a form as I could at that time (amongſt the Indians) for the benefit and aſſurance of the preſent and future inhabitants of the iſland.   This I mention, that as that truly noble Sir Henry Vane hath been ſo great an inſtrument in the hand of God for procuring of this iſland from the barba-rians, as alſo for procuring and confirming of the charter, ſo it may by all due thankful acknowledgment be remem-bered and recorded of us and ours which reap and enjoy the ſweet fruits of ſo great buſineſs, and ſuch unheard of liberties amongſt us.

To my honored, kind friend, Mr. John Winthrop, Governor, at Hartford, on Connecticut.

PROVIDENCE, 6, 12, 59–60.   [6th February, 1660.][1]

SIR,—Loving reſpeéts to yourſelf and Mrs. Winthrop, &c.   Your loving lines in this cold, dead ſeaſon, were as a cup of your Connecticut cider, which we are glad to hear abounds with you, or of that weſtern metheglin, which

, 3 *Maſſ. Hiſt. Col.*, voſl. x. p. 26; KNOWLES, p. 309.

you and I have drunk at Briſtol together, &c. Indeed, it
is the wonderful power and goodneſs of God, that we are
preſerved in our diſperſions among theſe wild, barbarous
wretches. I hear not of their excurſions this winter, and
ſhould rejoice if, as you hint, Uncas and his brother were
removed to Long Iſland, or any where, or elſe, as I have
ſometimes motioned, a truce for ſome good term of years
might be obtained amongſt them. But how ſhould we
expect that the ſtreams of blood ſhould ſtop among the
dregs of mankind when the bloody iſſues flow ſo freſh and
fearfully among the fineſt and moſt refined ſons of men and
ſons of God. We have not only heard of the four northern nations, Dania, Swedia, Anglia, and Belgium, all Proteſtants, (heretics and dogs, with the Pope, &c.,) laſt year
tearing and devouring one another, in the narrow ſtraits
and eminent high paſſages and turns of the ſea and world;
but we alſo have a ſound of the Preſbyterians' rage new
burſt out into flames of war from Scotland, and the independent and ſectarian army provoked again to new appeals to God, and engagements againſt them. Thus,
while this laſt Pope hath plied with ſails and oars, and
brought all his popiſh ſons to peace, except Portugal, and
brought in his grand engineers, the Jeſuits, again to Ven-
ice, after their long juſt baniſhment, we Proteſtants are
woefully diſpoſed to row backward, and bring our ſails
aback-ſtays, and provoke the holy, jealous Lord, who is a
conſuming fire, to kindle again thoſe fires from Rome and
hell, which formerly conſumed (in Proteſtant countries)
ſo many precious ſervants of God. The late renowned
Oliver, confeſſed to me, in cloſe diſcourſe about the Proteſtants' affairs, &c., that he yet feared great perſecutions
to the Proteſtants from the Romaniſts, before the downfall

of the Papacy.   The hiftories of our fathers before us, tell
us what huge bowls of the blood of the faints that great
whore hath been drunk with, in (now) Proteftant dominions.   Sure her judgment will ring through the world, and
it is hoped it is not far from the door.   Sir, you were, not
long fince, the fon of two noble fathers, Mr. John Winthrop and Mr. H. Peters.   It is faid they are both extinguifhed.   Surely, I did ever, from my foul, honor and love
them even when their judgments led them to afflict me.
Yet the Father of Spirits fpares us breath, and I rejoice, Sir,
that your name (amongft the New England magiftrates
printed, to the Parliament and army, by H. Nort. Rous,
&c.,) is not blurred, but rather honored, for your prudent
and moderate hand in the late Quakers' trials amongft us.
And it is faid, that in the late Parliament, yourfelf were
one of the three in nomination for General Governor over
New England, which however that defign ripened not, yet
your name keeps up a high efteem, &c.   I have feen your
hand to a letter to this colony, as to your late purchafe of
fome land at Narraganfett.   The fight of your hand hath
quieted fome jealoufies amongft us, that the Bay, by this
purchafe, defigned fome prejudice to the liberty of confcience amongft us.   We are in confultations how to anfwer that letter, and my endeavor fhall be, with God's help,
to welcome, with both our hands and arms, your intereft
in thefe parts, though we have no hope to enjoy your perfonal refidence amongft us.   I rejoice to hear that you
gain, by new plantations, upon this wildernefs.   I fear that
many precious fouls will be glad to hide their heads, fhortly, in thefe parts.   Your candle and mine draws towards
its end.   The Lord gracioufly help us to fhine in light and
love univerfally, to all that fear his name, without that mo-

nopoly of the affection to fuch of our own perfuafion only ;
for the common enemy, the Romifh wolf, is very high in
refolution, and hope, and advantage to make a prey on all,
of all forts that defire to fear God. Divers of our neighbors thankfully re-falute you We have buried, this winter,
Mr. Olney's fon, whom, formerly, you heard to be afflicted
with a lethargy. He lay two or three days wholly fenfelefs, until his laft groans. My youngeft fon, Jofeph, was
troubled with a fpice of an epilepfy. We ufed fome remedies, but it hath pleafed God, by his taking of tobacco,
perfectly, as we hope, to cure him. Good Mr. Parker, of
Bofton, pafling from Prudence Ifland, at his coming on
fhore, on Seekonk land, trod awry upon a ftone or ftick,
and fell down, and broke the fmall bone of his leg. He
hath lain by of it all this winter, and the laft week was
carried to Bofton in a horfe litter. Some fears there was
of a gangrene. But, Sir, I ufe too much boldnefs and prolixity. I fhall now only fubfcribe myfelf

Your unworthy friend,

ROGER WILLIAMS.

Sir, my loving refpects to Mr. Stone, Mr. Lord, Mr. Allen, Mr. Webfter, and other loving friends.

To my honored, kind friend, Mr. Winthrop, Governor of Con-
necticut, these presents.

PROVIDENCE, 8, 7, 1660. [September 8th, 1660.][1]

SIR,—A sudden warning gives me but time of this ab-
rupt salutation to your kind self and Mrs. Winthrop, wishing you peace. I promised to a neighbor, a former
servant of your father's, (Joshua Windsor,) to write a line,
on his behalf, and at his desire, unto you. His prayer to
you is, that when you travel toward Boston, you would
please to come by Providence, and spare one hour to heal
an old sore,—a controversy between him and most of his
neighbors, in which, I am apt to think, he hath suffered
some wrong. He hath promised to submit to your sentence. His opposite, one James Ashton, being desired by
me to nominate also, he resolves also to submit to your sentence, which will concern more will and stomach than
damage; for the matter only concerns a few poles of
ground, wherein Joshua have cried out of wrong these
many years I hope, Sir, the blessed Lord will make you
a blessed instrument of chiding the winds and seas; and I
shall rejoice in your presence amongst us. There are
greater ulcers in my thoughts at present, which, I fear, are
incurable, and that it hath pleased the Most Wise and Most
High to pass an irrevocable sentence of amputations and
cauterizations upon the poor Protestant party. The clouds
gather mighty fast and thick upon our heads from all the
Popish quarters. It hath pleased the Lord to glad the Ro-
mish conclave with the departure of those two mighty

---

[1] KNOWLES, *Memoirs of Roger Williams*, p. 312; 3 *Mass. Hist. Coll.* vol. x. p. 39.

bulwarks of the Proteſtants, Oliver and Guſtavus;[1] to unite, (I think by this time) all the Catholic kings and princes, for Portugal was like, very like, of late, to return to the yoke of Spain, whoſe treaſure from the Indies it hath pleaſed God to ſend home, ſo wonderfully great and rich this year, that I cannot but fear the Lord hath ſome mighty work to effeƈt with it. We know the Catholic King was in debt, but he now overflows with millions, which God is moſt like to expend againſt the Proteſtants or the Turks, the two great enemies, (the ſword-fiſh and the thraſher) againſt the Popiſh leviathan. The Preſbyterian party in England and Scotland is yet very likely to make ſome ſtruggle againſt the Popiſh invaſions; and yet in the end I fear (as long I have feared, and long ſince told Oliver, to which he much inclined,) the bloody whore is not yet drunk enough with the blood of the ſaints and witneſſes of Jeſus. One cordial is, (amongſt ſo many the merciful Lord hath provided) that that whore will ſhortly appear ſo extremely loathſome, in her drunkenneſs, beaſtialities, &c., that her bewitched paramours will tear her fleſh, and burn her with fire unquenchable. Here is a ſound that Fairfax,[2] and about two hundred of the Houſe with him, differ with the King. The merciful Lord fit us to hear and feel more. It is a very thick and dreadful miſt

---

[1] Oliver Cromwell, who died in 1658; and Guſtavus Adolphus, King of Sweden, the great champion of proteſtaniſm, who died many years before.

[2] Thomas, Lord Fairfax, was a diſtinguiſhed commander and leading charaƈter in the civil wars of England. When the diſputes between Charles I. and the Parliament terminated in open rupture, Fairfax eſpouſed the cauſe of the latter. He ſometimes differed from Cromwell and Parliament, yet adhered to their party and thus continued in employment, though more than ſuſpeƈted of diſaffeƈtion, till being ordered to march againſt the revolted Scotch Preſbyterians, he poſitively declined the command and retired awhile from public life.—*Biographia Britannica.*

and fwamp, with which the Lord hath a great while fuffered us to labor in, as hoping to wade out, break through,
and efcape fhipwreck.   In Richard Protector's Parliament,
they fell into three factions prefently : royalifts, protecto-
rians, (which were moft Prefbyterian, and earned it,) and
commonwealth's men.   The Prefbyterians, when General
Monk[1] brought in the fecluded members, carried it again,
of late, clearly, and fo vigoroufly againft the Papifts, that
ftricter laws than ever.   There muft furely, then, be great
flames, before the King can accomplifh his engagements
to the Popifh party.

You know well, Sir, at fea, the firft entertainment of a
ftorm is with, down with top-fails.   The Lord mercifully
help us to lower, and make us truly more and more low,
humble, contented, thankful for the leaft crumbs of mercy.
But the ftorm increafeth, and trying with our mainfails and
mizzens will not do.   We muft, therefore, humbly beg
patience from the Father of Lights and God of all mercies, to lay at Hull, in hope.   It was a motto in one of the
late Parliaments : cornets under a fhower of blood 'Tranf-
ibit.'

Sir, my neighbor, Mrs. Scott,[2] is come from England ;
and, what the whip at Bofton could not do, converfe with
friends in England, and their arguments, have, in a great

---

[1] Gen. George Monk, Duke of Albe-
marle, was diftinguifhed for the part he
took in the reftoration of Charles II.
During the Commonweath he had been
an adherent of Cromwell, whofe authority he maintained in Scotland, where
he was intimately connected with the
Prefbyterians. — Gorton, *Biographical
Dictionary.*

[2] Mrs. Scott.   This was doubtlefs the

wife of Richard Scott, one of the earlieft fettlers of the colony who received
a lot in Providence in 1636. Richard
Scott, who afterwards turned to the
Quakers, fays, "I walked with [Wil-
liams] in the Baptifts way about three
or four months, in which time he broke
up the Society, and declared at large the
reafons for it."—Backus, *Hift. of the
Baptifts,* vol. i. p. 108.

meafure drawn her from the Quakers, and wholly from
their meetings. Try the fpirits. There are many abroad,
and muft be, but the Lord will be glorious, in plucking up
whatever his holy hand hath not planted. My brother runs
ftrongly to Origen's notion of univerfal mercy at laft,
againft an eternal fentence.[1] Our times will call upon us
for thorough difcuffions. The fire is like to try us. It is
a wonderful mercy the barbarians are yet fo quiet. A portion of our neighbors are juft now come home, *re infecta.*
The Mohegans would not fally, and the Narraganfetts
would not fpoil the corn, for fear of offending the Englifh. The Lord mercifully guide the councils of the commiffioners. Mr. Arnold, Mr. Brenton, and others, ftrug-
gle againft your intereft at Narraganfett;[2] but I hope your
prefence might do much good amongft us in a few days.

Sir, I am, unworthy, yours,
ROGER WILLIAMS.

[1] Origen, of Alexandria, one of the moft eminent of the Chriftian Fathers who lived in the fecond and third centuries. He was deprived of his prieftly office, and excommunicated, the principal charge againft him being his denial of eternal punifhment. Origen is called the father of Biblical criticifm, and was a voluminous writer.

[2] Major Humphrey Atherton with others of Maffachufetts, and John Winthrop, of Connecticut, had purchafed lands in Narraganfett. At the May feffion of the General Affembly, 1660, it was voted "that William Brenton, Benedict Arnold, and others, are chofen a committee to ripen the matter concerning the purchafe made by the gentlemen of the Bay in Narraganfett, and draw up their refult thereon."

In October following, it was ordered

"that a committee be chofen to treat with thofe gentlemen that have made purchafes of lands in Narraganfett, with power to treat and fully agree with them in the prefent difference about their coming into our colony. . . . And that the commiffioners take care to write unto the gentlemen, viz.: Major Atherton and his affociates to defire them to appoint Commiffioners to treat with the aforefaid Commiffioners upon all the differences depending about their coming into, or poffeffing lands from the Indians within this colony's bounds."—*R. I. Col. Records*, vol. i., pages 429 and 435.

The lands purchafed as above, known as the "Neck purchafe" and "Bofton Neck," in the Narraganfett country, are fully defcribed in POTTER's *Narraganfett*, p. 269.

For his much honored kind friend Mr. John Winthrop, at his house, in Nameag, thefe.

27, 8, 60. (fo called.)   [27th October, 1660.]¹

I,OVING FRIENDS AND NEIGHBORS,—Divers of your-felves have fo cried out, of the contentions of your late meetings, that (ftudying my quietnefs) I thought fit to prefent you with thefe few lines. Two words I pray you to confider. Firft, as to this plantation of Providence: then as to fome new plantation, if it fhall pleafe the fame God of mercies who provided this, to provide another in mercy for us. 1. As to this town, although I have been called out, of late, to declare my underftanding as to the bounds of Providence and Pawtuxet; and, although divers have lands and meadows in poffeffion beyond thefe bounds, yet I hope that none of you think me fo fenfelefs as to put on any barbarian to moleft an Englifhman, or to demand a farthing of any of you.

2. If any do (as formerly fome have done, and divers have given gratuities, as Mr. Field, about Notaquoncanot and others,) I promife, that as I have been affiftant to fatisfy and pacify the natives round about us, fo I hope I fhall ftill while I live be helpful to any of you that may have occafion to ufe me.

Now, as to fome new plantation, I defire to propofe that which may quench contention, may accommodate fuch who want, and may alfo return moneys unto fuch as have of late difburfed.

To this purpofe, I defire that we be patient, and torment not ourfelves and the natives, (Sachems and people,) put-

---

¹R. I. *Colonial Records*, vol. i. p. 39; KNOWLES, *Memoirs Roger Williams*, p. 440.

ting them upon mifchievous remedies, with the great noife of twenty miles new or old purchafe.

Let us confider, if Nifwofakit and Wayunckeke, and the land thereabout, may not afford a new and comfortable plantation, which we may go through with an effectual endeavor for true public good. To this end, I pray you confider, that the inhabitants of thefe parts, with moft of the Cowefet and Nipmucks, have long fince forfaken the Narraganfett Sachems and. fubjected themfelves to the Maffachufetts. And yet they are free to fell their lands to any whom the Maffachufetts fhall not proteft againft. To this end (obferving their often flights, and to ftop their running to the Maffachufetts) I have parlied with them, and find that about thirty pounds will caufe them to leave thofe parts, and yield peaceable poffeffion. I fuppofe, then, that the town may do well to give leave to about twenty of your inhabitants (of which I offer to be one, and know others willing) to lay down thirty fhillings a man toward the purchafe. Let every one of this number have liberty to remove himfelf, or to place a child or friend there. Let every perfon who fhall afterward be received into the purchafe lay down thirty fhillings, as hath been done in Providence, which may be paid (by fome order agreed on) to fuch as lately have difburfed moneys unto the effecting of this. I offer, gratis, my time and pains, in hope that fuch as want may have a comfortable fupply amongft us, and others made room for, who may be glad of fhelter alfo.

Yours to ferve you,

ROGER WILLIAMS.

Testimony of Roger Williams relative to the purchase of lands at Seekonk and Providence.

PROVIDENCE, 13, 10, 1661. [13th December.][1]

1. I teſtify and declare, in the holy preſence of God, that when at my firſt coming into theſe parts, I obtained the lands of Seekonk of Ouſamaquin, the then chief Sachem on that ſide, the Governor of Plymouth (Mr. Winſlow) wrote to me, in the name of their government, their claim of Seekonk to be in their juriſdiction, as alſo their advice to remove but over the river unto this ſide, (where now, by God's merciful providence, we are,) and then I ſhould be out of their claim, and be as free themſelves, and loving neighbors together.[2]

2. After I had obtained this place, now called Providence, of Canonicus and Miantinomo, the chief Narraganſett Sachems deceaſed, Ouſamaquin, the Sachem aforeſaid, alſo deceaſed, laid his claim to this place alſo. This forced me to repair to the Narraganſett Sachems aforeſaid, who declared that Ouſamaquin was their ſubject, and had ſolemnly himſelf, in perſon, with ten men, ſubjected himſelf and his lands unto them at the Narraganſett: only now he ſeemed to revolt from his loyalties under the ſhelter of the Engliſh at Plymouth.[3]

---

[1] BACKUS, *Hiſt. of the Baptiſts*, vol. i. p. 73. Backus ſays "copied from the original in his own handwriting."

[2] This ſhows a great difference between the temper of Plymouth and Maſſachuſetts rulers, and of which we ſhall ſee more.—BACKUS, vol. i. p. 73.

[3] This perfectly agrees with the account we have of Maſſaſoit or Ouſamaquin's league made with the Plymouth people, the ſpring after their firſt coming, and of the Narraganſett's threatenings on that account.—PRINCE's *Chronology*, pp. 102–116.

This ſtatement, it will be perceived, was made twenty-five years after Williams croſſed the Seekonk river, and eſtabliſhed himſelf and his aſſociates at Providence.

3. This I declared from the Narraganfett Sachems to Oufamaquin, who, without any ftick, acknowledged it to be true that he had fo fubjected as the Narraganfett Sachems affirmed; but withal, he affirmed that he was not fubdued by war, which himfelf and his father had maintained againft the Narraganfetts, but God, he faid, fubdued me by a plague, which fwept away my people, and forced me to yield.

4. This conviction and confeffion of his, together with gratuities to himfelf and brethren and followers, made him often profefs, that he was pleafed that I fhould here be his neighbor, and that rather becaufe he and I had been great friends at Plymouth, and alfo becaufe that his and my friends at Plymouth advifed him to be at peace and friendfhip with me, and he hoped that our children after us would be good friends together.

5. And whereas, there hath been often fpeech of Providence falling within Plymouth jurifdiction, by virtue of Oufamaquin's claims, I add unto the teftimony abovefaid, that the Governor, Mr. Bradford, and other of their magiftrates, defcribed unto me, both by conference and writing, that they and their government were fatisfied, and refolved never to moleft Providence, nor to claim beyond Seekonk, but to continue loving friends and neighbors (amongft the barbarians) together.

This is the true fum and fubftance of many paffages between our countrymen of Plymouth and Oufamaquin and me.

ROGER WILLIAMS.

To the Town of Providence.

[No date.][1]

LOVING FRIENDS AND NEIGHBORS,—I have again con-
fidered on thefe papers, and find many confiderable things
in both of them.   My defire is, that after a friendly debate of particulars, every man may fit down and reft in
quiet with the final fentence and determination of the
town, for all experience tells us that public peace and love
is better than abundance of corn and cattle, &c.   I have
one only motion and petition, which I earneftly pray the
town to lay to heart, as ever they look for a blefling from
God on the town, on your families, your corn and cattle,
and your children after you ; it is this, that after you have
got over the black brook of fome foul bondage yourfelves,
you tear not down the bridge after you, by leaving no
fmall pittance for diftreffed fouls that may come after you.
What though your divifion or allotment be never fo fmall,
yet ourfelves know that fome men's diftreffes are fuch, that
a piece of a dry cruft and a difh of cold water, is fweet,
which, if this town will give fincerely unto God, (fetting
afide fome little portions for other diftreffed fouls to get
bread on) you know who hath engaged His heavenly word
for your reward and recompenfe.

Yours,   ROGER WILLIAMS.

[1] KNOWLES' *Mem. of Roger Williams,*
p. 402.
   This letter was copied for Mr. Backus, by the late Judge Howell, of Providence, and was accompanied by the following note in his handwriting: " This
remonftrance was fent in to the town,
upon their concluding to divide among
themfelves certain common lands, out of
which Roger Williams wanted fome to
remain ftill common, for the town afterwards to give occafionally to fuch as fled
to them, or were banifhed for confcience
fake, as he at firft gave it all to them."—
KNOWLES, p. 402.

To my honored kind friend Mr. Winthrop, Governor, at Hartford, prefent.

PROVIDENCE, 28, 3, 64. (fo called.) [May 28, 1664.][1]

SIR,—Meeting (this inftant before fun-rife, as I went to my field, &c.,) an Indian running back for a glafs, bound for your parts, I thought (fince *nihil fine Providentia*) that an Higher Spirit then his own, might purpofely (like Jonathan's boy) fend him back for this hafty falutation to your kind felf and your dear companion.

Sir, I waited for a gale to return you many cordial thanks for your many cordial expreffions of ancient kindnefs to myfelf, and the public peace and wellfare: I have fince been occafioned and drawn (being nominated in the Charter to appear again upon the deck,) from my beloved privacy; my humble defires are to contribute my poor mite (as I have ever, and I hope ever fhall) to preferve plantation and public intereft of the whole New England and not intereft of this or that town, colony, opinion, &c.

Sir, when we that have been the eldeft, and are rotting, (to-morrow or next day) a generation will act, I fear, far unlike the firft Winthrops and their Models of Love:[2] I fear that the common Trinity of the world, (Profit, Preferment, Pleafure) will here be the *Tria omnia,* as in all the world befide: that Prelacy and Papacy too will in this wildernefs predominate that God Land will be (as now it is) as great a God with us Englifh as God Gold was with the Spaniards, &c. While we are here, noble Sir, let us *Viriliter hoc agere, rem agere humanam, divinam, Chriftianam,* which I believe is all of a moft public genius.

---

[1] 4 *Mafs. Hift. Coll.* vol. vi. p. 295.
[2] This may be a reference to Gov. Winthrop's Model of Chriftian Charity, a fermon written on board the "Arbella." See 3 *Mafs. Hift. Coll.,* vol. vii., p. 33. Eds. *Winthrop Papers.*

Sir, thofe words in our Charter concerning the Narraganfett (notwithftanding a late grant to the colony of Connecticut,) &c., are fo taking with my neighbors, that Refolutions were up (this laft Court) of fetching old Mr. Smith prefently, becaufe of his new engagement to Connecticut : it pleafed God to help me to ftop that council, and to prevail that only a boat was fent, with a loving letter to invite him, and he came not, but faid well, viz. : that when the Colonies were agreed, he would fubmit. Sir, three days hence Major Denifon and Mr. Damport meet from the Bay with Mr. Greene of Warwick, and Mr Torrey of Newport,[1] at Seekonk, to compofe the ftrife between us ; I hope your honored felf and Major Mafon, and fome of the grave Elders, &c. will help on fuch work between yourfelves and us, alfo unto which I hope the Father of mercies will help me to be your and the country's fervant in all refpect, and faithfulnefs.

ROGER WILLIAMS.

Raptim.

On the outfide in Williams' handwriting.

Juft now I find this bearer to be Miantonomo's fon.

Indorfed by Gov. Winthrop, of Connecticut, " Mr. Rog: Williams rec : Saturday Jun: 25, 1664."

---

[1] Maffachufetts having appointed two agents to treat with Rhode Ifland in regard to Block Ifland and the Pequot country, John Greene and Jofeph Torrey were commiffioned to meet them at Rehoboth, on the laft day of the month. Roger Williams was one of the committee to prepare the inftructions for the commiffioners. Richard Smith, jr., and Thomas Gould, of Narraganfett, were bound over in the fum of four hundred pounds each ; and John Hicks and John Wood, of Newport, for two hundred pounds each, to appear when called for, upon the charge of feeking to bring in a foreign jurifdiction within the limits of the colony. Thefe bonds were afterwards releafed. A warrant for the fame offence was iffued againft John Greene, fen'r., who appeared and confeffed his

To the Right Honorable Sir Robert Carr, one of His Majefty's Honorable Commiffioners for New England, prefent.

PROVIDENCE, 1 March, 1665.[1]

SIR,—My humble and hearty refpeᴄts prefented, with humble and hearty defires of your prefent and eternal felicity.

Having heaad of a late confederacy among great numbers of thefe barbarians to affift Pumham, &c., I thought it my duty to wait upon your Honor with thefe humble falutations, and appreciations of the fafety of your perfon, not to be eafily hazarded amongft fuch a barbarous fᴄum and offscouring of mankind. Befides, Sir, this is an old ulcerous bufinefs, wherein I have been many years engaged, and have (in the behalf of my loving friends at Warwick) pleaded this caufe with the whole General Court of the Maffachufetts magiftrates and deputies, and prevailed with them to yield, that if I and Pumham would agree, they would ratify an agreement. But Pumham would not part with that Neck[2] on any terms. I crave leave to add (for the excufe of this boldnefs,) that the natives in this Bay do (by promife to them at my firft breaking of the ice in amongft them) expeᴄt my endeavors of preferving the public peace, which it hath pleafed God, mercifully to help

---

fault. Upon petition he was pardoned, and received again under proteᴄtion as a freeman of the colony. Richard Smith, fen'r., was written to, to appear before the court on a fimilar charge. He made no reply to the letter, but enclofed it to Capt. Hutchinfon, defiring him to inform Conneᴄticut of the affair, which he did. ARNOLD, *Hift. of Rhode Ifland*, vol. i., p. 307. For the letters written on the occafion and the aᴄtion of the General Affembly of Rhode Ifland on the fubjeᴄt, fee the *R. I. Col. Records*, vol. ii. pp. 44–49.

[1] J. CARTER BROWN's *Manufcripts*, vol. 1, No. 72.

[2] Warwick Neck. Gorton and others of the early fettlers called it "The Neck."

41

me to do many times (with my great hazard and charge), when all the colonies and the Maſſachuſetts, in eſpecial, have meditated, prepared and been (ſometimes many hundreds) among the march for war againſt the natives in this colony. Of this my promiſe and duty, and conſtant practice, mine own heart and conſcience before God; as alſo ſome natives put me in mind at preſent.

1. Firſt then (although I know another claim laid to this land yet,) Pumham being the ancient poſſeſſor of this Lordſhip, I humbly query whether it will be juſt to diſpoſſeſs him (not only without conſent, which fear may extort, but without ſome ſatisfying conſideration.) I had a commiſſion from my friends at Warwick, to promiſe a good round value, and I know ſome of them have deſired the natives, I thought it coſt them ſome hundred pounds.[1]

2. Your Honor will never effect by force a ſafe and laſting concluſion until you have firſt reduced the Maſſachuſetts to the obedience of his Majeſty, and then theſe appendants (towed at their ſtern) will eaſily (and not before) wind about alſo.

---

[1] The Commiſſioners of the United Colonies viſited Pettaquamſcut and Warwick for the purpoſe of ſettling the long exiſting controverſies between the inhabitants and the Indians. Pumham, the ſubject of Maſſachuſetts, who ſtill refuſed to leave Warwick Neck, although the land had been fairly purchaſed of his ſuperior Sachem many years before, was ordered by the Commiſſioners to remove within a year to ſome place to be provided for him either in Maſſachuſetts or by Peſſicus. Warwick was to pay him £20, but when he had received it, he refuſed to fulfil his contract or to obey of the order of the Commiſſioners, relying ſtill upon the protection of Maſſachuſetts.

John Eliot, the Apoſtle of the Indians, wrote to Sir Robert Carr in behalf of Pumham, who, he ſays, had "ſuffered much hard and ill dealings from ſome Engliſh," and begs him to "deal honorably by them." The correſpondence, with other papers on this ſubject, are contained in the Rhode Iſland manuſcripts, copied from the originals in the Britiſh State Paper Office, in the collection of John Carter Brown, Eſq., vol. i., Nos. 64 to 73.

3. The bufinefs as circumftantiated will not be effected without bloodfhed; barbarians are barbarians. There be old grudges betwixt our countrymen of Warwick and them. They are a melancholy people, and judge them- felves (by the former Sachem and thefe Englifh) oppreffed and wronged; you may knock out their brains, and yet not make them peaceably to furrender, even as fome oxen will die before they will rife; yet with patience, and gentle means will rife and draw, and do good fer- vice.

4. Thefe barbarians know that it is but one party in Warwick, which claim this Neck; the greateft part of the town cry out againft the other to my knowledge, and that of the natives alfo.

5. The natives know that this party in Warwick are not only deftitute of help, from their own townfmen, but of the other towns of this colony alfo.

6. They know that it would pleafe the Maffachufetts, and moft of the other colonies, that Mr. Gorton and his friends had been long ere this deftroyed.

7. They know that Ninigret and Pefficus are barbarians, and if it come to blood, and that at the firft, the worft be to the Englifh (in any appearances,) they will join to further the prey. However, if King Philip keep his promife, they will be too great a party againft the two Sachems.

8. Laftly, Sir, we profefs Chriftianity, which commends a little with peace; a dinner of green herbs with quietnefs; and if it be poffible, commands peace with all men. I therefore humbly offer, if it be not advifable (in this juncture of time) to lay all the blame on me, and on my interceffion and mediation, for a little further breathing to

the barbarians until harveſt, in which time a peaceable and loving agreement may be wrought, to mutual conſent and ſatisfaction."

Sir, I humbly crave your Honor's gracious pardon to this great boldneſs.

Your moſt obedient and bounden ſervants,

ROGER WILLIAMS.

To my much reſpected the Inhabitants of the Town of Providence.

PROVIDENCE, 10th February, 1667–8.][1]

LOVING FRIENDS AND NEIGHBORS,—Unto this day, it pleaſed the town to adjourn for the anſwering of the bill for the bridge and others. I have conferred with Shadrach Manton and Nathaniel Waterman, about their propoſal, and their result is, that they cannot obtain ſuch a number as will join with them, to undertake the bridge upon the hopes of meadow. I am, therefore, bold, after ſo many anchors come home, and ſo much trouble and long debates and deliberations, to offer, that if you pleaſe, I will, with God's help, take this bridge unto my care, by that moderate toll of ſtrangers of all ſorts, which hath been mentioned; will maintain it ſo long that it pleaſeth God that I live in this town.[2]

[1] KNOWLES, *Memoirs of Roger Williams*, p. 330.
[2] The Town of Providence, in June, 1662, had ordered a bridge to be built on Moſhaſſuck river, by Thomas Olney's houſe, which order was not accompliſhed. To this contemplated bridge, the letter doubtleſs refers. The late John Howland was of opinion that this bridge was intended to be built ſomewhere between

2. The town fhall be free from all toll, only I defire one day's work of one man in a year from every family, but from thofe that have teams, and have much ufe of the bridge, one day's work ot a man and team, and of thofe that have lefs ufe, half a day.

3. I fhall join with any of the town, more or few, who will venture their labor with me for the gaining of meadow.

4 I promife, if it pleafe God, that I gain meadow in equal value to the town's yearly help, I fhall then releafe that.

5. I defire if it pleafe God to be with me, to go through fuch a charge and trouble as will be to bring this to a fettled way, and then fuddenly to take me from hence, I defire that before another, my wife and children, if they defire it, may engage in my ftead to thefe conditions.

6. If the town pleafe to confent, I defire that one of yourfelves be nominated, to join with the clerk to draw up the writing.

ROGER WILLIAMS.

the prefent Great Bridge and Smith's Bridge, for the purpofe of getting accefs to the natural meadows at the head of the Cove. Mr. Howland, in a note to Mr. Knowles, fays, "I have frequently been told by Nathan Waterman, that teams and men on horfeback ufed to crofs the river (before his day) acrofs the clam-bed, oppofite Angell's land, at low tide, and land on the weftern fhore." The Thomas Olney lot was where the old Providence Hotel in North Main Street lately ftood, and extended down to the Cove. In front of this was a fhoal place, called the clam-bed.—KNOWLES, *Mem. of Roger Williams*, note p. 331.

To the General Court of the Maſſachuſetts Bay.

PROVIDENCE, 7th of May, 1668.[1]

I humbly offer to conſideration my long and conſtant experience, ſince it pleaſed God to bring me unto theſe parts, as to the Narraganſett and Nipmuck people.

Firſt, that all the Nipmucks were, unqueſtionably, ſubject to the Narraganſett Sachems, and, in a ſpecial manner to Mexham, the ſon of Canonicus, and late huſband to this old ſquaw Sachem, now only ſurviving. I have abundant and daily proof of it, as plain and clear as that the inhabitants of Newbury or Ipſwich, &c., are ſubject to the government of the Maſſachuſetts colony.[2]

2. I was called by his Majeſty's Commiſſioners to teſtify in a like caſe between Philip and the Plymouth Indians, on the one party, and the Narraganſetts on the other, and it pleaſed the committee to declare, that the King had not given them any commiſſion to alter the Indians' laws and cuſtoms, which they obſerved amongſt themſelves : moſt of which, although they are, like themſelves barbarous, yet in the caſe of their mournings, they are more humane, and it ſeems to be more inhumane in thoſe that profeſſed

[1] POTTER's *Hiſt. of Narraganſett*, p. 159; KNOWLES, *Memoirs of Roger Williams*, p. 331.

This letter is without any addreſs, but in the opinion of Mr. Knowles, was doubtleſs written to the government of Maſſachuſetts.

[2] "Maſſachuſetts, although her claims had been ſuperſeded by thoſe of Connecticut, and her right to interfere, even with the Indians had been denied by the royal commiſſioners, embraced an opportunity preſented by the Nipmucks, who acknowledged her ſupremacy, to impoſe terms on the Narraganſetts. The Nipmucks petitioned for redreſs for ſpoliations committed by the Narraganſetts. The General Court took up the matter, as of right, and ſettled the difficulty. It was a meaſure of peace and therefore commendable, but it does not admit of rigid ſcrutiny into the claim of juriſdiction over the Nipmuck country upon which the interview was baſed."— ARNOLD, *Hiſt. of Rhode Iſland*, vol i., p. 333.

subjection to this the very laft year, underfome kind of feigned protection of the Englifh, to be finging and dancing, drinking, &c., while the reft were lamenting their Sachems' deaths.[1]

I abhor moft of their cuftoms; I know they are barbarous. I refpect not one party more than the other, but I defire to witnefs truth; and as I defire to witnefs againft oppreffion, fo, alfo, againft the flighting of civil, yea, of barbarous order and government, as refpecting evéry fhadow of God's gracious appointments.

This I humbly offer as in the holy prefence of God.

ROGER WILLIAMS.

For John Whipple, jun., thefe.

PROVIDENCE, 8th July, 1669. (fo called.)[1]

NEIGHBOR WHIPPLE,—I kindly thank you, that you fo far have regarded my lines as to return me your thoughts, whether fweet or four I defire not to mind. I humbly hope, that as you fhall never find me felf-conceited nor felf-feeking, fo, as to others, not pragmatical and a bufybody as you infinuate. My ftudy is to be fwift to hear, and flow to fpeak, and I could tell you of five or fix grounds (it may be more) why I give this my teftimony againft this unrighteous and monftrous proceeding of Chriftian brethren helping to haul one another before the world, whofe fong was lately and loudly fung in my ears, viz.: the world would be quiet enough, were

---

[1] *Rhode Ifland Literary Repofitory*, vol. i., pp. 638–640; KNOWLES, *Memoirs of Roger Williams*, p. 332.

it not for thofe holy brethren, their divifions and content-ions. The laft night, Shadrach Manton told me that I had fpoken bad words of Gregory Dexter,[1] (though Shadrach deals more ingenuoufly than yourfelf faying the fame thing, for he tells me wherein,) viz.: that I faid he makes a fool of his confcience. I told him I faid fo, and I think to our neighbor Dexter himfelf; for I believe he might as well be moderator or general deputy or general affiftant, as go fo far as he goes, in many particulars; but what if I or my confcience be a fool, yet it is commendable and admirable in him, that being a man of education, and of a noble calling, and verfed in militaries, that his confcience forced him to be fuch a child in his own houfe, when W. Har. ftrained for the rate (which I approve of) with fuch imperious infulting over his confcience, which all confcientious men will abhor to hear of. However, I commend that man, whether Jew, or Turk, or Papift, or whoever, that fteers no otherwife than his confcience dares, till his confcience tells him that God gives him a greater latitude. For, neighbor, you fhall find it rare to meet with men of confcience, men that for fear and love of God dare

---

[1] Gregory Dexter was one of the earlieft fettlers of Providence. He received one of the home lots in 1637, and figned the firft compact in 1640. Was fubfequently one of the committee from Providence to form a government. For many years he was a commiffioner for that town, and a deputy in the Affembly. The reference to Mr. Dexter's refufal to pay his taxes, from confcientious fcruples fhows that Mr. Williams accurately difcriminated between the rights of confcience, and a perverfion of thofe rights. It is worthy of notice, too, that Mr. Williams condemned the conduct of Mr. Dexter, though an intimate friend; and approved, in part, at leaft, that of Mr. Harris, though a bitter hoftility exifted between them.

Mr. Dexter had been a printer and ftationer in London, and was the publifher of *Williams' Key into the* [*Indian*] *Language of America*. London: 1643. As he was in Providence feveral years before, his printing bufinefs may have been carried on after he left. SAVAGE, fays he died in 1700, at the age of ninety.—*Genealogical Dict.* vol. ii.

not lie, nor be drunk, nor be contentious, nor fteal, nor be covetous, nor voluptuous, nor ambitious, nor lazy-bodies, nor bufy-bodies, nor dare difpleafe God by omitting either fervice or fuffering, though of reproach, imprifonment, banifhment and death, becaufe of the fear and love of God.

If W. Wickenden[1] received a beaft of W. Field, for ground of the fame hold, I knew it not, and fo fpake the truth, as I underftood it. 2. Though I have not fpoke with him, yet I hear it was not of that hold or tenure, for we have had four forts of bounds at leaft.

Firft, the grant of as large accommodations as any Eng-lifh in New England had. This the Sachems always promifed me, and they had caufe, for I was as a right hand unto them, to my great coft and travail. Hence I was fure of the Tocekeunquinit meadows, and what could with any fhow of reafon have been defired; but fome, (that never did this town or colony good, and, it is feared, never will,) cried out, when Roger Williams had laid himfelf down as a ftone in the duft, for after comers to ftep on in town and colony, "What is Roger Williams? We know the Indians and the Sachems as well as he. We will truft Roger Wil-liams no longer. We will have our bounds confirmed us under the Sachems' hands before us."

2. Hence arofe, to my foul cutting and grief, the fecond fort of bounds, viz.: the bounds fet under the hands of thofe great Sachems Canonicus and Miantonomo, and were fet fo fhort (as to Mafhapaug and Pawtucket, and at that

---

[1] William Wickenden, removed to Providence from Salem, previous to Au-guft 20, 1637, and was a colleague with Chad Brown in the paftoral charge of the Baptift Church.—He died February, 23, 1670.—STAPLES' *note to* GORTON's *Simplicity's Defence*, p. 109.

42

time,) becaufe they would not intrench upon the Indians inhabiting round about us, for the prevention of ftrife between us.

The third fort of bounds were of favor and grace, invented, as I think, and profecuted by that noble fpirit, now with God, Chad Brown.[1] Prefuming upon the Sachems' grant to me, they exceeded the letter of the Sachem's deed, fo far as reafonably they judged, and with this promife of fatisfaction to any native who fhould reafonably defire it. In this third fort of bounds, lay this piece of meadow hard by Capt. Fenner's grounds, which, with two hogs, William Wickenden gave to W. Field for a fmall beaft, &c.

Befides thefe three forts of bounds, there arofe a fourth, (like the fourth beaft in Daniel) exceeding dreadful and terrible, unto which the Spirit of God gave no name nor bounds, nor can we in the firft rife of ours, only boundlefs bounds, or a monftrous beaft, above all other beafts or monfters. Now, as from this fourth wild beaft in Daniel, in the greater world, have arifen all the ftorms and tempefts, factions and divifions, in our little world amongft us, and what the tearing confequences it will be, is only known to the Moft Holy and Only Wife.

---

[1]Chad Brown was an affociate of Roger Williams, and one of the founders of Providence, having come from Maffachufetts in 1636. His name is among thofe who received a "home lot," and one of the four chofen in 1640 to prepare a form of government.—*Col. Records*, vol. i. pp 14 and 27.

He was paftor of the Baptift Church in 1642. He had children, John, who married a Holmes, daughter of the Rev. Obadiah Holmes; Daniel, who married a Herenden; James, Jeremiah, and Judah. The laft two removed to Rhode Ifland.—Staples' note to Gorton's *Simplicity's Defence*, p. 108.

The defcendants of Chad Brown have ever been among the moft enterprifing and public fpirited men of the State. They are equally diftinguifhed for their liberal benefactions to the literary and charitable inftitutions in Providence.

You conclude with your innocence and patience under my clamorous tongue, but I pray you not to forget that there are two bafins. David had one, Pilate another. David wafhed his hands in innocence, and fo did Pilate, and fo do all parties, all the world over. As to Innocence, my former paper faith fomething. As to patience, how can you fay you are patient under my clamorous tongue, when that very fpeech is moft impatient and unchriftian? My clamor and crying fhall be to God and men (I hope without revenge or wrath) but for a little eafe, and that yourfelves, and they that fcorn and hate me moft, may, (if the Eternal pleafe,) find cooling in that hot, eternal day that is near approaching. This fhall be the continual clamor or cry of

Your unworthy friend and neighbor,

ROGER WILLIAMS.

To my honored friend, Mr. John Winthrop, Governor of Connecticut, &c., thefe, at Bofton or elfewhere. Leave this at Major Leverett's.

PROVIDENCE, Auguft 19th, 1669. (fo called.)[1]

SIR,—Loving refpects to yourfelf and your deareft and other friends, &c. I have no tidings (upon my enquiry) of that poor dog, about which you fent to me. I fear he is run wild into the woods, though it is poffible that Englifh or Indians have him. Oh, Sir, what is that word that fparrows and hairs are provided for and numbered by

---

[1] 5 *Mafs. Hift. Coll.* vol. i. p. 414.

God ? then certainly your dog and all dogs and beaſts. How much more mankind. (He ſaveth man and beaſt.) How much more his ſons and daughters, and heirs of his crown and kingdom.

Sir, I have encouraged Mr. Dexter to ſend you a lime-ſtone, and to ſalute you with this encloſed. He is an intelligent man, a maſter printer of London, and conſcionable (though a Baptiſt), therefore maligned and traduced by William Harris (a doleful generaliſt.) Sir, if there be any occaſion of yourſelf (or others) to uſe any of this ſtone, Mr. Dexter hath a luſty team and luſty ſons, and very willing heart, (being a ſanguine, cheerful man) to do your-ſelf or any (at your word eſpecially,) ſervice upon my honeſt and cheap conſiderations; and if there be any oc-caſion, Sir, you may be confident of all ready ſervice from your old unworthy ſervant,

                                  ROGER WILLIAMS.

While you were at Mr. Smith's that bloody liquor trade (which Richard Smith[1] hath of old driven) fired the coun-try about your lodging. The Indians would have more liquor, and it came to blows. The Indians complained to Richard Smith. He told them he was buſy about your departure. Next day the Engliſh complained of ſome hurt and went with twenty-eight horſe (and more men) to

---

[1] Richard Smith's name firſt appears among the "inhabitants of Newport, ad-mitted ſince May 20, 1638," and pre-vious to 1639.—*R. I. Col. Records,* vol. i. p. 92. He and his ſon Richard Smith, jr., "traders, of Cocumcofuck," and Gov. Winthrop of Connecticut were among thoſe to whom Coganiquant, deeded the "Northern tract" in the Nar-raganſett country in 1659. They had a large trading houſe in Wickford. Both father and ſon were among the promi-nent men of that part of the colony. It would appear from Mr. Williams's let-ter, that they dealt largely in ſpirituous liquors.

fetch in the Sachem. The Indians with a fhout routed thefe horfes, and caufed their return, and are more infolent by this repulfe; yet they are willing to be peaceable, were it not for that devil of liquor. I might have gained thoufands (as much as any) by that trade, but God hath gracioufly given me rather to choofe a dry morfel, &c.

Sir, fince I faw you I have read Morton's Memorial,[1] and rejoice at the encomiums upon your father and other precious worthies, though I be a reprobate, *contemptâ vitior algâ.*   R. W.

PROVIDENCE, June 22, 1670, (*ut vulgo.*)[2]

MAJOR MASON,—My honored, dear and ancient friend, my due refpects and earneft defires to God, for your eternal peace, &c.

I crave your leave and patience to prefent you with fome few confiderations, occasioned by the late tranfactions between your colony and ours. The laft year you were pleafed, in one of your lines to me, to tell me that you longed to fee my face once more before you died. I embraced your love, though I feared my old lame bones, and yours, had arrefted traveling in this world, and therefore I was and am ready to lay hold on all occafions of writing, as I do at prefent.

The occafion, I confefs, is forrowful, becaufe I fee your-

------

[1] *New England's Memorial; or a Brief Relation of the moft Memorable and Remarkable paffages in the Providence of God manifefted in the Planters of New England in America,* etc., CAMBRIDGE, 1669.

[2] *Mafs. Hift. Coll.,* vol. i. p. 275; KNOWLES, *Memoirs of Roger Williams,* p. 393.

felves, with others, embarked in a refolution to invade and
defpoil your poor countrymen, in a wildernefs, and your
ancient friends, of our temporal and foul liberties.[1]

It is forrowful, alfo, becaufe mine eye beholds a black
and doleful train of grievous, and, I fear, bloody confequences, at the heel of this bufinefs, both to you and us.
The Lord is righteous in all our afflictions, that is a maxim; the Lord is gracious to all oppreffed, that is another;
he is moft gracious to the foul that cries and waits on him;
that is filver, tried in the fire feven times.

Sir, I am not out of hopes, but that while your aged
eyes and mine are yet in their orbs, and not yet funk
down into their holes of rottennefs, we fhall leave our
friends and countrymen, our children and relations, and
this land, in peace, behind us. To this end, Sir, pleafe
you with a calm and fteady and a Chriftian hand, to hold
the balance and to weigh thefe few confiderations, in much
love and due refpect prefented :

[1] The queftion of jurifdiction in the fouthweftern part of the colony led to the appointment of a committee by Connecticut, in May of this year, to confer with the authorities of Rhode If-land, and if the latter refufed to treat, they were authorized to reduce the peo-ple of Wefterly and Narraganfett to fubmiffion. A fpecial feffion of the Af-fembly of Rhode Ifland was called, and a committee appointed to confider the fubject. The two committees met at New London, but failed to agree upon terms of fettlement. The Connecticut men, the following day, formally pro-claimed the authority of their govern-ment over Wefterly, and fent officers warning the inhabitants eaft of Pawca-tuck river to appear at Stonington. The officers were arrefted and fent to New-port jail. To add to the troubles, Har-vard College fet up a claim to land in Wefterly. Arrefts were made on both fides, and another fpecial feffion of the Affembly took place in June, when agents were appointed to proceed to England, there to defend the charter againft the invafions of Connecticut. It was at this juncture that Mr. Williams wrote this letter to Major Mafon, who enclofed it to the Connecticut Commiffioners. Mr. Arnold in his *Hiftory of Rhode Ifland*, gives a lucid account of the controverfy in queftion; vol. i. pp. 341–348; while the documentary hiftory of it may be found at length in the *R. I. Colonial Re-cords*, vol. ii. pp. 309–328.

Firſt. When I was unkindly and unchriſtianly, as I be-lieve, driven from my houſe and land and wife and chil-dren, (in the midſt of a New England winter, now about thirty-five years paſt,) at Salem, that ever honored Gover-nor, Mr. Winthrop, privately wrote to me to ſteer my courſe to Narraganſett Bay and Indians, for many high and heavenly and public ends, encouraging me, from the free-neſs of the place from any Engliſh claims or patents. I took his prudent motion as a hint and voice from God, and waving all other thoughts and motions, I ſteered my courſe from Salem (though in winter ſnow, which I feel yet) unto theſe parts, wherein I may ſay Peniel, that is, I have ſeen the face of God.

Second, I firſt pitched, and began to build and plant at Seekonk, now Rehoboth, but I received a letter from my ancient friend, Mr. Winſlow, then Governor of Plymouth, profeſſing his own and others love and reſpect to me, yet lovingly adviſing me, ſince I was fallen into the edge of their bounds, and they were loath to diſpleaſe the Bay, to remove but to the other ſide of the water, and then, he ſaid, I had the country free before me, and might be as free as themſelves, and we ſhould be loving neighbors toge-ther. Theſe were the joint underſtandings of theſe two eminently wiſe and Chriſtian Governors and others, in their day, together with their counſel and advice as to the free-dom and vacancy of this place, which in this reſpect, and many other Providences of the Moſt Holy and Only Wiſe, I called *Providence.*[1]

---

[1] Finding himſelf upon lands claimed by Maſſachuſetts and Plymouth, Wil-liams embarked from Seekonk in a canoe, with five others, viz.: William Harris; John Smith, miller; Joſhua Verin, Tho-mas Angell and Francis Wickes. (*Moſes Brown in R. I. Regiſter* for 1828.) They are believed to have croſſed See-

Third. Sometime after, the Plymouth great Sachem, (Oufamaquin,) upon occafion, affirming that Providence was his land, and therefore Plymouth's land, and fome refenting it, the then prudent and godly Governor, Mr. Bradford,[1] and others of his godly council, anfwered, that if, after due examination, it fhould be found true what the barbarian faid, yet having to my lofs of a harveft that year, been now (though by their gentle advice) as good as banifhed from Plymouth as from the Maffachufetts, and I had quietly and patiently departed from them, at their motion to the place where now I was, I fhould not be molefted and toffed up and down again, while they had breath in their bodies; and furely, between thofe, my friends of the Bay and Plymouth, I was forely toffed, for one fourteen weeks, in a bitter winter feafon,[2] not knowing what bread or bed did mean, befide the yearly lofs of no fmall matter in my trading with Englifh and natives, being debarred from Bofton, the chief mart and port of New England.

konk river near where Central Bridge now croffes. As they approached the oppofite fhore, they were accofted by the Indians, with the friendly interrogation of "Whatcheer" a common Englifh phrafe, which they had learned from the colonifts, equivalent to "How do you do." (KNOWLES, p. 102.) Others fay this word meant "*Welcome.*" They probably landed on the rock which here juts out into the river, and remained for a fhort time. They then paffed round India Point and Fox Point, and proceeded up the river to a fpot near the entrance of the Mofhaffuck river, where the party landed. Tradition, fays, the landing place was near the fpring in the rear of the refidence of the late Gov. Philip Allen.

[1] William Bradford was the fecond Governor of Plymouth, John Carver, being the firft. He was one of the "Mayflower" Pilgrims. Was elected Governor in 1621, and annually re-elected until his death in 1657, excepting five years, when he declined the offer. He wrote a hiftory of Plymouth Colony from 1620 to 1647, which, after remaining in manufcript for more than two hundred years, was printed by the Maffachufetts Hiftorical Society, with notes by Charles Deane, in 1856.

[2] "Mr. Roger Williams," fays Gov. Bradford, "(a man godly and zealous, having many precious parts, but very unfettled in judgment) came over firft to the Maffachufetts, but upon fome difcontent left that place, and came hither,

God knows that many thoufand pounds cannot repay the very temporary loffes I have fuftained. It lies upon the Maffachufetts and me, yea, and other colonies joining with them, to examine, with fear and trembling, before the eyes of flaming fire, the true caufe of all my forrows and fufferings. It pleafed the Father of fpirits to touch many hearts, dear to him, with fome relentings; amongft which,

(where he was friendly entertained, according to their poor ability,) and exercifed his gifts amongft them, and after some time was admitted a member of the church; and his teachings well approved, for the benefit whereof I ftill blefs God. ... He this year began to fall into ftrange opinions, and from opinions to praftife, which caufed fome controverfy between the church and him, and in the end to fome difcontent on his part, by occafion whereof he left them fomething abruptly. Yet afterwards fued for his difmiffion to the church in Salem, which was granted. ... But he foon fell into more things there, both to their and the governments trouble and difturbance. I fhall not need to name particulars, they are too well known to all. ... But he is to be pitied, and prayed for, and fo I fhall leave the matter, and defire the Lord to fhew him his errors, and reduce him in the way of truth, and give him a fettled judgment and conftancy in the fame; for I hope he belongs to the Lord and that he will fhow him mercy."— *Hift. of Plymouth Plantation*, p. 310.

In conneftion with this fubjeft, and the remarks of Gov. Bradford, we quote an extraft from a letter of Sir William Martin to Gov. Winthrop, of Maffachufetts, enquiring about the ftate of the colony :

... "I am forry to hear of Mr. Williams's feparation from you. His former good affeftions to you and the Plantations, were well known unto me and make me wonder now at his proceedings. I have wrote to him effeftually to fubmit to better judgments, efpecially to thofe whom he formerly revered and admired ; at leaft to keep the bond of peace inviolable. This hath always been my advice ; and nothing conduceth more to the good of plantations. I pray fhow him what lawful favor you can, which may ftand with the common good. He is paffionate and precipitate, which may tranfport him into error. but I hope his integrity and good intentions will bring him at laft into the way of truth, and confirm him therein. In the meantime, I pray God to give him a right ufe of this affliftion."—*Hutchinfon Papers*, vol. i. p. 106.

There has been a queftion as to time when Williams left Salem ; but it is now generally acknowledged that it was in January, 1636. He was fourteen weeks journeying through the wildernefs, until he pitched his tent and began to plant at Seekonk. This was probably in May. The firft entry in the Providence records is dated the 16th of the 4th month, i. e. June [1636.]

43

that great and pious foul, Mr. Winflow, melted, and kindly vifited me, at Providence, and put a piece of gold into the hands of my wife, for our fupply.

Fourth. When the next year after my banifhment, the Lord drew the bow of the Pequod war againft the country, in which, Sir, the Lord made yourfelf, with others, a bleffed inftrument of peace to all New England, I had my fhare of fervice to the whole land in that Pequod bufinefs, inferior to very few that acted, for,[1]

1. Upon letters received from the Governor and Council at Bofton, requefting me to ufe my utmoft and fpeedieft endeavors to break and hinder the league labored for by the Pequods againft the Mohegans, and Pequods againft the Englifh, (excufing the not fending of company and fupplies, by the hafte of the bufinefs,) the Lord helped me immediately to put my life into my hand, and, fcarce acquainting my wife, to fhip myfelf, all alone, in a poor canoe, and to cut through a ftormy wind, with great feas, every minute in hazard of life, to the Sachem's houfe.

2. Three days and nights my bufinefs forced me to lodge and mix with the bloody Pequod ambaffadors, whofe hands and arms, methought, wreaked with the blood of my countrymen, murdered and maffacred by them on Connecticut river, and from whom I could not but nightly look for their bloody knives at my own throat alfo.

3. When God wondroufly preferved me, and helped me to break to pieces the Pequods' negotiation and defign, and to make, and promote and finifh, by many travels and charges, the Englifh league with the Narraganfetts and Mo-

---

[1] Gov. Bradford acknowledges the great fervice rendered by Mr. Williams in pacifying the Pequots at this time.— *Hiftory of Plymouth*, p. 364.

hegans againſt the Pequods, and that the Engliſh forces marched up to the Narraganſett country againſt the Pequods, I gladly entertained, at my houſe in Providence, the General Stoughton[1] and his officers and uſed my utmoſt care that all his officers and ſoldiers ſhould be well accommodated with us.

4. I marched up with them to the Narraganſett Sachems, and brought my countrymen and the barbarians, Sachems and captains, to a mutual confidence and complacence, each in other.

5. Though I was ready to have marched further, yet, upon agreement that I ſhould keep at Providence, as an agent between the Bay and the army, I returned, and was interpreter and intelligencer, conſtantly receiving and ſending letters to the Governor and Council at Boſton, &c., in which work I judge it no impertinent digreſſion to recite (out of the many ſcores of letters, at times, from Mr. Winthrop,) this one pious and heavenly prophecy, touching all New England, of that gallant man, viz.: "If the Lord turn away his face from our ſins, and bleſs our endeavors and yours, at this time againſt our bloody enemy, we and our children ſhall long enjoy peace, in this, our wilderneſs condition." And himſelf and ſome other of the Council motioned and it was debated, whether or no I had not merited, not only to be recalled from baniſhment, but alſo to be honored with ſome remark of favor. It is known who hindered, who never promoted the liberty of other men's conſciences. Theſe things, and ten times more, I could relate, to ſhow that I am not a ſtranger to the Pe-

---

[1] Iſrael Stoughton, of Dorcheſter, Maſs., commanded the Maſſachuſetts troops ſent againſt the Pequots. Was Captain of the Ancient and Honorable Artillery Company, and a commiſſioner to adminiſter the government of New Hampſhire. He was the father of Wm. Stoughton, the celebrated ſtateſman, who was Lieutenant-Governor and Chief Juſtice of Maſs.—Drake, *Biog. Dictionary.*

quod wars and lands, and poſſibly not far from the merit of a foot of land in either country, which I have not.

5. Conſidering (upon frequent exceptions againſt Providence men) that we had no authority for civil government, I went purpoſely to England, and upon my report and petition, the Parliament granted us a charter of government for theſe parts, ſo judged vacant on all hands. And upon this, the country about us was more friendly, and wrote to us, and treated us as an authorized colony; only the difference of our conſciences much obſtructed. The bounds of this, our firſt charter, I (having ocular knowledge of perſons, places and tranſactions) did honeſtly and conſcientiouſly, as in the holy preſence of God, draw up from Pawcatuck river, which I then believed, and ſtill do, is free from all Engliſh claims and conqueſts; for although there were ſome Pequods on this ſide the river, who, by reaſon of ſome Sachems' marriages with ſome on this ſide, lived in a kind of neutrality with both ſides, yet, upon the breaking out of the war, they relinquiſhed their land to the poſſeſſion of their enemies, the Narraganſetts and Niantics, and their land never came into the condition of the lands on the other ſide, which the Engliſh, by conqueſt, challenged; ſo that I muſt ſtill affirm, as in God's holy preſence, I tenderly waved to touch a foot of land in which I knew the Pequod wars were maintained and were properly Pequod, being a gallant country; and from Pawcatuck river hitherward, being but a patch of ground, full of troubleſome inhabitants, I did, as I judged, inoffenſively, draw our poor and inconſiderable line.

It is true, when at Portſmouth, on Rhode Iſland, ſome of ours, in a General Aſſembly, motioned their planting on this ſide Pawcatuck. I, hearing that ſome of the Maſſachuſetts reckoned this land theirs, by conqueſt, diſſuaded from the motion, until the matter ſhould be amicably debated and compoſed ; for though I queſtioned not our right, &c., yet I feared it would be inexpedient and offenſive, and procreative of theſe heats and fires, to the diſhonoring of the King's Majeſty, and the diſhonoring and blaſpheming of God and of religion in the eyes of the Engliſh and barbarians about us.

6. Some time after the Pequod war and our charter from the Parliament, the goverment of Maſſachuſetts wrote to myſelf (then chief officer in this colony) of their receiving of a patent from the Parliament for theſe vacant lands, as an addition to the Maſſachuſetts, &c., and thereupon requeſting me to exerciſe no more authority, &c., for they wrote, their charter was granted ſome few weeks before ours. I returned, what I believed righteous and weighty, to the hands of my true friend, Mr. Winthrop, the firſt mover of my coming into theſe parts, and to that anſwer of mine I never received the leaſt reply ; only it is certain, that, at Mr. Gorton's complaint againſt the Maſſachuſetts, the Lord High Admiral, Preſident, ſaid, openly, in a full meeting of the commiſſioners, that he knew no other charter for theſe parts than what Mr. Williams had obtained, and he was ſure that charter, which the Maſſachuſetts Engliſhmen pretended, had never paſſed the table.

7. Upon our humble addreſs, by our agent, Mr. Clarke, to his Majeſty, and his gracious promiſe of renewing our former charter, Mr. Winthrop, upon ſome miſtake, had entrenched upon our line, and not only ſo, but, as it is ſaid, upon the lines of other charters alſo. Upon Mr. Clarke's complaint, your grant was called in again, and it had never

been returned, but upon a report that the agents, Mr. Winthrop and Mr. Clarke, were agreed, by mediation of friends, (and it is true, they came to a folemn agreement, under hands and feals,) which agreement was never violated on our part.

8. But the King's Majefty fending his commiffioners among other of his royal purpofes) to reconcile the differences of, and to fettle the bounds between the colonies, yourfelves know how the King himfelf therefore hath given a decifion to this controverfy. Accordingly, the King's Majefty's aforefaid commiffioners at Rhode Ifland, (where, as a commiffioner for this colony, I tranfacted with them, as did alfo commiffioners from Plymouth,) they compofed a controverfy between Plymouth and us, and fettled the bounds between us, in which we reft.

9. However you fatisfy yourfelves with the Pequod conqueft, with the fealing of your charter fome weeks before ours; with the complaints of particular men to your colony; yet upon a due and ferious examination of the matter, in the fight of God, you will find the bufinefs at bottom to be,

Firft, a depraved appetite after the great vanities, dreams and fhadows of this vanifhing life, great portions of land, land in this wildernefs, as if men were in as great neceffity and danger for want of great portions of land, as poor, hungry, thirfty feamen have, after a fick and ftormy, a long and ftarving paffage. This is one of the gods of New England, which the living and moft high Eternal will deftroy and famifh.

2. An unneighborly and unchriftian intrufion upon us, as being the weaker, contrary to your laws, as well as ours, concerning purchasing of lands without the confent of the

General Court. This I told Major Atherton, at his firſt going up to the Narraganſett about this buſineſs. I refuſed all their proffers of land, and refuſed to interpret for them to the Sachems.

3. From theſe violations and intruſions ariſe the complaint of many privateers, not dealing as they would be dealt with, according to law of nature, the law of the prophets and Chriſt Jeſus, complaining againſt others, in a deſign, which they themſelves are delinquents and wrong doers. I could aggravate this many ways with Scripture rhetoric and ſimilitude, but I ſee need of anodynes, (as phyſicians ſpeak,) and not of irritations. Only this I muſt crave leave to ſay, that it looks like a prodigy or monſter, that countrymen among ſavages in a wilderneſs; that profeſſors of God and one Mediator, of an eternal life, and that this is like a dream, ſhould not be content with thoſe vaſt and large traſts which all the other colonies have, (like platters and tables full of dainties,) but pull and ſnatch away their poor neighbors' bit or cruſt; and a cruſt it is, and a dry, hard one, too, becauſe of the natives' continual troubles, trials and vexations.

10. Alas! Sir, in calm midnight thoughts, what are theſe leaves and flowers, and ſmoke and ſhadows, and dreams of earthly nothings, about which we poor fools and children, as David ſaith, diſquiet ourſelves in vain? Alas? what is all the ſcuffling of this world for, but, *come, will you ſmoke it?* What are all the contentions and wars of this world about, generally, but for greater diſhes and bowls of porridge, of which, if we believe God's Spirit in Scripture, Eſau and Jacob were types? Eſau will part with the heavenly birthright for his ſupping, after his hunting, for god belly; and Jacob will part with por-

ridge for an eternal inheritance. O Lord, give me to make Jacob's and Mary's choice, which fhall never be taken from me.

11. How much fweeter is the counfel of the Son of God, to mind firft the matters of his kingdom; to take no care for to-morrow; to pluck out, cut off and fling away right eyes, hands and feet, rather than to be caft whole into hell-fire; to confider the ravens and the lilies, whom a heavenly Father fo clothes and feeds; and the counfel of his fervant Paul, to roll our cares, for this life alfo, upon the moft high Lord, fteward of his people, the eternal God; to be content with food and raiment; to mind not our own, but every man the things of another; yea, and to fuffer wrong, and part with what we judge is right, yea, our lives, and (as poor women martyrs have faid) as many as there be hairs upon our heads, for the name of God and the fon of God his fake. This is humanity, yea, this is Chriftianity. The reft is but formality and picture, courteous idolatry and Jewifh and Popifh blafphemy againft the Chriftian religion, the Father of fpirits and his Son, the Lord Jefus. Befides, Sir, the matter with us is not about thefe children's toys of land, meadows, cattle, government, &c. But here, all over this colony, a great number of weak and diftreffed fouls, fcattered, are flying hither from Old and New England, the Moft High and Only Wife hath, in his infinite wifdom, provided this country and this corner as a fhelter for the poor and perfecuted, according to their feveral perfuafions. And thus that heavenly man, Mr. Haynes, Governor of Connecticut, though he pronounced the fentence of my long banifhment againft me, at Cambridge, then Newtown, yet faid unto me, in his own houfe at Hartford, being then in fome difference

with the Bay: "I think, Mr. Williams, I muſt now confeſs to you, that the moſt wiſe God hath provided and cut
out this part of his world for a refuge and receptacle for
all ſorts of conſciences. I am now under a cloud, and
my brother Hooker, with the Bay, as you have been, we
have removed from them thus far, and yet they are not
ſatisfied."[1]

Thus, Sir, the King's Majeſty, though his father's and
his own conſcience favored Lord Biſhops, which their
father and grandfather King James, whom I have ſpoke
with, ſore againſt his will, alſo did, yet àll the world may
ſee, by his Majeſty's declarations and engagements before
his return, and his declarations and Parliament ſpeeches
ſince, and many ſuitable actings, how the Father of ſpirits
hath mightily impreſſed and touched his royal ſpirit,
though the Biſhop's much diſturbed him, with deep inclination of favor and gentleneſs to different conſciences and
apprehenſions as to the inviſible King and way of his worſhip. Hence he hath vouchſafed his royal promiſe under
his hand and broad ſeal, that no perſon in this colony ſhall
be moleſted or queſtioned for the matters of his conſcience
to God, ſo he be loyal and keep the civil peace.[2] Sir, we
muſt part with lands and lives before we part with ſuch a
jewel. I judge you may yield ſome land and the govern-

---

[1] The Rev. Thomas Hooker, of Hartford, reſpecting whom ſee note on p. 84.

[2] The paſſage alluded to in the charter reads as follows: "That no perſon
within the ſaid colony, ſhall be anywiſe
moleſted, puniſhed or diſquieted, or
called in queſtion, for any differences in
opinion in matters of religion, who do
not actually diſturb the civil peace of our
ſaid colony; but that all and every perſon and perſons may, from time to time,
and at all times hereafter, freely and
fully have and enjoy his own and their
judgments and conſciences, in matters of
religious concernments, they behaving
themſelves peaceably and quietly," etc.,
etc.

44

ment of it to us, and we for peace fake, the like to you, as
being but fubjects to one king, &c., and I think the King's
Majefty would thank us, for many reafons.   But to part
with this jewel, we may as foon do it as the Jews with the
favor of Cyrus, Darius and Artaxerxes.   Yourfelves pretend liberty of confcience, but alas! it is but felf, the
great god felf, only to yourfelves.   The King's Majefty
winks at Barbadoes, where Jews and all forts of Chriftian
and Antichriftian perfuafions are free, but our grant, fome
few weeks after yours fealed, though granted as foon, if
not before yours, is crowned with the King's extraordinary favor to this colony, as being a banifhed one, in which
his Majefty declared himfelf that he would experiment,
whether civil government could confift with fuch liberty
of confcience.   This his Majefty's grant was ftartled at by
his Majefty's high officers of State, who were to view it
in courfe before the fealing, but tearing the lion's roaring,
they couched, againft their wills, in obedience to his Majefty's pleafure.

Some of yours, as I heard lately, told tales to the Archbifhop of Canterbury, viz.: that we are a profane people,
and do not keep the Sabbath, but fome do plough, &c.
But, firft, you told him not how we fuffer freely all other
perfuafions, yea, the common prayer, which yourfelves will
not fuffer.   If you fay you will, you confefs you muft fuffer more, as we do.

2. You know this is but a color to your defign, for, firft,
you know that all England itfelf (after the formality and
fuperftition of morning and evening prayer) play away
their Sabbath.   2d. You know yourfelves do not keep the
Sabbath, that is the feventh day, &c.

3. You know that famous Calvin and thoufands more

held it but ceremonial and figurative from Coloffians 2,[1] &c., and vanifhed; and that the day of worfhip was alterable at the churches' pleafure. Thus alfo all the Romanifts confefs, faying, viz. : that there is no exprefs fcripture, firft, for infants' baptifm ; nor, fecond, for abolifhing the feventh day, and inftituting of the eighth day worfhip, but that it is at the churches' pleafure.

4. You know, that generally, all this whole colony obferve the firft day, only here and there one out of confcience, another out of covetoufnefs, make no confcience of it.

5. You know the greatest part of the world make no confcience of a feventh day. The next part of the world, Turks, Jews and Chriftians, keep three different days, Friday, Saturday, Sunday for their Sabbath and day of worfhip, and every one maintains his own by the longeft fword.

6. I have offered, and do, by thefe prefents, to difcufs by difputation, writing or printing, among other points of differences, thefe three pofitions; firft, that forced worfhip ftinks in God's noftrils. 2d. That it denies Chrift Jefus yet to be come, and makes the church yet national, figurative and ceremonial. 3d. That in thefe flames about religion, as his Majefty, his father and grandfather have yielded, there is no other prudent, Chriftian way of preferving peace in the world, but by permiffion of differing confciences. Accordingly, I do now offer to difpute thefe points and other points of difference, if you pleafe, at Hartford, Bofton and Plymouth. For the manner of the difpute and the difcuffion, if you think fit, one whole day each month in fummer, at each place, by courfe, I am

---

[1] "Let no man judge you in meat, or of the new moon, or of the *Sabbath* in drink, or in refpect of an holyday, or *days.*"—Coloffians, ii. 16.

ready, if the Lord permit, and, as I humbly hope, affift me.

It is faid, that you intend not to invade our fpiritual or civil liberties, but only (under the advantage of firft fealing your charter) to right the privateers that petition to you. It is faid, alfo, that if you had but Mifhquomacuck and Narraganfett lands quietly yielded, you would ftop at Cowefet, &c.[1] Oh, Sir, what do thefe thoughts preach, but that private cabins rule all, whatever become of the fhip of common fafety and religion, which is fo much pretended in New England? Sir, I have heard further, and by fome that fay they know, that fomething deeper than all which hath been mentioned lies in the three colonies' breafts and confultations. I judge it not fit to commit fuch matter to the truft of paper, &c., but only befeech the Father of fpirits to guide our poor bewildered fpirits, for his name and mercy fake.

15. Whereas our cafe feems to be the cafe of Paul appealing to Cæfar againft the plots of his religious, zealous adverfaries, I hear you pafs not of our petitions and appeals to his Majefty, for partly you think the King will not own a profane people that do not keep the Sabbath; partly you think that the King is an incompetent judge, but you will force him to law alfo, to confirm your firft born Efau, though Jacob had him by the heels, and in God's holy time muft carry the birthright and inheritance. I judge your furmife is a dangerous miftake, for patents, grants and charters, and fuch like royal favors, are not laws of England, and acts of Parliament, nor matters of propriety and *meum* and *tuum* between

---

[1] With Connecticut's claim to Cowefet, i. e. to Eaft Greenwich Bay, and Maffachufetts and Plymouth clamoring for territory on the north, it was no eafy matter for the little colony of Rhode Ifland, to maintain a feparate exiftence. Maffachufetts alfo claimed a ftrip of territory eaft of Pawcatuck river, five or fix miles wide as her fhare in the divifion of the Pequot territory.

the King and his fubjects, which, as the times have been,
have been fometimes triable in inferior Courts; but fuch
kind of grants have been like high offices in England, of
high honor, and ten, yea twenty thoufand pounds gain per
annum, yet revocable or curtable upon pleafure, according
to the King's better information, or upon his Majefty's
fight, or mifbehavior, ingratefulnefs, or defigns fraudu-
lently plotted, private and diftinct from him

16. Sir, I lament that fuch defigns fhould be carried on
at fuch a time, while we are ftripped and whipped, and are
ftill under (the whole country) the dreadful rods of God,
in our wheat, hay, corn, cattle, fhipping, trading, bodies
and lives; when on the other fide of the water, all forts
of confciences (yours and ours) are frying in the Bifhops'
pan and furnace; when the French and Romifh Jefuits,
the firebrands of the world for their god belly fake, are
kindling at our back, in this country, efpecially with the
Mohawks and Mohegans, againft us, of which I know and
have daily information.[1]

17. If any pleafe to fay, is there no medicine for this
malady? Muft the nakednefs of New England, like fome
notorious ftrumpet, be proftituted to the blafpheming eyes
of all nations? Muft we be put to plead before his Majefty, and confequently the Lord Bifhops, our common
enemies, &c. I anfwer, the Father of mercies and God of all
confolations hath gracioufly difcovered to me, as I believe,
a remedy, which, if taken, will quiet all minds, yours and
ours, will keep yours and ours in quiet poffeffion and enjoyment of their lands, which you all have fo dearly

---

[1] This allufion is doubtlefs to the labors of the Jefuit miffionaries in Canada
and among the Mohawks and other Indian tribes in the northern parts of New
England, and in what is now the State of
New York.

bought and purchafed in this barbarous country, and fo long poffeffed amongft thefe wild favages; will preferve you both in the liberties and honors of your charters and governments, without the leaft impeachment of yielding one to another; with a ftrong curb alfo to thofe wild barbarians and all the barbarians of this country, without troubling of compromifers and arbitrators between you; without any delay, or long and chargeable and grievous addrefs to our King's Majefty, whofe gentle and ferene foul muft needs be afflicted to be troubled again with us. If you pleafe to afk me what my prefcription is, I will not put you off to Chriftian moderation or Chriftian humility, or Chriftian prudence, or Chriftian love, or Chriftian felf-denial, or Chriftian contention or patience. For I defign a civil, a humane and political medicine, which, if the God of Heaven pleafe to blefs, you will find it effectual to all the ends I have propofed. Only I muft crave your pardon, both parties of you, if I judge it not fit to difcover it at prefent. I know you are both of you hot; I fear myfelf, alfo. If both defire, in a loving and calm fpirit, to enjoy your rights, I promife you, with God's help, to help you to them, in a fair, and fweet and eafy way. My receipt will not pleafe you all. If it fhould fo pleafe God to frown upon us that you fhould not like it, I can but humbly mourn, and fay with the prophet, that which muft perifh muft perifh. And as to myfelf, in endeavoring after your temporal and fpiritual peace, I humbly defire to fay, if I perifh, I perifh. It is but a fhadow vanifhed, a bubble broke, a dream finifhed. Eternity will pay for all.

Sir, I am your old and true friend and fervant,

ROGER WILLIAMS.

To my honored and ancient friend, Mr. Thomas Prince,[1] Governor of Plymouth Colony, thefe prefent. And by his honored hand this copy, fent to Connecticut, whom it moft concerneth, I humbly prefent to the General Court of Plymouth, when next affembled.

Roger Williams to John Cotton, of Plymouth.

PROVIDENCE, 25 March, 1671. (fo called.)[2]

SIR,—Loving refpects premifed. About three weeks fince, I received yours, dated in December, and wonder not that prejudice, intereft, and paffion have lift up your feet thus to trample on me as on fome Mahometan, Jew, or Papift; fome common thief or fwearer, drunkard or adulterer; imputing to me the odious crimes of blafphemies, reproaches, flanders, idolatries; to be in the Devil's kingdom; a gracelefs man, &c.; and all this without any Scripture, reafon, or argument, which might enlighten my confcience as to any error or offence to God or your dear father. I have now much above fifty years humbly and earneftly begged of God to make me as vile as a dead dog in my own eye, fo that I might not fear what men fhould falfely fay or cruelly do againft me; and I have had long

---

[1] Thomas Prince came to America in 1621; was elected Governor of Plymouth in 1644; was again elected in different years until 1657, and was then chofen without intermiffion until 1672. He died in 1673, aged 73 years.—BLAKE, *Biog. Dict.*

[2] This John Cotton was the fon of the Rev. John Cotton with whom Roger Williams had had a controverfy. He was minifter at Plymouth, and was connected with the printing of ELIOT's Indian Bible, at Cambridge, in 1685, which he revifed and corrected.

[3] *Mafs. Hift. Soc. Proceedings,* 1858, p. 313.

experience of his merciful anſwer to me in men's falſe charges and cruelties againſt me to this hour.

My great offence (you ſo often repeat) is my wrong to your dear father,—your glorified father, &c.   But the truth is, the love and honor which I have always ſhowed (in ſpeech and writing) to that excellently learned and holy man, your father, have been ſo great, that I have been cenſured by divers for it.   God knows, that, for God's ſake, I tenderly loved and honored his perſon (as I did the perſons of the magiſtrates, miniſters, and members whom I knew in Old England, and knew their holy affeċtions, and upright aims, and great ſelf-denial, to enjoy more of God in this wilderneſs) ; and I have therefore deſired to waive all perſonal failings, and rather mention their beauties, to prevent the inſultings of the Papiſts or profane Proteſtants, who uſed to ſcoff at the weakneſſes—yea, and at the diviſions—of thoſe they uſe to brand for Puritans. The holy eye of God hath ſeen this the cauſe why I have not ſaid nor writ what abundantly I could have done, but have rather choſe to bear all cenſures, loſſes, and hardſhips, &c.

This made that honored father of the Bay, Mr. Winthrop, to give me the teſtimony, not only of exemplary diligence in the miniſtry (when I was ſatisfied in it), but of patience alſo, in theſe words in a letter to me : " Sir, we have often tried your patience, but could never conquer it."   My humble deſire is ſtill to bear, not only what you ſay, but, when power is added to your will, an hanging or burning from you, as you plainly intimate you would long ſince have ſerved my book, had it been your own, as not being fit to be in the poſſeſſion of any Chriſtian, as you write.

Alas! Sir, what hath this book merited, above all the many thoufands full of old Romifh idols' names, &c., and new Popifh idolatries, which are in Chriftians' libraries, and ufe to be alleged in teftimony, argument, and confutation?

What is there in this book but preffeth holinefs of heart, holinefs of life, holinefs of worfhip, and pity to poor finners, and patience toward them while they break not the civil peace? 'Tis true, my firft book, the "Bloody Tenent," was burnt by the Prefbyterian party (then prevailing); but this book whereof we now fpeak (being my Reply to your father's Anfwer)[1] was received with applaufe and thanks by the army, by the Parliament, profefsing that, of neceffity,—yea, of Chriftian equity,—there could be no reconciliation, pacification, or living together, but by permitting of diffenting confciences to live amongft them; infomuch that that excellent fervant of God, Mr. John Owen[2] (called Dr. Owen), told me before the General (who fent for me about that very bufinefs), that before I landed, himfelf and many others had anfwered Mr. Cotton's book already. The firft book, and the point of permitting Diffenters, his Majefty's royal father affented to; and how often hath the fon, our fovereign, declared himfelf indulgent toward Diffenters, notwithftanding the clamors and plottings of his felf-feeking bifhops! And, Sir,

---

[1] "*The Bloody Tenent yet more Bloody ;*" *by Mr. Cotton's endeavour to wafh it white in the Blood of the Lambe.* LONDON, 1652. Reprinted by Narragaufett Club, vol. iv.

[2] Dr. Owen was the author of more than eighty publications, all theological. A collected edition of thefe was publifhed in 1850–55 in twenty-four vols.

8vo. "His devotional and practical, and expofitory works are an invaluable treafure of divinity. . . . They are eminently fpiritual, devotional, edifying. He is full of Biblical learning, found expofition of doctrine, acutenefs and information." BICKERSTITH, *Chr. Student*, 1844, p. 268.

(as before and formerly), I add, if yourfelf, or any in public or private, fhow me any failing againft God or your father in that book, you fhall find me diligent and faithful in weighing and in confeffing or replying in love and meeknefs.

Oh! you fay, wrong to a father made a dumb child fpeak, &c. Sir, I pray forget not that your father was not God, but man,—finful, and failing in many things, as we all do, faith the Holy Scripture. I prefume you know the fcheme of Mr. Cotton's Contradictions (about Church-difcipline), prefented to the world by Mr. Daniel Cawdrey,[1] a man of name and note. Alfo, Sir, take heed you prefer not the earthen pot (though your excellent father) before his moft high eternal Maker and Potter. Bleffed that you were born and proceeded from him, if you honor him more for his humility and holinefs than for outward refpect, which fome (and none fhall juftly more than myfelf) put upon him.

Sir, you call my three propofals, &c., abominable, falfe, and wicked; but, as before, thoufands (high and holy, too, fome of them) will wonder at you. Captain Gookins,[2] from Cambridge, writes me word that he will not be my antagonift in them, being candidly underftood. Your honored Governor tells me there is no foundation for any difpute with Plymouth about thofe propofals; for you

[1] Daniel Cawdry, a non-Conformift divine, ejected from his living in Northamptonfhire. He was the author of feveral theological treatifes.—ALLIBONE, *Dictionary.*

[2] Daniel Gookins came to Maffachufetts in 1621, of which colony he became Major-General. He was Superintendent of the Maffachufetts Indians, and ftood forth as their friend and protector in all the wars and difficulties between them and the whites. He was the author of the *Hiftorical Collections of the Indians of New England.* He died in 1687, aged 75.

force no men's confcience. But, Sir, you have your liberty to prove them abominable, falfe, and wicked, and to dif-prove that which I have prefented in the book concerning the New England churches to be but parochial and na-tional, though fifted with a finer fieve, and painted with finer colors.

You are pleafed to count me excommunicate; and therein you deal more cruelly with me than with all the profane, and Proteftants and Papifts too, with whom you hold communion in the parifhes, to which (as you know) all are forced by the bifhops. And yet you count me a flave to the Devil, becaufe, in confcience to God, and love to God and you, I have told you of it. But, Sir, the truth is (I will not fay I excommunicate vou, but), I firft with-drew communion from yourfelves for halting between Chrift and Antichrift,—the parifh churches and Chriftian congregations. Long after, when you had confultations of killing me, but fome rather advifed a dry pit of banifh-ment, Mr. Peters advifed an excommunication to be fent me (after the manner of Popifh bulls, &c.); but this fame man, in London, embraced me, and told me he was for liberty of confcience, and preached it; and complained to me of Salem for excommunicating his diftracted wife, and for wronging him in his goods which he left behind him.

Sir, you tell me my time is loft, &c., becaufe (as I con-ceive you) not in the funclion of miniftry. I confefs the offices of Chrift Jefus are the beft callings; but generally they are the worft trades in the world, as they are practifed only for a maintenance, a place, a living, a benefice, &c. God hath many employments for his fervants. Mofes for-ty years, and the Lord Jefus thirty years, were not idle, though little known what they did as to any miniftry; and

the two prophets prophefy in fackcloth, and are Chrift
Jefus his minifters, though not owned by the public ordi-
nations. God knows, I have much and long and confcientioufly and mournfully weighed and digged into the differences of the Proteftants themfelves about the miniftry.
He knows what gains and preferments I have refufed in
univerfities, city, country, and court, in Old England, and
fomething in New England, &c., to keep my foul unde-
filed in this point, and not to act with a doubting confcience, &c. God was pleafed to fhow me much of this in
Old England; and in New, being unanimoufly chofen
teacher at Bofton (before your dear father came, divers
years), I confcientioufly refufed, and withdrew to Plymouth, becaufe I durft not officiate to an unfeparated people, as, upon examination and conference, I found them to
be. At Plymouth, I fpake on the Lord's days and week
days, and wrought hard at the hoe for my bread (and fo
afterward at Salem), until I found them both profeffing to
be a feparated people in New England (not admitting the
moft godly to communion without a covenant), and yet
communicating with the parifhes in Old by their members
repairing on frequent occafions thither.[1]

Sir, I heartily thank you for your conclufion,—wifhing
my converfion and falvation; without which, furely vain
are our privileges of being Abraham's fons, enjoying the

---

[1] Dr. Palfrey in fpeaking of this letter fays, " It is hard to fuppofe that,
when Williams made this ftatement, (forty years after this tranfaction, and when
he was fixty-five years old,) his memory
was mifled by his imagination. But on
the oppofie fuppofition, it is very extraordinary that the fact is not mentioned
in any record of the time. The records
of the Bofton church cannot be appealed
to in the cafe. The only entry they
contain previous to October, 1632, is
that of the covenant of church-mem-
bers."—*Hift. of New England*, vol. i. p.
406, note.

covenant, holy education, holy worſhip, holy church or temple; of being adorned with deep underſtanding, miraculous faith, angelical parts and utterance; thc titles of paſtors or apoſtles; yea, of being ſacrifices in the fire to God.

Sir, I am unworthy (though deſirous to be),

Your friend and ſervant,

ROGER WILLIAMS.

———————

PROVIDENCE, yᵈ 15th of the 5, [15 July,] 1672.[1]

To George Fox or any other of my Countrymen at Newport, who ſay they are the Apoſtles and Meſſengers of Chriſt Jeſus:—

In humble confidence of the help of the Moſt High, I offer to maintain in public, againſt all comers, theſe fourteen Propoſitions following, to wit: the firſt ſeven at Newport, and the other ſeven at Providence. For the time when, I refer it to G. Fox and his friends at Newport.

Only I deſire

1. To have three days notice, before the day you fix on.

---

[1] *Hiſt. Mag.* New York, 1858, p. 56; *George Fox digg'd out of his Burrowes,* 1676, p. 2.

The date of this letter is not given, where it appears in Williams's book, but is found in the original manuſcript preſerved among the archives of Connecticut, from which it was printed in the *Hiſtorical Magazine.*

As the ſubject matter of this letter and the diſcuſſion that grew out of it forms the principal ſubject of the celebrated book of Williams' called "*George Fox Digg'd out of his Burrowes,*" which was reprinted by the Narraganſett Club, (vol. v.) accompanied by an Introduction and Notes by Profeſſor Diman, it ſeems hardly neceſſary to enlarge upon

2. That without interruption (or many fpeaking at once) the Conference may continue from nine in the morning till about four in the afternoon ; and

3. That if either of the feven Propofitions be not finifhed in one day, the Conference may continue and go on fome few hours the next day.

it here. We can add nothing to that which the Profeffor has fo well faid in his introduction.

It appears that the letter, which was enclofed to Deputy Governor Cranfton, was not delivered to him until the 26th of July, feveral hours after George Fox had left. Williams charges Fox with having purpofely avoided him, which Fox denies in the moft emphatic language. Prof. Diman thinks there is no ground for the charge made by Williams that Fox "flily departed." "No characteriftic of Fox" he adds "was more marked than felf-confidence. At no time did he ever fhrink from meeting an adverfary ; he was now in the prime of life, and in the full flufh of his career as prophet of a new fect. No reafon can be conceived why he fhould be unwilling to meafure his ftrength with Roger Williams, a man paffed three fcore and ten, and wielding at this time but little influence."—*Introduction*, p. xvi.

The departure of Fox did not interfere with the propofed difcuffion. Stubbs, Burnyeat and other Quakers went to Providence, where they faw Williams and made an agreement to meet him at Newport, on the 9th of Auguft, "and God," he fays, "gracioufly affifted me in rowing all day with my old bones, fo that I got to Newport toward the midnight before the morning appointed."

When Williams made his appear-

ance at the hour appointed, he found his three opponents fitting together on an high bench. The diftinctive characteriftics of thefe whom he terms "able and noted preachers" are fketched in a few words. He had heard that John Stubbs "was learned in Hebrew and Greek," and he found him fo. Burnyeat he found "to be a moderate fpirit, and very able fpeaker." But Edmundfon feems to have aroufed his fpecial diflike. While Stubbs and Burnyeat were "civil and ingenious," Edmundfon "was nothing but a bundle of Ignorance and Boifteroufnefs," etc.— Prof. Diman, *Introduction*, p. xxx.

The debate which confumed three days on the firft feven propofitions drew together a great number of hearers, who eagerly watched the fortunes of the ftrife. The parties then adjourned to Providence, where the remaining propofitions were difcuffed ; ending in much the fame way as thofe at Newport, each fide apparently well fatisfied with the refult. Many accounts of the remarkable debate have been printed by contemporary writers; but thofe interefted in it who will not undertake to wade through the five hundred pages of Williams's book "*George Fox Digg'd out of his Burrowes,*" will find a clear and condenfed account of it in Prof. Diman's Introduction to that work in the fifth volume of the publications of the Narraganfett Club.

4. That either of us difputing, fhall have free uninter-
rupted liberty to fpeak (in Anfwers and Replies) as much
and as long as we pleafe, and thus give the oppofite the
fame liberty.

That the whole may be managed with that ingenuity
and humanity, as fuch an exercife, by fuch perfons in fuch
conditions, at fuch a time, ought to be managed and per-
formed, the Propofitions are thefe that follow:

Firft. That the people called Quakers, are not true Quakers according to the Holy Scriptures.

2. That the Chrift they profefs is not the true Lord
Jefus Chrift.

3. That the Spirit by which they are acted, is not the
Spirit of God.

4. That they do not own the Holy Scriptures.

5. Their principles and profeffions, are full of contradictions and hypocrifies

6. That their religion is not only an herefy in the matters of worfhip, but alfo in the doctrines of Repentance,
Faith, &c.

7. Their Religion is but a confufed mixture of Popery,
Armineanifme, Socineanifme, Judaifme, &c.

8. The people called Quakers (in effect) hold no God,
no Chrift, no Spirit, no Angel, no Devil, no Refurrection,
no Judgment, no Heaven, no Hell, but what is in man.

9. All that their Religion requires (external and internal) to make converts and profelites, amounts to no more
than what a reprobate may eafily attain unto, and perform.

10. That the Popes of Rome do not fwell with, and
exercife a greater pride, then the Quakers Spirit have
expreffed, and doth afpire unto, although many truly humble fouls may be captivated amongft them, as may be in
other Religions.

11. The Quakers' Religion is more obftructive and deftructive to the converfion and falvation of the fouls of people, then moft of the Religions this day extant in the world.

12. The fufferings of the Quakers are no true evidence of the Truth of their Religion.

13. That their many books and writings are extremely poor, lame, naked, and fwelled up only with high titles and words of boafting and vapor.

14. That the fpirit of their Religion tends mainly,

1. To reduce perfons from civility to barbarifm.

2. To an arbitrary goverment, and the dictates and decrees of that fudden Spirit that acts them.

3. To a fudden cutting off of people, yea of Kings and Princes oppofing them.

4. To as fiery perfecutions for matters of Religion and Confcience, as hath been or can be practifed by any Hunters or Perfecutors in the world.

Under thefe forementioned heads (if the Spirit of the Quakers dare civilly to argue) will be opened many of the Popifh, Proteftant, Jewifh and Quakers Pofitions, which cannot here be mentioned, in the Difpute (if God pleafe) they muft be alledged, and the examination left to every perfon's confcience, as they will anfwer to God, (at their own perils) in the great day approaching.

ROGER WILLIAMS.

Roger Williams to Samuel Hubbard.[1]

MY DEAR FRIEND, SAMUEL HUBBARD,—To yourſelf and aged companion, my loving reſpects in the Lord Jeſus, who ought to be our hope of glory, begun in this life, and enjoyed to all eternity. I have herein returned your little, yet great remembrance of the hand of the Lord to your-ſelf and your ſon, late departed. I praiſe the Lord for your humble kiſſing of his holy rod, and acknowledging his juſt and righteous, together with his gracious and mer-ciful diſpenſation to you. I rejoice, alſo, to read your hea-venly deſires and endeavors, that your trials may be gain to your own ſouls and the ſouls of the youth of the place, and all of us. You are not unwilling, I judge, that I deal plainly and friendly with you. After all that I have ſeen and read and compared about the ſeventh day, (and I have earneſtly and carefully read and weighed all I could come at in God's holy preſence) I cannot be removed from Calvin's mind, and indeed Paul's mind, Col. ii. that all thoſe ſabbaths of ſeven days were figures, types and ſhadows, and forerunners of the Son of God, and that the change is made from the remembrance of the firſt crea-tion, and that (figurative) reſt on the ſeventh day, to the remembrance of the ſecond creation on the firſt, on which

---

[1]BACKUS, *Hiſt. of the Baptiſts,* vol. i. p. 510.

Samuel Hubbard came to Salem in 1633; removed to Springfield, and was one of the five founders of the Baptiſt Church there. His name appears in the roll of freemen of Newport, in 1655. In 1664 he was choſen "Solici-tor." Backus ſays he was received in-

to the Baptiſt communion at Newport, in 1648, where he lived to a great age. His only ſon, Samuel, died late in 1671. SAVAGE, *Gen. Dict.* vol. ii. p. 485. As it is to the death of this ſon that Mr. Williams refers, we may place the date of this letter ſometime in 1672, after the diſpute with the Quakers at Newport, in Auguſt of that year.

46

our Lord arofe conqueror from the dead. Accordingly,
I have read many, but fee no fatisfying anfwer to thofe
three Scriptures, chiefly Acts 20, 1 Cor. 16, Rev. 1, in confcience to which I make fome poor confcience to God as
to the reft day.   As for thoughts for England, I humbly
hope the Lord hath fhowed me to write a large narrative
of all thofe four days' agitation between the Quakers[1]
and myfelf; if it pleafe God I cannot get it printed in
New England, I have great thoughts and purpofes for Old.
My age, lamenefs, and many other weakneffes, and the
dreadful hand of God at fea, calls for deep confideration.
What God may pleafe to bring forth in the fpring, his
holy wifdom knows.   If he pleafe to bring to an abfolute
purpofe, I will fend you word, and my dear friend, Obadiah Holmes, who fent me a meffage to the fame purpofe.
At prefent, I pray falute refpectively, Mr. John Clarke and
his brothers, Mr. Torrey,[2] Mr. Edes, Edward Smith,[3] William Hifcox,[4] Stephen Mumford, and other friends, whofe
prefervation, of the ifland, and this country, I humbly beg
of the Father of Mercies, in whom I am yours unworthy,

ROGER WILLIAMS.

[1] The difcuffion with the Quakers at
Newport : fee the two previous letters.
[2] Jofeph Torrey, admitted a freeman
of Newport, in 1653, was for many
years a prominent man in the colony.
He filled the offices of Deputy and Affiftant in the General Affembly, General
Recorder, Solicitor General, etc.

[3] Edward Smith, admitted a freeman of
Newport, in 1653, from which town he
was feveral times chofen an Affiftant and
Deputy.
[4] William Hifcox, admitted a freeman
of Newport, in 1671 : one of the Council of Advice in the Indian war, 1676.—
R. I. Col. Records, vol. ii. p. 557.

To my honored kind friend, Mr. John Winthrop, Governor of his Majefty's Colony of Connecticut, prefent.

From MR. RICHARD SMITHS, June 13, 1675.[1]

SIR,—Mr. Smith[2] being at Newport, I am occafioned to prefent my old and conftant love and refpects, as alfo Mrs. Smith's great thanks and fervice to you. Sir, Mr. Smith delivered me two letters, the one from Mr. Fitch, the other from Mr. John Mafon, praying me (according to the contents of the letters) to enquire of Mawfup, (now called Canonicus),[3] whether Uncas had ftirred him up againft the Wunnafhowatuckowogs, to kill them, &c. Sir, a fortnight fince I went to Canonicus his houfe, but he was gone twelve miles off: I fought him again yefterday, and found him five miles from his houfe : I fhewed him the letters : I ufed alfo your honored name, and the names of your honored Affiftants, both concerning the killing of the Englifh cattle in thefe parts ; as alfo concerning their carriage towards the Wunnafhowattuckoogs who are re-fpected by yourfelves.

Sir, Canonicus and other Sachems and his Council pro-fefs they will be careful of the Englifh and their cattle among them : alfo that they will fhow refpect to thofe Showatuks for your fake, and in particular (which an-fwers Mr. Fitch and Mr. Mafon's letters) Canonicus utter-ly denies that Uncas ever folicited him to kill or moleft thofe Showatuks. Withall he added two reafons. Firft, that it is not credible that fince Uncas killed his brother Miantunnomu, he (Canonicus) fhould be folicited by Un-

---

[1] 4 *Mafs. Hift. Coll.* vol. vi. p. 297.
[2] Smith's refidence was at Wickford,
where he eftablifhed himfelf in 1639 : fee note to letter on page 177.
[3] Better known by the name of *Peffacus.*

cas in fuch a bufinefs, or that he fhould gratify Uncas defires, &c.   2. Both himfelf, and Nananawtunu[1] (Miantunnomu's youngeft, very hopeful fpark) defired earneftly that
Tatuphofuwut, Uncas his fon, who hath killed a Wiyow
(or Sachem) one of their coufins, may fuffer impartially,
as now the Englifh have dealt with the three Indians which
killed John Soffiman.   Alfo they prayed me to add, that
yourfelf are not ignorant of Uncas his many foul practices, and how he treacheroufly fent an head (or heads) of
the Connecticut Indians to the Mawquawogs, and would
fend your heads alfo as prefents if he would come at them.
Sir, Nananawtinu added this argument for impartiality toward Tatuphofuit : I am (faid he) my father Miantunnomu's fon, as Tatuphofuit is to Uncas : if there fhould partiality be fhowed to him, and that money fhould buy out
men's lives, or that one of his men fhould die for him,
then all we young Sachems fhall have a temptation laid
before us to kill and murder, &c., in the hope of the like
impunity.

Sir, it is true that Philip fearing (apprehenfion) ftood
upon his guard with his armed barbarians.[2] Taunton,
Swanfey, Rehoboth, and Providence ftood upon ours, but
praifed be God, the ftorm is over, Philip is ftrongly fufpected, but the honored Court at Plymouth (as we hear)
not having evidence fufficient, let matters fleep, and the
country be in quiet, &c.

---

[1] Alias *Canonchet*, at this time the acknowledged Sachem of the Narraganfetts.

[2] Rumors of intended war on the part
of Philip, or Metacom, fon of Maffa-
foit, had been prevalent for feveral years,
and the Governor of Plymouth, had invited Philip to meet him at Taunton.

He refufed to go there unlefs Mr. Williams was a mediator.   Williams's agen-
cy in the matter was fuccefsful ; the Governor and the Sachem met; the latter
denied any hoftile defign and promifed
future fidelity.   The war was thus delayed four years.—KNOWLES, p. 341.

Sir, I conſtantly think of you, and ſend up one remembrance to heaven for you, and a groan from myſelf for myſelf, when I paſs Elizabeth's Spring.[1] Here is the ſpring ſay I (with a ſigh) but where is Elizabeth?[2] My charity anſwers, ſhe is gone to the Eternal Spring and Fountain of Living Waters: Oh, Sir, I beſeech the Father of Mercies and Spirits to preſerve your precious ſoul in life (long and long [*a portion of the letter and ſignature deſtroyed.*]

Sir, about a fortnight ſince your old acquaintance, Mr. Blackſtone,[3] departed this life in the fourſcore year of his age; four days before his death he had a great pain in his breaſt, and back, and bowels: afterward he ſaid he was well, had no pains, and ſhould live, but he grew fainter, and yielded up his breath without a groan. The Lord make us wait (with Job) for that great change.

---

[1] The ſpring ſo called from Governor Winthrop's lady, named Elizabeth, drinking at it as ſhe paſſed to Boſton.— Note probably by *John Winthrop*, F. R. S.

[2] Mrs. Elizabeth Winthrop, the wife of John Winthrop, Jr., died November 24, 1672.

[3] William Blackſtone, an Epiſcopal miniſter, and the firſt inhabitant of Boſton, ſettled there in 1625 or 1626, where he reſided when Gov. Winthrop arrived in 1630. At a Court held in April, 1633, fifty acres of land, near his houſe in Boſton, were granted him. The following year he ſold this eſtate and removed to the banks of a beautiful river which now bears his name. The place is known as Study Hill, in Cumberland, about ſix miles from Providence. It has been ſaid that Blackſtone was driven from Boſton, "an opinion" ſays Savage (note to *Winthrop's Journal*, i. 53,) "not to be entertained for a moment." His name is ſometimes ſpelled *Blaxton*. Williams ſpells it *Blackſtone*, which is undoubtedly correct. He died at his houſe on the 26th of May, 1675.

To my much honored kind friend Mr. John Winthrop, Governor of Connecticut, present.

FROM MR. SMITH'S AT NAHIGONSIK, June 25, 1675.[1]

SIR,—This incloſed of a former date comes to my hand again at Mr. Smith's. Mr. Smith is now abſent at Long Iſland. Mrs. Smith, though too much favoring the Foxians (called Quakers) yet ſhe is a notable ſpirit for courteſy toward ſtrangers, and prays me to preſent her great thanks foɪ your conſtant remembrance of her, and of late by Capt. Atherton.

Sir, this morning are departed from this houſe Capt. Hutchinſon[2] and two more of Boſton Commiſſioners from the Governor and Council of Boſton to the Narraganſett and Coweſit Indians. They came (three days ſince) to my houſe at Providence, with a letter to myſelf from the Governor and Council at Boſton, praying my advice to their Commiſſioners and my aſſiſtance, &c., in their negotiations with the Narraganſett Indians. I, within an half hour's warning) departed with them toward the Narragan-

---

[1] 4 *Maſs. Hiſt. Coll.* vol. vi. p. 299.

[2] "The Maſſachuſetts government ſent Capt. Hutchinſon as their commiſſioner to treat with the Narraganſetts. It was thought convenient to do it ſword in hand, therefore all the forces marched into the Narraganſett country. Connecticut afterwards ſent two gentlemen [Maj. Wait Winthrop and Richard Smith] and on the 15th of July they came to an agreement with the Narraganſett Indians, who favored Philip in their hearts, and waited only a convenient opportunity to declare openly for him, but whilſt the army was in their country were obliged to ſubmit to the terms impoſed upon them."—HUTCHINSON, *Hiſt. of Maſſachuſetts Bay,* vol. i. p. 288.

This agreement which is given at length by Hutchinſon, (pp. 289-291,) bears the ſignatures of ſix Sachems of the Narraganſetts. By it they were bound to ſeize and deliver to the Engliſh "any of Philip's ſubjects, living or dead; uſe all acts of hoſtility againſt Philip and his ſubjects; to ſearch out and deliver all goods ſtolen or taken from the Engliſh, at any time; to ceaſe from all manner of thefts and to be uſed as a guard about the Narraganſett country for the ſecurity of the Engliſh."

fett. We had one meeting that night with Quaunoncku, Miantunnomu's youngeft fon, and upon the opening of the Governor's letters, he readily and gladly affented to all the Governor's defires, and fent poft to Maufup, (now called Canonicus), to the Old Queen,¹ Ninicraft and Quawnipund, to give us a meeting at Mr. Smith's. They being uncivil and barbarous, and the Old Queen (efpecially timorous, we condefcended to meet them all near the great pond, at leaft ten miles from Mr. Smith's houfe. We laid open the Governor's letter : and accordingly they profeffed to hold no agreement with Philip, in this his rifing againft the Englifh. They profeffed (though Uncas had fent twenty to Philip, yet) they had not fent one nor would : that they had prohibited all their people from going on that fide, that thofe of their people who had made marriages with them, fhould return or perifh there : that if Philip or his men fled to them, yet they would not receive them, but deliver them up unto the Englifh.

They queftioned us why Plymouth purfued Philip. We anfwered : he broke all laws, and was in arms of rebellion againft that Colony, his ancient friends and protectors, though it is believed that he was the author of murdering John Soffiman,² for revealing his plots to the Governor of Plymouth, and for which three actors were

---

¹ *Quiapen*, afterwards called the Sunke Squaw, or Old Queen of the Narraganfetts. She was Ninigret's fifter and had been the wife of Meika the fon of Canonicus. She was taken prifoner by the Connecticut troops in July, 1676, and put to death.—Potter's *Hift. of Narraganfett*, p. 172.

² "*Sanfaman*, a friendly Indian, having given notice to the Englifh of a plot which he had difcovered amongft Philip's Indians againft the Englifh, was foon after murdered." "Three Indians, one a counfellor of Philip's, were convicted of the murder, at the Plymouth Court and executed."—Holmes' *Annals*, vol. i. p. 369 ; Hubbard, *Indian Wars*, p. 14.

two weeks fince executed at Plymouth, (though one broke
the rope, and is kept in prifon until their Court in October.)

2. They demanded of us why the Maffachufetts and Rhode
Ifland rofe, and joined with Plymouth againft Philip, and
left not Philip and Plymouth to fight it out. We
anfwered that all the Colonies were fubject to one King
Charles, and it was his pleafure, and our duty and engagement, for one Englifh man to ftand to the death by each
other, in all parts of the world.

Sir, two particulars the Moft Holy and Only Wife made
ufe of to engage (I hope and fo do the Commiffioners)
in earneft to enter into thofe aforefaid engagements.

Firft, the fenfe of their own danger if they feparate not
from Plymouth Indians, and Philip their defperate head.
This argument we fet home upon them, and the Bay's
refolution to purfue Philip (if need be) and his partakers
with thoufands of horfe and foot, befide the other Colonies, &c.

3. Their great and vehement defire of juftice upon Tatuphofuit, for the late killing of a Narraganfett young man
[*fic*] of account with them, which point while we were
difcourfing of, and their inftance with me to write to the
Governor and Council of Maffachufetts about it (which I
have this morning done by their Commiffioners) in comes
(as from Heaven) your dear fon Major Winthrop[1] to our
affiftance, who affirmed that he faw Tatuphofuit fent bound
to Hartford jail, and his father Uncas, taking boat with
him. The Sachems faid they knew it, and had written about
it (by my letter inclofed) to yourfelf: but they were in-

---

[1] Major Wait Winthrop, a commiffioner from Connecticut.

formed that he was fet free, and was keeping his Nicommo, or dance in triumph, &c. Your fon replied that either it was not fo, or if it were, it was according to your law of leaving Indians to Indian juftice, which if neglected you would then act, &c. In fine, their earneft requeft was that either Tatuphofuit might have impartial juftice, (for many reafons, or elfe they might be permitted to right themfelves, which the Commiffioners thought might be great prudence (in this juncture of affairs) that thefe two nations, the Narraganfetts and Mohegans might be taken off from affifting Philip (which paffionately he endeavors), and the Englifh may more fecurely and effectually profecute the quenching of this Philippian fire in the beginning of it.[1] The laft night they have (as is this morning faid) flain five Englifh of Swanfey, and brought their heads to Philip, and mortally wounded two more, with the death of one Indian. By letters from the Governor of Plymouth to Mr. Coddington, Governor of Rhode Ifland, we hear that the Plymouth forces (about two hundred) with Swanfey and Rehoboth men, were this day to give battle to Philip. Sir, my old bones and eyes are weary with travel and writing to the Governors of Maffachufetts and Rhode Ifland, and now to yourfelves. I end with humble cries to the Father of Mercies to extend his ancient and wonted mercies to New England, and am, Sir,

Your moft unworthy Servant,

ROGER WILLIAMS.

[1] Thefe were the firft open hoftilities in the war. "The Indians having fent their wives and children to the Narraganfetts for fecurity, began to alarm the Englifh at Swanzey, by killing their cattle and rifling their houfes." An Englifhman fired at them when they inftantly attacked the people of Swanzey, of which they flew nine. This took place on the 24th June. The alarm was now given and troops haftened forward from Bofton and Plymouth, joining forces at Swanzey on the 28th.—HUBBARD, *Indian Wars;* HOLMES' *Annals*, vol. i. p. 368.

47

Mrs. Smith earneſtly deſires your loving advice to hei huſband, to lay by his voyage to England : partly by rea-ſon of his inward grief, and alſo that his buſineſs may be tranſacted by delegation. She prays you alſo to conſider your own age and weakneſs, and not to lay your precious bones in England.

Sir, my humble reſpects to your honored Council.

ROGER WILLIAMS.

Roger Williams to John Winthrop, jr.

FROM MR. SMITH'S, 27 June, 75, (ſo called.)[1]

SIR,—Since my laſt (encloſed) the next day after the departure of Capt. Hutchinſon and the meſſengers from Boſton, a party of one hundred Narraganſett Indians, armed, marched to Warwick, which, as it frighted Warwick, ſo did it alſo the inhabitants here ; though ſince we heai that the party departed from Warwick without blood ſhedding : however, it occaſioned the Engliſh here (and myſelf) to ſuſpect that all the fine words from the Indian Sachems to us were but words of policy, falſehood and treachery : es-pecially ſince now the Engliſh teſtify, that for divers weeks (if not months) canoes paſſed to and again (day and night between Philip and the Narraganſetts)[2] and the Nar-raganſett Indians have committed many robberies on the

---

[1] 4 *Maſs. Hiſt. Coll.* vol. vi. p. 302.
[2] Hubbard ſays " the Narraganſetts promiſed to riſe with 4000 men in the ſpring of the year 1676."—*Hiſt. of the Indian Wars*, p. 126. This large num-ber is ſuppoſed to have included all the

Indians within the bounds of Rhode Iſ-land. Hutchinſon ſays " at the begin-ning of Philip's War, it was generally agreed that the Narraganſett tribe con-ſiſted of 2000 fighting men.—*Hiſt. of Maſſachuſetts*, vol. i. p. 458.

Englifh houfes. Alfo, it is thought that Philip durft not have proceeded fo far, had he not been affured to have been feconded and affifted by the Mohegans and Narraganfetts.

Two days fince, the Governor and Council of Rhode Ifland fent letters and meffengers to Maufup (Canonicus) inviting him to come to them to Newport, and affuring him of fafe condu&t to come and depart in fafety. His anfwer was, that he could not depart from his child which lay fick: but (as he had affured the Bofton meffengers) fo he profeffed to thefe from Newport, that his heart affe&ted and forrowed for the Englifh, that he could not rule the youth and common people, nor perfuade others, chief amongft them, except his brother Miantunnomu's fon, Nananautunu. He advifed the Englifh at Narraganfett to ftand upon their guard, to keep ftri&t watch, and, if they could, to fortify one or more houfes ftrongly, which if they could not do, then to fly. Yefterday, Mrs. Smith (after more, yea, moft of the women and children gone) departed in a great fhower, by land, for Newport, to take boat in a veffel four miles from her houfe. Sir, juft now comes in Sam. Dier in a catch from Newport, to fetch over Jireh Bull's wife and children, and others of Puttaquomfcutt[1] He brings word that laft night Caleb Carr's boat (fent on purpofe to Swanfey for tidings) brought word that Philip had killed twelve Englifh at Swanfey, (the fame Canonicus told us,) and that Philip fent three heads to them, but he advifed a

---

[1] Jireh Bull had a "garrifon houfe" at Pettequomfcut, which in December following was attacked by the Indians and burned. Ten Englifh men and five women were killed.—HUBBARD, *Indian Wars*, Bofton, 1677: p. 50. Jireh Bull was "Confervator of the Peace for King's Province."—*R. I. Col. Records*, vol. ii. The garrifon-houfe or fort was on Tower Hill, South Kingftown.

372 Letters of Roger Williams.

refusal of them, which some say was done, only the old Queen rewarded the bringers for their travel. Caleb Carr saith also, that one English sentinel was shot in the face and slain by an Indian that crept near unto him: that they have burnt about twelve houses, one new great one (Anthony Loes): that Philip had left his place, being a neck, and three hundred of Plymouth English, Swansey and others know not where he is, and therefore Capt. Oliver (being at Mr. Brown's) rode post to Boston for some hundreds of horse: that some hurt they did about Providence, and some say John Scot, at Pawtucket ferry, is slain. Indeed, Canonicus advised the English to take heed of remaining in lone out places, and of travelling in the common roads.

Sir, many wish that Plymouth had left the Indians alone, at least not to put to death the three Indians upon one Indian's testimony, a thing which Philip fears; and that yourselves (at this juncture) could leave the Mohegans and Narragansetts to themselves as to Tatuphusoit, if there could be any just way by your General Court found out for the preventing of their conjunction with Philip, which so much concerneth the peace of New England. Upon request of the Government of Plymouth, Rhode Island hath set out some sloops to attend Philip's motions by water and his canoes: it is thought he bends for an escape to the Islands. Sir, I fear the enclosed and this will be grievous to those visible spirits, which look out at your windows: mine, I am sure to complain, &c., yet I press them for your and the public sake, for why is our candle, yet burning, but to glorify our dreadful former, and in making our own calling and election sure, and serving God in serving the public in our generation.

Your unworthy servant,

ROGER WILLIAMS.

To Governor Leverett, at Bofton.

Providence, 11, 8, 75, fo accounted. [October 11, 1675.][1]

Sir,—Yours of the 7th I.gladly and thankfully received, and humbly defire to praife that Moft High and Holy Hand, invifible and only wife, who cafts you down, by fo many public and perfonal trials, and lifts you up again with any (*lucida intervalla*) mitigations and refrefhments. *Ab inferno nulla redemptio:* from the grave and hell no return. Here, like Noah's dove, we have our checker work, blacks and whites come out and go into the ark, out and in again till the laft, whom we never fee back again.

The bufinefs of the day in New England is not only to keep ourfelves from murdering, our houfes, barns, &c., from firing, to deftroy and cut off the barbarians, or fubdue and reduce them, but our main and principal *opus diei* is, to liften to what the Eternal fpeaketh to the whole fhip, (the country, colonies, towns, &c.) and each private cabin, family, perfon, &c. He will fpeak peace to his people; therefore, faith David, "I will liften to what Jehovah fpeaketh." Oliver, in ftraits and defeats, efpecially at Hifpaniola, defired all to fpeak and declare freely what they thought the mind of God was. H. Vane (then lain by) wrote his difcourfe, entitled "A Healing Queftion," but for touching upon (that *noli me tangere*) State fins, H. Vane went prifoner to Carifbrook Caftle, in the Ifle of Wight. Oh, Sir, I humbly fubfcribe (*ex animo*) to your fhort and long prayer, in your letter. The Lord keep us from our own deceivings. I know there have been, and are, many precious and excellent fpirits amongft you, if you take flight before me, I will then fay you are one of them, without daubing,) but *rebus fic ftantibus*, as the wind blows, the united colonies dare not permit, *candida et bona fide*, two dangerous fuppofed) enemies: 1. diffenting and non-conforming worfhippers, and 2. liberty of free (really free) dil putes, debates, writing, printing, &c. ; the Moft High hatl begun and given fome tafte of thefe two dainties in fome parts, and will more and more advance them when (as Luther and Erafmus to the Emperor, Charles V., and the Duke of Saxony,) thofe two gods are famifhed, the Pope's crown and the Monks' bellies. The fame Luther was wont to fay, that every man had a pope in his belly, and Calvin expreffly wrote to Melanéthon, that Luther made himfelf another Pope ; yet, which of us will not fay, Jeremiah, thou lieft, when he tells us (and from God) we muft not go down to Egypt?

Sir, I ufe a bolder pen to your noble fpirit than to many, becaufe the Father of Lights hath fhown your foul more of the myfteries of iniquity than other excellent heads and hearts dream of, and becaufe, whatever you or I be in other refpeéts, yet in this you will aét a pope, and grant me your love, pardon and indulgence.

Sir, fince the doleful news from Springfield, here it is faid that Philip with a ftrong body of many hundred cutthroats, fteers for Providence and Seekonk, fome fay for Norwich and Stonington, and fome fay your forces have had a lofs by their cutting off fome of your men, in their paffing over a river. *Fiat voluntas Dei,* there I humbly reft, and let all go but himfelf. Yet, Sir, I am requefted by our Capt. Fenner[1] to give you notice, that at his farm,

---

[1] Arthur Fenner firft appears on the roll of freemen of Providence, in 1655. He was one of the moft prominent of the inhabitants, and for many years refented the town as a Commiffioner, Deputy or Affiftant in the Affembly. He

in the woods, he had it from a native, that Philip's great de-
(fign is among all other poffible advantages and treacheries)
to draw Capt. Mofely[1] and others, your forces, by training and drilling, and feeming flights, into fuch places as
are full of long grafs, flags, fedge, &c., and then environ
them round with fire, fmoke and bullets. Some fay no
wife foldier will fo be caught; but as I told the young
prince, on his return lately from you, all their war is com-
mootin; they have commootined our houfes, our cattle,
our heads, &c., and that not by their artillery, but our weapons; that yet they were fo cowardly, that they have not
taken one poor fort from us in all the country, nor won,
nor fcarce fought, one battle fince the beginning. I told
him and his men, being then in my canoe, with his men
with him, that Philip was his cawkakinnamuck, that is,
looking glafs. He was deaf to all advice, and now was

was a Captain in Philip's war, and was
by the General Affembly appointed
"Commander of the King's garrifon at
Providence, and of all other private garrifon or garrifons there, not eclipfing
Captain Williams's power in the exercife of the Traine Band there." His
commiffion is printed at length in *Colonial Records*, vol. ii. p. 547.

Mr. Williams alfo held a commiffion
as Captain, as appears by the Records,
(vol. ii. p. 548,) notwithftanding his age.
It certainly difplayed great fpirit and
patriotifm for a man of feventy-feven
years to engage in a military campaign
againft the Indians. The following appears on the records of Providence: "I
pray the town, in the fenfe of the bloody
practices of the natives, to give leave to
fo many as can agree with William Field,
to beftow fome charge upon fortifying

his houfe, for fecurity to women and
children. Alfo to give me leave, and fo
many as fhall agree, to put up fome defence on the hill, between the mill and
the highway, for the like fafety of the
women and children in that part of the
town." Various fums were fubfcribed
to defray the coft of this fortification,
the largest of which was £2.6., except
that of Mr. Williams which was £10.
The propofed fort was probably to be
placed at the head of what is now Conftitution Hill.

[1] Samuel Mofely, of Dorchefter, a captain in the war with Philip, fhowed gallant fpirit and had great fuccefs in de-
ftroying the Indians. He was, by fome,
thought to take too great delight in that
exercife.—SAVAGE, *Genealogical Dictiona
ry*, vol. iii. p. 179.

overfet, Coofhkowwawy, and catched at every part of the country to fave himfelf, but he fhall never get afhore, &c. He anfwered me in a confenting, confidering kind of way, Philip Coofhkowwawy. I went with my great canoe to help him over from Seekonk (for to Providence no Indian comes) to Pawtuxet fide. I told him I would not afk him news, for I knew matters were private; only I told him that if he were falfe to his engagements, we would purfue them with a winter's war, when they fhould not, as mufketoes and rattlefnakes in warm weather, bite us, &c.

Sir, I carried him and Mr. Smith a glafs of wine, but Mr. Smith not coming, I gave wine and glafs to himfelf, and a bufhel of apples to his men, and being therewith (as beafts are) caught, they gave me leave to fay anything, acknowledged loudly your great kindnefs in Bofton, and mine, and yet Capt. Fenner told me yefterday, that he thinks they will prove our worft enemies at laft. I am between fear and hope, and humbly wait, making fure, as Hafelrig's motto was, fure of my anchor in heaven, *Tantum in Coelis*, only in heaven. Sir, there I long to meet you.

Your moft unworthy,

ROGER WILLIAMS.

To Mrs. Leverett, and other honored and beloved friends, humble refpects, &c.

Sir, I hope your men fire all the woods before them, &c.

Sir, I pray not a line to me, except on neceffary bufinefs; only give me leave (as you do) to ufe my foolifh boldnefs to vifit yourfelf, as I have occafion. I would not add to your troubles.

For my honored kind friend Mr. John Winthrop, Governor of Connecticut Colony, at Boston or elsewhere, present. Leave this at my loving friends Dan: Smith, at Rehoboth.

PROVIDENCE, 18, 10, 75, (*et vulgo.*) [December 18th, 1675.][1]

SIR,—If you are ſtill in Boſton (which owes you more and your precious name, then it is like to pay you) pleaſe you to paſs by, that I have not troubled you with a late ſalutation. The preſent revolutions of the wonderful and all ſighted wheels (Ezek. 1.) rouſe up my ſleepy ſpirits to muſe and write, and to preſent yourſelf and others with what I believe to be the mind and voice of the Moſt High amongſt us. Others think otherwiſe (and ſome clean contrary); unto whom I ſay at preſent, let them take the pains which God mercifully hath helped me to take, to find out where's the difference: let them ſuffer what (and ſo long) God hath helped me to bear for their belief and conſcience : let them debate freely, calmly, &c., as I hope God hath helped me and will help me to do, (without the Pope's ſword, which Chriſt commanded Peter to put up in his matters.)

Sir, I have heard that you have been in late conſultations, *ſemper idem, ſemper pacificus*, and I hope therein *beatus.* You have always been noted for tenderneſs toward men's ſouls, eſpecially for conſcience ſake to God. You have been noted for tenderneſs toward the bodies and infirmities of poor mortals. You have been tender too, toward the eſtates of men in your civil ſteerage of government, and toward the peace of the land, yea, of theſe wild ſavages. I preſume you are ſatisfied in the neceſſity of theſe preſent hoſtilities, and that it is not poſſible at preſent to keep

---

[1] 4 *Maſs. Hiſt. Col.* vol. vi. p. 305.

peace with thefe barbarous men of blood, who are as juftly
to be repelled and fubdued as wolves that affault the fheep.
It was . . . *in* . . . *eft* . . . *rium :*[1]   God hath helped
yourfelf and other [*torn*] with wonderful felf-denial and
patience to keep off this neceffity.   But God (againft
whom only is no fighting) is pleafed to put this iron yoke
upon our necks, and (as he did with the Canaanites) to
harden them againft Jofhua to their deftruction.   I fear
the event of the jufteft war : but if it pleafe God to deliver them into our hands, I know you will *antiqum obti-
nere*, and ftill endeavor that our fword may make a difference, and *parcere fubjeftis*, though we *debellare fuperbos.*
God killeth, deftroyeth, plagueth, damneth none but thofe
that will perifh, and fay (as thefe barbarians now fay) Nip-
pittoi ; though I die for it, &c.

   Sir, I hope the not approach of your dear fon with his,
(your forces of Connecticut,) &c., is only through the in-
tercepting of the pofts : for we have now no paffing by
Elizabeth's Spring without a ftrong foot.   God will have
it fo.   Dear Sir, if we cannot fave our patients, nor relations, nor Indians, nor Englifh, oh let us make fure to fave
the bird in our bofom, and to enter in that ftraight door
and narrow way, which the Lord Jefus himfelf tells us,
few there be that find it.   Sir, your unworthy

                                   ROGER WILLIAMS.

[1] This fentence has been carefully erafed.

To the much honored Governor Leverett at Bofton, prefent.

PROVIDENCE, 14 Jan. 1675, (fo called.)[1]

SIR,—This night I was requefted by Capt. Fenner and other officers of our town to take the examination and confeffion of an Englifh man who hath been with the Indians before and fince the fight : his name is Jofhua Tift[2] and he was taken by Capt. Fenner this day at an Indian houfe half a mile from where Capt. Fenner's houfe (now burned) did ftand. Capt. Fenner and others of us propofed feveral queftions to him, which he anfwered, and I was requefted to write, which I did, and thought fit having this bearer (Mr. Scott) brought by God's gracious hand of Providence to mine, to prefent you with an extract of the pith and fubftance of all he anfwered to us.

He was afked by Capt. Fenner, how long he had been with the Narraganfetts. He anfwered about twenty-feven days, more or lefs.

He was demanded how he came amongft them. He faid that he was at his farm a mile and a half from Puttuckquomfcut, where he hired an Indian to keep his cattle, himfelf propofing to go to Rhode Ifland, but that day which he purpofed and prepared to depart, there came to his houfe, Nananawtenu (the young Sachem) his elder brother Paupauquivwut, with their Captain Quaquackis and a party of men, and told them he muft die. He faid that he begged for his life, and promifed that he would be fervant to the Sachem while he lived. He faid the Sachem

---

[1] *4 Mafs. Hift. Coll.* vol. vi. p. 307.

[2] "Jofhua Tifft, a renegade Englifhman of Providence, that upon fome difcontent had turned Indian, married a fquaw, renounced his religion, nation and natu- ral parents, fighting againft them. He was wounded in the knee, and taken prifoner. After examination he was condemned to die the death of a traitor."—HUBBARD, *Narrative,* p. 162.

then carried him along with him, having given him his life as his flave. He faid that he brought him to their fort, where was about eight hundred fighting men and about two hundred houfes. He faid the Indians brought five of his cattle and killed them before his face: fo he was forced to be filent, but prayed the Sachem to fpare the reft: who anfwered him what will cattle now do you good; and the next day they fent for the reft and killed them all, whereof eight were his own.

Being afked whether he was in the Fort in the fight,[1]

[1] "The great Narraganfett fight." "On the 2d of November, 1675, the Commiffioners of the United Colonies declared the Narraganfetts to be "deeply acceffory in the prefent bloody outrages" of the Indians that were at open war, and determined that 1000 more foldiers be raifed for the Narraganfett expedition. Thefe troops were accordingly raifed. Thofe of Maffachufetts confifting of fix companies of foot and a troop of horfe. Connecticut fent 300 foldiers and 150 Mohegan and Pequod Indians. Gov. Winflow of Plymouth, was commander-in-chief. Rhode Ifland took no part in the fight.

"On the 8th December, the Maffachufetts forces marched from Bofton, and were foon joined by thofe of Plymouth. The troops from Connecticut joined them on the 18th at Pettaquamfcot. At break of day the next morning, they commenced their march through a deep fnow, toward the enemy, who were about fifteen miles diftant in a fwamp, at the edge of which they arrived at one in the afternoon. The Indians, apprized of an armanent againft them, had fortified themfelves ftrongly within the fwamp. The Englifh at once marched forward in queft of the enemy's camp. Some Indians appearing, were no fooner fired on by the Englifh, than they returned the fire and fled. The whole army now entered the fwamp and followed the Indians to their fortrefs. It ftood on a rifing ground in the midft of the fwamp, and was compofed of pallifades, encompaffed by a hedge. It had but one practicable entrance which was over a log, four or five feet from the ground; and that aperture was guarded by a block-houfe. The Englifh captains entered it at the head of their companies. The two firft, with many of their men were fhot dead at the entrance, and four other captains were alfo killed. When the troops had effected an entrance, they attacked the Indians, who fought defperately, and beat the Englifh out of the fort. After a hard fought battle of three hours, the Englifh became mafters of the place, and fet fire to the wigwams. The number of them was 500 or 600, and in the conflagration many Indian women and children perifhed. The furvivors fled into a cedar fwamp, at a fhort diftance, and the Eng-he faid yes, and waited on his mafter the Sachem there, until he was wounded, (of which wound he lay nine days and died.) He faid that all the Sachems were in the Fort and ftaid two vollies of fhot, and then they fled with his mafter, and paffed through a plain, and refted by the fide of a fpruce fwamp, but he faid himfelf had no arms at all. He faid that if the Mohegans and Pequods had been true, they might have deftroyed moft of the Narraganfetts : but the Narraganfetts parlied with them in the beginning of the fight, fo that they promifed to fhoot high, which they did, and killed not one Narraganfett man, except againft their wills.

He faid that when it was dufkifh, word was brought to the Sachems that the Englifh were retreated. Upon this they fent to the Fort to fee what their lofs was, where they found ninety-feven flain and forty-eight wounded, befide what flaughter was made in the houfes and by the burning of the houfes, all of which he faid were burnt except five or fix or thereabouts. He faid the Indians never came to the Fort more, that he knows of. He faid they found five or fix Englifh bodies, and from one of them a bag of about one pound and a half of powder was brought to the Sachems; and he faid that abundance of corn, and pro-vifions, and goods were burnt alfo. He faid fome powder belonging to the young Sachem, which was in a box, was blown up, but how much he cannot tell.

He faid the Narraganfett's powder is (generally) gone and fpent, but Philip hath fent them word that he will

lifh retired to their quarters. Of the Eng-lifh there were killed and wounded about two hundred and thirty; of which eighty-five were killed. Of the Indians, one thoufand are fuppofed to have perifhed." HOLMES, *Annals,* vol. i. p. 575–376. The fwamp where this battle took place is three or four miles weft of the village of Kingfton.

furnifh them enough from the French. He faid they have carried New England money to the French for ammunition, but the money he will not take, but beaver or wampum. He faid that the French have fent Philip a prefent, viz.: a brafs gun and bandoliers fuitable. He faid alfo that the Narraganfetts have fent two bafkets of wampum to the Mohawks (Mauquawogs) where the French are, for their favor and affiftance.

He fays that the Sachems and people were about ten miles northweft from Mr. Smith's, whether the Cowefets and Pumham and his men brought to the Sachems all the powder they could, but Canonicus faid it was nothing, for they had four hundred guns (befide bows) and there was but enough for every gun a charge. The young Sachem faid that had he known that they were no better furnifhed, he would have been elfewhere this winter.

He faid that while they were in confultation, an Indian fquaw came in with a letter from the General. Some advifed to fend to Philip for one of his counfellors to read it, but at laft they agreed to fend a councellor to the General, who brought word that the General faid that there had been a fmall fight between them, and afked him how many Indians were flain, and how the Sachems liked it. That he defired the Sachems would fhow themfelves men, and come and parley with him : that if they feared they might bring what guard they pleafed, who might keep at a diftance from ours who fhould not offer them any affront, while the Sachems were at the houfe with the General, from whom they fhould depart in peace, if they came to no agreement.

Their councillors faid that the Englifh did this only in policy to entrap the Sachems, as they had done Philip many times, who, when he was in their hands, made him yield to what they pleafed.

Nananawtenu (the young Sachem) faid he would not go, but thought it beft to ufe policy, and to fend word to the General, that they would come to him three days after; but Canonicus faid that he was old, and would not lie to the Englifh now, and faid if you will fight, fight; for tis a folly for me to fight any longer. The young prince faid he might go to Mr. Smith's then, but there fhould never an Indian go with him. Their chief Captain alfo faid that he would not yield to the Englifh fo long as an Indian would ftand with him. He faid he had fought with Englifh, and French, and Dutch, and Mohawks, and feared none of them, and faid that if they yielded to the Englifh they fhould be dead men or flaves, and fo work for the Englifh. He faid that this Quaquackis bears chief fway, and is a middling thickfet man, of a very ftout, fierce countenance.

Being afked whether he was prefent at this confultation, he faid no; but that Quaquackis acquainted the people what the fum of the confultation was.

He faid that Philip is about Quawpaug, amongft a great many rocks, by a fwampfide: that the Narraganfetts have been thefe three days on their march and flight to Philip: that he knows not what number Philip hath with him, and that this day the laft and the rear of the company departed : that they heard the General was purfuing after them, and therefore feveral parties, to the number of four hundred, were ordered to lie in ambufcadoes : that feveral parties were left behind, to get and drive cattle after them : that the young prince and chief captain were in a houfe four miles from Providence, where Captain Fenner (with fifteen or sixteen of Providence, seeking after cattle) took this Joshua Tift, who saith that the rest of the party (about forty-one) were not far off, and toward Pawtuxet.

Being asked what was the English child which was brought into the General : he said that Pumham's men had taken it at Warwick. Also he said that there is an English youth amongst them (his name he forgot :) one that speaks good Indian, and was wounded and taken in the fight, whom they spake of killing with torture, but he was yet with Quawnepund.

Sir, you may suppose it now to be past midnight, and I am to write forth the copy of this, to go to-morrow to the General, and therefore I dare not add my foolish comment, but humbly beg to the Father of Mercies for his mercy sake to guide you by his counsel (Psal. 73.) and afterward receive you unto Glory.

Your most unworthy,
Roger Williams.

My humble respects presented to such honored friends to whom your wisdom may think fit to communicate, &c.

Sir, Joshua Tift added that this company intend to stay with Philip till the snow melt, and then to divide into companies.

Also that many of Ninicraft's men fought the English in the Fort, and four of the Mohegans are now marched away with the Narragansetts.

Sir, since I am oft occasioned to write upon the public business, I shall be thankful for a little paper upon the public account, being now near destitute.

Sir, I pray present my humble respects to the Governor Winthrop, and my thanks for his loving letters, to which I cannot now make any return.

To the much honored the Governor Leverett, at Boſton, or the Governor Winſlow, at Boſton, preſent.

PROVIDENCE, 16, 8, 76, (*ut vulgo.*) [Oct. 16.][1]

SIR,—With my humble and loving reſpects to yourſelf and other honored friends, &c. I thought fit to tell you what the Providence of the Moſt High hath brought to my hand the evening before yeſterday. Two Indian children were brought to me by one Thomas Clements, who had his houſe burnt on the other ſide of the river. He was in his orchard, and two Indian children came boldly to him, the boy being about ſeven or eight, and the girl (his ſiſter) three or four years old. The boy tells me, that a youth, one Mittonan, brought them to the ſight of Thomas Clements, and bid them go to that man, and he would give them bread. He ſaith his father and mother were taken by the Pequods and Mohegans about ten weeks ago, as they were clamming (with many more Indians) at Coweſet ; that their dwelling was and is at a place called Mittaubſcut ; that it is upon a branch of Pawtuxet river to Coweſet (their neareſt ſalt water) about ſeven or eight miles ; that there are above twenty houſes. I cannot learn of him that there are above twenty men, beſide women and children ; that they live on ground nuts, &c., and deer ; that Aawayſewaukit is their Sachem ; and twelve days ago, he ſent his ſon, Wunnawmeneeſkat to Uncas, with a preſent of a baſket or two of wampum. I know this Sachem is much related to Plymouth, to whom he is ſaid to be ſubject, but he ſaid (as all of them do) he depoſited his land. I know what bargains he made with the Brown's

[1] 3 *Maſs. Hiſt. Col.* vol. i. p. 70.

and Willet's and Rhode Ifland and Providence men, and the controverfies between the Narraganfetts and them, about those lands. I know the talk abroad of the right of the three united colonies (by conqueft)[1] to this land, and the plea of Rhode-Ifland by the charter and commif-fioners. I humbly defire that party may be brought in ; the country improved (if God in mercy fo pleafe ;) the Englifh not differ about it and complaints run to the King (to unknown trouble, charge and hazard, &c.,) and there-fore I humbly beg of God that a committee from the four colonies may (by way of prudent and godly wifdom) pre-vent many inconveniences and mifchiefs. I write the fum of this to the Governors of Connecticut and Rhode Ifland, and humbly beg of the Father of Mercies to guide you in Mercy, for his mercy fake.

Sir, your unworthy,

ROGER WILLIAMS.

Excufe my want of paper.

This boy faith, there is another town to the north-eaft of them, with more houfes than twenty, who, 'tis like, correfpond to the eaftward.

---

[1] Rhode Ifland took no part in the ex-termination of the Narraganfetts. In a letter to the King, Rhode Ifland fays : " The war between King Philip and the colony of New Plymouth was profecuted by the United Colonies as they term them-felves. . . . But this your majefty's colo-ny, not being concerned in the war only as neceffity required for the defence of their lives and what they could of their estates, and as countrymen, did, with our boats and provifions, affift and relieve our neighbors, we being in no other ways concerned."

After the extermination of this once powerful tribe, the United Colonies claimed the King's Province as a con-quered territory, to which, Rhode Ifland for this reafon, among others, had no ti-tle. Connecticut magnanimoufly offered peace upon a divifion of territory, fay-ing that, " although our juft rights, both by patent and conqueft extend much fur-ther, yet our readinefs to amicable and

To the Court of Commiffioners of the United Colonies.

PROVIDENCE, 18, 8, [Oct. 18,] 1677.[1]

HONORED GENTLEMEN,—My humble refpects prefented, with congratulations and prayers to the Moft High, for your merciful prefervations in and through thefe late bloody and burning times, the peaceable travelling and affembling amongft the ruins and rubbifh of thefe late defolations, which the Moft High hath juftly brought upon us. I crave your gentle leave to tell you, that I humbly conceive I am called of God to prefent your wifdoms with what light I can, to make your difficulties and travails the eafier. I am fore grieved that a felf-feeking contentious foul, who has long afflicted this town and colony, fhould now, with his unfeafonable and unjuft clamor, afflict our Royal Sovereign, his honorable Council, New and Old England, and now your honored felves, with thefe his contentious courfes. For myfelf, it hath pleafed God to vouchfafe me knowledge and experience, of his providence in thefe parts, fo that I fhould be ungratefully and treacheroufly filent at fuch a time. When his Majefty's Commiffioners, Col. Nichols, &c., were here, I was chofen by this colony, one of the commiffioners to treat with them and with the commiffion-

---

neighborly compliance is fuch, (that for peace fake,) we content ourfelves to take with Cowefit (that is from Apponaug to Connecticut line,) to be the boundary between your colony and ours, if his Majefly pleafe to indulge us therein, and yourfelves fhall fpeedily exprefs to us your defire and agreement to have it fo." *R.'I. Colonial Records*, vol. ii. p. 584–585. [1]KNOWLES, *Memoir of Roger Williams,* p. 407 ; POTTER'S *Narraganfett,* p. 164.

The original manufcript of this letter was in the hands of the late John Howland, and was firft printed by Mr. Knowles in his Memoirs of Williams. In a letter to Mr. Knowles, Mr. Howland ftates, that all here given was on one fheet, and that there muft have been a fecond fheet that is loft. Some portions of what remain have become illegible where the paper is folded. It is wholly in the handwriting of Mr. Williams.

ers from Plymouth, who then were their honored Governor deceafed, and honored prefent Governor, about our bounds. It then pleafed the Father of mercies, in whofe moft high and holy hands the hearts of all men are, to give me fuch favor in their eyes, that afterward, at a great affembly at Warwick, where (that firebrand) Philip, his whole country, was challenged by the Narraganfett Sachems, I was fent for, and declared fuch tranfactions between Old Canonicus and Oufamaquin, that the commiffioners were fatisfied, and confirmed unto the ungrateful monfter his country. The Narraganfett Sachems (prompted by fome Englifh) told the commiffioners that Mr. Williams was but one witnefs, but the commiffioners anfwered that they had fuch experience of my knowledge in thefe parts, and fidelity, that they valued my teftimony as much as twenty witneffes.

Among fo many paffages fince W. Harris, (fo long ago) kindled the fires of contention, give me leave to trouble you with one, when if W. Harris had any defire by equal and peaceable converfe with men, this fire had been quenched; our General Court, Mifhauntatuk men, and W. Harris, agreed that arbitration fhould heal this old fore.[1] Arbitrators were chofen, and Mr. Thomas Willet[2] was chofen

[1] "In October, 1677, the Commiffioners from the feveral colonies met at Providence, to fettle the long contefted difputes between Mr. Harris and others about lands. Mr. Harris laid before the Court a long ftatement, in which he preferred heavy charges againft Mr. Williams, and the latter made counter ftatements in a fimilar ftyle. The refult of the examination was favorable to the claims of Mr. Harris and his friends, who obtained five verdicts from a jury. But the difputes were not fettled, till more than thirty years afterwards."— KNOWLES' *Memoir*, p. 348.

[2] Thomas Willet, came to Plymouth in 1632. Was an Affiftant from 1651 to 1654, and when the Englifh conquered New York, he accompanied them and was made Mayor. He returned not long after and took up his refidenec in Rehoboth and Swanzey, dying at the latter place Auguft 4, 1674 —SAVAGE, *Genealogical Dictionary*, vol. iv. p. 557.

umpire. He, when they met, told them that the arbitrators fhould confider every plea with equity, and allot to every one what the arbitrators' confciences told them was right and equal. Mifhauntatuk men yielded, W. Carpenter then one with W. Harris, yielded. W. Harris cried out, no ; he was refolved all or none ; fo the honored foul, Mr. Willet (as he himfelf told me) could not proceed, but was forced to draw up a proteft to acquit himfelf and the arbitrators from this truft, that the obftruction might only be laid on W. Harris his fhoulders, concerning whom a volume might be written, of his furious, covetous, and contentious domineering over his poor neighbors. I have prefented a character of him to his Majefty, (in defence of myfelf againft him) in my narrative againft George Fox, printed at Bofton. I think it not feafonable here to trouble your patience with particulars as to the matter.[1] I humbly refer myfelf to my large teftimony, given in writing, at a Court of Trials on the Ifland, before the honored gentleman, deceafed, Mr. W. Brenton, then Governor. At the fame time Mr. William Arnold, father to our honored prefent Governor, and Stukely Weftcott,[2] father to our

---

[1] Mr. Williams's book here referred to " *George Fox Digged out of his Burrowes*" fo abounds with abufe of Wm. Harris, as well as of all others oppofed to him in this controverfy that we cannot point out any particular paffage which refers to his character. " Mr. Harris foon after went to England, on this bufinefs, but the veffel was captured by an Algerine or Tunifian corfair, and he was fold for a flave. His family in Rhode Ifland redeemed him at the coft of about $1200, by the fale of a part of his property. After travelling through Spain and France, he arrived in London in 1680, where he died the third day after. He was an able, and we may hope, a good man, notwithftanding fome infirmities. His quarrels with Roger Williams were very difcreditable to them both. On which fide the moft blame lay, we cannot now decide."—KNOWLES, *Memoir of Williams*, p. 349, note ; STAPLES' *Gorton*, p. 113, note.

[2] STUKELY WESTCOTT, removed to Providence, in April, 1638, and was the firft named in Williams's firft deed. He figned the compact at Providence in 1640.

Governor's wife, gave in their teftimony with mine, and
W. Harris was caft. In that teftimony, I declare not only
how unrighteous, but alfo how fimple is W. Harris his
ground of pleading, viz.: after Miantinomo had fet us our
bounds here in his own perfon, becaufe of the envious
clamors of fome againft myfelf, one amongft us (not I) recorded a teftimony or memorandum of a courtefy added
(upon requeft) by the Sachem, in thefe words, *up ftream
without limits.* The courtefy was requefted and granted,
that being fhortened in bounds by the Sachem becaufe of
the Indians about us, it might be no offence if our few
cows fed up the rivers where nobody dwelt, and home again
at night. This hafty, unadvifed memorandum W. H. in-
terprets of bounds fet to our town by the Sachems; but
he would fet no bounds to our cattle, but up the ftreams fo
far as they branched or run, fo far all the meadows, and at
laft all the uplands, muft be drawn into this accidental
courtefy, and yet, upon no confideration given, nor the
Sachem's knowledge or hand, or witneffes, nor date, nor
for what term of time this kindnefs fhould continue.

Second. In my teftimony, I have declared that Miantonomo having fet fuch fhort bounds (becaufe of the Indians)
upon my motion, payments were given by us to Alexander and Philip, and the Narraganfett Sachems, near two
hundred and fifty pounds, in their pay for inland enlarge-
ments, according to leave granted us by the General Court
upon our petition. This after purchafe and fatisfaction to
all claimers, W. Harris puts a rotten title upon it, and calls

He afterwards removed to Warwick, and
for many years was Commiffioner from
that town. Staples fays, " He held to
entire and rigid feparation from the
Church of England, and defired the
Churches of Maffachufetts to be true
churches; for which the Church at Salem paffed " the great cenfure " on him
as early as July 1, 1639."—Note to *Simplicity's Defence,* p. 117.

it confirmation, a confirmation of the title and grant of *up ftreams without limits;* but all the Sachems and Indians, when they heard of fuch an interpretation, they cried *commoobin,* lying and ftealing, as fuch a cheat as ftunk in their pagan noftrils.

Honored Sirs, let me now add to my teftimony, a lift of feveral perfons which the right and difpofing of all or confiderable part of thefe Narraganfetts, and Cowefet and Nipmuck lands, &c.

Firft. The colony of Connecticut, by the King's grant and charter, by the late wars, wherein they were honorably affiftant.

Second. The colony of Plymouth, by virtue of Tacommaicon's furrender of his perfon and lands to their protection, and I have feen a letter from the prefent Governor Winflow, to Mr. Richard Smith, about the matter.

Third. The colony of Rhode Ifland and Providence Plantations, by grant from his Majefty and confirmation from his Majefty's commiffioners, who called thefe lands the King's Province, and committed the ordering of it to this colony, until his Majefty further order.

Fourth. Many eminent gentlemen of the Maffachufetts and other colonies, claim by a mortgage and forfeiture of all lands belonging to Narraganfett.

Fifth. Our honored Governor, Mr. Arnold, and divers with him, are out of a round fum of money and coft, about a purchafe from Tacummanan.

Sixth. The like claim was and is made by Mr. John Brown, and Mr. Thomas Willet, honored gentlemen and their fucceffors, * * * from purchafe with Tacummanan, and I have feen their deeds, and Col. Nichols his confirmation of them, under hand and feal, in the name of the King's Majefty.

Seventh. William Harris pleads *up ftreams without limits*, and confirmation from the other Sachems of the *up ftreams, &c.*

Eighth. Mifhuntatuk men claim by purchafe from Indians by poffeffion, buildings, &c. * * * * [*worn out and obliterated.*] * * *

Ninth. Capt. Hubbard and fome others, of Hingham * * * by purchafe from the Indians.

Tenth. John Tours, of Hingham, by three purchases from Indians.

Eleventh. William Vaughan,[1] of Newport, and others, by Indian purchafe

[The next following No. is 13; there is no 12.]

Thirteenth. Randall, of Scituate,[2] and White, of Taunton, and others, by purchafe from Indians.

Fourteenth. Edward Inman, of Providence, by purchafe from the natives.

Fifteenth. The town of Warwick, who challenge twenty miles, about part of which, William Harris contending with them, it is faid, was the firft occafion of W. Harris falling in love with this his monftrous Diana *up ftreams without limits*, fo that he might antedate and prevent (as he fpeaks) the blades of Warwick.

Sixteenth. The Town of Providence, by virtue of Canonicus' and Miantonomo's grant renewed to me again and again, viz.: of as large a plantation and accommodation as

---

[1] William Vaughan's name appears on the roll of the freemen of Newport, in 1655. He was one of the purchafers from the Sachem *Socho*, of Mifquamacock, the neck of land eaft of Pawcatuck river in Wefterly, in 1660.—*R. I. Colonial Records*, vol. i. p. 450.

[2] The Scituate here mentioned, muft be in Maffachufetts, as there was no town of that name in Rhode Ifland until 1730.

any town in the country of New England. It is known what favor God pleafed to give me with old Canonicus, (though at a dear-bought rate) fo that I had what I would (fo that I obferved my times of moderation ;) but two or three envious and ungrateful fouls among us cried out, What is R. Williams? We will have the Sachem come and fet our bounds for us; which he did, and (becaufe of his Indians round about us) fo fudden and fo fhort, that we were forced to petition to our General Court for enlarge-ment.

Honored Sirs, there be other claims, and therefore I prefume your wifdoms will fend forth your proclamations to all the colonies, that all the claims may come in before your next meeting ; and Oh ! that it would pleafe the Moft High to move the colonies hearts to empower you, and move your hearts to be willing, (being honorably rewarded) and the hearts of the claimers to acquiefce and reft in your determination. And Oh, let not the colonies of Connec-ticut and Rhode Ifland to be offended, if I humbly be-feech them, for God's fake, for the King's fake, for the country of New England's fake, and for their own fouls' and felves' and pofterity's fakes to prevent any more com-plaints and clamors to the King's Majefty, and agree to fubmit their differences to the wifdoms of fuch folemn commiffioners chofen out of the whole country. I know there are objections, but alfo know that love to God, love to the country and pofterity, will conquer greater matters, and I believe the King's Majefty, himfelf, will give us thanks for fparing him and his honorable Council from being troubled with us.

Honored gentlemen, if his Majefty and honorable Coun-cil knew how againft all law of England, Wm. Harris

50

thus affects New and Old England, viz. : that a vaft country fhould be purchafed, and yet be but a poor courtefy
from one Sachem, who underftood no fuch thing, nor they
that begged it of him, who had not, nor afked any confideration for it, who was not defired to fet his hand to it,
nor did; nor are there the hands of witneffes, but the parties themfelves, nor no date, nor term of time, for the ufe
of feeding cows, up ftreams without limits, and yet thefe
words, (*up ftreams without limits*) by a fudden and unwary
hand fo written, muft be the ground of W. Harris this
raifing a fire about thefe thirty years unquenchable.   If his
Majefty and Council knew how many of his good fubjects are claimers and competitors to thefe lands and meadows up the ftreams of Pawtuxet and Pawtucket, through
only one comes thus clamoring to him, to cheat all the
reft.   If his Majeftv and Council knew this confirmation
W. Harris talks of, what a grand cheat it is, ftinking in the
noftrils of all Indians, who fubfcribed to and only confirmed only fuch bounds as were formerly given us, and
W. Harris clamors that they confirmed Miantonomo's
grant of up ftreams without limits, a thing which they
abhor to hear of, and (amongft others) was one great occafion of their late great burning and flaughtering of us."
    *   *   *   *   *   *   *   *   *

¹*To the much honored* Mr. *Thomas Hinckley*² *and the reft of the much honored Commiffioners from the refpeftive colonies, affembled at Providence,* October 4th, 1678. (*ut vulgo.*)

MUCH HONORED SIRS :—Your wifdoms know that this town is liable to many payments: that moneys will be drawn like blood from many amongft us : for fome of us have appeared legally in town meetings to anfwer the charge and fummons and declaration of the plaintiff againft the town of Providence. Others have not appeared at our town meetings ; or, appearing have diffented from the major vote, which hath always (in all thefe tranfactions) carried on matters in juft order and quietnefs. The non-appearers and diffenters will not pay, as being none of the town in this cafe.

We had much heat in our laft town-meeting, I motioned a fufpenfion of proceedings until the fitting of this high court. Both parties yielded and propofed to fubmit to your decifion, in active or paffive obedience. We were hot ; fo no addrefs was orderly prepared, &c.: and therefore I hold it my humble duty, in the town's name, to pray your favorable and moft feafonable help unto us. I prefume not to add a word as to our matters ; no, not to urge to your remembrance the maxim of Queen Experience (*fecunda cogitationes meliores.*) Only I pray you to remember that all lands and all nations are but a drop of a bucket in

¹ 4 *Mafs. Hift. Coll.* vol. v. p. 21.
²Thomas Hinckley was the laft Governor of Plymouth. He came to Scituate, Mafs., in 1635. He foon became prominent in the affairs of the colony and held various public offices and was

Governor from 1681, (except during the interruption of Andros,) till the union with Maffachufetts colony in 1682. He was alfo a Commiffioner of the two colonies from 1673 to 1692.

the eyes of that King of kings, and Lord of lords, whom
I humbly befeech to adorn your heads with that heavenly
crown at your parting from us. *Beati pacifici.*
    So prays your moft unworthy fervant,
                                ROGER WILLIAMS.

_____

To the moft honored Thomas Hinckley, Commiffioner for the
Colonies.

                        PROVIDENCE, July 4, 1679. (*ut vulgo.*)[1]

    SIR,—Your heavenly meditations on that heavenly Mr.
Walley, I kindly and thankfully received, and pray your
leave to fay four words : Firft, you hold forth in your own
foul a bright character of a true fon of God, who attribute to your deep diftreffes, &c., to His all-wife and His
moft gracious hand eternal. *Una eademque, manus,* &c.
    2. Though a natural fpirit will pretend high to fpirituals,
yet I rejoice to fee you (with rejoicing) predicating fuch
graces in the deceafed, as hoping that a fpiritual light hath
given yourfelf that fpiritual eye as clearly to fee and rejoice in that image of God in another.
    3. I praife God for that heavenly ftirring-up of your-
felf and others to an humble enquiry after thofe coals of
jealoufly which have kindled fuch a fire of jealoufly in the
noftrils of the Moft High againft you ; and I pray your
patience to fuffer me to fay, that, above thefe forty years
in a barbarous wildernefs, driven out on pain of death, I

[1] 4 *Mafs. Hift. Coll.* vol. v. p. 29.

have, (as I believe) been the Eternal his poor witnefs in fackcloth againft your churches, and miniftries, as being but State politics and a mixture of golden images, unto which (were your carnal fword fo long) you would muficaly perfuade, or by fiery torments compel, to bow down as many as (that great type of inventors and perfecutors) Nebuchadnezzar did. I have ftudioufly avoided clamoroufnefs; and yet (being called) I have divers times, and efpecially in the *Bloody Tenent yet more Bloody*, humbly offered my reafons, and to Mr. Nathaniel Morton[1] before this laft winter (upon his charges on me): and I humbly and heartily defire, in the fear of the Moft High, to ponder (in the double weights of the King Eternal) the fharpeft rebukes or cenfures, and to prefent my thoughts in love, patience and meeknefs.

4. Can you fay, with a true broken heart and contrite fpirit (deeply diftreffed Mr. Thomas Hinckley,) and not confider how, not many weeks or months before, myfelf and fo many other innocent fouls, as to W. Harris, you deeply diftreffed by your adding gall to our (mine own above) forty years vinegar in countenancing that prodigy of pride and fcorning W. Harris, who, being an impudent morris-dancer in Kent, under the cloak of (fcurrilous) jefts againft the bifhop, got into a flight to New England, and, under a cloak of feparation, got in with myfelf, till his felf-ends and reftlefs ftrife, and at laft his atheiftical

---

[1] Nathaniel Morton emigrated to America in 1623. Was clerk of the Judicial Court in Plymouth from 1645 to his death in 1685. He wrote a brief Ecclefiaftical Hiftory of Plymouth, which has been preferved in Young's Chronicles of the Pilgrims; but he was better known by his *New England Memorial*, firft publifhed in 1669, in 4to. Other editions were printed in 1721; 1772; 1825; in 1826 with valuable notes by John Davis, and one by the Congregational Board in 1855.

denying of heaven and hell, made honeſt ſouls to fly from
him ?   Now he courts the Baptiſts; then he kicks them
off and flatters the Foxians; then the drunkards (which
he calls all that are not of the former two amongſt us);
then knowing the prejudices of the other Colonies againſt
us, he dares to abuſe his Majeſty and Council, to bring
New England upon us ; and when your noble ſelf diſ-
cerned and diſowned his old and only monſtrous ſong, *Hoc
eſt Corpus meum* (up ſtreams without limits,) how hath he
ıun about the world again to force my conſcience to give
him more up Wanaſquatucket than the bounds ſo punc-
tually ſet us by the Sachems in our grand deed.   It is not
queſtionable, is that, if he be not ſatisfied with his poor
bone he hath ſo long fancied, he will ſtamp on yourſelf,
and his Majeſty and Council too, and make Rome, if he
can (bloody Rome), his ſanctuary ; for he ſaith he can go
to Maſs : yea (*flectere ſi nequeam,* &c.), he will go down to
devils and witches ; for he ſaith he can go to the witch of
Endor for a piece of bread.   I am not ſenſible of his long
thirſting after my blood.   I humbly pray the bleſſed Lord
to return him or rebuke him, and to deliver my ſoul and
yours from all our diſtreſſes.   So daily prays, Sir,

Your moſt unworthy ſervant,

Roger Williams.

My humble reſpects to your honored Governor, Major
Cudworth, &c.

Teſtimony of Roger Williams relative to the firſt ſettlement of the Narraganſett Country by Richard Smith.

NARRAGANSETT, 21 July, 1679.[1]

Roger Williams, of Providence, in the Narraganſett Bay, in New England, being (by God's mercy) the firſt beginner of the mother town of Providence, and of the colony of Rhode Iſland and Providence Plantations, being now near to fourſcore years of age, yet (by God's mercy) of ſound underſtanding and memory; do humbly and faithfully declare, that Mr. Richard Smith, ſenior, who for his conſcience to God left fair poſſeſſions in Gloceſterſhire, and adventured, with his relations and eſtate, to New-England, and was a moſt acceptable inhabitant, and a prime leading man in Taunton and Plymouth colony; for his conſcience ſake, many differences ariſing, he left Taunton and came to the Narraganſett country, where, (by God's mercy and the favor of the Narraganſett Sachems) he broke the ice at his great charge and hazard, and put up in the thickets of the barbarians, the firſt Engliſh houſe amongſt them. 2. I humbly teſtify, that about forty years from this date, he kept poſſeſſion, coming and going him-ſelf, children and ſervants, and he had quiet poſſeſſion of his houſing, lands and meadow; and there, in his own houſe, with much ſerenity of ſoul and comfort, he yielded up his ſpirit to God, (the Father of ſpirits) in peace. 3. I do humbly and faithfully teſtify as aboveſaid, that ſince his departure, his honored ſon, Capt. Richard Smith, hath kept poſſeſſion, (with much acceptance with Engliſh and pagans) of his father's houſing, lands and meadows, with great improvement alſo by his great coſt and induſtry.

[1]BACKUS, *Hiſt. of the Baptiſts in New England*, vol. i. p. 421.

And in the late bloody Pagan war, I knowingly teſtify and declare, that it pleaſe the Moſt High to make uſe of him-
. ſelf in perſon, his houſing, goods, corn, proviſions and cattle, for a garriſon and ſupply for the whole army of New England, under the command of the ever to be honored General Winſlow,[1] for the ſervice of his Majeſty's honor and country of New England.   4. I do alſo humbly declare, that the ſaid Captain Richard Smith, junior, ought, by all the rules of equity, juſtice and gratitude, (to his honored father and himſelf) to be fairly treated with, conſidered, recruited, honored, and, by his Majeſty's authority, confirmed and eſtabliſhed in a peaceful poſſeſſion of his father's and his own poſſeſſions in this pagan wilderneſs, and Narraganſett country. The premiſes I humbly teſtify, as now leaving this country and this world.

ROGER WILLIAMS.

To Mr. Daniel Abbott, Town Clerk of Providence.[2]

PROVIDENCE, 15th January, 1680–81. (ſo called.)

MY GOOD FRIEND,—Loving remembrance to you. It has pleaſed the Moſt High and Only Wiſe, to ſtir up your ſpirit to be one of the chiefteſt ſtakes in our poor hedge. I, therefore, not being able to come to you, preſent you with a few thoughts about the great ſtumbling-block to them that are willing to ſtumble and trouble themſelves,

---

[1] Joſiah, ſon of Edward Winſlow, Governor of Plymouth Colony, was alſo Governor from 1673 to 1680. During Philip's war, being commander of the Plymouth forces, he ſhowed him- ſelf to be a brave ſoldier.—BLAKE, *Biographical Dictionary.* [2] KNOWLES, *Memoir of Roger Williams,* p. 350.

our rates. James Matifon had one copy of me, and Thomas Arnold another. This I fend to yourfelf and the
town, (for it may be I fhall not be able to be at meeting.)
I am grieved that you do fo much fervice for fo bad recompenfe; but I am perfuaded you fhall find caufe to fay,
the Moft High God of recompenfe, who was Abraham's
great reward, hath paid me.

Confiderations prefented touching rates.

1. Government and order in families, towns, &c., is the
ordinance of the Moft High, Rom. 13, for the peace and
and good of mankind. 2. Six things are written in the
hearts of all mankind, yea, even in pagans: 1st. That
there is a Deity; 2d. That fome actions are nought; 3d.
That the Deity will punifh; 4th. That there is another
life; 5th. That marriage is honorable; 6th. That mankind cannot keep together without fome government. 3.
There is no Englifhman in his Majefty dominions or elfewhere, who is not forced to fubmit to government. 4.
There is not a man in the world, except robbers, pirates
and rebels, but doth fubmit to government. 5. Even
robbers, pirates and rebels themfelves cannot hold together,
but by fome law among themfelves and government. 6.
One of thefe two great laws in the world muft prevail,
either that of judges and juftices of peace in courts of
peace, or the law of arms, the fword and blood. 7. If it
comes from the courts of trials of peace, to the trial of
the fword and blood, the conquered is forced to feek law
and government. 8. Till matters come to a fettled government, no man is ordinarily fure of his houfe, goods,
lands, cattle, wife, children or life. 9. Hence is that ancient maxim, *It is better to live under a tyrant in peace, than*

51

under the *sword, or where every man is a tyrant.* 10. His
Majesty sends governors to Barbadoes, Virginia, &c., but to
us he shews greater favor in our charter, to choose whom
we please. 11. No charters are obtained without great
suit, favor or charges. Our first cost a hundred pounds
(though I never received it all;) our second about a thousand; Connecticut about six thousand, &c. 12. No government is maintained without tribute, custom, rates,
taxes, &c. 13. Our charter excels all in New England,
or, *in the world, as to the souls of men.* 14. It pleased God,
Rom. 13, to command tribute, custom, and consequently
rates, not only for fear, but for conscience sake. 15. Our
rates are the least, by far, of any colony in New England.
16. There is no man that hath a vote in town or colony,
but *he hath a hand in making the rates by himself or his deputies.* 17. In our colony the General Assembly, Governor,
magistrates, deputies, towns, town clerks, raters, constables,
&c., have done their duties, the failing lies upon particular persons.[1] 18. It is but folly to resist, (one or more,
and if one, why not more?) God hath stirred up the
spirit of the Governor, magistrates and officers, driven
to it by necessity, to be unanimously resolved to see the
matter finished; and it is the duty of every man to
maintain, encourage, and strengthen the hand of authority.
19. Black clouds (some years) have hung over Old and
New England heads. God hath been wonderfully patient
and long suffering to us; but who sees not changes and
calamities hanging over us? 20. All men fear, that this

---

[1] In 1679, the General Assembly ordered a rate to be levied of sixty pounds,
which was apportioned as follows: Newport, eighteen; Portsmouth, eleven;
Providence, four; Kingstown, six; Warwick, four; Westerly, four; New Shore-
ham, four; East Greenwich, six; James-
town, six.

blazing herald from heaven[1] denounceth from the Moſt High, wars, peſtilence, famines; it is not then our wiſdom to make and keep peace with God and man?

Your old ůnworthy ſervant,

ROGER WILLIAMS.

To my much honored, kind friend, the Governor Bradſtreet,[2] at Boſton, preſent.

PROVIDENCE, 6 May, 1682, (*ut vulgo.*)[1]

SIR,—Your perſon and place are born to trouble as the ſparks fly upward; yet I am grieved to diſturb your thoughts or hands with any thing from me, and yet am

---

[1] Referring to the remarkable comet of 1680, which created a great ſenſation throughout the world, Increaſe Mather wrote an eſſay on the ſubject, ſhowing the remarkable events which followed the appearance of comets; and Bayle wrote two ſmall volumes on the comet of 1680, wherein his views are quite at variance with thoſe of the Puritan divine.

[2] Gov. Bradſtreet was one of the Commiſſioners of the United Colonies. In 1662, he and Mr. Norton were ſent to congratulate King Charles on his reſtoration. In 1679 he was elected Governor, which office he held till 1686, when the charter was annulled and Dudley commenced his adminiſtration as Preſident of New England. He was replaced in office in 1689 and held it until 1692. He died in 1697 at the age of 94.

[1] 2 *Maſs. Hiſt. Col.* vol. iii. p. 196.

Mr. Williams when near the cloſe of his life, occupied his leiſure in preparing the diſcourſes he had delivered during his miſſionary efforts as will appear from this letter. "It affords" too " additional proof, writes Dr. Elton, of the writer's diſintereſted benevolence and ſelf-denying ſpirit. With ample opportunities of enriching himſelf—to uſe the words of his ſon—he gave away his lands and other eſtate to them that he thought were moſt in want, until he gave away all. His property, his time, and his talents, were devoted to the promotion of the temporal and ſpiritual welfare of mankind, and in conducting to a glorious iſſue the ſtruggle to unlooſe the bonds of the captive daughter of Zion."—*Life of Williams*, p. 148.

refreſhed with the thought, that ſometimes you ſubſcribe [your willing ſervant:] and that your love and willingneſs will turn to your account alſo.

Sir, by John Whipple[1] of Providence, I wrote lately (though the letter lay long by him) touching the widow Meſſinger's daughter, Sarah Weld, of Boſton, whom I believe Joſeph Homan, of Boſton, hath miſerably deluded, ſlandered, oppreſſed (her and his child) by barborous inhumanity, ſo that I humbly hope your mercy and juſtice will glorioufly in public kiſs each other.

Sir, this encloſed tells you that being old and weak and bruiſed (with rupture and colic) and lameneſs on both my feet, I am directed by the Father of our ſpirits, to deſire to attend his infinite Majeſty with a poor mite, (which makes but two farthings.) By my fire-ſide I have recollected the diſcourſes which (by many tedious journeys) I have had with the ſcattered Engliſh at Narraganſett, before the war and ſince. I have reduced them unto thoſe twenty-two heads, (encloſed) which is near thirty ſheets of my writing: I would ſend them to the Narraganſetts and others; there is no controverſy in them, only an endeavor of a particular match of each poor ſinner to his Maker. For printing, I am forced to write to my friends at Maſſachusetts, Connecticut, Plymouth, and our colony, that he that hath a ſhilling and a heart to countenance and promote ſuch a foul work, may truſt the great Paymaſter (who is beforehand with us already) for an hundreth for one in this life. Sir, I have many friends at Boſton, but pray you to call in my kind friends Capt. Brattle and Mr.

---

[1] John Whipple was a Deputy from Providence to the General Aſſembly as early as 1666, to which office he was at many times re-elected. He was an inhabitant of Dorcheſter, Maſs., in 1632; removed to Providence in 1659.

Seth Perry, who may, by your wife difcretions, eafe yourfelf of any burthen. I write to my honored acquaintance at Roxbury, Mr. Dudley[1] and Mr. Eliot, and Mr. Stoughton,[2] at Dorchefter, and to Capt. Gookins, at Cambridge, and pray yourfelf and him to confult about a little help from Charleftown, where death has ftripped me of all my acquaintance. Sir, if you can return that chapter my reply to G——ton, concerning New England, I am advifed to let it fleep, and forbear public contefts with Proteftants, fince it is the defign of hell and Rome to cut the throats of all the proteftors in the world. Yet I am occafioned, in this book, to fay much for the honor and peace of New England.[3]

[1] Jofeph Dudley, Governor of Maffachufetts, held many important offices in that colony. He was at the battle with the Narraganfetts in December, 1675, and was one of the Commiffioners who dictated the terms of a treaty with them. By a commiffion from King James he was exalted to the office of Prefident of New England, in which capacity he had much to do with Rhode Ifland. He fell into trouble in the revolution of 1680, being imprifoned in Bofton as one of the friends of Andros. Being fent to England with Andros, Queen Anne received him with favor, and made him Chief Juftice of New York. When in England in 1693, he was made Lieut. Governor of the Ifle of Wight and in 1701 elected to Parliament. The following year he returned to Maffachufetts as Governor, including the colonies of New Hampfhire and Maine, which office he held till 1715 when he retired to his home in Roxbury, where he died in 1720 aged 72 years.—*New Eng. Hift. and Gen. Regifter*, vol. x. p. 337.

[2] Ifrael Stoughton. See note 10 Letter of Iune 22, 1670.

[3] "The foregoing letter," fays Knowles, "furnifhes proof that Mr. Williams, even after Philip's War, and confequently after he had paffed his 77th year, went to Narraganfett and delivered difcourfes. His zeal for the falvation of men was not extinguifhed by his age, nor was he prevented from efforts to fave them, by his theory refpecting the miniftry. That zeal is difplayed in his defire to print thefe difcourfes, after difeafe confined him to his home. The letter, too, leads us to infer his poverty. He would not, probably, have folicited aid to print fo fmall a work, if he had poffeffed the means. A letter from his fon to the Town of Providence, dated Aug. 24, 1710, printed in Knowles's Memoir, (p. 110) intimates that his father had been dependent on his children to fome extent, during the latter years of his life." *Memoir of Roger Williams*, p. 148.

Sir, I fhall humbly wait for your advice where it may be beft printed, at Bofton or Cambridge, and for how much, the printer finding paper.   We have tidings here of Shafts-bury's and Howard's beheading, and contrarily, their re-leafe, London manifeftations of joy, and the King's call-ing a Parliament.   But all thefe are but fubluniaries, tem-poraries and trivials.   Eternity (O eternity!) is our bufinefs, to which end I am moft unworthy to be

Your willing and faithful fervant,

ROGER WILLIAMS.

My humble refpects to Mrs. Bradftreet, and other hon-ored friends.

Teftimony of Roger Williams relative to his firft coming into the Narraganfett country, dated

, NARRAGANSETT, June 18, 1682.[1]

I teftify, as in the prefence of the all-making and all-feeing God, that about fifty years fince, I coming into this Narraganfett country, I found a great conteft between three Sachems, two, (to wit, Canonicus and Miantonomo) were againft Oufamaquin, on Plymouth fide, I was forced to travel between them three, to pacify, to fatisfy all their and their dependents' fpirits of my honeft intentions to live peaceably by them.   I teftify, that it was the general and conftant declaration, that Canonicus his father had three fons, whereof Canonicus was the heir, and his

---

[1]KNOWLES, *Memoir of Roger Williams*, p. 411.

youngeft brother's fon, Miantonomo, (becaufe of youth,)
was his marfhal and executioner, and did nothing without
his uncle Canonicus' confent ; and therefore I declare to
pofterity, that were it not for the favor God gave me with
Canonicus, none of thefe parts, no, not Rhode Ifland, had
been purchafed or obtained, for I never got any thing out
of Canonicus but by gift.   I alfo profefs, that very inquifitive of what the title or denomination Narraganfett fhould
come, I heard that Narraganfett was fo named from a little ifland between Puttiquomfcut and Mufquomacuk on
the fea and frefh water fide.   I went on purpofe to fee it ;
and about the place called Sugar Loaf Hill, I faw it, and
was within a pole of it, but could not learn why it was
called Narraganfett.   I had learned, that the Maffachufetts was called fo, from the Blue Hills, a little ifland
thereabout ;. and Canonicus' father and anceftors, living in
thefe fouthern parts, transferred and brought their authority
and name into thofe northern parts, all along by the fea-
fide, as appears by the great deftruction of wood all along
near the fea-fide and I defire pofterity to fee the gracious
hand of the Moft High, (in whofe hands are all hearts)
that when the hearts of my countrymen and friends and
brethren failed me, his infinite wifdom and merits ftirred
up the barbarous heart of Canonicus to love me as his fon
to his laft gafp, by which means I had not only Miantonomo and all the loweft Sachems my friends, but Oufamaquin alfo, who becaufe of my great friendfhip with him
at Plymouth, and the authority of Canonicus, confented
freely, being alfo well gratified by me, to the Governor
Winthrop and my enjoyment of Prudence, yea of Providence itfelf, and all the other lands I procured of Canonicus which were upon the point, and in effect whatfoever I

defired of him ; and I never denied him or Miantonomo whatever they defired of me as to goods or gifts or ufe of my boats or pinnace, and the travels of my own perfon, day and night, which, though men know not, nor care to know, yet the all-feeing Eye hath feen it, and his all-powerful hand hath helped me.   Bleffed be his holy name to eternity.

ROGER WILLIAMS.

September 28th, 1704.   I then, being at the houfe of Mr. Nathaniel Coddington, there being prefented with this written paper, which I atteft, upon oath, to be my father's own hand writing.   JOSEPH WILLIAMS, *Affiftant.*

February 11th, 1705.   True copy of the original, placed to record, and examined per me.

WESTON CLARKE, *Recorder.*

INDEX.

www.ingramcontent.com/pod-product-compliance
Lightning Source LLC
Chambersburg PA
CBHW020859130726
47900CB00014B/1128